HORROR NEEDS NO PASSPORT:
20th CENTURY HORROR FICTION OUTSIDE THE UNITED STATES AND GREAT BRITAIN

by Jess Nevins

copyright © 2018 Jess Nevins

Contents

Acknowledgments

Introduction   1

Part One: 1900-1939
    Chapter One. Africa: Angola, Lesotho, Nigeria, South Africa.   5
    Chapter Two. The Americas: Argentina, Brazil, Chile, Costa Rica, Cuba, Honduras,
        Jamaica, Mexico, Peru, Uruguay, Venezuela.   10
    Chapter Three. Asia: China, India, Indonesia, Japan, Korea, Philippines.   20
    Chapter Four. Europe: Austria, Belgium, Croatia, Czech Republic, Denmark, Finland,
        France, Germany, Italy, Latvia, Poland, Portugal, Romania, Russia, Spain.   34
    Chapter Five. The Middle East: Egypt, Iran, Turkey.   63

Part Two: 1940-1970
    Chapter Six. Africa: Angola, Congo, Guinea, Ivory Coast, Lesotho, Nigeria, Senegal,
        Sierra Leone, South Africa.   65
    Chapter Seven. The Americas: Argentina, Barbados, Bolivia, Brazil, Chile, Colombia,
        Costa Rica, Cuba, Ecuador, Guyana, Mexico, Québéc, Uruguay, Venezuela.   75
    Chapter Eight. Asia: India, Indonesia, Japan, Malaysia, Pakistan, Philippines.   96
    Chapter Nine. Europe: Belgium, Czech Republic, France, Germany, Italy, Portugal,
        Spain.   107
    Chapter Ten. The Middle East: Israel, Syria, Turkey.   118

Part Three: 1971-2000
    Chapter Eleven. Africa: Congo, Ghana, Guinea, Kenya, Libya, Mauritania, Mauritius,
        Nigeria, Rwanda, Senegal, Sierra Leone, South Africa.   120
    Chapter Twelve. The Americas: Argentina, Brazil, Chile, Colombia, Costa Rica, Cuba,
        Ecuador, El Salvador, French Guiana, Guatemala, Guyana, Mexico, Peru, Puerto
        Rico, Québéc, Venezuela.   132
    Chapter Thirteen. Asia: Bangladesh, China, India, Indonesia, Japan, Malaysia, Pakistan,
        Philippines, Singapore, South Korea, Taiwan, Thailand   152
    Chapter Fourteen. Europe: Austria, Belgium, Czech Republic, Denmark, Finland, France,
        Germany, Italy, Latvia, Poland, Portugal, Russia, Serbia, Spain, Sweden,
        Switzerland, Ukraine.   175
    Chapter Fifteen. The Middle East: Egypt, Israel, Jordan, Kuwait, Syria, Turkey.   195

Bibliography   199

Index   212

Acknowledgments

What began as mental itch and curiosity about the non-existence of a book (or monograph or even scholarly article) on this subject turned into a years-long journey through a very large number of primary and secondary sources. As is always the case with books like these, the author (i.e., me) is grateful to other authors and critics for a variety of insights; any errors in interpretation are my own fault.

This book could not have been written without the Interlibrary Services department of the Harris County Public Library System, who always came through where my own college's ILL department would not. Similarly, I'm grateful to the librarians at the Harry Ransom Center at the University of Texas at Austin, to the librarians at Texas A&M University, and to the librarians at Sam Houston State University.

My thanks to all the many people on Facebook and Twitter–too many to name–who responded in some way to my statements and queries about this book. Writing is usually a solitary activity, but social media can make it less so, and provide help and encouragement besides.

Lastly, I have to thank my wife Alicia and my son Henry, who as usual had to put up with me being physically and mentally elsewhere during the long hours spent researching and writing this book. Without their love, tolerance, and support, I'd never be able to write anything of consequence.

This book is dedicated to the great writers of horror, past and present.

Introduction

Precepts, Justifications, Definitions, and Purposes

This book was born out of irritation. I was deep in the writing of my book *A Chilling Age of Horror: How 20th Century Horror Fiction Changed the Genre* (Praeger, 2020) and continually encountering difficulties in finding useful information on non-Anglophone horror literature and horror writers. As a lazy writer, my first impulse was to look for books or scholarly articles on the topic that I could mine for information, but I found, to my increasing dismay and exasperation, that there were no such books or articles. When I wanted to find information on a particular non-Anglophone horror writer or story or book, I had to search out individual works of criticism on those authors and texts, and in many cases that required no small amount of effort. "Why," I pouted and sulked, "hasn't someone put this all together in a book? Don't they know how inconvenienced I am?" Such a book seemed like a valuable thing to have, and a worthy thing to exist–after all, there was a great deal of horror literature written during the twentieth century in non-Anglophone countries. The United States and the United Kingdom might have written the best-known and most influential horror literature during the century, but there were any number of non-English language horror authors creating works in their own countries and their own languages. Why hadn't someone compiled a list of them and written something approaching a literary history of them?

No one had, though, likely due to a combination of the difficulty in doing research on those authors and works and a prejudice against them as somehow being unequal to their American and UK counterparts. Even the best and longest reference works on horror literature, like the S.T. Joshi- and Stefan Dziemianowicz-edited *Supernatural Literature of the World* (Greenwood, 2005), have a limited number of entries on non-Anglophone horror writers, and of those most are well-known French and German authors. Similarly, Joshi, the most prominent contemporary critic of horror fiction, confines himself to a scant handful of French and German authors in his works of criticism, ignoring the fine work done in the rest of the world. In *Supernatural Literature*, the cause is likely an inability by the contributing authors to access the right resources; in the case of Joshi, whose academic rigor is too often cartoonishly narrow harshness and bias in favor of his favorites, the cause is likely intellectual prejudice. Neither of which is ultimately excusable, to my way of thinking, but they are at least contributing reasons to the lack of a book on non-Anglophone horror literature.

Ultimately I came to the conclusion that I was going to have to write such a book myself, if I wanted to see such a book exist. And so here I am.

Despite the overwhelming U.S. and U.K. bias of most horror criticism[1], horror literature

---

[1] S.T. Joshi's *Unutterable Horror*, whose subtitle is the definitive-sounding "A History of Supernatural Fiction," devotes seven pages out of 783 to a select few French and German writers. The *St. James Guide to Horror, Ghost & Gothic Writers* does somewhat better, with 25 entries, though nearly all are European and most are French and German. The *Supernatural Literature of the World* (again, a definitive-sounding title) ventures a little further: six Belgian, two Danish, twenty-one French, twenty-nine German and Austrian, two Italian, nine Japanese, four "Latin

has traditionally not been restricted to English-language countries. Many countries in which there has been a flourishing market for popular literature have seen natively-written horror literature. This is true in familiar European countries like France and Germany, whose horror writers are given at least a cursory mention in the broader types of horror criticism. But this is also true in less familiar European countries, and in fact in a broad range of countries outside the "Anglosphere," the term I'm using to cover all the countries in which English is the dominant language. A *thorough* history of non-English language horror is beyond the space restrictions of this work. Instead, what follows is a more limited coverage of non-English language horror in the years 1901-1939.

The question of "what is horror?" needs to be addressed. A part of the difficulty of writing about the horror genre lies in defining it. The commonly accepted definition of the horror genre is that, unlike other genres, the core definition of horror lies not in its content but in its effect. Westerns must have a certain setting; romances must have certain emotions; mysteries must have certain illegal acts; science fiction must have a set of assumptions about technology and society. But horror, because of its mutability, and its ability to nest, cuckoo-like, in any other genre, does not have content limitations or requirements. Works of horror can be fantastic or mimetic; they can be set in any place or time; they can involve any characters; they can be supported by any pot. To qualify as horror, all that a text must contain is the ability to create an effect in its reader: the feeling of dread, fear, horror, or terror (or, as Stephen King once put it, "the gross-out."[2]).

But even this generally accepted definition has its disputants. John Clute's *The Darkening Garden* describes fiction written to evoke fear, dread, etc. as "affect horror," and writs that

> the theory of AFFECT HORROR–crudely, that texts may be defined as Horror if they generate certain emotions–works more satisfactorily with non-fantastic Horror than with Fantastic Horror...locating non-fantastic Horror in this fashion makes it easier to concentrate here on the special nature of Fantastic Horror, which is described in this lexicon as a pattern of story moves deeply and at times grotesquely responsive–like all genres of the Fantastic–to the nature of the world since 1750; attendance to the world precedes affect.[3]

I'm loth to disagree with the formidable Mr. Clute, but as he himself notes, his definition is predicated on a Western historical orientation: "Horror is (in part) a subversive response to the

---

American," four Russian, one Pole, one Norwegian, one South African, one Greek, one Chinese–out of hundreds of entries.

[2]Stephen King, *Danse Macabre* (New York: Berkeley, 1981), 25.

[3]John Clute, *The Darkening Garden* (Cauheegan, WI: Payseur & Schmidt, 2006), 87.

falseness of that Enlightenment ambition to totalize knowledge and the world into an imperial harmony...Horror–and the Fantastic as a whole–are conceived in contradiction of the imperialisms of the West. The Fantastic is Enlightenment's dark, mocking Twin."[4] As this book shows, there was a substantial amount of *fantastika* horror published outside the West that did not rely upon the Enlightenment for its conception and execution.

So my definition is mostly in accord with the "affect horror" definition, but with one crucial difference. I'm including works in which evoking horror was only the secondary or even tertiary intent of the author. I don't believe that any text is ever of just one genre, or that a writer has only one intent in mind when writing a work. I tend to agree with Jacques Derrida and Avitall Ronell, who wrote "As soon as genre announces itself, one must respect a norm, one must not cross a line of demarcation, one must not risk impurity, anomaly, or monstrosity,"[5] and that "every text participates in one or several genres, there is no genreless text; there is always a genre and genres, yet such participation never amounts to belonging."[6] A horror text can be many things: romance-horror, science fiction-horror, edifying-horror, and so on.

Before we begin, a few notes:

- I rather liberally make use of John Clute's term *"fantastika,"* which he defines at http://www.sf-encyclopedia.com/entry/fantastika:

> A convenient shorthand term employed and promoted by John Clute since 2007 to describe the armamentarium of the fantastic in literature as a whole, encompassing science fiction, Fantasy, fantastic horror and their various subgenres.

It's clearly a term with manifold uses in this work, and I've happily appropriated it.

- A substantial amount of material in this work appeared originally in a language other than English. All translations in this work are mine.

- The question of whether to use a novel or short story's original title or the title translated into English was a vexing one. The English titles would be most convenient for the majority of my readers. But using English titles by default would be to make an unpleasant political statement, and ultimately one I chose not to make. So, in general, I use the original title of the work, although I do provide the English translation. However, if the work is much more famous in English than in the original, I'm using the English title. It'd be an act of mulish perversity to write "Mikhail Bulgakov's Мácтep и Маргарѝта" rather than "Mikhail Bulgakov's *Master and Margarita*," and not, ultimately, helpful to the reader.

- My apologies to readers who were expecting a narrative or narratives. I would have loved to have been able to write this as a proper literary history. But with all the will in the world

---

[4]Clute, *Darkening Garden*, 88.

[5]Jacques Derrida and Avitall Ronell, "The Law of Genre," *Critical Inquiry* 7, no. 1 (1980): 57.

[6]Derrida and Ronell, "The Law of Genre," 65.

I couldn't relay a narrative that doesn't exist, or construct one that is inaccurate. Each country's literary history is unique, and while certain countries share partial histories–the development of magic realism throughout Latin America, for example–they weren't enough to build a narrative around. Africa, for example, is simply too big, with too many countries, for there to be any one narrative or historical thread combining all of the countries and writers together. So *Horror Needs No Passport* isn't a narrative history. It's 141 capsule narratives and literary critiques, instead.

Part One: 1901-1939

Chapter One: Africa

The colonial status of most African countries in the 1901-1939 period meant that the literature produced in those countries was primarily produced in the language of the colonizers rather than in the native languages. Moreover, the colonial governments had severe restrictions on the kinds of literature that could be produced by natives; genre fiction with any kind of independence or anti-colonial implications was strictly forbidden. And the novel and short story, being alien imports into primarily oral cultures, were slow to catch on in most African countries before World War Two.

All of which is to say that those looking for horror literature in African countries before World War Two will turn up precious little. To a large degree the history of genre literature in Africa starts with the end of World War Two and the beginning of the African independence movements, and the history of horror literature in Africa starts in the 1950s. That being said, there area few countries that produced horror literature during the 1901-1939 time period.

Angola

The Angolan intellectual and liberation movements of the late nineteenth century did not give rise to a substantial body of literature, and the first serious Angolan novelist, António de Assis Júnior, did not begin publishing until the 1910s. De Assis Júnior, "Angola's first important black or *mestiço* writer of prose fiction,"[1] was best-known in his time as an activist lawyer, but his *O Segredo da Morta* (*The Secret of the Dead*, as a serial, 1929, as a novel, 1934) is a first for Angolan literature: activist fiction, a *roman feuilleton*, a history and ethnography of a time and place in Angolan history, and a work of journalism complete with editorial comments. The plot concerns a witch who dies of sleeping sickness and then returns from the dead to haunt the living and punish and kill those who stole from her while she was dying. *O Segredo da Morta* is a weakly-plotted melodrama, modeled on the novels of Victor Hugo and Anatole France, and suffers from "superficial erudition...and pedantic passages."[2] But to modern readers' eyes it is effective in using African oral traditions and folktales to create frightening moments of supernatural horror.

Lesotho

One of the first Basotho collections of short stories was Edward Motsamai's *Mehla ea malimo* (*The Days of the Cannibals*, 1912). Halfway between fictional narratives and recitations

---

[1]Russell G. Hamilton, *Voices from an Empire: A History of Afro-Portuguese Literature* (Minneapolis: University of Minnesota, 1975), 30.

[2]Hamilton, *Voices from an Empire*, 31.

of Basotho folktales, the stories in *Mehla ea malimo* "deal with memories from precolonial days, and it is significant that they are imbued with a strong sense of fear and horror. Five of them describe frightening encounters between human beings and the ferocious beasts of the jungle."[3]

Thomas Mofolo's novel *Chaka* (1925) is a fictionalized biography of the life of the Zulu conqueror Shaka kaSenzangakhona. Mofolo adds in Faustian elements in the Mephistophelean figure of the sorcerer Isanusi, who is sorcerously responsible for Shaka losing his way and descending into evil and sinful ways. *Chaka* was not Mofolo's first attempt at horror-inflected literature; another novel, never published, bore the French title *L'Ange déchu* (*The fallen angel*). But *Chaka* is far and away Mofolo's best-known novel and is one of the landmarks of pre-independence sub-Saharan African literature.

Nigeria

Nigerian literature in the 1930s was still largely dominated by British authors and colonial forms and modes. The nineteenth century tendency to transcribe Yoruba folktales had been supplanted, thanks to the western education instituted by the British colonial system, by a vogue for realism in fiction, especially in the late 1940s, when literary scholars at the University College of Ibadan formed an unnamed movement to promote and propagate the realist form as a replacement for folktales. Despite this movement, *fantastika* in various forms continued to appear in Nigerian literature, most notably in Chinua Achebe's classic *Things Fall Apart* (1958), with its Igbo folklore, to the work of Amos Tutuola to Daniel O. Fagunwa's *Ogboju Ode ninu Igbo Irunmale* (*The Forest of a Thousand Daemons,* 1938), which was the first significant novel written in Yoruba.

Fagunwa was a novelist, short story writer, editor, and biographer, and a devout Christian convert; his work was a landmark both in Nigeria and in sub-Saharan Africa as a whole, and he has been dubbed by critics the "master ancestor to the institutional category we have come to call modern African literature."[4] *Ogboju Ode ninu Igbo Irunmale* is generally seen as Fagunwa's masterpiece, although he continued writing until just before his death. It is loosely autobiographical, although both the framing story and the folktales the narrator tells are largely mythical, dealing with a world of supernatural being of all varieties. The novel is a formidable synthesis of Yoruba folklore, Fagunwa's own creations, and Christian sensibilities. Told in a rich, vivid, evocative language, the stories have a realistic portrait of the Yoruban environment, both literal and metaphysical, where the supernatural lives cheek by jowl with the mundane. Unfortunately for the protagonist, a hunter, he is forced to travel through the titular forest, a location full of malign beings, supernatural and human, armed only with his gun, his own witchcraft, and an unshakeable faith in God. Although Fagunwa combines folkloric aesthetics and Christian sermonizing, and further has his narrator intrude into the novel at random

---

[3] Albert S. Gérard, *Four African Literatures: Xhosa, Sotho, Zulu, Amharic* (Berkeley, CA: University of California Press, 1971), 137-38.

[4] Olakunle George, "Compound of Spells: The Predicament of D.O. Fagunwa (1903-1963)," *Research in African Literatures* 28, no. 1 (Spring 1997): 78.

moments, Fagunwa's use of the details of traditional folklore helps create imagery and moments that can frighten the unwary. That was not his primary intention, which was to tell a picaresque story using folktales for the ultimate purpose of convincing readers to convert to Christianity. But terror from specific horrible concepts and moments was generated nonetheless.

South Africa

The origin of written South African[5] horror literature began centuries ago, with the seventeenth century colonization of the region by the Dutch and the later development of the Boer people:

> From 1652 a continuous stream of ghost religions - a blend of pre-Christian German religions, forbidden Catholic views, witchcraft and public legends - swung with white settlers from Europe to South Africa. At the Cape, it was brought into the interior by a diverse group of distributors - colonial officials, adventurers, cattle farmers, hunters, drosters and smuses. Along with campfires, communion festivals, armor kings and commandos, these stories were exchanged and kept alive, so that 'a fixed narrative style and structure eventually developed around these traditions...a ghost liturgy arose around the ways stories were typically composed and exchanged.'[6]

But more than in most countries, the South African horror stories of the 1901-1939 period were the product of several different cultures, merging together however unwillingly. There were the oral folklore traditions of the native South African peoples, which often contained supernatural elements or ghosts. "These entertaining didactic folk stories and ballads are part of the earliest examples of written Afrikaans texts."[7] There was the British spiritualist tradition established during the nineteenth century, which manifested itself in early- and mid-twentieth-century South African Gothics. There were East Indian folk stories, that came mainly from the Malaysian and Indonesian slaves who were brought to South Africa from 1658. There were traditional folk horror stories of vampires and werewolves and witches brought to South Africa by Dutch and German settlers. And there was the German Faust legend.

The end result of this cultural transfer were three main types of South African horror literature during the 1901-1939 period: European-style horror stories, Afrikaans Gothic, and

---

[5]Unless otherwise noted, I'm using "South African" to mean *white* South African in this section. Later sections will contain information on native South African horror literature, but there is none to describe from the 1901-1939 period.

[6]J.B. de Villiers, *Agter die somber gordyn: 'n onthullende studie oor die vergete geskiedenis van die Afrikaanse spiritisme* (Kaapstad: Griffel Media, 2011), 46.

[7]Gerda Taljaard-Gilson, "Die inslag van die Gotiese in die Afrikaanse literatuur: 'n ondersoek na 'n eiesoortige Afrikaanse Gotiek aan die hand van die Faust-motief," *LitNet Akademies* 13, no. 1 (May 2016): 191.

Afrikaans magical realism.

Most common of the three were the European-style horror stories, which often made use of European horror tropes, motifs, and plots, and whose writers, like most South African writers of the period, were heavily influenced by European and American writers and critics. But even in the European-style horror stories, substantial South African (meaning the combination of all cultures in South Africa) elements appeared, so that the South African horror story of the 1901-1939 period, regardless of its European trappings, has its own distinctive character. Afrikaans communities, rather than European ones, are the usual setting. Farms–farm houses, farmlands–are "the characteristic space of the Afrikaans ghost story–the majority of Afrikaans ghost stories play in a deserted farm, in a dilapidated farmhouse or on abandoned farm roads."[8] Stories emphasizing oral accounts of witchcraft or supernatural events–both popular topics–drew upon, respectively, the Dutch fear of witches, which led to the investigation several cases of witchcraft by the Dutch Reformed Church between 1906 and 1912, and "successive retellings of the initiation of white Afrikaans-speaking children by an African, Bushman or Malay servant, into the workings of the natural or supernatural world."[9]

Foremost among the South African horror story writers of the pre-WW2 period was C. Louis Leipoldt. Leipoldt was one of the leading poets of South Africa's "Second Afrikaans Movement," the post-1902 movement to make Afrikaans rather than Dutch the primary language of South Africa. Leipoldt was a versatile writer, prolific as a poet, novelist, children's book writer and author of non-fiction, and is still considered one of South Africa's greatest poets and writers. But despite being very much a part of the literary mainstream in South Africa during the 1901-1939 period, Leipoldt also wrote a number of genre works, including a series of detective novels and three collections of ghost stories, *Waar spoke speel* (*Where ghosts play*, 1924), *Wat agter le en ander verhale* (*What lies behind and other stories*, 1927), and *Die rooi rotte, en ander kort verhale* (*The red rats and other stories*, 1932). Leipoldt's horror fiction bears the influence of Poe; Poe was one of Leipoldt's primary influences, and Leipoldt's detective novels, like his horror stories, are informed by Poe's theories of and practices in those genres.[10] Leipoldt's plots and tropes are Poe-esque, but his characters and fictional communities are thoroughly South African, as occasionally are his motifs, such as the ominous white puppy in "Die wit hondjie" ("The White Puppy," 1924). Other South African writers wrote in the vein of Poe–Reenen van Reenen published two anthologies of Poe-esque horror stories in 1919 and 1920–but Leipoldt was the most aesthetically successful of them.

Another major South African poet, C.J. Langenhoven, also wrote horror short stories,

---

[8]Mariëtte Van Graan, "Die rol van ruimte in Afrikaanse spookstories" (PhD diss., Noordweis-Universiteit, 2008), 7.

[9]Sandra Swart, "'Bushveld Magic' and 'Miracle Doctors'–an Exploration of Eugene Marais and C. Louis Leipoldt's Experiences in the Waterberg, South Africa, c. 1906-1917," *Journal of African History* 45 (2004): 249.

[10]Riaan N. Oppelt, "C. Louis Leipoldt and the Making of a South African Modernism" (PhD diss., Stellenbosch University, 2013), 81.

albeit less successfully than Leipoldt. Langenhoven's first collection, *Geeste op aarde* (*Spirits on earth,* 1924), contains stories that range from rationalized supernatural to overtly supernatural, all set in Afrikaans communities and usually centered on a dilapidated farmhouse or abandoned farm. His second collection, *Aan Stille Waters* (*On quiet waters*, 1930), are purportedly genuine South African ghost stories that the collection's fictional narrator collected by traveling around the countryside and interviewing older Afrikaners. These stories are more traditionally South African, mingling Afrikaner settings and characters with native South African or Malaysian ghosts and monsters. A similarly mixed approach to the South African ghost story appeared in T.L. Kemp's newspaper stories in the early 1920s and in Marie Linde's and I.D. Du Plessis' stories in popular South African magazines later in the decade. Eugene Marais, in his *Dwaalstories en ander vertellings* (*Mistletoe stories and other stories*, 1927, originally published in journals in 1921), used the native stories told to him by Hendrik, a member of the San people, as the source for his horror stories.

Marais' short novel *Die boom in die middle van die tuin* (*The tree in the middle of the garden,* 1933) is a fine example of the Afrikaans Gothic. As Gerda Taljaard-Gilson describes, the Afrikaans Gothics

> contain unique Gothic effects such as mystery, fear and horror within a distinctive South African environment (such as deserted farmsteads, drought-ridden areas) with authentic South African characters (including farmers, Khoisan rainmakers and Boer soldiers). These aspects, in combination with the influence of indigenous occult traditions, bring about a distinctive Afrikaans Gothic literature. In other words, Afrikaans Gothic is not a mere imitation of European traditions, but has original attributes.[11]

Marais' Gothic in particular draws upon the Faust motif, using the Mephistopheles figure, also named Mephistopheles, to criticize the widespread poverty in South Africa during the global Depression. Marais uses the elements of the Faust legend but incorporates indigenous dialogue and occult traditions as well as the native settings and characters of authors like Leipoldt and Langenhoven.

Least common of the three types of South African horror literature is magic realism, which though increasingly commonly used by South African writers of all ethnicities and cultures as the twentieth century progressed was rarely used for horror by writers; when horror was called for during the 1901-1939 period, the Afrikaans Gothic or the more uniquely Afrikaans horror story was used.

---

[11] Taljaard-Gilson, "Die inslag van die Gotiese," 186.

Chapter Two: The Americas

Very often, Latin American horror resides on the borderlines between different genres, permeating a number of nonnaturalistic types of narrative—such as science fiction, fantasy, or crime thriller—and a great deal of horror literature and film embraces parody by means of comedy or experimental works...if the ideal of a pure genre has rarely or perhaps never truly been identified in classical contexts, Latin American horror demonstrates that impurity might be one—that is, if there even is one—distinctive trait of the production of this genre on the Latin American continent.[1]

Argentina

For Argentina, the Gothic was a dominant mode of long-form horror for most of the 1901-1939 period, in large part because post-independence Argentine history is, as Diana Ferrero put it, "a Gothic novel in its own right because of the degree of violent horror, from the massacres of the rebellious gauchos in the 19th century to the political massacres of the 70's [sic], just thirty years ago."[2] Ferraro notes that the Argentine Gothic springs from internal contradictions and cross-currents:

> The influence of the Enlightenment was present in the first writers post Independence, who were nurtured with its values; Romanticism's wave took its own local color in the Río de la Plata; and Surrealism made later its own way in the minds of writers who were ready, because of their distance from the great capitals of the world, to recreate the universe according to new laws. Since the beginning, the tension between the local barbarity and the aspiration to civilization created the intense emotional basement for an Argentine Gothic, in which the ghosts always come from the repressed, in an eternally split culture.[3]

At the turn of the twentieth century a new Argentine social elite, well-read in European and American writers, changed matters. Particularly influenced by Edgar Allan Poe as well as nostalgia for Europe, these Argentine writers began writing Gothic novels that partook of the American Gothic tradition as well as the British/European Gothic tradition.

---

[1] Alfredo Luiz Suppia, "Horror in Literature and Film in Latin America," Oxford Bibliographies, last modified July 24, 2013, http://www.oxfordbibliographies.com/view/document/obo-9780199766581/obo-9780199766581-0124.xml.

[2] Diana Ferraro, "The Argentine Gothic," The Continental Blog, last modified Nov. 17, 2017, http://dianaferraroenglish.blogspot.com/2007/11/argentine-gothic.html.

[3] Ferraro, "The Argentine Gothic."

Occasionally set against the more mainstream Gothics were various short stories or collections which relied on different sources to produce horror. The modernist Leopoldo Lugones, a leader of the Argentine modernist movement at the turn of the century, specialized in de Maupassant-like *contes cruel*, but leavened with the trappings of modernity, whether scientific or spiritualist:

> Lugones's stories of the turn of the century, collected in *Las fuerzas extrañas* (*Strange forces*, 1906) were outstanding for passages in which the narrators described in detail abnormal information they had obtained through their senses. In one story, a participant in a terrifying séance tells of being covered with glacial cold as he sat at the spirit-summoning table. In another, the friend of a mad scientists discovers the experimenter's brains evenly buttered across a wall in the wake of some ill-advised labwork. In a story not collected during the author's lifetime, "Cábala práctica" (Practical Kabbalah), the entire plot leads up to a lengthy descriptive passage giving the narrator's sensation as he grabbed hold of a friend and, with his fingers sinking into her, suddenly realized that she had no skeleton.[4]

Brazil

Brazilian historians and critics of horror literature have lamented the fact that there seems to be no tradition of horror literature in the country: "Brazilian literature, from romanticism through realism, had been taken over by the project of building a national identity, which consequently restrained any other theme considered unsuitable for such a purpose."[5]

But Brazil, like other Latin American countries, was influenced by the Gothics, which circulated heavily in Brazil in the first half of the nineteenth century[6] and which influenced Brazilian authors directly during the nineteenth century and more indirectly during the twentieth. French intellectual models were more respected and respectable in Brazil during the nineteenth century, but a large number of British and German Gothics were published in Brazil under French or Portuguese titles, with the end result being that the Brazilian novel of the nineteenth century absorbed elements from both French and British/German literature.[7] Notable nineteenth century Brazilian Romantic authors like José de Alencar and Álvares de Azevedo wrote heavily

---

[4]Naomi Lindstrom, "Argentina," in *Handbook of Latin American Literature*, ed. David William Foster (New York: Routledge, 2014), 17.

[5]Julio França and Luciano Cabral da Silva, "A Preface to a Theory of Art-Fear in Brazilian Literature," *Ilha do Desterro* 62 (Jan/Jun 2012): 348.

[6]Sandra Guardini T. Vasconcelos, "Leituras Inglesas no Brasil oitocentista," *Crop* 8 (2002): 235-36.

[7]Daniel Sá, "Tropical Gothic I," The Gothic Imagination, last modified April 5, 2012, http://www.gothic.stir.ac.uk/guestblog/tropical-gothic-i/.

Gothic novels, and elements of the Gothic persisted into twentieth century literature. Additional influences, to a greater or lesser degree, were the works of Edgar Allan Poe, via French critics, and native/indigenous folklore, especially the motif of the revenant corpse, which was common during the nineteenth century.

The first significant Brazilian horror fiction of the twentieth century was the late work of Joaquim Maria Machado de Assis. Machado de Assis was a writer of short stories, novels, poetry and plays, and is generally regarded as Brazil's greatest writer of the nineteenth and early twentieth century. Of his roughly two hundred short stories, roughly twenty make use of *fantastika* and an additional twenty, overlapping somewhat with his *fantastika* work, can be counted as horror literature, with a number of those appearing after 1900. Machado de Assis' horror stories reject the naturalism so common among mainstream Brazilian fiction of the time and embrace perverse characters of dubious and unstable sanity and skewed and possibly unreliable viewpoints. Many of the stories are satire or allegories, using traditional tropes like the *femme fatale* as vehicles for the delivery of the point of the satire or allegory, in particular the oppression of women and a condemnation of the entire system of patriarchal thinking.[8] His work is narratively complex and often difficult, but is rewarding, and merits the comparison with Twain.

However, despite his later critical acclaim, Machado de Assis was little known after his death and cannot be counted as influential on the Brazilian horror writers who followed him. Over the next twenty years a number of short story writers would produce horror fiction of less elevated stature, not as well written as Machado de Assis' work but also less difficult to read and influenced by different writers. The typical Brazilian writer of horror fiction during the 1901-1939 period was influenced by the *contes cruel*, by the work of Edgar Allan Poe, and by the carnivalesque;[9] these writers wrote works in more naturalistic and modern prose, but with macabre and cruel twist endings. Júlia Lopes de Almeida's "A colha" ("The reaping," 1903) describes a boy who is teased because of his one-eyed mother, and resents her for it, until learning that he himself, as an infant, was responsible for stabbing her in the eye. João Simões Lopes' "Contrabandista" ("Smuggler," 1910) is about a ninety-year-old smuggler who struggles to find a white wedding dress for his adult daughter, and ends up shot dead by the police, who suspect him of wrongdoing in this, the only good thing he has tried to do in his life. Paulo Barreto's short novel *O bebe de tarlatana rosa* (*The baby of Tarlatana Rosa,* 1912), structured along the traditional lines of the heroic quest, features a descent into the underworld of Rio de Janeiro's carnival and a macabre encounter with a woman who is ultimately revealed to be other

---

[8] Jordan B. Jones and James R. Krause, "The *Femme Fragile* and *Femme Fatale* in the Fantastic Fiction of Machado de Assis," *Revista Abusões* 1, no. 1 (2001): 72.

[9] 9. Mikhail Bakhtin's *Rabelais and His World* (Bloomington, IN: Indiana University Press, 1984) is the starting point for studies of the "carnivalesque" cultural dynamic, which can be summed up as a culturally-approved inversion of worldly restraints on sexuality, behavior, dress, obedience, food, and drink, taking place during a limited period of time on a "carnival" or holiday.

than what she seems.[10] Lima Barreto's "Sua Excelencia" (1920) tells the story of a minister of state whose carriage trip takes him not through Rio de Janeiro but instead through a hellish afterworld–again, the carnivalesque ethos of death democratizing all the dead and reducing all social positions and aspirations to nothing is evident. Barreto's "A nova Califórnia" ("A new California," 1921) allegorically describes how a chemist who has found a way to turn human bones into gold reduces the town he has newly moved to into murderous chaos. And Monteiro Lobato's "Negrinha" ("Sissy," 1923) uses the tragic story of a little African-Brazilian orphan girl who is adopted by a wealthy family but dies of a broken hear to condemn the legacy of slavery.

Coelho Neto was a Renaissance Man of his time: a writer of fiction and non-fiction, a critic and playwright, a politician and a professor. Although he was forgotten about soon after his death in 1934 due to the actions of his long-time enemies, the Modernists, his work has slowly been rediscovered. In 1908, during his prolific heyday as a writer, he wrote *Esfinge* (*The Sphinx*), a Gothic Symbolist novel about an Asian scientist–a correspondent of Victor von Frankenstein–who, after a tragic accident involving a brother and sister, saves the brother's body and the sister's head and sews them together, creating a kind of transsexual Frankenstein's Creature. As much a tragic romance as a Gothic novel, *Esfinge* includes a love story, of sorts, to accompany the Gothic shocks and general Gothic architecture of the novel. Although the language of *Esfinge* is formal and old-fashioned–and was when it was written–once the reader adjusts to it they will find the novel well written and Gothic aspects of the novel well-wrought: "each scene is carefully assembled, the supernatural degree of each fantastic event calculated to support the suspense, and the dialogues contribute to the characterization of the characters, giving each one a proper voice."[11]

João do Rio was a journalist, playwright, and short story author. He was a creature of urban Rio de Janeiro, and through his writings was largely responsible for the Brazilian conception of Rio in the belle époque. His horror stories, mainly collected in *Dentro da noite* (*Inside the night*, 1910), portray "the urban space...as a privileged space for the manifestation of modern evils."[12] These evils are not supernatural in origin; they are entirely mortal, if dangerously deranged. Do Rio emphasizes the claustrophobia of the city and the impotence of those caught in it, the cruelty and sexual decadence of the wealthy, the randomness of deadly crimes and the fact that, in Rio de Janeiro, the danger can come from anywhere, or anyone, at all.

Humberto de Campos was a politician, journalist, and author who was best known for his autobiographical writings. In 1932 he published *Monstro e outro contos* (*The Monster and Other Tales*), a collection of horror stories. Campos' horror narratives are conventional, if well-told: an

---

[10] Julie Jones, "Paulo Barreto's 'O bebê de tarlatana rosa': A Carnival Adventure," *Luso-Brazilian Review* 24, no. 1 (Summer, 1987): 27.

[11] Roberto de Sousa Causo, *Ficçãa científica, fantasia e horror no Brasil 1875 a 1950* (Belo Horizonte: Editora UFMG, 2003), 112-13.

[12] Aline Pires de Morais, "João do Rio e o medo no espaço da cidade," Anais do CENA 2, no. 1 (2016), accessed June 19, 2018, http://www.ileel.ufu.br/anaisdocena/wp-content/uploads/2016/01/Aline-Pires-de-Morais.pdf.

eye operation gives a patient x-ray vision, but the patient eventually rips his eyes from their sockets; a man whose request for marriage is denied vows to eat the woman's heart, and eventually succeeds; a beheaded head that receives a kiss that it did not get while alive; and so on. His stories have dark atmospheres and macabre endings, and while some contain too many cliches others are narrated in a dreamlike fashion, adding to the horror of the events. Campos set his stories in the countryside and rural areas of Brazil and in the jungles of the Amazon, but he did not use traditional Brazilian folklore, instead telling modern (by the standards of the day) horror stories that could be set anywhere.

Chile

The *criollismo*—the use of realism to focus on the scenes, customs, and manners of the countryside—which was the prevailing literary trend and fashion in Chile during the 1901-1939 period produced a wide range of quality literature, including a Nobel prize for the poetry of Gabriela Mistral. However, *criollismo* was limiting when it came to *fantastika*. Little science fiction or fantasy was written during this period, especially compared to Argentina and other Latin American countries, and only two writers produced any amount of notable horror fiction.

Mistral wrote a set of six short stories between 1904 and 1911 which can only be considered as horror fiction. Mistral did not think much of these stories, later dismissing them as juvenile work (they were started when she was fourteen), and Mistral's critics and biographers tend to focus on her poetry. Nonetheless, the sextet of stories, though uncharacteristic of her work as a whole, is worth noting. The theme of the stories is the violence, physical, mental, and emotional, inflicted on women by men, manly women, or inanimate objects with male characteristics. Allusions to revenge, physical violence, and rape are common in the stories.

> Unlike Mistral's more objective prose poems or texts, some referred to as "Recados," they are tales that all have a female character who must endure suffering, madness, or death, usually inflicted on them by men or malelike protagonists. Perhaps because they share themes common to folk tales or nineteenth-century stories influenced by Edgar Allan Poe and Baudelaire, these stories are not easy tales to enjoy. Instead, they dislocate the reader into the realms of agony and pain, where sinister meanings and unreal circumstances bring the characters (mostly men) to commit bizarre and unexpected acts of violence.[13]

Her choice of horror as the genre in which to write, and her choice of horrors to write about, are unlikely to have been consciously taken from Baudelaire or Poe, however. Mistral was well-read, and an indirect influence is certainly possible, but her stated influences are Latin American authors like Ruben Dario and José Maria Vargas Vila.

Eduardo Barrios was a poet, journalist, and an acclaimed writer of short stories and novels. He was also a master of grotesque narratives, although Barrios' use of the grotesque was often intended to heighten the shock of the awful real, of the gruesome and often horrifying

---

[13]Karen Peña, "Violence and Difference in Gabriela Mistral's Short Stories (1904-1911)," *Latin American Research Review* 40, no. 3 (2005): 71-72.

realities of life for the less fortunate, rather than the terrifying supernatural. In some stories and novels, the grotesque is merely the trapping of the story, with the plot being oriented toward social activism. In other stories and novels, Barrios makes the grotesque an inseparable part of the plot and setting; writing of the descent of a child into madness, or the experiences of a teenager working in a mortuary, or the macabre tales of a doctor, Barrios uses the grotesque not as trapping or set dressing, but as the world-motive itself. The shock of the grotesque, in Barrios' work, disintegrates the reader's reality and reinscribes a much darker reality in its place.

The 1935 publication of Jorge Luis Borges' collection *Historia universal de la infamia* (*Universal History of Infamy*) was revolutionary, not just in Argentina but in all the more literate countries of Latin America. "With Borges as pathfinder and moving spirit, a group of brilliant stylists developed around him. Although each evidenced a distinct personality and proceeded in his own way, the general direction was that of magical realism."[14] The writer Maria Luisa Bombal was among them, although she had actually met Borges before the publication of his collection. In the last years of the 1930s Bombal wrote a set of supernatural, oneiric stories. They qualify as horror because of their main theme, the treatment of women in the patriarchal societies of Latin America. Subjective, experimenting with time, language, and perspective, and creating an ambiguous reality that is "a mysterious and polyfaceted conglomerate in which there are no limits between factual events and dreams,"[15] Bombal's stories horrify not because of her use of the supernatural or the nightmarish, but because of the purely factual and mimetic way in which she shows the mistreatment of women.

Costa Rica

The world of Costa Rican letters did not have much room for *fantastika* in either the nineteenth or the first four decades of the twentieth century. Examples of *fantastika*, particularly horror, stand out as rare exceptions compared to the mass of realistic and nation-building literature written during those years. Arguably the first Costa Rican horror writer–and unarguably its first novelist–was Manuel Argüello Mora, who published, during the 1880s and 1890s, stories involving monsters from traditional Costa Rican and Central American folklore, monsters like the siren and La Llorona and the Cadejos.

But Mora did not spawn influences or imitate other writers, and when Jenaro Cardona–a diplomat and writer of realist literature–published "La caja del doctor" ("The Doctor's Box," 1929) he was, as Mora had been, essentially alone. "La caja del doctor" is a story about an evil occult scientist who is eventually killed by the skeleton of the wife he had murdered. The scientist and the setting and environment of "La caja del doctor" are sophisticatedly imagined,

---

[14] Angel Flores, "Magical Realism in Spanish American Fiction," *Hispania* 38, no. 2 (May 1955): 189.

[15] Angel Flores, *Spanish American Authors: The Twentieth Century* (New York: H.W. Wilson and Co., 1992), 113.

leading José Ricardo Chaves to call the story "the cosmopolitization of the fantastic"[16] in Costa Rican prose. But like Mora, Cardona was not influential, and "La caja del doctor" is little known compared to the rest of his work.

Cuba

The Caribbean, like Brazil, was a site in which the Gothic was of signal importance: "it is finally in Caribbean writing that a postcolonial dialogue with the Gothic plays out its tendencies most completely and suggestively…the Caribbean, it turns out, is a space that learned to 'read' itself in literature through Gothic fiction."[17] In Cuba, the foremost Gothicist of the 1901-1939 period was Alfonso Hernández Catá, a Spanish-Cuban diplomat, journalist, writer and playwright. Between 1907 and 1938 he wrote a series of Gothic stories and novellas in which the then-prevalent naturalist style is yoked to memorable portrayals of the monstrous Other. In Catá's Gothic fiction,

> the monstrous is represented as a mental illness or as a physical deformity…the Gothic is manifested in the grotesque body that is initially located outside of a social structure. The threat and entry of these bodies into the narrative, therefore, implies the destabilization of the established order in spaces such as the city, the bourgeois home, the hospital or the religious mission.[18]

Catá's purpose was to explore the forbidden, the insane, the transgressive, and the grotesque, but also to generate fear—the ideological purposes of his fiction, especially his anti-Asian plots, were secondary to his desire to create emotions in his readers. The method by which he achieved this was the use of twisted madmen, "hysterical and lustful women, tormented homosexuals, incestuous brothers, and sinister or monstrous children."[19] Vampiric (or incestuous or bigamous or murderous) *femmes fatale*, lepers, haunted houses, and lust-filled Asians are also used by Catá in his horror fiction.

Honduras

---

[16]José Ricardo Chaves, "Monstruos fantásticos en la literatur a Costarricense," *Revista de Filología y Lingüística de la Universidad de Costa Rica* 42 (2016): 83.

[17]Lizabeth Paravisni-Gebert, "Colonial and Postcolonial Gothic: the Caribbean," in *The Cambridge Companion to Gothic Fiction*, ed. Jerrold E. Hogle (Cambridge: Cambridge University Press, 2012), 233.

[18]Sandra M. Casanova-Vizcaino, "Monstruos, Maniobras y Mundos: Lo Fantástico en la Narrativa Cubana, 1910-2010" (PhD diss., University of Pennsylvania, 2012), 23.

[19]Casanova-Vizcaino, "Monstruos, Maniobras y Mundos," 39.

Literature came to Honduras relatively late compared to the other Latin American countries, with Romanticism reaching Honduras only in the late nineteenth century and Modernism not long thereafter. Honduran popular literature essentially matched Honduran serious literature, with the usual genres, such as adventure and romance, being produced in large numbers and with horror fiction–popular with readers rather than intellectuals–being confined to serial fiction. One exception to this was Froylán Turcios' *El vampiro* (*The vampire*, 1910). Turcios was an important intellectual of his time and an author, poet, journalist, and politician, but most of his fiction was Modernist. *El vampiro* is a tragedy, a doomed love story about a priest-vampire who sexually preys upon a teenage girl who is in love with her cousin. The first Latin American novel with a vampire character, *El vampiro* is imitative of *Dracula* structurally but otherwise places far more emphasis on the romance plot and on Modernist elements such as the transgressive and queer sexuality of the three main characters than on the creation of fear, although there are several frightening moments in the novel.

Jamaica

The years between 1890 and 1914 were important ones for the development of the short story in Jamaica. Jamaica, then a British colony, was the recipient of substantial fiction from Great Britain, in the form of both short story collections and the popular magazines that were publishing high quality short fiction.[20] Not surprisingly, several Jamaican writers had their work published in American and British magazines, while numerous others had their work published in the Jamaican literary journals and newspapers at this time. A wide range of genres and story types were written and published during the 1890-1914 period, including horror literature. The English influence on Jamaican horror stories of the period is heavy, with a number having Jamaican settings but otherwise being imitations of Sheridan Le Fanu, Margaret Oliphant, or Robert Louis Stevenson. Many other writers, however, reworked featured or reworked folklore or oral stories from the island's native and African past, to create stories that had English trappings but purely Jamaican content.

In 1929 Herbert George de Lisser, a journalist and novelist, published *The White Witch of Rosehall*. De Lisser primarily wrote romances, "the central plot of Jamaican literature until 1949;"[21] *The White Witch* is his only work of *fantastika*. A heavily fictionalized story about the legendary–but thoroughly historical–monster Annie May Palmer, *The White Witch* is a Gothic romance of good quality. Still readable (and widely read) today, *The White Witch* horrifies not only via Palmer's spells (which are hinted to be mesmerism rather than outright magic) but also because of her treatment of her slaves; although written in the late 1920s, and therefore discrete rather than explicit in its depiction of sex and violence, even the hints of the terrible reality that

---

[20]It is with good reason that Roger Lancelyn Green dubbed the 1880-1914 period "the age of the storytellers." Roger Lancelyn Green, "Introduction," in *The Prisoner of Zenda* (London: J.M. Dent & Sons, 1966), ix.

[21]Leah Rosenberg, "Modern Romances: the short stories in Una Marson's 'The Cosmopolitan' (1928-1931)," *Journal of West Indian Literature* 12, no. ½ (Nov. 2004): 172.

de Lisser includes are horrifying enough.

Mexico

Defying the trend toward Modernism in Mexican literature in the 1900-1914 years were the popular and commercial writers of genre stories, who primarily published their work in newspapers. The foremost writer of horror stories among these commercial writers was Alejandro Cuevas, a lawyer, composer, and playwright. In the latter half of the 1900s he "appalled and delighted readers of the illustrated Sunday supplement to *El Diario* with his series of 'Cuentos macabros,' which combine elements of violence, evil, and eroticism."[22] Cuevas' influences were primarily French, and ranged from Dumas to Zola; Cuevas' narratives usually featured realistic settings and people assailed by the grotesque or the supernatural. In Cuevas' stories people are buried alive or eaten by rats; there are wax museums run by insane doctors, spider-vampires, and mad scientists.

Peru

Manuel Ricardo Palma Soriano was a giant of nineteenth century Peruvian letters, creating a separate genre of short stories known as *tradiciones* which mixed history and fiction for educational purposes. His son Clemente was an important and influential literary critic and short story writer, regarded as one of the founders of the modern short story form in Peruvian literary history. Clemente Palma wrote two collections of "malevolent tales" in 1904 and 1925. His fiction was in most respects the opposite of his father's, being neither historical nor educational. Clemente Palma's horror fiction shows the influence of Poe and Nietzsche as well as the French symbolists and decadents, although their most obvious influence is Villiers de l'Isle-Adam and his *contes cruel*. Clemente Palma's horror stories are darkly humorous, sardonically blasphemous, deeply pessimistic, and filled with the supernatural.

Quite different in his horror work was Manuel Augusto Bedoya y Lerzundi, one of the most prolific of all Peruvian authors, although his work was not always of the best quality. His *La señorita Carlota* (1915) is a relatively simple tragedy about a woman who is turned into a vampire and eventually commits suicide. Much more complicated and interesting is Bedoya's *El tirano Bebevidas. Monstruo de America* (*The tyrant Bebevidas. Monster of America*, 1939). A political allegory about the despotic Peruvian regime of General Oscar Benevides, *El tirano Bebevidas* places the action in a boys' school, and has the gay vampire headmaster prey on the young boys in order to cure an incurable disease. *El tirano Bebevidas* uneasily combines a standard romance plot with the inclusion of paraliterary texts such as pamphlets whose point is to make the political metaphors and allegory clear; the vampire's appearance is relatively limited (a trick taken from Stoker's *Dracula*) but the frightening scenes of the aftermath of the attack are many.

---

[22]Ross Larson, *Fantasy and Imagination in the Mexican Narrative* (Tempe, AZ: Center for Latin American Studies, 1977), 12-13.

Uruguay

Perhaps the most famous pre-World War Two Latin American writer of horror stories is Horacio Quiroga, who alone of the pre-1939 Latin American writers appears in the standard American reference works on horror literature. Quiroga, who "is a serious contender for the symbolic title 'father of the Latin American Short Story,'"[23] published in prestigious Uruguayan magazines during his lifetime but did not achieve nearly the renown that he gained post-mortem. This is especially so in the field of horror literature, where the comparisons to Poe–Quiroga's self-acknowledged first teacher–Kipling, and de Maupassant are especially apt. "In his tales death is just as pervasive, protean and arbitrary, serving finally to portray human life as a pre-ordained struggle that, however valiant, affirms inglorious destiny and the futility of individual action. In Quiroga, hope is foolish illusion, a lie to which we cling even knowing full well the awful and mortal truth it hides."[24] Quiroga's horror stories usually have settings in the wild; "with Jack London, Quiroga was probably the greatest writer of *natural* horror stories, chronicling the terror that can occur when man finds himself in the midst of a natural environment he cannot understand or cope with."[25] Quiroga shares with London (and Kipling, another writer Quiroga modeled himself upon) a terse, lean style possessed of powerfully barbed endings. Quiroga's stories are dark and powerful, set in an uncaring universe full of merciless natural settings, in whose environs men and women usually come to bad ends. In many respects Quiroga is a "Spanish language de l'Isle Adam possessed by the *contes cruel*."[26]

Venezuela

Julio Calcaño was an author, translator, journalist and critic, best known critically as an important Venezuelan poet. His 1913 collection *Cuentos escogidos* (*Selected stories*) contained a number of stories featuring vampires, pacts with the devil, Gothicisms, and other elements of traditional horror stories. Calcaño's strength is both the psychological depth he lends to his characters and the atmosphere of his stories, thick with an asphyxiating dread and fear. Too, he regularly ratchets up the narrative tension in his stories and makes adroit use of moments of surprise in his plots.

---

[23]Paul W. Borgeson, Jr., "Quiroga, Horacio, 1878-1937," in *Concise Encyclopedia of Latin American Literature*, ed. Verity Smith (New York: Routledge, 2000), 525.

[24]Borgeson, Jr., "Quiroga, Horacio, 1878-1937," 525.

[25]Lawrence Greenberg, "Quiroga, Horacio (1878-1937)," in *St. James Guide to Horror, Ghost & Gothic Writers*, ed. David Pringle (Detroit: St. James Press, 1998), 676.

[26]Jessica Amanda Salmonson, "Some Ghostly Tales from South America," Violet Books, last accessed June 19, 2018, https://web.archive.org/web/20130629032050/http://www.violetbooks.com/magic-realist.html.

20

Chapter Three: Asia

China

China's tradition of horror fiction is ancient. Jing Cao and Linda Dryden argue that the Chinese form of the Gothic dates to *The Classic of Mountains and Seas* (circa 300 B.C.E.). Jing and Dryden note that in both England and China Gothic fictions "revealed the aristocracy's upper class corruption, erosion and pleasure, meanwhile also reveal the hardship, pain and resistance of the lower level labors and 'division exacerbated by huge gulf between poor and rich.'[12] Unequal distribution, broken psychology, inner imbalance and Schizophrenia became the main reason and topic in the gothic fiction."[1] The Chinese Gothic is in some ways the opposite of the English Gothic, being more about romance than horror, relatively short, and usually being stories collected from peasants' oral accounts. With the Qing government's ban on contacts with the outside world, the Chinese Gothic stayed in these stories, with the sources of horror being ghosts, monsters, and evil animals, and it was only in the late Qing period, when Western cultural forms began to affect Chinese literature, that the Chinese Gothic began evolving.

Zhiguai, stories of the strange and the supernatural, appeared in the Warring States period (475 B.C.E.-221 B.C.E.) and flourishing as early as the Six Dynasties period (220-589 C.E.), and *chuanqi*, "accounts of marvels," emerging during the Tang period (618-907). *Zhiguai*, simpler in narrative structure and style, are generally seen as less artistically sophisticated than the *chuanqi*, which have deeper characterization and fuller plots. One particularly notable collection of *zhiguai* was Duan Chengshi's *Youyang zazu* (circa 860), which not only tell relatively sophisticated stories of strangeness and horror, but contain a strain of cosmic horror similar to what Lovecraft evoked:

> The focus of these stories is, in fact, that some hidden, mysterious force is at work behind certain phenomena through a process unknown to us. The law and order of the human world become insignificant when contrasted against the background of unknown spheres and powers. For Lovecraft, such alien contact evokes a profound sense of dread and a subtle attitude of awe. In *Youyang zazu*, contact with unknown forces often takes the form of a distinctive narrative structure: a strange event takes place, and then after a certain length of time something horrible happens. No explicit interpretations are offered with regard to the connection of the two incidents; however, an accompanying relationship between them is implied through their juxtaposition...these stories are not motivated by political, religious, or moral purposes; rather, they are more appropriately subject to what Lovecraft has described as "literature of cosmic fear" which features phenomena beyond our comprehension—whose scope extends beyond the narrow field of the mundane. The mysterious nature of the causal agent, the process and the surprisingly meaningful outcome can be better understood in terms of the fundamental thesis that Lovecraft developed in the cultivation of cosmic fear: the human microcosm is contained in the

---

[1]Jing Cao and Linda Dryden, "Comparison of Gothic Genre in both English and Chinese Fictions," *International Journal of Social Science and Humanities* 1, no. 1 (April 2012): 19.

magnitude and malignity of the macrocosm.²

The *Youyang Zazu* was the significant collection of *zhiguai* for centuries, much commented upon by literary critics from the Tang to the Qing periods and much copied by other authors and collectors of *zhiguai*. The landmark Chinese modern book of horror stories, Pu Songling's *Strange Tales from a Chinese Studio*, was published in 1715. *Strange Tales* is full of *zhiguai* and *chuanqi* and stories of fox fairies, ghosts, and demons, based on native Chinese folktales and legends, but full of the author's "strong but subtle criticism of social injustice, his steadfast support for love and freedom."³ *Strange Tales* was an immediate success, spawning dozens of imitation anthologies, and its influence on later Qing writers of horror cannot be overstated. But in the late Qing period, around the turn of the twentieth century, the "response to the strange and supernatural became stereotyped: fantasy was confined by a body of traditional lore, inventions limited to the incidental and peripheral, and the prose style lacked liveliness and zest and elegance and wisdom."⁴

During the 1901-1939 period all of these trends–the Gothic, cosmic horror, the politically-neutered *zhiguai*, and the influence of Western elements and trends–emerged in matured form, in horror fiction in short form and in poems. Four writers in particular stood out as important and influential.

Li Jinfa was the foremost Chinese Symbolist poet. Heavily influenced by Charles Baudelaire and especially Baudelaire's "Les Fleurs du Mal," Li Jinfa wrote a series of poems collected in *Wei yu* (*Light rain*, 1925). The poems in *Wei yu* are symbolist in approach and offer a great deal of macabre imagery, from corpses to skeletons to bloodstains, muddy roads, and dead leaves. Similar in approach to the English graveyard poetry, Li Jinfa's poetry uses the grotesque imagery and vocabulary of death to evoke and appeal to melancholic emotions. "Like Baudelaire, Li aestheticizes the unseemly and turns it into the sublime."⁵

Lu Xun, a noted Chinese man of letters following the 1919 May Fourth Movement, published *Ye cao* (*Wild grass*), a collection of prose-poems, in 1926. In the prose-poems Lu Xun infused supernatural events and a dreamlike atmosphere and narrative with a Freudian approach to the subconscious. The subconscious becomes "a place of strong emotional intensity expressive of otherwise repressed or surrealist images and desires. The effect is one of underscoring the discrepancy between the inner and outer world, and of highlighting the complexity of individual

---

²Lin Wang, "Celebration of the Strange: *Youyang Zazu* and its Horror Stories" (PhD diss., University of Georgia, 2012), 22-23.

³Xiaohuan Zhao, *Classical Chinese Supernatural Fiction: A Morphological History* (Lewiston, NY: E. Mellen Press, 2005), 129.

⁴Xiaohuan, *Classical Chinese Supernatural Fiction*, 147.

⁵Li-hua Ying, *Historical Dictionary of Modern Chinese Literature* (Lanham, MD: Scarecrow Press, 2009), 100.

psychology."[6] Further, in several of the stories the dreams, in disturbing fashion, attempt "imagistic distortion as an artistic way to project the suppressed traumas of the inner psyche."[7]

Stories by Shi Zhecun, a professional author and journal editor, likewise merge the *zhiguai* and Freudian insights. In a series of stories published in 1932 and 1933, Shi Zhecun used the vocabulary of psychology "to translate the classical *zhiguai* tale into a type of Chinese surrealist fiction."[8] His stories often refer back to older works, from Pu Songling's *Strange Stories* to the stories of Sheridan Le Fanu to Shi Nai'an's *Water Margin* (circa 1250 C.E.). Shi Zhecun's stories range from full-blown fantasies involving the appearance of a ghostly woman in black who acts as a omen of death to historical tales set in the mythical past to stories set in the present, in a Shanghai that is figuratively and possibly literally haunted by its past. In the stories "the supernatural events are clearly utilized to symbolize repressed forces of sexuality or guilt in the individual psyche,"[9] and history becomes an irruption of the irrational: "a large measure of the disturbing power of Shi's fiction...lies in the returns within its narratives not only of the destructive desires of its characters, but also of disruptively heterogeneous elements of a Chinese past that seemed to many in need of repression in the search for modernity."[10]

Xu Dishan was a public intellectual and an author, translator, and folklorist. Among literary critics he is known for his novels focusing on the common people of south China and Southeast Asia, but he is more generally known for his religious studies and his connection of the I Ching to occult predecessors, including Chinese witchcraft, numerology, and astrology. During the 1930s he wrote a series of ghost stories; the stories were collected and published in 1994. Xu Dishan was a proponent of Rabindranath Tagore's works, translating and promoting them to Chinese audiences, and Xu Dishan's horror stories are similar to Tagore's, being combinations of traditional folklore and Gothic architecture, elements, or tropes. In at least one of his ghost stories Xu Dishan addressed his Christian faith, and incorporated it into the greater world of Chinese supernatural beliefs.[11]

---

[6]Anne Wedell-Wedellsborg, "Haunted Fiction: Modern Chinese Literature and the Supernatural," *The International Fiction Review* 32, no. 1-2 (2005), accessed June 19, 2018, https://journals.lib.unb.ca/index.php/IFR/article/view/7797/8854.

[7]Lee Oufan Lee, *Voices from the Iron House: A Study of Lu Xun* (Bloomington, IN: Indiana University Press, 1987), 92.

[8]Wedell-Wedellsborg, "Haunted Fiction."

[9]Wedell-Wedellsborg, "Haunted Fiction."

[10]William Schaefer, "Kumarajiva's Foreign Tongue: Shi Zhecun's Modernist Historical Fiction," *Modern Chinese Literature* 10, no. 1/2 (Spring/Fall 1998): 27.

[11]Archie C.C. Lee, "The Bible in Chinese Christianity: Its Reception and Appropriation in China," *The Ecumenical Review*, 67, no. 1 (March 2015): 98-99.

India

In India, traditional cultures had no lack of ghosts, vampires, and other horror icons and motifs in their folklores, and it was to be expected that when Indians began to write prose in modern forms–short stories and novels–they would draw upon these icons and motifs for their horror fiction. However, during the middle of the nineteenth century, at the height of the British control over the Indian subcontinent, Western literary models and writers made a major impact on most of the Indian literary cultures, so that not only were the novel and the short story rapidly adopted by Indian authors, so too were contemporary Western movements like realism, contemporary Western issues like the oppression of the poor, and contemporary Western authorial tactics like an emphasis on the psychology of characters. These two competing forms–the natively folklorish and the imitation of the Western novel or short story–were the shapes into which Indian horror fiction was formed for the first decades of the twentieth century. Indian horror literature was not a coherent genre during the 1901-1939 time period, not in the way that Indian detective literature and science fiction was during those years; Indian horror literature instead consisted of individual works and authors laying the groundwork for the works and authors to come.

The most significant, if not influential, of the nineteenth century Indian horror novels is Toru Dutt's *Le Journal de Mademoiselle d'Arvers* (*The Journal of Miss d'Arvers*, 1879). Written when Dutt was only a teenager, *Le Journal* is a Gothic novella about a young woman who suffers silently for the crimes of a man she loves, and is ultimately martyred for her pains. The language is old-fashioned and sentimental, and the plot and characterization is melodramatic, but the novel is full of Gothic paraphernalia, including premonitory dreams and visions, ghosts, and an obsession with Death. Likely Dutt was influenced during the writing of *Le Journal* by the Gothic and sensation novels she read; the end result is a very Western Gothic novel, with little of Dutt's native India in it. *Le Journal* was an example for later Indian women writers, and several decades after its writing Indian horror writers would return to the Gothic form, but in the near term horror writers did not emulate Dutt's example.

Troilokyanath Mukhopadhyay was a civil servant, museum curator, and popular author in both English and Bengali. Most of his fiction was light and humorous, and his ghost stories, written from the 1890s through the 1920s, were in this category. Although the ghosts are traditionally Indian, grotesque, and frightening to characters, Mukhopadhyay wrote the stories as light-hearted satire, and the cumulative effect of his stories is not fear but amusement. An author who similarly wrote ghost stories to amuse was Upendrakishore Raychowdhury, best known as a great innovator in printing technology, as a children's author, and as the grandfather of Satyajit Ray. Raychowdhury wrote ghost stories in the 1900s and 1910s, but his ghosts, like Mukhopadhyay, are harmless, fun-loving, and benevolent.

Bengal proved to be among the leaders in the modernization of Indian literature during the nineteenth century, so that during the first four decades of the twentieth century a surprising amount of Western genre literature was produced, from science fiction to horror. On the folklorish side were a number of books aimed at children, collections of Bengali folktales and fairy tales which contained horror of a basic sort. The classic collection of this sort is Dakshinaranjan Mitra Majumder's *Thakurmar Jhuli* (*Grandmother hangs*, 1907), which features an array of different supernatural creatures in simplistic good-and-evil terms appropriate for a youthful audiences.

Written for more mature audiences was Panchkari Dey's "The Poet's Lover" (1914) and *Mayabini* (1928). Dey was by profession a writer of detective novels, and was quite successful at it, being famous in his time. His "The Poet's Lover," a folkloric horror story, was unusual for him. More usual was his *Mayabini* (1928), in which one of Dey's series detectives duels with a shapeshifting *femme fatale*; the horror in *Mayabini* arises from a combination of her ruthlessness and her yoga-granted supernatural power, which she puts to use in the course of committing crimes, including murders.

The stories in S. Mukerji's *Indian Ghost Stories* (1914) were typical of a certain type of Indian horror story of the 1910s: "in compliance with the generic requirements of the English Victorian and Edwardian ghost story,"[12] lacking all but a fraction of Indian characters, folklore, or environment, and "largely anecdotal, aped the discursive style of Victorian literature, and replicated the ennoblement of Western rationalism and civilization through discrimination against the superstitious, ghost-fearing 'natives.'"[13]

Certainly the most prominent Indian writer of the 1901-1939 era was Rabindranath Tagore, who was awarded the Nobel Prize in Literature in 1913. Tagore, both extremely literate in Bengali literature and an ardent patriot, began writing short stories in 1877 and, influenced by both traditional Bengali literature and realist-heavy Western literature, began writing politically-charged horror stories in 1892; he continued writing horror stories, among many other works, for the next thirty years. Tagore's horror stories are not in the realist genre, but rather are Gothics, a genre that, for indigenous writers, offers "neither the literary exorcism of a monstrous Other nor a path back to an original identity through such an exorcism. However, as a genre that favors narratives of fragmentation and disjunction and that emphasizes the uncanny, the Gothic is particularly suited for explorations of hybridity."[14] This hybridity–characters combining traditional and modern ways, English and Indian ways–and Tagore's exploration of the "ambiguities and poignancy of changing gender relations in nineteenth-century colonial Bengal"[15] are the dominant themes of Tagore's horror, although in his "The Lost Jewels" (1919) he uses psychological suspense rather than the tropes of the Gothic.

---

[12]Katarzyna Ancuta, "Asian Gothic," in *A New Companion to the Gothic*, ed. David Punter (Chichester, West Sussex: Blackwell Publishing, 2012), 432.

[13]Andrew Hock-soon Ng, "South Asia," in *The Ashgate Encyclopedia of Literary and Cinematic Monsters*, ed. Jeffrey Andrew Weinstock (Burlington, VT: Ashgate, 2014), 269.

[14]Sumangala Bhattacharya, "Between Worlds: The Haunted Babu in Rabindranath Tagore's "Kankal" and "Nishite," *Nineteenth-Century Gender Studies* 6, no. 1 (Spring 2010), accessed June 19, 2018, http://www.ncgsjournal.com/issue61/bhattacharya.htm.

[15]Bhattacharya, "Between Worlds."

Tagore's use of horror fiction to express his social and political views presented Indian horror writers with new possibilities for horror fiction. Muhammad Habib's *The Desecrated Bones and Other Stories* (1925), is one such collection of horror stories. Habib's sympathy with the poor and oppressed is clear in the stories, whose guiding philosophy is Sufism, and his combination of folklore motifs with a more modern sensibility makes clear the influence of Tagore. A writer of horror stories (among many other things) in the 1930s, Bibhutibhushan Bandopadhyay, also took a political slant in his horror fiction, focusing on class injustices. Hemendra Kumar Roy, a notable Bengali children's writer and detective writer, contributed a number of stories in the 1930s and 1940s and a collection, *Names Feared By All* (1932); the stories in the collection were localized Bengali ghost and horror stories (vampires, mummies, unearthly *femmes fatale*, mad scientists, etc.) with unsubtle political commentaries, similar to Roy's detective fiction.

Tagore's writing of horror literature also paved the way for other horror writers who weren't so politically passionate and who told stories that combined traditional folklore and folkloric motifs and tropes with twentieth century prose style. Notable among these were Sankara Krishna Chettur's *Muffled Drums and Other Stories* (1927) and *The Cobras of Dharma Sevi and Other Stories* (1937).

Tagore was the most prominent Indian horror writer of the time period, but the most widely-read were the writers who appeared in the *Indian State Railways Magazine* in the 1920s and 1930s. *Indian State Railways Magazine* was a cheap publication sold at railway stations and containing items that might interest, inform, and appeal to railway travelers. The publication numbers of the *Magazine* are unknown, but considering how many people rode the railways during the 1920s and 1930s, the numbers of people who read the stories in the *Magazine*, or had them read to them, would be in the millions if not the tens of millions. Interestingly, the *Magazine* carried stories of the supernatural in nearly every issue. These horror stories were not aesthetically superior works of art, and many of them were written by Anglo-Indians rather than Indians, but they were nonetheless popular. The horror itself is of the standard nineteenth century British variety, often with an Indian environment and cast of characters and occasionally making use of Indian folklore.

Indonesia

The Indonesian (then the "Dutch East Indies") dime novels (*majalah roman*, or *roman picisan* as they were later disparagingly called) of the 1920s and 1930s, when they published horror fiction, used traditional Chinese horror stories--*zhiguai* or *chuanqi*–or serialized novels that combined martial arts with horror, in stories that were geared toward a mass readership. More common in the *majalah roman* were detective and crime stories, but even there horror sometimes slipped through. In the popular *majalah roman Doenia Pengalaman* in 1939, Sumatran Malay writer and editor S. Djarens published a series of stories about Dr. Zin, a German Jew who performs a series of nasty experiments on Christian Jews. Ultimately he is exposed and forced to flee to Indonesia, where a local detective apprehends him. The Dr. Zin stories are as horrific and graphic as Djarens could make them while still obeying the colonial Dutch censorship laws.

Japan

As with China, Japan's literary involvement with the supernatural and with horror fiction long predates the twentieth century. From the erotically terrifying spirits in Murasaki Shikibu's *The Tale of Genji* (circa 1015) to the frightening encounters between man and the supernatural—heavily influenced by the Chinese *zhiguai*--in the *Konjaku Monogatarishū* (circa 1120) to the ominous ghosts of the *Heike Monogatari* (circa 1300) to the spirits of Ueda Akinari's *Ugetsu Monogatari* (1776), which made use of *zhiguai*, *chuanqi*, and Japanese folklore, the strange and frightening, especially in proto-Gothic form,[16] have always been a part of Japanese literature. This accelerated in the Meiji era (1868-1912), when the influx of Western values, technology, and cultural artifacts, including literature, exercised a powerful influence over Japanese culture, and Japanese horror writers in particular chose Western models to emulate, including modern writers of Gothics.

Almost immediately after the arrival of Commodore Perry in 1853 and the prying open of Japan in 1854, Japan underwent two separate popular crazes, one for all things Western and one for the supernatural, the strange, and anything not encountered in everyday Japanese life. Both fads lasted well into the twentieth century, but the fad for Western culture and technology provoked a backlash against the West among Japanese intellectuals. As part of this backlash, a movement arose by which these intellectuals attempted to halt the influx of Western culture and technology and to popularize a return to traditional Japanese values and folkways. Many modern Japanese writers and artists turned to the supernatural as a reaction to Western bourgeois capitalist values and scientific positivism.

This backlash, and turn toward the use of the supernatural and the traditional Japanese form of the Gothic, can be seen in the foremost Japanese horror writers of pre-WW2 years.

Kyōka Izumi, one of the premier literary stylists of his time, was heavily influenced by both Poe and the supernatural elements of traditional Japanese literature. "In terms of his mastery of such traditional supernatural elements as ghosts, monsters, and demonic females, all set within an appropriately eerie atmosphere, Kyōka Izumi is the greatest of twentieth-century Japanese fantasists."[17] He also had a strong, negative reaction to the positivism and bourgeois capitalism of the Meiji era, and expressed his views in a variety of Gothic stories, written from the late 1890s into the 1930s. Kyōka's stories combine a complex and sophisticated prose style with an obsession with the supernatural and a series of Romantic and surrealist critiques of mainstream

---

[16]Regarding the reasonable claim that the application of the term "Gothic" to non-Western literature is a form of colonialism, "the Japanese Gothic shares with the West its subversion of religious and social norms, an obsession with sex and death, and a fear of the supernatural or unknown. These are human qualities, not the province of one culture." Henry J. Hughes, "Familiarity of the Strange: Japan's Gothic Tradition," *Criticism* 42, no. 1 (Winter 2000): 60.

[17]Susan Napier, *The Fantastic in Modern Japanese Literature: The Subversion of Modernity* (London: Routledge, 1996), 240.

Meiji values, especially those concerning class, sexuality, and marriage. The stories are heavily supernatural, and are usually ghost stories about unfulfilled sexual desire, *doppelgängers*, and eroticized suicides; one of Kyōka's strengths was to take archetypal tropes like the demonic/nurturing woman and breathe new life into them. Moreover, Kyōka introduces the uncanny into the Tokyo metropolis in his stories, similar to the work of Shi Zhecun, creating a Tokyo that sees traditional ghosts haunting modern city streets in what functions as a rebuke of the then-popular positivist subjectivism in fiction and the process by which newcomers to Tokyo were transforming the city from a location to the center of the nation.[18] Traditional Japan, in these stories, avenges itself on modernity via the fantastic.

Natsume Sōseki is generally considered to be the greatest novelist in post-Meiji Restoration Japanese history. Primarily a novelist, Sōseki has exerted and continues to exert a significant influence on most major Japanese writers. He was a critic of the rapid mechanization that Japan was undergoing in the early 1900s, as well as Japan's attempts to imitate the West. This attitude manifested itself in his *Yume jūya* (*Ten Nights of Dream*, 1908), a set of ten dreams set in various time periods and described in visionary terms. The "Dream of the Sixth Night" is about the narrator watching Unkei, a historical master sculpture, carving guardian gods. Inspired by what he sees, the narrator attempts, in increasingly frenzied terms, to imitate Unkei. "Dream of the Sixth Night" is like the other dreams in *Yume jūya*, only more so: hazy, dreamlike, poignant, eerie, even uncanny in its portrayal of character and the conclusion that guardian gods will never be found in modern wood–that the modern person is isolated and abandoned by the gods. "In its effective development of a surreal atmosphere of Otherness, combined with its imaginative use of the notion of dream itself, the work creates a liminal literary world which is clearly that of the twentieth century."[19]

Hyakken Uchida was one of Sōseki's disciples, and eventually became a major literary figure in his own right. While best known for his matter-of-fact writings about wartime life in Tokyo, his first book, *Meido* (*Realm of the Dead*, 1922), is a collection of nightmarish vignettes. Uchida's stories are *koan*-like in their abruptness and hidden or submerged epiphanies, but Uchida's clean and uncluttered style renders them easy to read and effective in their frightening impacts. "The stories defy psychology and symbolism but seem to float on the surface of their own weirdness. As with poems, the surface *is* the experience. But if the details are strange and

---

[18]Chiyoko Kawakami, "The Metropolitan Uncanny in the Works of Izumi Kyōka: A Counter-Discourse on Japan's Modernization," *Harvard Journal of Asiatic Studies* 59, no. 2 (Dec. 1999): 559.

[19]I'm using "weird" as a categorical term, akin to "horror" and "mystery" and "science fiction," in the same sense and with much the same meaning as Jeff Vandermeer, who wrote "'Weird' refers to the sometimes supernatural or fantastical element of unease...an element that could take a blunt, literal form or more subtle and symbolic form and which was...combined with a visionary sensibility." Jeff Vandermeer, "The New Weird: 'It's Alive?'" in *The New Weird*, eds. Ann VanderMeer and Jeff VanderMeer (San Francisco, CA: Tachyon Publications, 2008), ix.

unreal, the epiphanies are not."[20]

The most famous of these Japanese writers of the supernatural was Edogawa Rampo, whose work was superficially detective fiction, which he began publishing in 1923, but which was also a part of the *ero-guro-nansensu* movement (see below). Rampo's short fiction, macabre and deviant, was heavily influenced by Poe, and although elements of his detective fiction were inspired by the Sherlock Holmes stories of Arthur Conan Doyle, Rampo let the Poe-esque perversity reign supreme in those stories. In his non-detective work he emphasized perversity and abnormal psychology with results that evoked a sense of the uncanny; these stories cannot be counted as horror *per se*, but are instead in the category of the "frightening weird."[21] In works like "The Red Chamber" (1925), "The Human Chair" (1925), "The Hell of Mirrors" (1926), and "The Caterpillar" (1929), Rampo writes about perverse sexuality, body horror, and the cruelty of fate in *contes cruel* and psychological horror stories. To exist, in Rampo's stories, is to transgress, not just against contemporary Japanese mores (which were conservative and emphasized tradition), but against the supposedly scientific psychological standards of the West. In his horror fiction Rampo rebelled against his own society and the foreign influences in it; Rampo, through *ero-guro-nansensu*, is following his own perverse muse–but his muse's path leads him into open revolt against current Japanese society.

Tanizaki Junichirō, whose work spanned a fifty year period, was in some ways an outsider to Japan. Phyllis I. Lyons compares him to Lafcadio Hearn, the white writer who did so much to introduce Japan to the West: "if Hearn can be faulted as an Orientalist for seeing Japan as mysterious, exotic, and aesthetically fascinating—so, too, can Tanizaki."[22] Tanizaki was a master storyteller, but the stories he told were not of Japan as it was, but Japan as he imagined it to be; he "built a self-sustained world of his own *monogatari*, a Japanese narrative genre of storytelling close to that of romance, exploring the realm of classical Japanese literature, folktales, and legends."[23] He began his career under the spell of the West, with the influences of Poe, Baudelaire and Wilde being pronounced, but the lure of traditional Japanese literatures of the seventeenth and eighteenth centuries, especially the erotic and sadistic plots of *kabuki* plays, overwhelmed the influences of Western writers, and by 1926 Tanizaki's writing was thoroughly Japanese in style. In character and content, however, his work never varied:

> …"desire"—emotional, intellectual, artistic and sexual—is his subject matter. His stories are filled with obsessions and fetishes, emotional abuse and mayhem, and also with tender yearnings, lyrical celebrations of beauty, and reverence for the elegance of

---

[20]Phyllis I. Lyons, "Tanizaki Junichirō," in *Modern Japanese Writers*, ed. Jay Rubin (New York: Charles Scribner's Sons, 2001), 385.

[21]Lois Davis Vines, *Poe Abroad: Influence, Reputation, Affinities* (Iowa City, IA: University of Iowa Press, 2002), 244.

[22]Lyons, "Tanizaki Junichirō," 385.

[23]Vines, *Poe Abroad*, 246.

tradition. Without psychological jargon (but with an early and deep study of Krafft-Ebing's nineteenth-century analyses of sexual pathologies) Tanizaki's imagination soared to the highest of ideals, even as many of his stories wallowed in cesspools of degradation.[24]

The "degradation" Lyons writes of is usually sexual masochism or sadism, or some combination of the two, and usually of a desire-obsessed male at the hands of a *femme fatale*; "in Tanizaki's works the themes of the discovery of perversity in human nature and the masochistic desire for self-destruction are intertwined."[25] Here the rebellion is against the sexual order of Meiji society.

Akutagawa Ryūnosuke was the foremost exponent of the short story during his short lifetime, and became known after his death as the "Father of the Japanese short story." "Critics have interpreted his works as reflecting bourgeois traditionalism, disintegrating modernism, and a disturbing combination of both."[26] Influenced by a variety of Western writers, including Poe, Gogol, Baudelaire, and Bierce, as well as by the *Konjaku Monogatarishū*, Akutagawa produced psychologically brutal tales of terrifying events, told in a lyrical style that was the opposite of the naturalist approach favored during his lifetime. Often graphically described, Akutagawa's horror fiction, written from 1915 to the year of his death in 1927, can achieve a hallucinatory quality, an intensity similar to that of Poe's finest works. Akutagawa's work lacks the perverseness of Edogawa Rampo, the masochism and sadism of Tanizaki Junichirō, or the attacks on society of Izumi Kyōka; what Akutagawa's work has instead is raw brutality and harshness, told in splendid prose. Akutagawa's rebellion against Meiji society and Western values was confined to the literary sphere; where Western realism was in vogue, Akutagawa instead chose to write nightmares.

Less famous writers wrote works exemplifying the rebelliousness and anti-Western attitudes of the intellectual elite. Yumeno Kyūsako, a writer of "irregular detective fiction,"[27] wrote his masterpiece, *Dogura magura* (1935), about a paranoid mental patient who may be a murderer, but who ultimately discovers that he's a fetus inside his mother's womb, suffering from a nightmare. Yumeno was known for his avant-garde Gothic narratives, but *Dogura*

---

[24]Howard Hibbett, "Akutagawa Ryūnosuke," in *Modern Japanese Writers*, ed. Jay Rubin (New York: Charles Scribner's Sons, 2001), 19.

[25]"…'irregular detective fiction' (*henkaku tantei shosetsu*), so called because it differed from the more objective and rational methods of 'regular detective fiction' (*honkaku tantei shôsetsu*).² Because of its frequent scientific themes, this category of 'irregular detective fiction' is now treated as the forerunner of contemporary Japanese science fiction.³" Miri Nakamura, "Horror and Machines in Prewar Japan: The Mechanical Uncanny in Yumeno Kyûsaku's Dogura magura," *Science Fiction Studies* 29, no. 3 (Nov. 2002): 364.

[26]Miri, "Horror and Machines in Prewar Japan," 366.

[27]Miri, "Horror and Machines in Prewar Japan," 364.

magura, with its critique of Western scientific culture and its blurring of the distinctions between human bodies and robots, between the biological and the mechanical, is unusually direct. In pre-WW2 Japan machines were seen as both examples of social progress and symbols of degeneration; in the 1990 words of Unno Hiroshi (quoted in Miri 2002), prewar literature depicting machines was in "a constant flux between a utopian dream of machines on one hand and a pessimistic nightmare of them on the other."[28] Yumeno "envisioned machines as fearful entities tearing apart human bodies and...evoked mechanical imagery to strike fear into the heart of reader,"[29] coming down squarely on the anti-Western side of the issue. In his other work, which were hybrid detective/horror novels, "an international cast of androgynes and hermaphrodites involved with family curses and love beyond death populate Yumeno Kyūsaku's sinister but entertaining fantasies."[30]

Yumeno and fellow "irregular detective fiction" writers Oguri Mushitarō and Unno Jūza took this further in their portrayal of "agents of science," including research scientists, engineers, and doctors, as mad scientists. This criticism of contemporary Japanese scientism, the general overconfidence in the possibilities of science and in the presumptuous merging of science and ethics, were "at odds with both the contemporary state ideology toward and the popular understanding of science."[31] Yumeno, Oguri, Unno, and other writers like them instead wrote horror stories of science run amok.

More broadly, these authors can be considered to be members of Japan's Gothic tradition; despite objections to the use of the term to describe canonical Japanese authors,[32] there is what Henry J. Hughes calls a "remarkable continuity in the Gothic tradition beginning with [Ueda] Akinari and branching into the work of Kyōka, Akutagawa, and [Yukio] Mishima."[33] There is the violent eroticism through which the Gothic story portrays the struggles of the spirit and the flesh; there is the confrontation with a Faust figure or a dangerous, supernatural being; there is the use of the figure of the *doppelgänger*; there is the portrayal of religious institutions as corrupt and priests as lust-filled or even murderous; there is the subversion of social norms; and there is a fear of the supernatural and the unknown.

But there are substantial differences between the two traditions as well. For protagonists in Western Gothics, individualism is paramount, but for protagonists in Japanese Gothic novels,

---

[28]Sari Kawana, "Mad Scientists and Their Prey: Bioethics, Murder, and Fiction in Interwar Japan," *The Journal of Japanese Studies* 31, no. 1 (Winter 2005): 89.

[29]Hughes, "Familiarity of the Strange," 60.

[30]Napier, *The Fantastic in Modern Japanese Literature*, 242.

[31]Hughes, "Familiarity of the Strange," 69.

[32]Hughes, "Familiarity of the Strange," 74.

[33]Hughes, "Familiarity of the Strange," 75.

the quest for enlightenment and transcendence, the "explosion of self into psychic collectivity,"[34] is all-important. In the Japanese Gothic, the confrontation with the Faustian or supernatural enemy does not result in death, but the emptying of desire; "unlike Doctor Frankenstein's, the self in the Japanese Gothic is not reaffirmed by the consumption or destruction of the other, especially an other it has helped create."[35] The discovery that life is suffering prompts a quite different reaction in the Japanese Gothic hero, who "looks within and finds peace in *mu*. Whereas the Christian worries that an idle or empty mind invites the devil, the Buddhist empties the mind and glimpses Nirvana."[36]

One specific movement in Japanese society that contributed significantly to Japanese horror fiction in the 1901-1939 period was the "erotic, grotesque, nonsense" movement, "the prewar bourgeois cultural phenomenon that devoted itself to explorations of the deviant, the bizarre, and the ridiculous."[37] The movement, popularly known through the shorthand compound phrase *ero-guro-nansensu*, had constituent elements in various texts in the 1920s but coalesced into an articulated movement in the 1930s. *Ero-guro* texts were aimed primarily at adolescents but at the same time were perceived as avant-garde. In the *ero-guro* stories, which Edogawa Rampo was the leading author of but which Tanizaki and Akutagawa both wrote substantial amounts of, emphasize transgression: of social norms, of gender roles, of the law, of the expected and socially demanded heteronormative sexuality, of prevailing aesthetic codes, of Meiji scientism. "In other words, the culture of *ero, guro, nansensu* allowed rebellion in some small way against the constraints of standard aesthetic, moral, and legal codes and enabled readers to indulge, at least vicariously, in those erotic, thanatotic, and seemingly 'irrational' urges ordinarily suppressed by the logical, civilizing superego of social ethics."[38]

A very different movement in Japanese horror fiction took place during the 1930s: vampire fiction. The first work of foreign vampire fiction to be translated into Japanese was published in Japan in 1930,[39] giving rise to a kind of craze for vampire fiction which reached its

---

[34]Hughes, "Familiarity of the Strange," 75.

[35]Jim Reichert, "Deviance and Social Darwinism in Edogawa Ranpo's Erotic-Grotesque Thriller 'Kotō no oni,'" *The Journal of Japanese Studies* 27, no. 1 (Winter 2001): 114.

[36]Jeffrey Angles, "Seeking the Strange: 'Ryōki' and the Navigation of Normality in Interwar Japan," *Monumenta Nipponica* 63, no. 1 (Spring 2008): 102-3.

[37]Sone Seunghee, "The Mirror Motif in the *Crow's-Eye View* (*Ogamdo*) Poems*," *Seoul Journal of Korean Studies* 29, no. 1 (June 2016): 194-95.

[38]Adam Lifshey, *Subversions of the American Century* (Ann Arbor: University of Michigan Press, 2016), 102.

[39]Mari Kotani, "Techno-Gothic Japan: From Seishi Yokomizo's *The Death's-Head Stranger* to Mariko Ohara's *Ephemera the Vampire*," in *Blood Read*, eds. Joan Gordon and Veronica Hollinger (Philadelphia: University of Pennsylvania Press, 1997), 189.

height in 1939, when "the prototype of Japanese vampire literature, mystery writer Seishi Yokomizo's *Dokuro-Kengyo* (*The Death's-Head Stranger*, 1939),"[40] was published. Japanese vampire writers during this craze were "deeply conscious of the binary opposition between their national culture and foreign culture,"[41] and strove–usually successfully–to tell purely Japanese vampire stories. The craze came to an end with the beginning of World War Two and the restrictions on the use of paper, and was not renewed for another forty years.

Korea

The Korean newspapers of the 1920s and 1930s, one of the main sources of modern fiction for Korean readers during those decades, were not allowed to print horror fiction by the occupying Japanese, and for the most part printed romances and serialized detective novels. However, there were two Korean authors of note who published works with horror elements. Yi Sang, one of the foremost Korean poets of the 1930s, was the first to combine psychological realism with surrealist techniques, resulting in poetry collections like *Kkamagwiui Siseon (Crow's Eye View*, 1934). *Crow's Eye View* is both modernist and quintessentially Yi Sang, with striking visual imagery, an ominous repetition of signs and lines, and an "irreconcilable combination of dark mood and playful tone."[42] In poems like "Poem No. 1," the playful mood is limited to Yi's experimentation with form; the dark mood–the horror of terrified (or worse, terrifying) children–is all. Yi's subject matter, in both his short stories and his poetry, is anxiety and alienation, the latter manifesting as horror of self and the universe.

A more straightforwardly horrific story is Kim Tongni's "Munyŏ-do" (1936), about the confrontation between Christianity and Korean shamanism. "Munyŏ-do" was written by Tongni, perhaps the most prolific novelist in the history of Korea, early in his career, but shows him, typically, to be both cosmopolitan and Korean at the same time. In the story a shaman mother and Christian son grimly struggle to exorcize each other of alien spirits; the forces of nature in "Munyŏ-do," those who are using the mother, are shown to be very dark indeed.

Philippines

In the Philippines, the production of literature steadily rose after the American occupation following the end of the Spanish-American War in 1898, as a combination of educational reforms and post-Hispanic nationalism spurred the creation of literature, whether popular, mainstream, or explicitly nationalistic and propagandistic. One of the major writers of the period was Guillermo Gómez Windham, who wrote articles, stories, and poems for newspapers and then a series of novels, for which he was the winner of the Zóbel Prize, for best Filipino literature in the Spanish language, in 1922. In 1924 he published "Tía Pasia" ("Aunt Pasia"), the first Filipino

---

[40]Mari, "Techno-Gothic Japan," 189.

[41]Mari, "Techno-Gothic Japan," 190.

[42]Sone, "Mirror Motif," 195.

horror story of note, about a hard-edged widow, Pasia, who repels her neighbors through her unkindness and is eventually haunted for her actions. Gómez Windham was usually a realist, and "Tía Pasia" is a substantial departure for him. The haunting of Pasia is literal, but the symbolism is plentiful and ambiguous, and "its Gothic ambience and themes of sadism and vengeance rely on affect as a dominant mode."[43] "Tía Pasia" is an anti-colonial story, but a subversive one in which colonial forces are portrayed in mixed terms and it's a Filipina who compels them to action–the ghost that haunts Pasia is metaphorically the ghosts of 1898. "The result is a text of particular literary depth, compelling in its strangenesses and the perplexing catharsis with which it ends."[44]

The events of the Second World War were cataclysmic for the Asian countries, as they were for most of the rest of the world, and it would take some time for most of the Asian countries to return to the pre-war state in which horror fiction was able to be published, much less welcome.

---

[43]Lifshey, *Subversions of the American Century,* 102.

[44]Lifshey, *Subversions of the American Century,* 102.

Chapter Four: Europe

Austria

In Austria, the nineteenth-century realist movement did not in turn produce a twentieth-century naturalist movement. Rather, what followed in the 1901-1939 period in Austrian letters, especially for writers located in Vienna, were the *Jugendstil* (art nouveau) and expressionist movements. The latter movement, in which reality is presented subjectively rather than objectively, with the ultimate goal being to produce emotions and moods, was influential on writers of both mainstream literature and genre literature; the protagonists of genre *heftromane* ("hero-novels," the Austrian and German equivalent of the American pulps) like *Billy Dogg, Der Blinde Meisterdetektiv* (1931) or *Weltenbummler. Die Vier Musketiere* (1935-1937) displayed unusual expressionist and art nouveau elements.

In horror literature, however, authors drew upon different movements: advances in psychology, medicine, technology, and the occult and pseudosciences, French decadence, the *fin-de-siècle*, and German "black Romanticism" or "neo-Romanticism," as well as the rediscovery of the works of E.T.A. Hoffmann, the discovery of the works of Edgar Allan Poe, and a renewed interest in painters like Pieter Breughel the Elder and Hieronymous Bosch. Drawing on these diverse elements, three major German-language authors crafted memorable horror stories: the Germans Hanns Heinz Ewers and the Austrians Karl Hans Strobl and Gustav Meyrink. Meyrink, Ewers, and Strobl are usually grouped together as the triumvirate of writers who ushered in the writing of German-language supernatural and horror literature, and certainly the three were influential and widely-read as a group. But the Austrian *fantastika* and horror which followed Strobl and Meyrink's work were more than just German horror-manqué; there were specifically Austrian attributes to them that the German authors who followed the triumvirate lacked, and

Strobl wrote four collections of horror short stories (1901, 1904, 1907, 1911), and two novels (both in 1920), all well-received by critics and the audience. Strobl wrote other things besides horror–he was a working writer from 1917, but before that he wrote poetry, plays, and historical novels–but it was for his horror fiction that he became best-known, and it was his horror fiction that he was proudest of, to the point of claiming to have solely reinvented the horror genre that E.T.A. Hoffmann began, rather than having been influenced by and a successor to Ewers, as was commonly assumed (not without some justification). Besides the influence of Ewers, Strobl's fiction was also influenced by Poe's work, and like Poe Strobl's horror fiction is usually macabre and grotesque with an end toward frightening or appalling the reader, although a gallows humor occasionally makes its appearance as well. Strobl's work, though, is ultimately a fatalistic acceptance of an amoral universe, some distance from the underlying message of much of Poe's work. After the mid-1920s and the rise of the *neue Sachlichkeit* (new Objectivist) movement, Strobl stopped writing horror fiction to concentrate on other genres.

Strobl's contemporary, Gustav Meyrink, began writing in 1901 and was a full-time professional writer from 1904. But where Strobl claimed to be the inheritor of the mantle of *the* German horror writer from E.T.A. Hoffmann, Meyrink actually was, carrying forward Hoffmann's tradition of allegorical and hallucinatory fantasy-horror. Strobl's style was more

Poe-esque, while Meyrink, especially in his stories–which he essentially stopped writing in favor of novels by 1910–was Hoffmann-esque, albeit combined with influences from Franz Kafka and the other writers of the "Prague school." Meyrink, like the other German-language writers of the Prague school, was a cultural and linguistic minority in Prague, heartily disliked by the Czechs, and this isolation "contributed decisively to their sense of alienation and their feeling of lostness of the individual...Meyrink was typical of the Prague writers in two respects, in his language and in his solution to the problem of the alienated, endangered individual,"[1] which was withdrawal into mysticism and a search for transcendence. Also typical of the Prague writers was Meyrink's style; like the other Prague writers, Meyrink responded to his linguistic isolation by "resorting to a highly embellished style. Every noun was preceded by tiringly repetitious adjectives, and tasteless, forced similes abounded."[2]

Meyrink's style has not aged well, but his content remains relevant. He is the "most respected German-language writer in the field of supernatural fiction,"[3] both for his short stories, with their savage satire and dark moralism, and for his novels, which combine apocalyptic dread, phantasmagoric imagery, and a gallows hopefulness that destruction–whether of the city or the world–will be "an occult cleansing of the material world so that higher unions of the spirit can be achieved."[4] Later novels left real-world concerns behind to embrace Meyrink's occult philosophy, but in his best work, like *Der Golem* (1915), he creates essential works of German expressionism.

Meyrink's counterpart as a visual artist was Alfred Kubin, arguably the foremost Austrian artist in the field of the grotesque, the fantastic, and the weird. Kubin's literary output was tiny: only one novel. But that novel, *Die Andere Seite* (*The other side*, 1909), is remarkable, perhaps the most important work of *fantastika* in the entirety of twentieth century German literature. Influenced by Meyrink, the early stories of Franz Kafka, and the work of the surrealists, *Die Andere Seite* is a landmark Lost World novel in which a Western narrator finds an Asian utopia and witnesses its eventual destruction. Its theme is the transition from pleasant dream to ugly reality, and Kubin lades the novel with surreal imagery and sexual symbolism and with a dreamlike tone. The end result is the best-written Lost World novel in any language and the signature work of German-language *fantastika* from the 1901-1939 period.

Less significant, if far more prolific, was Bodo Wildberg, who wrote a number of *fantastika* short stories and adventure novels, and whose early work helped initiate neo-

---

[1] Verna Schuetz, "The Bizarre Literature of Hanns Heinz Ewers, Alfred Kubin, Gustav Meyrink, and Karl Hans Strobl" (PhD diss., University of Wisconsin, 1974), 88.

[2] Schuetz, "The Bizarre Literature," 89.

[3] Marco Frenschkowski, "Meyrink, Gustav," in *Supernatural Literature of the World: An Encyclopedia*, eds. S.T. Joshi and Stefan Dziemianowicz (Westport, CT: Greenwood Press, 2005), 803.

[4] John Clute, "Meyrink, Gustav," in *The Encyclopedia of Fantasy*, eds. John Clute and John Grant (New York: St. Martin's Press, 1997), 642.

Romanticism in Germany, but who is little-known today. His first collection, in 1894, was compared to the work of Poe and Hoffmann, and his later work, with its focus on mentally unstable protagonists and "the transmutation from man to animal and vice-versa,"[5] was an able mix of the commercial and the fantastic.

Never a part of the Prague school, but an important Austrian novelist nonetheless, was Leo Perutz. Perutz, who is best known as a fantasist, wrote historical novels interwoven with fantastic elements which confuse the protagonist(s) and create numerous possible and contradictory interpretations for the apparently or actual supernatural events. But on occasion Perutz added horror to his novels and his short stories, either through the evocation of psychological deterioration and psychopathology, through ominous surreality, or through the use of Jewish folklore and legend. Perutz's most famous novel, *Der Meister des Jüngsten Tages* (*Master of the Day of Judgment*, 1921), is coldly cruel in its treatment of the characters and the reader.

Never a writer of the supernatural, Franz Kafka is nonetheless a vitally important writer of horror fiction. The elements of *fantastika* in his work are ambiguous and generally small, "The Metamorphosis" (1915) aside; what mattered for Kafka are the horrors of the real world, and what those horrors imply about the state of reality:

> There is a sense that, as with Borges, FK's vision of the world can be understood as gnostic...the material world may be an error, a falling from true being, but if there ever was a God from whom we fell there is none now; the Pleroma...is beyond reach, or null. The world is recursive, and it refers back only to itself. If FK can be understood as a religious writer, his religion addresses a Universe from which God has been evacuated.[6]

He created the subgenre of bureaucratic horror, which has its surrealistic and absurd elements but which continually reminds the reader of its too-real plausibility. In "The Metamorphosis" and his other short horror stories, dreamlike events become reality, never losing their paranoid, nightmarish edge but otherwise becoming flawlessly (and frighteningly) incorporated into the real. But, again, the horror in Kafka's narratives is not supernatural: "it is instead the horror of despair, the terrifying fragility of men's loyalty and love, and the frightening ability of the absurd to isolate, insulate, and entrap."[7]

The last significant Austrian horror writer before the advent of the *neue Sachlichkeit* was Paul Busson, a poet, novelist, and short story writer best known for a small collection of "sinister

---

[5]Robert N. Bloch, "Wildberg, Bodo (1862-1942)," in *Supernatural Literature of the World: An Encyclopedia*, eds. S.T. Joshi and Stefan Dziemianowicz (Westport, CT: Greenwood Press, 2005), 1206.

[6]John Clute, "Kafka, Franz (1883-1924)," in *The Encyclopedia of Fantasy*, eds. John Clute and John Grant (New York: St. Martin's Griffin, 1997), 528.

[7]Jack Sullivan, "Franz Kafka," in *The Penguin Encyclopedia of Horror and the Supernatural*, ed. Jack Sullivan (New York: Viking, 1986), 238.

tales" and his historical fantasy and (in Robert Hadji's words) "Gothic phantasmagoria"[8] *Die Wiedergeburt des Melchior Dronte* (*The rebirth of Melchior Dronte* 1921). Busson was an expressionist with similarities–stylistically, at least–to Hanns Heinz Ewers. But Busson's work, though dabbling in horror, ultimately has a hopeful bent, despite the inclusion of infernal powers, ghosts, witches, demons, and black magic. His narratives, both short and long, are an "extraordinary amalgam of historical romance and Gothic fantasy, strongly influenced by the *schauer-romantik* of Hoffmann and Tieck, but expressed in terms of a modern, and distinctly personal, ethos of the supernatural."[9]

Belgium

Literature in Belgium is a relatively recent innovation, the first significant Belgian work of fiction only having been published in 1867 and Belgian's "literary renaissance" having taken place as recently as 1880-1900. Among the many Francophone Belgian[10] writers of the literary renaissance were a quintet of writers who made use of *fantastika*, whether the witches and warlocks of local folklore, grotesque and macabre elements, or full-blown Symbolist work. These five writers--Camille Leonnier, Georges Eekhoud, Emile Verhaeren, Georges Rodenbach, and Maurice Maeterlinck–were the grandfathers of what has come to be known as *l'ecole belge de l'etrange*, "the Belgian school of the strange," whose start is usually located in the 1920s and which has been developing ever since. Its influences are several: French (and, surprisingly, American) writers of *fantastika*, what Kim Connell calls "the macabre myths of Catholicism–the Virgin Mary, the ghostlike holy spirit, the dead returning to life, and the notion of life beyond the tomb, of Judgment Day,"[11] the grotesque art of Belgians Hieronymous Bosch and Jan and Pieter Brueghel, and the nineteenth and early twentieth century Belgian writers of the bizarre, the strange, the uncomfortable, and the grotesque.

Two of the fathers of *l'ecole belge de l'etrange* were Jean Ray and Franz Hellens. Interestingly, though both were direct inspirations for Belgian writers of *fantastika*, only Hellens' horror work was in the quiet style of *l'ecole belge de l'etrange*. The most apposite comparison for Jean Ray is one of the more imaginative American pulp writers–Norvell Page, perhaps.

---

[8]Robert Hadji, "Paul Busson," in *The Penguin Encyclopedia of Horror and the Supernatural,* ed. Jack Sullivan (New York: Viking, 1986), 65.

[9]Hadji, "Paul Busson," 65.

[10]The Dutch-speaking Walloons were generally excluded from the Belgian literary renaissance, and did not contribute any horror writers of note.

[11]Kim Connell, "Introduction," in *The Belgian School of the Bizarre*, ed. Kim Connell (Cranbury, NJ: Associated University Presses, 1998), 12.

Ray is described as "Belgium's most important writer of weird fantasy"[12] and "the Belgian Edgar Allan Poe."[13] The latter designation is arguable, but the former is not. Ray wrote prolifically and influenced a number of Belgian writers who followed him, and presented both the Belgian public and other Belgian writers with the image of what a professional Belgian writer of *fantastika* could be, beginning with his first collection of *fantastika*, in 1925. But as a writer Ray was the opposite of Poe in most respects, deserving the comparison only in terms of being *primus inter pares* among Belgian *fantastika* writers, as Poe is to American and French *fantastika* writers. Ray wrote continuously from 1929 to the invasion of Belgium in 1940, but the great majority of his work is coarsely written, quite some distance from Poe's much more careful craftsmanship and much closer to the work of the American pulp writers. Too, Ray was an extremely commercial writer, far more so than Poe, and customarily wrote to the market. Ray was a professional, of course, and his work is always competent, even in the dime novel detective stories he churned out by the dozens. But with the exception of *Malpertuis* (1943) Ray was never inspired to create Art, as Poe was and did.

What Ray did achieve, though, was a fecund production of colorfully imagined stories reveling in the creation of overt terror in their characters and readers. In his dime novel work, he often made use of the flashy trappings of the supernatural–werewolves, ghost trains, curses and death rays–to great effect, most famously in his Harry Dickson stories. In his horror stories, he combined unsubtle supernaturalism with black humor and a lean, laconic style comparable to Jack London. It was only in his longer work, *Malpertuis* and the other novels and novellas, that he attempted to develop a sinister and *unheimlich* atmosphere.

Franz Hellens, conversely, was an entirely more subtle writer of horror–more subtle, and more talented. Hellens was nominated for the Nobel Prize four times and earned the praise of no less than Vladimir Nabokov. Hellens, through his writing and the literary magazines, was influential not just on other writers of *l'ecole belge de l'etrange* but on the world of Belgian letters more generally. Hellens' horror work is as mentioned much quieter than Ray's; Hellens does not tell tales of murder, monstrosity, and destruction, but instead edification and enrichment. Hellens' horror work ultimately shows that everything can be *fantastika*, as long as the reader truly focuses and ignores mental distractions. Like the later writers of *l'ecole belge de l'etrange*, Hellens uses surrealistic imagery–*avant la lettre*, Hellens' surrealistic work beginning in 1906–to great effect, as well as subtle use of the incongruous and the humorous.

The combination of Ray's fecundity and Hellens' style influenced other Belgian writers to create *l'ecole belge de l'etrange*, also known as "*le fantastique réel*, realistic fantasy, which often concerns itself with the staid middle class."[14] But in typical Belgian style Belgian *fantastika* is

---

[12]Brian Stableford, "From Baum to Tolkien, 1900-1956," in *Fantasy and Horror*, ed. Neil Barron (Lanham, MD: Scarecrow Press, 2000), 129.

[13]Hubert van Calenbergh, "Ray, Jean," in *Supernatural Literature of the World: An Encyclopedia*, eds. S.T. Joshi and Stefan Dziemianowicz (Westport, CT: Greenwood Press, 2005), 932.

[14]Connell, "Introduction," 21.

also marked by its humor, its surreal images laid on to realistic situations and environments, and its magical realism; the fantastic and horrific, when it appears, is spoken with a whisper, not a shout.

Croatia

The traditional influence of a German education on Serbo-Croatian writers faded around the turn of the twentieth century, when a passionate independence movement succeeded in establishing a national literary vocabulary and literature. The leading representative of the new literary generation, the "Modern School," was Antun Gustav Matoš, who though dying early in 1914 proved to be influential posthumously as well as during his lifetime. Matoš began writing in 1892, under the self-acknowledged influence of Prosper Merimée, Guy de Maupassant, and especially Edgar Allan Poe; like the other members of the Modern School, Matoš turned away from the Germans and toward the French and those authors the French literary world approved of. In 1909 Matoš published *Umorne Priče* (*Tired stories*), a collection of macabre stories showing the influence of Poe and de Maupassant. Matoš' horror stories are not like his mainstream work, being less concerned with the social problems of his time and place and focusing instead on the twisted psychology of his characters. The result is a set of vivid and macabre tales which have earned critical comparison to the work of Mikhail Bulgakov, although Matoš' work is more Symbolist.

Czech Republic

At the beginning of the twentieth century Czech writers no longer felt the need to subordinate their work to the needs of the nation or to limit themselves to educating and serving the Czech people. Consequently, Czech authors began writing literature, both High Art and Low, for its own sake or as part of schools like naturalism and impressionism.

One important early twentieth century Czech writer was Jiri Karásek ze Lvovic, a poet, author, and literary critic, and perhaps the foremost representative of the Decadents in Czech literature. While most of what Karásek ze Lvovic was purely Decadent in nature and without much *fantastika*, his "Romány tří mágů" ("Novels of the Three Mages") trilogy, published in 1907, 1908, and 1925, has substantial elements of *fantastika* and horror. The trilogy is a "fragmented narrative [which] describes the tormented wanderings of fey young men in the decaying cityscapes of Prague, Venice and Vienna, and their encounters with the occult."[15] The three novels of the trilogy feature cursed portraits, poison rings, magic formulae which will create golems, and nightmarish visions which haunt the protagonists. There are also Gothic elements in the three novels:

> These three Karásekové novels follow on the tradition of the Gothic novel and represent a kind of its update in the context of modernism of the early 20th century. We can give

---

[15]Ivan Adamovič and Cyril Simsa, "Czech Republic," in *The Encyclopedia of Fantasy*, eds. John Clute and John Grant (New York: St. Martin's Griffin, 1998), 242.

some Gothic characters and compare it to the trilogy. The Gothic novel usually takes place in a mysterious space (in the Prague trilogy magical, Venice), in ancient settlements hiding something ominous (Manfred's the palace, Marcel's home with a family tomb, a house from the time of Rudolph II). The predominately feature male characters of mysterious origin, often demonic criminals..."a noble aristocrat" carrying an ancestral curse (murders, sexual perversions, madness) corresponds to the type of the Gothic novel. Fantastic facts are explained irrationally or logically....fantastic phenomena are inexplicable, but understandable within the occult efforts of the magi. They are a means for a shocking reader, forcing them to push the boundary of imagination....in the case of Karásek's trilogy, we can speak of it being a "modernist Gothic novel."[16]

Emanuel Lešehrad was a writer, poet, playwright, critic and translator, and was an important propagator of Freemasonry among the Czechs. His poetry leans heavily on the "cursed poet" trope and makes substantial use of occult elements; in his story collections *Démon a jiné povídky* (*The Demon and Other Stories*, 1911) and *Záhadné životy* (*Mysterious Lives*, 1919) he includes a number of horror stories, with titles like "The Demon," "The Old Mirror's Memories," and "The Love of Aunt Zofia." His horror narratives tend toward the Lovecraftian end of supernatural horror rather than the Poe end–one story, "Rainbow Wonder," involves a researcher in exotic mushrooms who finds a particularly rare specimen which ultimately transforms him into a duplicate of itself–and include occult mysteries and nightmares as plot devices.

Joe Hloucha was a writer and art collector. In his *Pavilón hrůzy* (*Pavilion of Horror*, 1920), one of a number of works reflecting Hloucha's extensive knowledge of traditional Japanese culture and folklore, he describe an initiation ritual, an *Ohimachi*, involving the sons of samurai. The children are told seven stories, intended to teach moral lessons and the benefits of revenge. The stories are heavily supernatural and most are frightening, involving traditional Japanese supernatural creatures, from ghosts to witches to revenants, and have titles like "The Doll Under the Hat."

Josef Váchal was a novelist and poet as well as an artist, sculptor, and woodworker. As a writer, his works were influenced by the Expressionist movement. His 1924 *Krvavý román* (*Bloody Novel*) contains two sections. The first is a study of and apologia for the penny bloods, which were especially popular with Czechs in the second half of the nineteenth century. The second section of *Krvavý román* is Váchal's attempt at writing a kind of Modernist penny dreadful. The fiction section of *Krvavý román* concerns the struggle between the Jesuits and the Inquisition–who are both portrayed as wicked in cliched and stereotyped terms, as was *de rigueur* in the penny bloods–and the heroic Freemasons. In addition to the requisite blood, gore, and turgid horror–again, *de rigueur* for the penny bloods--*Krvavý román* also contains satires of modern art, communism, and writers like Váchal himself. The product of psychic automatism, *Krvavý román* does not resolve the fates of some of its characters nor the resolution of several plot strands.

Ladislav Klíma was a philosopher and novelist. Despite being influenced by Nietzsche,

---

[16] Adéla Hazuchová, "Romány Tří Mágů Jiřího Karáska Ze Lvovic" (PhD diss., Univerzita Palackého V Olomouci, 2013), 52-53.

Klíma's fiction usually emphasized, in strongly expressed terms, traditional moral and cultural values. However, his final work, *Utrpení knížete Sternenhocha* (*The suffering of Prince Sternenhoch*, 1928), is an expressionist narrative that Klíma described as a "grotesque novel." *Utrpení knížete Sternenhocha* is a kind of expressionist riff on Goethe's *The Sorrows of Young Werther*, influenced by it but also satirizing it. About a wealthy, degenerate nobleman and the woman he loves and so badly mistreats, *Utrpení knížete Sternenhocha* is a grotesque novel with substantial horror elements, from Sternenhoch's cruelty and the murder of his child by his mother to nightmares about ghosts to the return of his wife from Hell and his act of necrophilia with her. Klíma's prose is expressionistic and well-wrought, but the content ranges philosophical musings to base lewdness to the horrific.

Vítězslav Nezval was the co-founder of the Surrealist movement in Czechoslovakia and was one of the most prolific avant-garde Czech writers of the first half of the twentieth century, penning poetry, plays, and novels. Most of his work is non-*fantastika*, but there is one exception: the trippy experimental phantasmagoria *Valérie a týden divů* (*Valerie and a Week of Wonders*, 1935). *Valérie a týden divů* can be thought of as the Czech forerunner to Stephanie Meyer's best-selling vampire romance *Twilight* (2005). Like *Twilight*, *Valérie* depicts a romance between a teenaged girl and an older vampire, but *Valérie* also contains an evil grandmother sucking the youth out of Valérie, a talking puppy, a description of Valérie's menstruation, and hallucinogenic mushrooms. Nezval intended *Valérie a týden divů* to be a tribute to the Gothics of his youth, and includes themes and tropes ranging from Shelley's *Frankenstein* to M.G. Lewis' *The Monk* to the F.W. Murnau film *Nosferatu*.

Denmark

Although Danish literature during the 1901-1939 period was for the most part going through a nationalist, regionalist, and realism/social realism phase, there was one prominent exception: Isak Dinesen. Dinesen was influenced both by the Danish fairy tale tradition, best personified by Hans Christian Andersen, and by the Scandinavian Gothic tradition, which ran throughout most of the nineteenth century and into the twentieth. But Dinesen's style–smooth, polished, mannered, and erudite–owed little to either fairy tales or her Gothic predecessors, instead being influenced by Shakespeare, Shelley, and the best of the Danish writers of the nineteenth and early twentieth centuries. Her stories, both the overt Gothics and the fables that come very close to being Gothics, are more concerned with the non-horror aspects of the Gothic, the nostalgia for the past, "the ambiguous attempt either to ward off the unpredictable future by celebrating past and passing beauty, or, failing that, to derive a sense of glory from that very passing."[17] Dinesen took a more modern, liberal approach to traditional Gothic conventions and moral codes as well as injected them with a feminist sensibility. Nonetheless, there are frights to be found in those stories, albeit liberally mixed with wit. As Brian Stableford writes, they are

---

[17]David Punter, *The Literature of Terror: Volume 2: The Modern Gothic* (New York: Routledge, 1996), 125.

"fine examples of mannered grotesquerie,"[18] combining a Gothic atmosphere, memorable scenes, psychological insight, and a generally subtle and haunting approach.

Finland

In the first decades of the twentieth century Finland underwent a number of changes, both social (rapid population growth and the increasing industrialization of the country) and political (gaining independence from Russia in 1917, followed by the civil war). While mainstream Finnish literature was focused on portraying and discussing these changes, Finnish genre literature flourished.

Konrad Lehtimaki, a politician and the best-known "proletarian writer" of the pre-World War Two era, wrote politically-motivated fiction. But Lehtimaki did not limit himself to mimetic fiction, and wrote an excellent work of pacifist Utopian near-future science fiction as well as a collection of romantic horror stories, *Kuolema* (*Death*, 1915). The stories in *Kuolema*, inspired by the work of Edgar Allan Poe, tend towards sentimentality, with good always triumphing over evil and revenge, when it is successfully taken, being purely of the non-violent variety. However, the stories are much concerned with death, and there are frightening scenes interwoven with the sentimental and romantic outcomes.

One of Finnish literature's greats, Mika Waltari, would as an adult write in a number of different genres and achieve mainstream success with titles like *Sinuhe, egyptiläinen* (*The Egyptian,* 1945). As a teenager he began writing various stories for a Finnish pulp magazine, including horror stories, and as a seventeen year old he published a collection of eleven horror stories, *Kuollen silmä* (*The dying eye*, 1926). The obvious inspiration for Waltari in writing these stories was Edgar Allan Poe, although the stories reflect Waltari's interest in current events; "Mummy," about ancient Egypt, is clearly written in response to the then-current enthusiasm for all things ancient Egyptian following the discovery of King Tut's tomb. Another story, "The Red Triangle," is not just full of erotic horror but also a touch of Lovecraftian cosmic horror, although it's highly unlikely that Waltari had heard of Lovecraft at this time. A third, "The Isle of the Setting Sun," is sword-and-sorcery with fantastic elements and phantasmagoric overtones that remind the modern reader of the work of Clark Ashton Smith. The other stories in the collection are more standard adventure-horror, obviously written in imitation of Poe, although "The Black Orchids," with its enormous supernatural black dog, may have been written with the model of Arthur Conan Doyle's "The Hound of the Baskervilles" in mind.

Waltari was not alone in writing horror in Finland during the 1901-1939 period, of course. Numerous horror short stories appeared in the cheaper Finnish literary magazines, the Finnish equivalent of the American pulps. A typical horror story of this kind was Leo Anttila's "Destiny" (1925), a look at the depraved vampires of Paris' decadent nightlife. "Destiny" would not have been out of place in *Weird Tales*, being imaginative if not particularly well-written. A work of horror of an altogether different and better sort was Aino Kallas' *Sudenmorsian* (*The wolf-bride*, 1928). Kallas, a Finno-Estonian, wrote in a complex and highly archaicized style similar to a medieval chronicler's and quite unlike what her contemporaries, under the sway of

---

[18]Stableford, "From Baum to Tolkien," 117.

neo-Romanticism, were writing. By the mid-1920s she was the most widely translated and internationally best-known living Finnish writer. *Sudenmorsian*, a dreamy, symbolic story colorfully told, is set in seventeenth century Estonia and is about the wife of a forester; the wife, Aalo, is a werewolf, and is ultimately tragically killed. Kallas' point in writing the novel was to describe what she called "the slaying Eros," the love that kills, and to critique from a feminist's standpoint the patriarchal control of women, and she uses Aalo's status as a werewolf as a vehicle for the feminist critique. The horror in *Sudenmorsian* comes not from Aalo's actions as a werewolf, but from the actions of the men reacting to her, and the destruction of Aalo, who only wants the freedom to pursue her dreams and sexual and emotional satisfaction.

France

In France, the nineteenth century's appetite for *romans fantastique*, whether *populaire*, *littéraire,* or *frénétiques*, heightened as the century turned. The period from the 1880s to the 1930s was one in which *fantastika* was common in France, whether at novel-length or in the many wide-circulation periodicals of the time which published *fantastika*. But science fiction, under the name of "anticipations," were the favored genre of the wide-circulation periodicals; *romans noir* and stories of horror generally appeared at novel-length. As in the United States, the market for popular fiction began to fragment into genres as the cleavage between the *fantastique populaire* and the *fantastique littéraire,* Low and High Art, widened. Supernatural fiction and supernatural horror became seen as the province of the *fantastique populaire*, with even the most refined authors of it being equated with the horror hacks. However, in the 1920s the Surrealists, following the Symbolists, made substantial use of the supernatural, so that there was a certain percentage of the *romans littéraire* which made use of the elements of horror while not being horror themselves.

Jean Lorrain was in his time famous as a Decadent—perhaps *the* Decadent of Paris, if only because of his affectations, dress, and the way in which he put himself forward as the primary Decadent of the city and therefore of France as a whole. Certainly he enthusiastically took part in the *fin-de-siècle* and the Decadent movement, although there was always a part of Lorrain that was a savage critic of what he saw, as could be seen in his journalism, and modern biographers and critics have carefully shown how much of Lorrain's Decadence was actually a pose. Critics differ on how his weird and horror fiction should be valued—as powerful and authentic, or as the ultimate expression of a scene hanger-on? His 1890s horror stories are certainly Decadent, about the nightmarish effects of ether and pedophiliac lesbian vampires, and fit more or less neatly into the category of the *conte cruel*. But what Lorrain is remembered for are his Decadent novels, especially *Monsieur de Phocas* (1901), the best "retrospective summary of the Decadent Movement and the world that had given birth to it."[19] A deliberate homage to J.K. Huysmans' *À Rebours* (1884), the landmark work of Decadence, *Monsieur de Phocas* partly pastiches Huysmans' work and partly subverts it. With Huysmans and E.T.A. Hoffmann as his model, Lorrain creates a powerfully phantasmagoric work, including "one of the most elaborate

---

[19]Brian Stableford, *Glorious Perversity: The Decline and Fall of Literary Decadence* (Rockville, MD: Wildside Press, 2008), 75.

literary accounts of a nightmarish hashish dream."[20]

A writer of horror of an altogether different sort was Maurice Renard. Little-known in America, even today, Renard was the French H.G. Wells, and no less than Pierre Versins described Renard as "the best French sf writer of the years 1900-1930."[21] Renard's science fiction is rarely pure sf, however; he is ultimately a hybrid writer whose work continually crosses the line into "Gothic fiction, mythological fantasy, detective fiction, and the fantastic in general."[22] Renard's science fiction usually has horror elements—the reverse is also accurate—and throughout all his fiction is clear evidence of a prolific, ingenious imagination at play. Renard's influences include Poe, Hoffmann, Erckmann-Chatrian, J-H Rosny aîné, and Gaston Leroux; stylistically, Renard wrote in whichever style and mode was most fitting for an individual narrative, though always skillfully. In his *Doctor Moreau*-esque *Le docteur Lerne, sous-dieu* (*Doctor Lerne, undergod*, 1908) he tells the story of a mad scientist who practices cross-species organ transplants, including putting a human brain into a bull's body. In *Le Peril Bleu* (*The Blue Danger*, 1910) he describes a civilization of alien beings who live on the top of the world's atmosphere and fish for prey into the lower reaches of the atmosphere, catching humans. In *Les mains d'Orlac* (*The hands of Orlac*, 1920) he describes the unfortunate results of the transplantation of hands. His short work is similarly colorful and imaginative, and makes use of a wide array of science fictional concepts, from clones to vampire bats to mutated intelligent sharks, for horrific ends.

Gaston Leroux, popular in his time, was one of the writers whose work had some influence on Maurice Renard. But Renard was a far better writer than Leroux, whose work has aged poorly. An author who wrote primarily serials for magazines and the French equivalent of dime novels and pulps, Leroux tended to make stuff up as he went along, to the detriment of his stories. The endless requirement to keep the stories interesting meant that Leroux was continually adding colorful or spicy elements to the stories, which can led them a feverish or nightmarish feel, and in his shorter work he effectively draws upon the Grand Guignol plays of Maurice Level, but generally Leroux's horror work is crude and on the level of the poorer of the *Weird Tales'* writers. Even *Le fantôme de l'opéra* (*The Phantom of the Opera*, 1910), read in the original, is poor stuff.

One of Renard's and Leroux's horror fiction contemporaries was Maurice Level, who is as different from the both of them as Leroux is from Renard. Level was a top contributor to the Grand-Guignol Theatre in Paris and was surprisingly popular in the United States and Great Britain thanks to the 1911 and 1923 translations of two of his novels and the 1920 publication of

---

[20]Brian Stableford, "The Cosmic Horror," in *Icons of Horror and the Supernatural*, ed. S.T. Joshi (Westport, CT: Greenwood Press, 2007), 77.

[21]Pierre Versins, "Maurice Renard," in *Encylopédie de l'utopie, des voyages extraordinaires, et de la science fiction*, ed. Pierre Versins (Lausanne: L'Age d'Homme, 1984), 734.

[22]Arthur B. Evans, "The Fantastic Science Fiction of Maurice Renard," *Science Fiction Studies* 21 (1994): 380.

a collection of short stories. That Level is forgotten today, both in the Anglophone world and in France itself, is a regrettable example of the cruelty of posterity, for Level deserved his fame. Level was "a master of the *conte cruel*, though he was a less subtle exponent of the art"[23] than Villiers de L'Isle-Adam, with de Maupassant and Poe the primary influence on Level. Level wrote a number of twisty, dark, and cruel short stories which ended up as Grand Guignol plays. Level specialized in violent stories about abnormal psychology, obsession, and ironic, wrenching, surprise endings. Level was resolutely non-supernatural, however, being more concerned with the violent and wicked ways that humans being treat each other than with ghosts, vampires, and other supernatural threats. Level's fiction is stripped-down, lean, with never a word out of place; they "reveal such an economy of means that nothing could be added to or extracted from them without destroying their very fabric."[24] During and after World War One Level added a certain level of social concern and poignancy to his stories, the effect on him of the war being clear.

Henri Béraud is known today for his collaboration with the Germans during World War Two, but there was a reason so many French authors intervened on his behalf with the French government following the war, when Béraud was sentenced to death. Béraud was an author of rare skills, called in his heyday "the cleanest writer in France" and "the French G.K. Chesterton." His *Lazare* (*Lazarus*, 1924), a riff on Ambrose Bierce's "An Encounter at Owl Creek Bridge," is a gripping, poignant tale, beautifully told, about an amnesiac who after sixteen years leaves an insane asylum only to find the world outside unrecognizable and himself changed beyond recognition, his personality irrevocably altered and full of new anxieties and doubts. His past pursues him, increasingly frighteningly and insanely, and on the last page of *Lazare* we learn that the amnesiac has never left his bed in the asylum, and that the entire terrifying experience was inside his head. *Lazare* is a delicate, artistic novel which was also a self-acknowledged influence on H.P. Lovecraft's "The Shadow Out of Time" (1936).

Two notable mainstream authors who also wrote genre work were Pierre Frondaie and Frédéric Boutet. Frondaie's collections (1930, 1935, 1946) of the *fantastique* contained a number of horror stories narrated by Jean Pharg, a ghost-buster in the vein of William Hope Hodgson's occult detective Carnacki the Ghost-Finder. The stories, with titles like "The story of a ghost and the two arms of Venus" and "The Dancing Dead," are Hodgson-like. Boutet's novels (1921, 1922, 1927) are influenced by Poe. Less notable as an author, though more entertaining than either Frondaie or Boutet, was Édouard Letailleur, who wrote a dozen Gothic mystery-horror novels between 1932 and 1939. Their titles–*La Demeure de Satan* (*The House of Satan*), *Perkane, le Démon de la Nuit* (*Perkane, the Night Demon*), and *Le Squelette de la rue Scribe* (*The Skeleton of Scribe Street*)–only hint at the over-the-top frights and thrills to be found in Letailleur's work.

Last of the major French works of horror was Andre Maurois' *Le peseur d'âmes* (*The weigher of souls,* 1931). Maurois, a biographer and novelist, wrote in a number of genres, including science fiction, but *Le peseur d'âmes* was his only work to venture into horror. The

---

[23]Stableford, "From Baum to Tolkien," 125.

[24]S.T. Joshi, "Introduction," in *Thirty Hours with a Corpse; and Other Tales of the Grand Guignol*, ed. S.T. Joshi (Mineola, NY: Dover Publications, 2016), viii.

novel, about an English doctor who captures souls from the bodies of the dying, places the souls in hollow glass globes, and then performs experiments on them, is simultaneously frightening, suspenseful, awe-inspiring, and tragic.

Although he never reached the artistic heights of Level, Béraud, or Maurois, André de Lorde, a prolific playwright and social novelist whose fame, during the 1910s and 1920s, was the equal of a Dumas or a de Goncourt, wrote a number of horror plays for the Grand-Guignol theater and gained the nickname "the Prince of Terror."

> Lorde became the Grand Guignol writer *par excellence* and probably the first best-selling gore writer in the genre's history. Lorde's own brand of terror relied on medicine and psychiatry rather than the supernatural. For him, a man who saw ghosts or conversed with spirits was a dangerous lunatic, possibly a potential murderer, not someone who communicated with the occult.[25]

Germany

In Germany, the 1900-1930 period was a span of years full of high quality *fantastika*. What followed the realist movement of the nineteenth century in Germany was expressionism and symbolism in the mainstream. For German writers of *fantastika*, especially writers of horror, neo-Romanticism was a strong influence. German neo-Romanticism "opposed late nineteenth-century rationalism and materialism by eclectically appealing, in a vaguely 'romantic' manner, to different periods and traditions of the past, including Romanticism."[26] Accompanying this was the influence of the *fin-de-siècle* and especially French Decadence, with French Decadent authors like J.K. Huysmans, Théophile Gautier, and Villiers de L'Isle-Adam being used as models. Edgar Allan Poe became interesting to the Germans for the first time, and the French interest in E.T.A. Hoffmann sparked a German re-evaluation of his work.

Not all German horror writers of the 1901-1939 period were influenced by the French Decadents, of course. A prominent example of an author drawing upon different sources is Eufemia von Adlersfeld-Ballestrem, in her time a quite popular writer of romances. In most things von Adlersfeld-Ballestrem was conservative; her novels generally take place in an aristocratic milieu and are approving of the monarchy. Of the more than fifty novels she wrote, roughly half of which were written before the turn of the century, most skip past the French Decadents and go to traditional German fiction. Von Adlersfeld-Ballestrem wrote Gothic romances, similar to if preceding Daphne Du Maurier but with substantially more supernatural content. The supernatural in these novels hearken back to the German Gothic tradition: visions, prophetic dreams, ghosts, secret rooms, poisoned rings, Italian *femmes fatale*, etc. But von

---

[25] Jean-Marc Lofficier and Randy Lofficier, *French Science Fiction, Fantasy, Horror and Pulp Fiction* (Jefferson, NC: McFarland, 2000), 356.

[26] Margarete Kohlenbach, "Transformations of German Romanticism 1830-2000," in *The Cambridge Companion to German Romanticism*, ed. Nicholas Saul (Cambridge: Cambridge University Press, 2009), 262

Adlersfeld-Ballestrem took from more than the German Gothic. Several of her short stories and two of her novels, *Ca'Spada* (1904) and *Die dame in gelb* (*The lady in yellow,* 1908), are pure ghost stories in the British manner, quite similar to and possibly influenced by M.R. James' work. Her outright horror fiction is suspenseful and frightening, skillfully told, with romantic plots that in no way impede or hamper the production of terror.

Georg von der Gabelentz was another author who made substantial use of the supernatural in his novels and short stories, although he was not as prolific as von Adlersfeld-Ballestrem. (Few were). Von der Gabelentz was more overt in his use of the supernatural and told more straightforward ghost and horror tales. His "Gelber Schädel" ("Yellow skull," 1909) involves the cursed, talking head of Cagliostro, stolen from its tomb. *Das Rätsel Choriander* (*The puzzle Choriander*, 1929) is about a psychic vampire. Other stories, obviously influenced by E.T.A. Hoffmann, describe supernaturally dark doings in mysterious and sometimes surreal fashion. Von der Gabelentz was another writer who, like von Adlersfeld-Ballestrem, eschewed the influence of the French Decadents to tell stories in his own style, which was gloomy, elegant, and skilled to the highest degree.

Radically unlike von Adlersfeld-Ballestrem and von der Gabelentz was Hanns Heinz Ewers, one of the three major German-language Decadent horror writers of the period, alongside Karl Hans Strobl and Gustav Meyrink. Ewers was the best-known and most popular of the three, both domestically and internationally, and is in many ways the archetypal Decadent. (Whether or not Ewers' Decadence was the genuine thing or the act of an imitative poseur is something which critics and biographers differ on). Ewers' association with the Nazis in the late 1920s and early 1930s brought him into disrepute, and his name today remains tainted, but this should not cloud critical judgment of his work, which is often excellent. The "salaciously provocative and self-indulgent decadence of his earlier stories make them repulsive to some readers… but they are undeniably powerful."[27] His work, from his Frank Braun trilogy to his *contes cruel*, is often grotesque, but it is powerful. Ewers worked within the German Gothic tradition, making use of traditional Gothic frights, but added Expressionism and Decadent depravity, abnormal or twisted psychology, and a languidness purely his own, in horrors ranging from supernatural horror to sadism to grotesquerie. The result is powerful, desolating, and a *sui generis* mixture of ecstasy and horror.

Georg Heym is best known for his expressionist poetry and his early death, but a posthumous collection of horror stories, *Der dieb* (*The thief*), was published in 1913. As in his poetry, which lyrically portrays war—Heym saw the coming European war all too clearly—in horrific, densely packed terms, Heym's stories, which contain the themes of madness, disease, pain, and murder, are ultimately about the end of the world, whether one person's or everybody's.

> The times were such, Heym felt, that 'nice' literature was no longer possible. He sensed the approach of a cataclysm; the boredom that is so often mentioned in his later diary entries was the ominous calm before the storm. 'Why doesn't something happen?' he asked in 1910. 'Why doesn't somebody cut the balloon-seller's string?' He did not live to

---

[27]Stableford, "From Baum to Tolkien," 118.

see the string cut, but in his work he had already foreseen all that would ensue when it was.[28]

Heym rarely used the supernatural in his description of the madness of crowds and individuals, the cruelty of authority, and the plague, but he does not need to—the horror of the mundane is quite sufficient to frighten the reader.

Another expressionist of the era, Alexander Moritz Frey, also wrote horror, although Frey made substantial use of the supernatural in his grotesque and powerful fantasies. Frey produced quiet stories, controlled and full of unanswered questions, that used the fable form to attack the conservatives and reactionaries, from before World War One up through the appearance of the Nazis. Frey artfully begins with everyday reality and gradually introduces the fantastic until his stories are full-blown *fantastika*. Frey "adapts the fable's techniques of defamiliarization, reductio ad absurdum, and especially its conflation of the animal and the human, to expose what he regarded as the most pernicious effect of fascism: its degradation of the human to brute beast, domestic animal, even inanimate tool."[29]

Alfred Döblin was a German physician, novelist, and essayist, best known for his *Berlin Alexanderplatz* (1929). Döblin is one of the most important figures in pre-WW2 German Modernism; prolific, his work spanned many genres. In 1924 he published *Berge Meere und Giganten* (*Mountains, Seas, and Giants*), a Future History/Dystopia/science fictional horror novel. About the twentieth through the twenty-seventh centuries, *Berge Meere und Giganten* shows humanity developing advanced technology and a dystopic world government in response to overpopulation, racism, and rampant economic migrations. What follows, after seven centuries of dystopic rule, is an underclass-fomented world war and then a drive to make Greenland arable. Unfortunately, when the Greenland icecap is melted, giant monsters emerge, and plants and animals mutate to dangerously giant sizes. Eventually humanity goes underground. "Günter Grass once described it as "written as if under visionary influence." Döblin clarified his goal: to write so that "Jules Verne would roll over in his grave."[30] The book is difficult for modern readers to get through, having experimental stylistic, structural, and thematic elements. But those who struggle through will be rewarded with a work of substantial science fictional horror, first of the realistic variety (the images of men mangled by machines, the overpopulation, racism, economic migration, and dystopic government) and then of the imaginative sort (the prehistoric

---

[28]Allen G. Blunden, "Heym, Georg (1887-1912)," in *Columbia Dictionary of Modern European Literature*, ed. Jean Albert Bédé and William Benbow Edgerton (New York: Columbia University Press, 1980), 362.

[29]Paola Mayer and Ruediger Mueller, "Fascism as Dehumanization: Alexander Moritz Frey's Political Fables," *Oxford German Studies* 46 (2017): 58.

[30]Carolyn Taratko, "'Jules Verne Would Roll over in His Grave,' or Döblin on the Future," *JHIBLOG*, last modified Mar. 11, 2015, https://jhiblog.org/2015/03/11/jules-verne-would-roll-over-in-his-grave-or-doblin-on-the-future/.

monsters unearthed by the melting Greenland icecap, and the plant and animal mutations). The more science fictional the horrors get, the more the readers are likely to be put in mind of H.P. Lovecraft's later work, both in imagery and the scope of *Berge Meere und Giganten*.

Italy

The *Scapigliatura* movement in Italy of the late nineteenth and early twentieth century sought to bring foreign elements and inspirations into Italian culture as a way to revivify and rejuvenate Italian literature, music, and art. Among these foreign influences were German Romantics, French authors like Théophile Gautier and Gérard de Nerval, and especially the poetry of Charles Baudelaire and the prose and poetry of Edgar Allan Poe. The result was what can be thought of as Italian bohemian art and artists and literature. In horror fiction, the *Scapigliatura* movement resulted in a wave of horror written in imitation of French and German masters, particularly Hoffmann, and of Poe, though within a few years Italian Decadence and the *Crepuscolari* movement would displace the bohemianism of the *Scapigliatura* and lead to more original and essentially Italian work.

Typical in some respects of the *Scapigliatura*-influenced horror writers was Carolina Invernizio. Invernizio is not generally known as a horror writer, instead having gained fame for her many (130+) romances. Invernizio's novels were *romanzo d'appendice*, or *feuilleton*-like serialized novels, and were quite popular during and after her lifetime. Invernizio wrote hybrid novels which combined detective, romance, and horror elements, and though she is best known for the former two–she wrote the first Italian detective novel with a female detective–the latter should not be overlooked. Her horror was of the Gothic variety, but pitched high and pushing at the limits of good taste and general acceptability, so that sadism, necrophilia, and repressed sexuality often make an appearance. Her *La Vergine dei veleni* (*The poison virgin,* 1917) owes obvious an obvious debt to Hawthorne's "Rappaccini's Daughter;" other novels show the weight of the French *feuilletonists* upon her. "Her apolitical novels are dark stories about infamous crimes, dazzling redemptions, and lifeless characters with an aura of sanctity."[31]

For female Italian writers at the turn of the twentieth century, realism was the dominant mode expected of them. But a number of these women read Northern European Gothics and *fantastika* and saw in them "alternative models to the ethos and closed linear narrative structure prescribed by realism."[32] Among the writers these women read were Gautier, Hoffmann, Poe, M.G. Lewis, Ann Radcliffe, Clara Reeve and Mary Shelley. One of the writers heavily influenced by these non-Italian writers was Matilde Serao, best known as the founder of a literary magazine and a novelist who was nominated for the Nobel Prize six times. Serao's fiction, in the late

---

[31] Anna Bogo, "Carolina Invernizio," in *The Encyclopedia of Italian Literary Studies*, ed. Gaetana Marrone (New York: Routledge, 2007), 961.

[32] Francesca Billiani, "The Italian Gothic and Fantastic: An Inquiry into the Notions of Literary and Cultural Traditions (1869-1997)," in *The Italian Gothic and Fantastic. Encounters and Rewritings of Narrative Traditions*, ed. Francesca Billiani and Gigliola Sulis (Cranbury, NJ: Rosemont Publishing and Printing Corp., 2007), 15.

nineteenth century, began as what Joan Lidoff describes as "domestic gothic,"[33] or fiction in which "everyday matters relating to the home become magnified to nightmare proportions, framed by recognizably Gothic tropes and presented in the language of excess."[34] Serao's later, twentieth-century fiction shucked its domestic trappings and its apparent realism became full-blowing Gothic novels, what Ursula Fanning calls "dramatic Gothics."[35] This shift was not one which most mainstream male Italian writers were willing or able to engage in, but was one which Italian women did take part in. Serao's Gothics, particularly *Il delitto di via Chiatamone* (*The crime of via Chiatamone,* 1908) and *La mano tagliata* (*The cut hand,* 1912), have numerous references to and reworkings of the Gothics of Walpole, Radcliffe, and Shelley; she uses the *doppelgänger*, the Wandering Jew, and Frankenstein's monster-like characters; "melodramatic and supernatural elements are added to the motif of intrigue and transgression;"[36] and she experiments with and reconfigures Gothic conventions, so that the innocent and pure blonde woman dies while the stronger, darker woman survives and triumphs.

Quite a different kind of horror writer was Guido Gozzano, one of the *Crepuscolari* and a poet initially influenced by the European symbolists and by Oscar Wilde. Following the advice of a professor while studying law, Gozzano returned "back to the sources" of Italian literature and ended up creating a hybrid form of horror fiction, nineteenth century in content, twentieth century in style and approach. Gozzano's horror narratives are usually *contes cruel*, obviously written in homage to Poe and de Maupassant, but with the delicate style of the *Crepuscolari* and an underlying message of tragic absurdity. Gozzano's style, usually written in the first person, is stripped-down and lean, almost under-written, and the cause of his terrors both weird encounters, long-buried mysteries, and Gothic atmospheres, as well as a general sense of the *unheimlich*. The tone is Hemingway; the content and effect is Shirley Jackson.

Alberto Savinio was a kind of Renaissance man in pre-World War Two Italy. He was a writer, painter, musician, journalist, playwright, set designer, and composer. His fiction shows a fine style and irony, never more so than in his haunted house novel *La casa ispirata* (*The haunted house,* 1920), which was well-received in its time. Using a humorously satirical tone, Savinio tells the story of a house, haunted by ghosts, in which everything rapidly decomposes, including the food one eats, and in which the unconscious fantasies of the characters have

---

[33]Joan Lidoff, *Christina Stead* (New York: Ungar, 1982), 123-24.

[34]Elaine Hartnell-Mottram, "Domestic Gothic," in *The Encyclopedia of the Gothic*, eds. William Hughes, David Punter, and Andrew Smith (Chichester: John Wiley and Sons, 2016), 185.

[35]Ursula Fanning, "From Domestic to Dramatic: Matilde Serao's Use of the Gothic," in *The Italian Gothic and Fantastic. Encounters and Rewritings of Narrative Traditions*, eds. Francesca Billiani and Gigliola Sulis (Cranbury, NJ: Rosemont Publishing and Printing Corp., 2007), 120.

[36]Gabriella Romani, "Matilde Serao," in *The Encyclopedia of Italian Literary Studies*, ed. Gaetana Marrone (New York: Routledge, 2007), 1734.

terrifying consequences. Savinio's approach is light, but the atmosphere is ominous, the details sinister and horrifying, and the ultimate impact is nightmarish. *La casa ispirata* is psychological horror which makes reality itself ambiguous.

> A gloomy Paris serves as the tableau for a revelation of death and of the monstrosity of daily life. Objects, behaviors, and meals are transformed into a dark yet comic representation, mirroring a reality suspended between dream and nightmare--between the fantastic and the hyperreal. In such a way Savinio transforms the real into an ambiguous structure that continuously undergoes metamorphosis, multiplying and becoming multiform.[37]

Less overtly horrifying, but no less disquieting in their way, are the stories in Ada Negri's collections *Le strade* (*The roads*, 1926) and *Di giorno in giorno* (*Day by day*, 1932). Negri, a prominent poet, uses feverishly-depicted visual sensations, similar to those in her poems, to describe her experiences traveling the roads of Italy and her encounters with a range of Italians, from famous actresses to ordinary children. What disquiets the reader is the "oscillations between the world of experience and the world of unreality, and the coexistence of multiple selves and different temporal dimensions within one single consciousness."[38] The stories are ultimately a kind of psychological horror, lacking the supernatural but unnerving for their ontological ambiguity.

Latvia

While Latvian literature was going through a heavily Modernistic phase during the early part of the twentieth century, horror as a genre began appearing in Latvian literature at the same time, albeit in poetry—specifically ballads—rather than in prose. It wasn't until the 1920s and 1930s that horror fiction began appearing in any numbers. Foremost among these Latvian writers of horror literature was Augusts Saulietis, an author of poetry and prose, plays and memoirs, who wrote a variety of stories "in which the traditional, realistic storyline is interrupted by inexplicable and incomprehensible phenomena from the world beyond the grave."[39] Saulietis' horror narratives, written from 1925 to the end of his life in 1933, can be considered High Art Horror, but the presence of supernatural beings such as ghosts is undeniable in his stories, unlike a number of other Latvian authors:

---

[37]Maria Elena Gutiérrez, "Alberto Savinio," in *Italian Prose Writers, 1900-1945*, ed. Luca Somigli and Rocco Capozzi (Farmington Hills, MI: Gale, 2002), 280.

[38]Cristina Della Coletta, "Fantastic," in *The Feminist Encyclopedia of Italian Literature*, ed. Rinaldina Russell (Westport, CT: Greenwood Press, 1997), 86.

[39]Bārbala Simsone, "A Cloud of Vapour, the Cool of the Cellar: the Horror Genre in Latvian Literature," *Interlitteraria* 19, no. 2 (2014), 310.

it should be added that figures representing the Devil, spirits of the dead and demons do occur earlier in Latvian prose, but the presence of a supernatural being in itself does not classify a work as belonging to the genre of horror, because such figures can also be interpreted in a symbolic, allegorical or even psychological sense (as is often the case with the demons referred to by the Decadents), or else they can be folkloristic or mythical, not being at all frightening.[40]

Other Latvian authors who wrote horror fiction of the 1920s included Jānis Ezeriņš and Kārlis Zariņš. While both authors were excellent short story writers, their horror work was heavily Poe-influenced, as was the case for a number of their horror writer colleagues. Typical of these Poe-inspired stories was Zariņš' story "Remember You Will Die, Heidenkranc!"

> The whole story is pervaded by an atmosphere of inescapable death that is characteristic of the works of the horror classic, even though the hero's suffering and fear, when hanging by the edge of his coat at the top of a three hundred-metre tower, results not from some kind of supernatural intervention, but simply from the cruelty of his fellow human beings, just as in Poe's story.[41]

Aleksandrs Grīns, a writer, translator, and officer in the Latvian army, was best known for his historical novels, but he wrote a substantial amount of fiction, both short stories and novel-length, with extensive horror apparatuses, both mystical/supernatural and purely historical. Grīns extensively uses witches, the Inquisition's torture chambers, ghosts and revenants in his work.

> These stories, overflowing with passion, often include as elements of horror quite modern, medical factors, such as venereal disease and its outward signs, often physically repulsive. Grīns succeeds admirably in creating an oppressive atmosphere of terror by means of stylistically eloquent description, where practically every detail is intended to heighten the suspense....[42]

The best of the female writers of horror during these years was Mirdza Bendrupe. Better known as a novelist and poet, she wrote a number of short stories in the mid- and late-1930s which departed from the tradition of being inspired by Poe and instead used the tropes, motifs, creatures, and plots of Latvian folklore and legends old and new. Bendrupe's story "Helēna" (1939), for example, is based on the urban legend of a man meeting a beautiful woman in a cemetery and falling in love with her, only to discover later that the woman died a decade beforehand.

---

[40] Simsone, "A Cloud of Vapour," 310.

[41] Simsone, "A Cloud of Vapour," 310-11.

[42] Simsone, "A Cloud of Vapour," 311.

Poland

The Młoda Polska, or "Young Poland" movement (1890-1918), was for Polish literature similar to the neo-Romantic and Decadent movements being experienced in other countries. The movement's emphasis was variously on symbolism, modernism, a contempt for the bourgeoisie, a decadence verging on nihilism, and the pursuit of art for art's sake. A number of writers took part in this movement, producing works of varying quality. Some of the most powerful came from Stefan Grabinski, who somewhat erroneously gained the nickname "the Polish Poe" but should better be known as the foremost Polish author of the supernatural in the twentieth century. Neither a commercial nor a critical success, Grabinski nonetheless produced highly accomplished stories and novels of horror, both psychological and Gothic. Although the common comparisons for Grabinski are Poe and H.P. Lovecraft, Grabinski is more appositely compared to Bruno Schulz and Franz Kafka. Like them, Grabinski tells psychologically rich, allegorical tales of horror. Grabinski has a particular talent for atmosphere and strangeness, for portraying dark Gothic landscapes and obsessed and warped personalities, for unerotic sexual frankness, and for surrealism and dark humor. His short stories tend to be horrific or ironic, while his novels tend toward diffuseness and mysticism. A recurring theme in his work is the negative psychological effects of modern life, especially trains and the determinism and mechanism of bourgeois society. In some respects Grabinski can be considered a regionalist similar to Lovecraft, as both use fictional locations set in their home regions; too, both authors, though Gothic in many ways, use contemporary settings rather than imaginary locations in the unspecified distant past. But Grabinski is not Lovecraft. Grabinski is a cerebral writer, influenced by Freud, with expressionist and modern elements quite alien to Lovecraft's deliberately antiquarian mind set. Ultimately, Grabinski is a writer of a kind of contemporary horror, showing modern concerns and modern themes. As China Miéville writes, "here is a writer for whom supernatural horror is manifest precisely in modernity—in electricity, fire-stations, trains: the uncanny as the bad conscience of today."[43]

Władysław Stanisław Reymont, who won the Nobel Prize for literature in 1924 and is best known for his realist, naturalist work, also had a fascination for aspects of the Young Poland movement, particularly its interest in esoterica like Theosophy and spiritualism. Out of this fascination came his novel *Wampir* (*Vampire*, 1904). *Wampir*, despite its title, is not about a literal vampire. What is sucked from the main character is the *elan vital*, either psychically or by supernatural forces—Reymont leaves matters ambiguous. The plot is about a Polish writer who moves to a gloomy London, full of decadent men and women, and becomes entangled with a group of mystics, spiritualists, a Hindu guru, and a beautiful *femme fatale*. Ultimately the writer changes from ambitious into a young man full of misery, despair, corruption and addiction, in a story about those who mistake the spiritual and occult for the scientific. *Wampir* is beautifully told in a darkly atmospheric and poetic style.

Franciszka Pika Mirandoli was a writer, poet, and translator. Although associated with the Impressionist and Expressionist movements in Poland, he's today remembered as one of the

---

[43]China Miéville, "Trainspotting," *The Guardian*, accessed June 19, 2018, https://www.theguardian.com/books/2003/feb/08/featuresreviews.guardianreview20.

first Polish authors of science fiction and horror. His 1919 collection *Tropy* (*Tracks*) is a collection of allegorical narratives. Told in a poetic, almost mannered style, and making ample use of *fantastika*, Mirandoli's stories "often result in the effect of not so much horror but strangeness and the unusual."[44]

After the end of the Young Poland movement natively-produced Polish literature surged, with energetic production of literature on all levels, from the avant-garde to the popular. One of the more cutting-edge poets and authors was Stanisław Baliński, among whose work was the story collection *Miasto księżyców* (*City of moons,* 1924). Baliński's work is not outright horror; his work is more ambiguous, straddling genres, the sort of fiction the term *fantastika* was invented for. There are ghosts, witches, and other traditional evils from Polish folklore, but Baliński treats them in new, modern ways, depicting them and their world in hazy and elliptical ways, sometimes dreamlike and sometimes nightmarish. Well-traveled and widely-read, Baliński was influenced by Hoffmann and Poe and sometimes brought in themes and motifs, like transcendence, fatalism, and unreliable narrators, that were not native to the Polish literary tradition.

Less poetic and lyrical and altogether more popular were the horror collections of Janusz Meissner, a decorated air ace in the Polish-Soviet War of 1920 who went on to write forty-eight novels and story collections on topics ranging from aviation to piracy to hunting. Meissner's horror fiction–four collections' worth–is similar to the horror fiction of the American pulp *Weird Tales*. Meissner wrote horror stories set in the air, on planes or in the skies, and where Grabinski made trains his recurring motif and *idée fixe*, Meissner used planes. His work is shallow and pulpy, but also reveals a subconscious or perhaps unconscious fear of the empty places in the sky, which are often portrayed in his stories as being home to ghosts or demons or other frightening entities.[45]

As with any popular horror writer, Meissner attracted imitators–in his case, a satirizer, and an edged one. Like Meissner, Jerzy Sosnkowski wrote about the mysteries of the unexplored skies and the undiscovered places on Earth. But Sosnowski, in his 1926 collection *Żywe powietrze* (*Living air*), tells stories, in mock-Meissner tones, of geometric monsters, "intelligences of the skies," and cosmic horrors not unlike those Lovecraft was writing about. Sosnowski's satire of Meissner was witty and unkind, mocking his style while giving readers much more imaginative monsters and frights to enjoy.

Portugal

In Portugal the Modernist wave that was affecting the other European capitals in the first years of the twentieth century struck hard, inspiring a group of poets, writers, and painters to form the Geração de Orpheu, which introduced Modernism to Portugal through the short-lived

---

[44]Jakub Knap, "Niesamowitość i groza w literaturze polskiej dwudziestolecia międzywojennego: (rekonesans badawczy)," *Annales Universitatis Paedagogicae Cracoviensis. Studia Historicolitteraria* 8 (2008): 48.

[45]Knap, "Niesamowitość i groza," 47.

journal *Orpheu* (1915).

One of the Geração de Orpheu was Fernando Pessoa, who became not just the quintessential Modernist but the greatest Portuguese poet since the sixteenth century. The vast majority of critical attention is paid to his poetry, but when he was nineteen, in 1907, he published a collection of short stories, *Um jantar muito original* (*A very original dinner*). At the time in thrall to Poe and the English writers he was reading, Pessoa "was especially interested in perversity and made several attempts in the realm of horror, from the sophisticated supernatural of the communication with another world to the most degrading macabre horror of human condition, cannibalism."[46]

Another member of the Geração de Orpheu was Mário de Sá-Carneiro, a poet and author whose father was the unwilling sponsor of *Orpheu*. Sá-Carneiro committed suicide in 1916, at the age of twenty-six, but before he died he wrote a small body of fiction–short stories and one novel–in which the influence of Poe, Hoffmann, French Decadence and the English aesthetes can clearly be seen. Sá-Carneiro wrote stories on the model of the French *contes fantastique*: "everything is odd, worrying, even incomprehensible both to author and reader, and the incidence of the *merveilleux* in narrative action, too, is frequent and striking: characters appear from nowhere, disappear as surprisingly, create other people out of thin air, have a sixth sense, bear uncanny resemblances to each other, go to other worlds, die from no apparent physical cause."[47] Unlike the *contes fantastique*, however, Sá-Carneiro chooses explanations of his universes which are Poe-like in their logical irrationality.

Romania

The 1901-1939 time period was the "golden age" of Romanian letters, with an enormous number of publications by Romanian novelists and short story writers and a vigorous debate between Romanian traditionalists and the "Westernizing" group which sought to bring Romanian culture closer to the cultures of western Europe, especially France.

1933 was the so-called "miracle year" of Romanian novels. During that year Ionel Teodoreanu published the second novel in his Gothic trilogy, *Golia*. (The first, *Fata din Zlataust* (*The Girl from Zlataust*) was published in 1931 and the third, *Turnul Milenei* (*Milena's Tower*) was published in 1934). "The novels make up a kind of Gothic triptych, very different from each other, and form one of the few coherent attempts in Romanian prose to develop Gothic fiction, aiming to conquer the general public and impose a fantastic prose."[48] Teodoreanu's attempt at

---

[46] Maria Leonor Machado de Sousa, *O <<horror>> na literatura portuguesa* (Amadora, Portugal: Instituto de Cultura Portuguesa), 74.

[47] Pamela Bacarisse, "Sá-Carneiro and the Conte Fantastique," *Luso-Brazilian Review* 12, no. 1 (Summer, 1975): 66.

[48] Elisabeta Lăsconi, "Taina Romanului Gotic," *Viața Românească*, accessed June 19, 2018, http://www.viataromaneasca.eu/arhiva/70_via-a-romaneasca-1-2-2011/53_carti-paralele/798_tai

creating a Gothic for the Romanian reading audience, influenced by the work of the Brontës and by the general 1930s enthusiasm for the Gothic (which would later result in Du Maurier's *Rebecca* (1938)), resulted in a work which has most of the traditional Gothic touchstones: a suspiciously close pair of siblings, a haunted ancient mansion, a formerly grand family fallen on hard times, a book of cryptic messages, an incest theme, and hidden mysteries in general.

Russia & Soviet Union

The nineteenth century was Russia's "Golden Age" of literature. What followed it was Russia's "Silver Age," which was in large part a continuation of the trends of the nineteenth century established by Tolstoy and Dostoyevsky and Chekhov. However, a number of Russian authors veered away from the realist and naturalist modes to create hybrid works that combined the supernatural with realist or naturalist approaches, or Expressionist or Symbolist works. While there was no individual school for these authors, one element that they do have in common is the use of horror in ways unprecedented in Russian fiction, which in the nineteenth century was either purely folklorish (as in Gogol's "Viy" (1835)) or purely naturalistic (as in Dostoyevsky's *Crime and Punishment* (1866)).

One of these avant-garde authors was Leonid Andreyev, who from 1901 to 1914 published proto-Expressionist work–Andreyev is considered by critics to be the father of Russian Expressionism, although a common critical association is also with the Symbolists. (Andreyev combines realist, naturalist, and Symbolist tendencies in his work). Andreyev's work is "uniquely harrowing,"[49] in the words of Brian Stableford; with little recourse to supernaturalism, he creates stories that horrify and lead the empathetic reader to terrifying places. (His *Chernye maski* (*Black masks*, 1907) and "Dnevnik Satany" ("The diary of Satan," 1919) are rare exceptions in their use of the supernatural to terrify). Andreyev's approach is to combine very detailed realist or naturalist prose with psychological portraits of his protagonists. Unlike Dostoyevsky, however, Andreyev does not show ordinary people in stressful and depressing circumstances. Andreyev's characters are usually gripped by extreme emotions, leaving them in psychological states akin to if not the same as madness. Isolated and assured of the futility of their lives, they are unable to understand or control their own worst impulses. This psychological extremity lends Andreyev's work a feverish and even nightmarish quality quite unlike anything Russian literature had seen before. "In spite of Andreyev's obvious bombast and mostly superficial language, he is eminently readable as the unconcealed manipulator of the literary horror machine."[50]

Zinaida Gippius was an important and even formative figure for Russian men and women

---

na-romanului-gotic.html.

[49]Stableford, "From Baum to Tolkien," 111.

[50]Isabelle de Wyzewa, "Andreyev, Leonid Nikolayevich (1871-1919)," in *Columbia Dictionary of Modern European Literature*, eds. Jean Albert Bédé and William Benbow Edgerton (New York: Columbia University Press, 1980), 23.

of letters in the early part of the twentieth century. A poet, playwright, short story writer, essayist, and critic, she organized literary soirées and encouraged the free exchange and creation of new ideas. She was a Symbolist, but an influential one within the movement rather than one slavishly devoted to it. She is best-known for her poetry and her incisive and sometimes savage literary criticism, but she wrote prose as well, and it is in her prose work that horrific elements can be found. Her prose has Decadent and even visionary qualities accompanying intelligent plotting and psychological portrayals, although her overt ideological or political schematicism tends to detract from the horrifying effects. But in works like "Sumasshedsha" ("The Madwoman," 1906), which "charts the attempts at 'colonizing' a young woman's mind and body on the part of her husband,"[51] Gippius' ideology *adds* to the horrifying effect, just as Charlotte Perkins Gilman's "The Yellow Wallpaper" is beneficially augmented by Gilman's feminist intent. Gippius, like the other Symbolists, used supernaturalism when it was appropriate. Her "Ivan Ivanovich I chert" ("Ivan Ivanovich the devil," 1906) and *Chertova kukla* (*The bloody doll*, 1908) make use of the Devil, whether as a Mephistophelean tempter, in the former, or as a diabolical puppet-master, in the latter.

Valeri Bryusov was a poet, critic, novelist, and translator. He was a leading member and organizer of the Russian Decandent (later Symbolist movement), and through his *fiats* and criticism helped push Russian letters in the direction of European Decadents and away from traditional Russian literary schools. Far better known as a poet than prose writer, Bryusov wrote short stories and two novels, one of which, *Ognennyi angel* (*Fiery angel*, 1907-1908) is a historical fantasy with substantial horrific elements. The novel, about a young man's adventure in sixteenth-century Germany and his affair with a passionate woman, is seen as an allegory of Bryusov's real life affair with the poet Nina Petrovskaia. It's also about a demonic possession, black magic and black masses, and the imprisonment, trial, condemnation and death of the woman as a witch. *Ognennyi angel* is well-researched, both in its history and in its occult matter, and portrays the uneasy balance and tension between sexuality and spirituality that occupied so many Russian men and women of letters at the time Bryusov wrote the novel. Elements of *Ognennyi angel* have earned comparison to Bulgakov's *Master and Margarita* (1928) and J.K. Huysmans' *Là-bas* (1891), but *Ognennyi angel*'s horrifyingly described "psychoerotic episodes of demonic possession,"[52] sadomasochistic undercurrents, and detailed descriptions of demonic possession and the witches' Sabbath are Bryusov's own.

Andrei Bely was a leading theorist and poet of the Russian Symbolist movement as well as a novelist and literary critic. *Peterburg* (1913) is thought to be his masterpiece, and was highly praised by Nabokov among others. Bely's first novel, *Serebrianiyi golub'* (*Silver Dove*, 1909), is a prime example of the occult interests and movement of the Russian intelligentsia in the early twentieth century, when the revival of interest in the occult in *fin-de-siècle* Europe, especially the

---

[51] Julie W. De Sherbinin, "'Haunting the Center': Russia's Madwomen and Zinaida Gippius's 'Madwoman,'" *The Slavic and East European Journal* 46, no. 4 (Winter 2002): 733.

[52] Kristi Groberg, "'The Shade of Lucifer's Dark Wing'; Satanism in Silver Age Russia," in *The Occult in Russian and Soviet Culture*, ed. Bernice Glatzer Rosenthal (Ithaca, NY: Cornell University Press, 1997), 120-21.

Satanism of French Symbolist and Decadence, merged with the Russian fear of female sexuality and the "resurgent popularity of the Gothic novel, Goethe, and Poe, the theme of Satan as the projection of intellectual pride in the works of prominent Russian novelists, and the discovery of Nietzsche. The result was a convergence of the occult with religious and philosophical questions about the nature of evil, as well as a preoccupation with evil for its own sake."[53] Bely's novel is about the effort of a religious sect to produce a "Dove child," an infant who will redeem the world. Unfortunately for the protagonist of *Serebrianiyi golub'*, a sex-obsessed member of the intelligentsia, the lascivious peasant woman he has become obsessed with is linked with the sect, who are occult- and demonically-fixated, and the protagonist is ritually sacrificed. *Serebrianiyi golub'* has musical prose and accurate occult knowledge to accompany its frightening moments.

Shloyme Zanul Rappoport, who wrote under the pseudonym "S. Ansky," was an important–perhaps the important–ethnographer of the eastern European Jewish population before World War Two, as well as a socialist activist and writer of folklore-influenced fiction. Ansky's best-known and most important work of fiction is his play *Tsvishn tsvey veltn--der dibek* (*Between Two Worlds--the Dybbuk*, 1914). *The Dybbuk*, set amongst the Jews of the Russian Pale, is about a woman's possession by the spirit of her undead beloved. The worst of the horrors of possession happen off-stage; Ansky intellectualizes the action, holding emotion (so vital to the creation of the horrified effect) at arm's length. Nonetheless, Ansky's approach inspires fright simply through the presentation of the concept of the evil spirit's possession and the scene in which Leah, the victim, is seen to be possessed.

At the same time that avant garde authors were using horror elements in progressive works, more traditional-minded authors were writing Gothics. "The centrality of the Gothic-fantastic to Russian fiction is almost impossible to exaggerate."[54]

Ivan Bunin, Nobel Prize winner, wrote a Gothic in the years before the Revolution, which forced him to flee from Russia for good:

> "Sukhodol" ("Dry Valley," 1911) is a realist re-imagining of Gothic space in provincial Russia. Sukhodol is the Khrushchev family's gloomy mansion, sited on a neglected estate, guarded by a destitute, half-insane relative. Its history includes destructive scenes of rape and murder which descend as terrifying rumours to subsequent generations. Ancient patterns of revenge are repeated upon innocent descendants of those most harmed by Sukhodol's ambience of mental and physical suffering, such as the Khrushchevs' housekeeper, are nonetheless drawn irresistibly back.[55]

Aleksandr Chaianov was best known as an agrarian economist and an amateur historian of art and architecture. He also wrote fiction, and between 1918 and 1928 published five Gothic

---

[53] Groberg, "'The Shade of Lucifer's Dark Wing,'" 99-100.

[54] Muireann Maguire, *Stalin's Ghosts: Gothic Themes in Early Soviet Literature* (New York: Peter Lang, 2012), 14.

[55] Maguire, *Stalin's Ghosts*, 52.

short stories and novellas. Chaianov likely intended them to be meditations on the Revolution and its after-effects, and disguised them under the Gothic trappings, the pastiches of Russian literary traditions, and the references to Pushkin, Gogol, Hoffmann and Gautier. One of Chaianov's stories, "Veneditkov" (1921), would go on to influence Bulgakov in the writing of *The Master and Margarita*. Horrific elements include the aforementioned Gothic elements, psychic possession, diabolical forces, card-playing demons, ominous mirrors, sinister mesmerists, female ghosts, and *doppelgängers*.

Fyodor Sologub was a prolific Symbolist poet, a novelist, a playwright, and an essayist. Critics have charged that he was the first Russian author to introduce the morbid, pessimistic, depressing elements of European *fin-de-siècle* literature into Russian prose, a charge that is difficult to rebut. Sologub is best known for *Melkii bes* (*The petty demon*, 1905), about Peredonov, a schoolteacher who dreams of promotion but who is also the personification of *poshlost*, an untranslatable Russian word meaning "petty, banal, self-satisfied and self-serving evil." Peredonov is filled with lust, sadism (he enjoys the whipping of the boys he teaches), and corruption. He is also mad, a madness which takes the form of a grey demon which hisses at Peredonov with increasing regularity. Peredonov eventually sets a building on fire and murders his best friend. *Melkii bes* is a modernist novel, plotless and intertextual. As Peredonov loses his grasp on his sanity the novel becomes increasingly Gothic, strange, and even nightmarish, and the influence of Poe, Hoffmann, and Gogol become increasingly clear. Nonetheless, the language is poetic and evocative, and *Melkii bes* is a classic work of psychological horror.

Boris Pilniak was a Russian author, known for his various short stories, novels, travelogues, and his anti-modernist, anti-urbanist stances. His novella "Mat' syra-zemlia" ("Mother Earth," 1924) is about the conflict between two well-intentioned, if naive, Bolsheviks and the stubbornly ignorant, yet natural and authentic peasants, as well as nature in the form of a wolf that the two Bolsheviks attempt to domesticate. "Mat' syra-zemlia" is also a Gothic, reflecting Pilniak's growing reservations about both the Bolshevik revolution and the peasant culture he saw behind the revolution: "'Mother Earth' emphasizes revolutionary terror and violence rather than revolution's potential for renewal."[56] "Mat' syra-zemlia" is very much a post-revolution Gothic. While it features the "emphasis on the returning past, its fascination with transgression and decay, and its interest in exploring the aesthetics of fear–the preoccupations that characterize 'Mother Earth,'"[57] all basic elements of the Gothic, "Mat' syra-zemlia" also focuses on the return of the repressed past (the injustices of pre-revolutionary Russia), the ambivalence toward social change, and the emphasis on the traumas of history. "Exposing the social roots of the revolutionary nightmare, "Mother Earth" nevertheless conclusively depicts the peasant community as 'naturally' predisposed to deception, darkness, and violence. In addition, the novella connects the gothic with the feminine, creating a relationship between changing

---

[56]Irina Anisimova, "The Terrors of History: Revolutionary Gothic in 'Mother Earth' by Boris Pilniak," *The Slavic and East European Journal* 55, no. 3 (Fall 2011): 376.

[57]Anisimova, "The Terrors of History," 377.

gender roles and the mechanized violence of the state."[58] "Mat' syra-zemlia" is well-written, combining expressiveness and rhythmic, euphonious prose, and its frightening Gothic moments are smoothly assimilated into the readable and engaging whole.

Gleb Alekseev was a journalist and author. His *Podzemnaia Moskva* (*Underground Moscow*, 1925), is a "striking early Soviet parallel" to the early traditional Gothic trip underground:

> a Soviet archaeologist and his companions thread the labyrinthine catacombs under Moscow's Kremlin to eventually discover the lost library of Ivan IV. Their quest unearths historical treasures that can be used as symbols to legitimize Soviet power; but in the process, they encounter numerous cliches of Gothic horror - including chained skeletons, an underground graveyard, and a damaged manuscript left by a boyar whose wife was raped and murdered by Ivan.[59]

Little is known about Maks Zhizhmore, a Jewish poet and playwright of the 1920s and 1930s. His 1929 play *Grob*, performed as *Posledniaia zhertva* (*The Last Victim*), is one of the foremost Soviet Gothic plays of the twentieth century: "*Grob* fulfils most of the narrative perquisites of Female Gothic: a beautiful heroine betrayed by her family, a lubricious, sadistic villain, and a plot pivoted on an act of sexual sacrifice. (Its hero is even called Naiman.) Moreover, the plays' action transpires in stereotypically Gothic loci: a coffin-maker's workshop and a (Jewish) cemetery."[60]

Spain

Traditionally there were far fewer Spanish horror texts, much less Spanish horror writers, than in other countries. This was so for a variety of reasons, starting with a cultural disapproval of fantasy (dating back to the Renaissance), the 1492 ascension of Catholicism as the official religion of Spain, and continuing through the Inquisition's banning on novels in 1799 as a way to stop Gothic novels from infecting Spain. Although the ban was lifted in 1830 and the Inquisition abolished in 1834, Realism's appearance in Spain in the late nineteenth century meant that fantasy and horror were "particularly targeted, being criticized on the basis of their inferior quality."[61] (That the same authors who wrote horror texts were also writing acclaimed realist works was either not noticed or ignored by critics of horror and fantasy).

---

[58] Anisimova, "The Terrors of History," 379.

[59] Maguire, *Stalin's Ghosts*, 44.

[60] Maguire, *Stalin's Ghosts*, 33.

[61] Clara Palleja-López, "Houses and Horror: A Sociocultural Study of Spanish and American Women Writers" (Thesis, University of Auckland, 2010), 155.

If, as Antonio Cruz Casado claims, the fantastic literature of the early-twentieth century in Spain was everything but homogenous, Spanish Gothic was strongly affected by the spiritualist craze that had taken over Europe in the nineteenth century....there was a curiosity about the spectral from canonical writers who were active as part of the Modernist movement.[62]

Among these canonical authors who, tourist-like, played with the supernatural and the Gothic in some of their stories while still remaining mainstream and respected were: Pio Baroja, who published genuinely *unheimlich* stories in *Vidas sombrías* (*Darkened lives*, 1900) and a hallucinatory and nightmarish novel in *El hotel del cisne* (*The swan hotel*, 1945); Miguel de Unamuno, who wrote Gothic short stories in 1908 and 1921; and Ramón del Valle-Inclan, whose *Jardín umbrio* (*The shadowy garden*, 1920), contains a Gothic short story and one portraying demonic possession, and whose *Tirano Banderas* (*The tyrant Banderas*, 1926) "takes place in a synthetic, composite dystopia ruled by a grotesque and ghostly dictator."[63] Most effective of the Spanish Gothic spiritualist tales in evoking horror, fear, and unease were the short stories published in Angeles Vicente's *Los cuentos de Sombras* (*The tales of shadows*, 1911); one story, "Sombras," depicts a group of spirits taking the form of a terrifying giant spider which then eats the protagonist.

Emilia Pardo Bazán was one of the first Spanish women writers to become internationally known. She was a novelist, literary critic, poet, playwright, and translator, and is best known as the innovator of Spanish naturalism and as an early and outspoken advocate for Spanish women's rights. Her earlier work is more naturalistic, her later work tending more toward symbolism and political advocacy. Around the turn of the century, she began writing horror stories, which like her other fiction of the time embodies her feminist ideals, to the point that the stories deserve inclusion in any anthology of feminist horror stories. Her pre-1900 horror fiction makes use of Gothic and Romantic settings, while her post-1900 horror stories use more realistic settings. In her horror stories she uses classic horror fiction monsters—vampires, ghosts, etc—but often in unusual roles, as protagonists or secondary characters rather than antagonists. Her "Vampiro" (Vampire; 1901), about a wealthy old man who marries a poor young woman and drinks her blood, thereby regaining his youth and vigor. "Here issues such as class difference and gender relationships are tackled by refracting them through the conventions of a horror tale."[64] And Pardo Bazán's "La resucitada" ("The resurrected woman," 1908), is about a woman who wakes up in her family chapel after what seems to have been a cataleptic seizure, but when she returns home, she is treated by everyone with fear and disgust, and she notices that her flesh is pale and she has the odor of decomposition about her. "'La resucitada' resonates with

---

[62]Xavier Aldana Reyes, *Spanish Gothic: National Identity, Collaboration and Cultural Appropration* (London: Palgrave Macmillan, 2017), 135-36.

[63]Persephone Braham, *From Amazons to Zombies: Monsters in Latin America* (Lewisburg, PA: Bucknell University Press, 2015), 135.

[64]Palljá-López, "Houses and Horror," 166.

patriarchy's validation of women's worth and identity as depending on their roles as mothers and wives."[65] Pardo Bazán's prose is straightforward, and her horror comes from concepts rather than moments, but the end result is an able combination of horror and ideology.

Eduardo Zamacois began as a writer of erotic material but quickly began creating socialist fiction. In 1910 he wrote *El Otro* (*The Other*), which is generally seen by critics as one of the most accomplished Spanish Gothics of the twentieth century. One of the few examples of early twentieth century Spanish novels whose explicit intent is to terrify, *El Otro* is about the protagonist, his lover, and the ghost of the lover's husband, who the protagonist helped murder and who haunts the protagonist. However, the existence of the ghost is left ambiguous, and is felt but never seen. Zamacois focused on the psychology of those who could perceive the ghost and the psychology of guilt, what he called "metaphysical fear." The result was psychological horror more than it was supernatural horror.

Emilio Carrere was the rare Spanish writer of the 1910s and 1920s who wrote primarily Gothic fiction. An unashamedly pulp writer with a passion for the occult, the spiritualist, and Gothic fiction, Carrere wrote numerous stories and novels with the horrific *fantastika* in them or that were Gothic in genre. Although he sometimes wrote ambiguously supernatural stories, most of them feature the world of ghosts, witchcraft, Satanism, black masses, demonic possession, and appearances of the Devil Himself.

Carmen de Burgos was a journalist, writer, translator, and women's rights advocate. A modernist and professional writer, she was known in her lifetime not only for the quantity of her work but also for her fictional treatment of homosexuality, transvestism, feminism, and other controversial topics. Like Pardo Bazán, Burgos' horror fiction was a sidelight to the majority of her writing, but like Pardo Bazán Burgos wrote horror fiction with a greater purpose than to simply entertain. For Burgos, even horror fiction had to include the political messages she fought all her life to convey. In her "La mujer fría" ("The Cold Woman," 1923) a beautiful dead woman unaware of her own nature attracts all the men who see her but sucks the life out of those who kiss her. It is overtly feminist work, about the rootlessness of women, who depend on men for survival; the titular woman is forced to wander around Spain because of the string of dead people behind her, and only finds temporary homes, in hotels and rented apartments, because of the interest men have in her. In Burgos' "El perseguidor" ("The Pursuer," 1917) a woman who hates to be restrained or limited, and who loves freedom above all else, is stalked by a mysterious cloaked man. The woman ultimately gives up her freedom and independence in exchange for safety by marrying a man who she had formerly despised. "Matilde's refusal to be contained in a home, which is gradually eroded by a male character who stands for social pressure, constitutes the essence of the narrative."[66] Burgos, unlike Pardo Bazán, was not a pure realist, and made use of vivid and occasionally surreal imagery and concepts in her short work. It is the moments as much as the concept that deliver fright in Burgos' stories.

---

[65]Pallejá-López, "Houses and Horror," 168.

[66]Pallejá-López, "Houses and Horror," 184.

Chapter Five: Middle East

Egypt

Egyptian literature began its transformation into modern literature during *al-Nahda*, the national cultural renaissance of the late nineteenth century. The *Nahda* was partly inspired by the shock of Napoleon's invasion of Egypt in 1798, but more largely the result of the nineteenth century reformation of the Ottoman Empire and internal political, economic, and social changes in Egypt throughout the second half of the nineteenth century. The result of the *Nahda* in literature was the establishment of modern literary criticism in Arabic, the return of the literary salon, the publication of the first novel—in essence, the creation of a modern world of letters for Egyptian writers and readers.

Naturally, given the history of Egypt during these years—an Ottoman subject through 1882, a British protectorate thereafter—Low Art, what was popular and widely-read (as opposed to High Art, the product of the patriotic and nationalistic intelligentsia), was influenced not only by native literary movements but also by what was being produced in England and across Europe, especially in France. By the turn of the twentieth century Egyptian newspapers were publishing translations and imitations of French popular literature, including romances, thrillers, spy stories, and, later, detective stories. Fifteen periodicals in Egypt and Lebanon specialized in publishing translations and original works of fiction.

The result was the first Egyptian horror literature, inspired by translations of Poe, Gautier, Hoffmann, and other authors from the French. These stories were for the most part crude imitations of Western horror stories, just as the first Egyptian detective fiction modeled itself on American dime novels rather than the far better work of Doyle.

Iran

Sadeq Hadāyat was a Persian intellectual, translator, and author. Although he wrote widely, he is best-known for his novel *Būf-e Kūr* (*The Blind Owl*, 1937). Hadāyat was greatly conversant with the masters of European literature, and was influenced by Poe, de Maupassant, Kafka, Chekhov and Dostoyevsky—all of which helps explain the pessimism of *Būf-e Kūr*, which is nominally a series of confessions of an unnamed pen case painter, addressed to a shadow which looks like the titular owl. But *Būf-e Kūr* also makes use of several Poe elements, including the general premise (the unnamed narrator relating an incident), allusions to disease, a descent into madness, an unreliable narrator, and an ethereal beauty.[1] *Būf-e Kūr* further uses a dreamlike atmosphere not unlike that of Kafka. *Būf-e Kūr* is enigmatic, absurdist, and nightmarish, with elements common to the Gothic and the *contes fantastique* as well as motifs from Persian folklore and myth. A combination of modern, Sartre-esque alienation and malaise and a more Persian outlook, *Būf-e Kūr* is a splendidly-wrought and very personal nightmare of a

---

[1] Rouhollah Zarei, "Axes of Evil Live Evermore: Brother Poe in Iran," *The Edgar Allan Poe Review* 4, no. 2 (Fall 2003): 16.

descent into the depths of horror and corruption.

Turkey

While Turkish literature of the 1901-1939 period did not have horror literature as such–the closest it came were the more gruesome and chilling detective/mystery dime novels–it did have the Gothic novel. There was no Turkish tradition of the Gothic in the early 19th century, nor did the Turks' folklore feature the Western spooks which appeared in Western Gothics. (Turks' folklore was primarily Anatolian- and Islamic-based). But the religious elements and social conditions of Turkish society during the nineteenth and early twentieth century gave rise to a very Turkish Gothic, one which was influenced by the European Gothic (as the Turkish intelligentsia looked to Europe for modernization) but with particularly Turkish mind sets, environments, and horror elements.

One early Turkish Gothic writer was Hüseyin Rahmi Gürpınar, a popular novelist whose works were mainly realist and social commentary, designed to educate the reading public and raise the level of their consciousnesses. This is reflected in the two novels he wrote–*Cadı* (*Witch*, 1912) and *Gulyabani* (*Ghoul*, 1913)–which were Turkish Gothics but at the same time rationalized horror of the Ann Radcliffe sort. In *Cadı* a young widow hears frightening rumors about her new fiancée; in *Gulyabani* sinister occurrences beset a farm located in a desolate spot. In both novels Gürpınar ladled on the appropriate frights and horror elements, but made sure to explain every one of them by the novels' ends.

65

Part Two: 1940-1970

Chapter Six: Africa

Angola

Despite the work of earlier authors, like Antonio de Assis Junior, Angolan fiction at the century's halfway mark was largely in thrall to the model of traditional Portuguese fiction. Oscar Ribas helped to change that. A popular folklorist and spokesman–with the government's official imprimatur–for native Angolan traditions, Ribas wrote both fiction and non-fiction about traditional Angola and the Kimbundu, especially Angola at the turn of the twentieth century. In two of his works, *Uanga (Feitiço)* (1951) and "O Praga" (1951), Ribas incorporated substantial amounts of Kimbundu beliefs about witchcraft and sorcery, making the plots heavily dependent on evil magic for their twists and turns and resolutions. Ribas' style is sophisticated, much more so than Assis Junior's, and his handling of Luanda's African heritage is delicate and knowledgeable, but he makes too much use of cliche, and his characters are primarily vehicles for Ribas to lecture the audience on Angolan culture and folkways. The supernatural horror elements in both works are a part of those. Ribas did not write horror literature–that is, his primary intention was not to frighten the reader, although that was a secondary intention. His primary intention was to defend traditional Angolan society against the Portuguese colonials. The horror he achieves is conveyed is primarily conceptual, about what happens to its victims. Ribas is a straightforward storyteller whose works' horror elements are conveyed in a folkloric manner. That they frightened his readers was a good thing, to Ribas, but not the best thing.

Congo

Literature in the Congo in the late 1940s was entirely under the sway of the Belgian literary establishment. Paul Lomami-Tshibamba changed that, publishing in 1948 the first work of Congolese literature and a work that, in its devotion to the description both the Congolese way of life and the world of Congolese mythology, expressed an innately Congolese (rather than Belgian) viewpoint. The book, *Ngando le Crocodile* (*Ngando the Crocodile*) won a Congolese literary award and subtly expressed the anti-colonialist politics of its author, who was both a writer and a literary activist, while also vividly telling the story of a supernatural journey through a spirit-haunted land. *Ngando le Crocodile* is a poetic and even mythic work possessed of detailed description of everyday life and psychologically realistic portraits of its protagonists. Unlike other retellings of native myths, as in the work of Oscar Ribas and Birago Diop, Lomami Tshibamba's work is dark. *Ngando le Crocodile* explores Congolese metaphysics and legends, depicting a belief system of opposing supernatural good and evil forces who are omnipresent and active. "The destructive power is in the hands of invisible beings who inhabit a mysterious world hidden from man"[1] and are always ready to intervene. Death is ever-present, and usually arrives

---

[1]Dorothy S. Blair, *African Literature in French: A History of Creative Writing in French from West and Equatorial Africa* (Cambridge, UK: Cambridge University Press, 1976), 69.

in a shockingly unexpected and frightening manner, in *Ngando*, and readers are similarly chilled by the more horrible of the supernatural beings. *Ngando*'s ultimate purposes were to tell a Congolese folktale and to criticize the Belgian colonial regime, but without meaning to Lomami Tshibamba created one of the earliest works of Francophone African horror fiction.

Maurice Kasongo, a trade union leader and author, wrote *Kongono, esclave des nains-démons de la forêt* (*Kongono, slave of the dwarf-demons of the forest*, 1948) for the same contest that Lomami-Tshibamba's *Ngando le crocodile* won. The two have a number of points in common:

> ...the reversal of the pre-colonial order following the arrival of the whites is rendered by a choice of spatial order. The opposition between the African world and the Western world is not yet openly declared, but is transposed metaphorically to a mythical level. The restitution of the traumatic experience of the colonial impact which...breaks the "circle of mythologies"...remains in the deepest archetypal stage of binary oppositions between above and below, sphere of the gods and from hell, a staircase that leads to heaven and the sunken world....the polarization between the forest and a rather vague but promising "north" (at Kasongo), and between the river (and its islands) and the city that appears in its middle (at Lomami Tchibamba), is not the consequence of the irremediable fracture introduced upon the arrival of Europeans in the world of ancestors. And indeed, the ancestors die because the contact of modernity indirectly disturbs the world of tradition: the danger creeps within the very space of origin, which is no longer known or recognizable, nor organized in hierarchies. It is a world in which the good has fallen back into some pockets of resistance, threatened by the outside world; a world whose slogans and taboos (Musemvola, the father of the little boy kidnapped by the crocodile, died precisely for not having known how to respect one) have been forgotten.[2]

But *Kongono* is markedly different in an important way. The novel is about two children, born to old parents, who live in a world of supernatural beings. They are raised to fear the evil spirits that live in the forest—the dwarf-demons of the novel's title—and end up being bewitched by them. The two have a series of adventures, with rescues and heartbreaks, until the author interrupts the narrative to sing the praises of the white men in an "apology for colonization. Such an apology now appears to be ideological conformism."[3]

Guinea

In the 1960s Guinean literature, and that of Francophone African literature more generally, was going through a period in which literature was expected to be political as well as

---

[2]Silvia Riva, *Nouvelle histoire de la littérature du Congo-Kinshasa* (Paris: L'Harmattan, 2006), 56-57.

[3]Kadima Nzuji Mukala, *La littérature zaïroise de langue française: 1945-1965* (Paris: Éditions Karthala, 1984), 203.

well-crafted. Works of fiction which looked backwards in time or which contained elements of *fantastika* were seen as embarrassments that were of no use to Guineans. The author Camara Laye began writing in the 1950s, when Guinea was still a colony of France, and produced two works which are generally described by critics as being among the classics of African literature during the colonial period. During the 1960s, Camara–a political activist and writer, first in Guinea and then in exile in Senegal–began adding elements of *fantastika*–specifically that of the African oral narrative tradition--to his fiction, which had been generally autobiographical. First in *Dramouss* (1966) and then in a serial written for the Nigerian literary journal *Black Orpheus* in 1967, Camara wrote hybrid fiction, part-Modernist and part-*griot*-influenced. *Dramouss* and the serial are generally seen as Camara's weakest work, being uneasy combinations of social commentary, *fantastika*, autobiography, and ethnography. The works, while important to Francophone African literature, are flawed in style and weakly plotted. The *fantastika* in both of them is of the dark variety, tending toward horror. The serial is a haunting allegory in which the supernatural is a part of a dreadful reality. In *Dramouss* the supernatural is a part of reality, though not a menacing part. However, the final section of the novel is about a nightmarish Orwellian dream the protagonist has, in which he is trapped in a Kafka-esque prison and a giant preys on a helpless Guinea. Unlike much of *Dramouss*, the nightmare sequence is memorably written, with surreal elements adding to the fright; it is an allegory for Guinea as it was under the reign of the tyrant Sékou Touré, which is meaningless to current readers but to contemporary readers was a disquieting reminder of a terrifying reality.

Ivory Coast

The fiction of the Ivory Coast in the 1950s was much like Angolan fiction during Oscar Ribas' heyday: unduly influenced by the models of its colonizer's novels and short stories. In 1955 Ivory Coast had not yet achieved independence, but there was a substantial anti-colonial, pro-independence movement. The fiction writer Bernard Dadié was a part of this movement. In his life he would become one of Africa's most distinguished man of letters, prolifically writing novels, plays, and poetry; after independence he would serve the Ivorian government as the Ministry of Culture. In 1955 he had already published a novel and a collection of Ivorian folktales. But *Le pagne noir* (*The black loincloth,* 1955) was an advance on his previous work. His second collection of retellings of Ivorian folktales and legends, *Le pagne noir* is told in a fluid, enjoyable style that strikes an admirable balance between the requirements of the modern *conte* and the requirement to present the folktales as if they were transcriptions of live performances of *griots*. The stories are colorful and linguistically vivid stories of a pastoral people, and admirably fulfill Dadié's intention of preserving traditional Ivorian culture. However, they are not innocent, nor are several of them light-hearted. A number of the stories deal with matters of life and death, Faustian bargains, frightening talking animals, and loved ones turned revenants. Although good triumphs and evil is punished in these stories, Dadié does not scant on adding tension and frightening imagery and concepts, so that these traditional legends and folktales, much like their European counterparts, generally have happy endings to redeem the dreadfulness that the protagonists undergo. As with the work of Oscar Ribas, the stories in *Le pagne noir* are intended to teach moral lessons, with the horror effect on the reader being an enjoyable second-order effect.

Lesotho

In the 1950s Sesotho letters were vibrant for the first time in a generation, thanks to a politicized group of authors who wrote novels objecting to the apartheid policies of neighboring South Africa's National Party government–policies which had a drastically adverse effect on the many Basotho immigrants who moved to South African cities in search of work. Protest literature was the dominant genre for the Basotho, with fiction that didn't contain political elements looked down upon and deemed irrelevant or unnecessary. In 1953, when poet, dramatist, and school teacher J.G. Mocoancoeng published *Meqoqo ea phirimana* (*Evening Stories*), he felt it necessary to format the book as a group of improving moral essays dealing with the evils of imperialism, colonialism, and apartheid. But Mocoancoeng added more to his essays on "modern themes" than political messages:

> they contain...a great number of fantastic and hair-raising elements, depicting, for examples, the appearance of huge water snakes believed to cause tornadoes, ghosts, and the *thokolosi*, a supernatural being resembling a man who can only be seen by the person to whom he is sent.[4]

Mocoancoeng has a fluid and lyrical style which adds to the chill felt by the reader when reading about these creatures' appearances.

A more straightforwardly fictional book of horror stories appeared in 1961, written by the poet and translator Z.L. Hoeane. *Pale tse hlomolang le tse tshehisang* (*Sad and Jocular Stories*) is an able combination of horror, humor, and tragedy, making use of both Basotho legends and contemporary situations.

Another trend in Basotho horror fiction during the mid-century decades was the religious fantasy. The main goal of such works was to promote Christianity in the face of Basotho resistance—animist beliefs were still common, especially outside of Maseru, the capital, and were moreover seen as part of the resistance against the British colonizers. But Basotho religious fantasy stories, novellas, and novels often combined Christian ideals with settings in Lesotho and creatures from Basotho folklore. D.P. Lebakeng's *Sekoting sa lihele* (*In the Depths of Hell*, 1956) uses both Satan and a variety of demonic figures out of Basotho folklore to torment sinners from Lesotho.

Nigeria

Seven years after David Fagunwa's *Ogboju Ode ninu Igbo Irunmale* was published, a Yoruba writer, Amos Tutuola, wrote his first full-length novel, *The Palm Wine Drinkard*. The

---

[4] Josh R. Maseia, "Southern Sotho Literature," in *Literatures in African Languages: Theoretical Issues and Sample Surveys*, eds. B. W. Andrzejewski, S. Pilaszewicz, W. Tyloch (Cambridge, UK: Cambridge University Press, 1985), 618.

novel was not published for another six years, in 1952, but when it was published it came from the London publishing house Faber and Faber, making it the first African novel published in English outside of Africa. It was an immediate success, garnering praise from V.S. Pritchett and, most notably, Dylan Thomas, and launched not just Tutuola's career as a writer but modern west African literature as a whole. Tutuola drew heavily on Fagunwa's work as a resource, although the inspiration for and most of the stuff of *The Palm Wine Drinkard* is derived from Yoruba folktales. A successful attempt to transplant oral folklore into the printed form, *Palm Wine Drinkard* is told in a uniquely idiosyncratic form of pidgin English, but the wonder and horror of the novel is felt not despite the pidgin narrative voice, but because of it. *Palm Wine Drinkard* initially came in for a great deal of criticism from Nigerian critics—western critics were far more generous—on the grounds that the pidgin narrative voice made Nigerians look poorly educated and ignorant, but with the space of sixty years' time it can be see that the pidgin narrative voice is poetic and even lyrical, not a "macédoine of malapropisms."[5] The grammar and spelling can be messy, but the cumulative effect of the Tutuola's pidgin narrative voice is poetic, enthralling—and terrifying. *Palm Wine Drinkard* bears no relation to western forms (although it is an epic, episodic saga-quest), nor does its content map easily on to western horror motifs, tropes, and concepts. What *Palm Wine Drinkard* is instead is a presentation of Yoruba folktale—unfamiliar, enigmatic, and strange to Western eyes—which is ultimately nightmarish, containing vivid frightening and grotesque imagery and moments, grim themes, and cruel elements in an odyssey filled with pain. The final result is a beautiful nightmare, filled with realism, humor, beauty, and the macabre, grotesque, and evil.

Four years later another work of *fantastika* with substantial horror elements was published. Like *The Palm Wine Drinkard*, this book—*Ibu Olokun* (*The Deeps Where Olokun Reigns Supreme*, 1956), written by J. Ogunsina Ogundele, a school teacher—was heavily influenced by Fagunwa's *Ogboju Ode ninu Igbo Irunmale*. It is a loosely episodic saga about a man with superhuman abilities who is forced to go on a long trip from the Earth to the heavens by way of the deeps of the sea. During the journey he encounters a variety of frightening supernatural threats, and overcomes them all using his superhuman powers. The most terrifying of all of these is the goddess Olokun herself, trapped at the bottom of the sea after she became enraged with humanity (Ogundele here makes use of an existing Yoruba myth about Olokun), and against her the protagonist is forced to rely on help from friendly spirits. *Ibu Olokun* is roughly in the Fagunwa tradition, but Ogundele is a stricter writer and keeps a much tighter grasp on his plot and is more disciplined in his deployment of the frightening supernatural. Ogundele's second novel, *Ejigbede Lona Isalu Orun* (*Ejigbede on his way from Heaven to Earth*, 1957), is more of the same, albeit the protagonist wants to return to Heaven after jumping from there on to Earth, rather than traveling from Earth to Heaven and back. In *Ejigbede*, the horrific supernatural beings are Earthly creatures, as opposed to *Ibu Olokun*'s residents of liminal spaces.

A decade later another writer tapped the Fagunwa vein. D.J. Fatanmi's *K'orimale ninu igbo Adimula* (*K'orimale in the Forest of Adimula*, 1967) is even more imitative of Fagunwa's *Ogboju Ode ninu Igbo Irunmale* than *Palm Wine Drinkard* or *Ibu Olokun* was, being about a

---

[5]Steven G. Kellman, *The Translingual Imagination* (Lincoln, NE: University of Nebraska Press, 2000), 41.

brave hunter who encounters supernaturally threatening creatures in a mysterious, forbidding forest. But Fatanmi was far more influenced in the writing of the book by his Christian upbringing and added passages of sermonizing and a clear moral at the end of the novel, as well as allegorical material not present in Fagunwa.

Quite a different writer from the preceding Nigerians was Obi Egbuna, a novelist, playwright, and political activist. His *Daughters of the Sun and Other Stories* (1970) is a collection of four short stories whose intent is to show the superiority of native African culture to that of white interlopers and foreigners. As part of his story-telling, however, Egbuna uses the tactics of fear literature to horrify his white readers, who are likely to identify with the white characters in the stories and to be horrified by the bad ends they come to. "An elderly catechist challenges the power of the village 'Divinity' with terrible results; a right-wing settler clashes with a Black Power leader; an American medical student discovers that a 'witch doctor' has powers greater than his own."[6]

Senegal

In the late 1940s Senegalese literature, much like Ivorian literature of the 1950s, was dominated by the expectations that writers would imitate French writers and avoid the influence of traditional Senegalese culture. One of the writers who changed this state of affairs was Birago Diop, a Senegalese poet who published three collections of folktales and legends in 1947, 1958, and 1963. While some of these tales were from Mali and Burkina Faso, the majority of them were from the Wolof of Senegal. Diop's intention was to present, in clear French, African oral literature in a written form. Diop succeeded marvelously, providing Francophone African with seminal models of native oral stories, and became an important member of the first generation of Francophone African writers. Diop's greatest achievement was not to tell African stories to a white audience; nearly all of his stories are aimed the Wolof and Senegalese audiences rather than white readers. Diop's greatest achievement is creating a well-written prose equivalent to the living realities of the griots' oral performances. Vivid and engaging, Diop's retellings of these oral stories include all the griots' nuances of dialogue and gesture, while also making use of a variety of storytelling techniques, including those Diop learned from western literature. Diop's prose style is elegant. The stories themselves are a combination of realism, humor, satire, and fantasy, and work as fables and legends, as moral lessons, and as allegories for the ordinary human condition. Many of them are animal fables, though a number, more generally serious, lack animals and replace them with malign spirits. These stories use both chilling concepts and effects and tragic irony and the sudden reversal of fortune to frighten the reader into learning the right lesson. Like Oscar Ribas and Bernard Dadié, Diop's work is primarily intended to teach–frightening the reader happens to be one of the good teaching methods.

Abdoulaye Sadji was one of the best-known of the Senegalese authors who followed in the footsteps of Diop, Léopold Séddar Senghor, and Ousmane Socé. Unusually, Sadji's attempts

---

[6]"*Daughters of the Sun and Other Stories*," in *A New Reader's Guide to African Literature*, eds. Hans M. Zell, Carol Bundy, and Virginia Coulon (New York: Holmes & Meier Publishers, 1983), 147.

at realist fiction were less successful than his more fantastic work, where the former's "turgid over-emphasis...[is replaced by] genuine poetic charm."[7] Sadji's *Tounka* (1946), about a legendary epic hero's marriage to a sea-princess and his downfall, brought about by his own hubris, is unusual in that it is a fabular work with "unflagging dramatic tension...[Sadji] indicates the ever-present mystery and menace of the supernatural that hangs over the nameless tribe's daily existence."[8]

Sierra Leone

Poet Lenrie Peters wrote only one novel: *The Second Round* (1965). That novel was enough to provoke controversy, as its subject matter–rape, incest, madness, matricide, violence, acedia–was deemed both inappropriate for a novel by an African author, and not African enough, meaning it didn't deal with specifically African issues such as colonialism, imperialism, and racism. About an alienated doctor returned to Freetown after years away, *The Second Round* is a thoroughly–and non-supernaturally–Gothic novel, the first in West African letters and one that, as Charles Larson argues, is "removed from African tradition"[9] and–in defiance of the trends of the time in serious African literature, universal in application.

South Africa

South African horror literature in the mid-century decades largely fell into the three categories described in Chapter One: European-style horror stories, Afrikaans Gothic, and Afrikaans magical realism. One of the foremost practitioner of European-style horror stories in both the 1930s and the 1940s was I.D. du Plessis, an academic (later government official) and writer of everything from poetry (for which he was acclaimed) to ethnographies to novels to biographies. In the field of horror he published four collections of short stories, the first (in 1935) retellings of Afrikaner folklore and the other three (1941, 1942, 1966) a mixture of folktales and original work. Du Plessis' ghost stories are in the vein of Leipoldt, Marais, and Langenhoven, being a mix of Afrikaner, native South African, and Malay concepts, creatures and settings. Du Plessis' original work has also been described as Afrikaner neo-Gothic, with mysterious and supernatural elements, including vampires, ghosts, and hauntings.

A much different writer writing European-style horror stories was Maria Elizabeth Rothmann, a journalist and social worker who served on the Carnegie Committee. Under the pseudonym of "M.E.R." she wrote a variety of novels, short stories, and essays and pieces for local newspapers. Her collection *Uit en Tuis* (*Out and Home*, 1946) is a collection of pieces

---

[7]Dorothy S. Blair, *Senegalese Literature: A Critical History* (Boston: Twayne Publishers, 1984), 75.

[8]Blair, *Senegalese Literature*, 75.

[9]Charles R. Larson, "Patterns of African Fiction," (PhD diss., Indiana University, 1971), 245.

written for newspapers and magazines over the preceding two decades. A number of the pieces are sensitive sketches which delicately handle the dynamics of difficult relationships, whether between men and women, mothers and daughters, or sisters and girlfriends. But a number of the pieces are short stories dealing with the lives of native South Africans. In those stories she wrote with great compassion about those lives, although she could often be didactic and paternalistic. This didacticism was abandoned in the horror stories in the collection, which in the words of Gerda Taljaard are "ghost stories for black workers who have a grudge against their employers."[10] Afrikaans ghost stories of the mid-century decades, both before 1948 and after, often express similar racial fears, but Rothmann's stories were the first to express not only sympathy for the workers rather than for management–needless to say, a radical stance in conservative post-war South Africa–but sympathy for the blacks in the story rather than the whites. As in her mainstream work, Rothmann tells her ghost stories with an uncommon touch for relationships, with a marked sympathy for women (especially those in mixed marriages), and with a careful touch for the proper deployment and use of the frightening concept or moment.

Different still from both Rothmann and du Plessis was the horror work of Eric Rosenthal. An Afrikaner freelance journalist, broadcaster, biographer and writer of reference books, Rosenthal had an appetite for "true" South African stories of the fantastic, adventurous, and terrifying. In 1951 he published *They Walk By Night,* a collection of "real" ghost stories, supposedly as told to him by his fellow Afrikaners (and, in one memorable case, a native South African). Like his British counterpart Elliott O'Donnell–an unacknowledged influence on Rosenthal's work, perhaps–Rosenthal's stories were actually fiction, whether his own creation or fictionalized accounts of actual ghost stories and folktales. The stories in *They Walk By Night* are generally told in a light-hearted narrative voice, but the matter of the stories, the concepts and warnings, are very dark indeed. One typical description is as follows:

> There is in Basutoland a little creature of whom all stand in awe. He is not much bigger than a baboon, but is minus the tail, and is perfectly black, with a quantity of black hair on his body. He has hands and feet like an ordinary mortal, but is never heard to speak. He shuns the daylight, and abhors clothing, even in the coldest weather. Evidently he is above such sensations as heat and cold. This wonderful creature is "Tokolosh,' the Poisoner, the Evil One, whose deeds are cruel, revengeful, apparently unlimited. He has power to kill, to afflict in every imaginable way, to send mad, or to visit with unknown sickness; but to do good is beyond his power. There are several of these little people in the country. They generally are employed by the witch doctors to do their dirty work.[11]

The history of theater in South Africa is a long one, going back into the nineteenth century, but theater by black writers and for black audiences in South Africa began only in 1925. Plays by black writers and for black audiences were popular in urban areas in the 1930s and 1940s, and flourished after the war. In 1956 the "New Drama" phase of native South African

---

[10]Taljaard-Gilson, "Die inslag van die Gotiese," 194.

[11]Eric Rosenthal, *They Walk By Night* (Cape Town: Timmins, 1951), 159-60.

theater began. "New Drama" plays made a serious effort to break away from the British tradition of colonial theater and to show native faces, native thought, native tongues, and native resistance to apartheid. Four years before "New Drama" began, however, S.M. Mofokeng wrote a play, *Senkatana*, which allegorically tackled the same issues which "New Drama" would make explicit. Although he died young, Mofokeng produced enough high quality work to be generally acclaimed as the greatest playwright and essayist in the Sotho language. *Senkatana* is based on a native legend about the "swallowing monster" kgodumodumo, a kind of dragon-snake who swallowed up many Basotho until it was slain by the boy Senkatana. *Senkatana* expands this on this legend; in the play the kgodumodumo has swallowed up the entire Basotho nation, and Senkatana is the only man left alive. In the play Mofokeng made the Senkatana legend into both a Christian allegory, with Senkatana representing Christ and kgodumodumo representing sin, and an allegory for apartheid, with kgodumodumo representing the apartheid regime which has "swallowed" the Basotho people, and Senkatana representing a future liberator of the Basotho. Although the kgodumodumo never appears on stage, it is described by a figure embodying both the Seer and the Chorus of Greek theater (a deliberate invocation on Mofokeng's part) in vivid, terrifying phrases designed to frighten the audience.

Henriette Grové was an award-winning writer of plays and prose. She began making a name for herself by writing romance serials for women's magazines under the name "Linda Joubert." One of her earliest novels, *Meulenhof se Mense* (*Meulenhof's People*, 1956), was a special kind of romance, however. Literary prejudice caused *Meulenhof se Mense* to be dismissed as just a romance novel, but critics have come to regard it as one of the foremost South African Gothic romances of the mid-century decades. An epistolary novel, *Meulenhof se Mense* is well-written, nicely balancing the competing demands of the romance novel, the epistolary novel, and the Gothic. More than that, however, is Grové's eager embrace of the techniques of the Gothic novel used by Gothic authors to create tension and fear in their readers. *Meulenhof se Mense* is a feverish, intense novel, full of overheated melodrama, suppressed emotion and eroticism, and the usual Gothic elements:

> Like Charlotte Brontë in *Jane Eyre*, Grové also makes a strong Gothic feature used to create a sense of nuisance for the reader. Continual delusions of evil, spot descriptions characterized by dark and shadow (11), the threatening presence of the enigmatic Josephine who has no eyeshadow or eyebrows do not have (15), tattoos in the mirrors in the living room (22-23) and grave descriptions (33) create a threatening Gothic atmosphere that is "dark and full of fear."[12]

Wessels' invocation of *Jane Eyre* is apt, as there are deliberately-created parallels between *Meulenhof se Mense* and *Jane Eyre*, Emily Brontë's *Wuthering Heights*, and Daphne Du Maurier's *Rebecca*. These parallels, and the general inspiration which Grové drew from those classics, give *Meulenhof se Mense* a sense of familiarity but also allowed Grové to take form those three works techniques of making the audience uneasy, tense, and frightened. Grové adds

---

[12] Andries Wessels, "Intertekstualiteit en modernistiese kompleksiteit in Henriette Grové se Linda Joubert-romans," *Tydskrif vir letterkunde* 48, no. 2 (2011): 38.

specifically South African elements to *Meulenhof se Mense*, though, including witchcraft and a sinister midwife.

P.J. Nienaber was one of South Africa's leading men of letters during his heyday, which ran from the mid-1930s to 1990. Most of what he wrote and edited was non-fiction literary history and criticism, but he wrote a substantial amount of poetry as well. In 1966, unusually for Nienaber, he made an attempt at writing horror stories, in *Geeste en gedaantes* (*Spirits and Shapes*). At the time of the collection's writing there had been a substantial gap in the production of horror stories in South Africa: "ghost stories – after Langenhoven and Leipoldt – disappeared almost entirely from Afrikaans literature."[13] Nienaber, an academic as well as a critic, seemingly felt that what the South African marketplace needed was a collection of ghost stories that mixed Poe with Langenhoven, Leipoldt, and Marais. The result was only intermittently frightening or successful, and did not spark a wave of imitators.

In 1969, with South African drama going through a turbulent period of full of protest theater, P.G. du Plessis (no relation to I.D. du Plessis) wrote what quickly became the standout protest play of the 1960s, *Die nag van Legio* (*The Night of Legion*), which reportedly brought Pretoria to a standstill in its first week of performances. Du Plessis would go on to become an important Afrikaans writer, playwright, and academic, but *Die nag van Legio* is his best-known work. About five patients stuck in a psychiatric hospital, one of whom is evil, *Die nag van Legio* was groundbreaking not just for its message, a furious shout against the South African status quo and the reigning National Party, but also for its stagecraft. While *Die nag van Legio* is inherently political, and about South Africa in 1969, its message about the omnipresence of evil and the wickedness of corrupt leaders has been able to be stressed in recent productions without any loss from the original play. *Die nag van Legio* is magical-realism theater, about psychiatric illness, emotional trauma, and murder. Of relevance to this work is the fact that the evil antagonist, Dogoman, is not merely evil, but possessed by dozens of demons and capable of black magic, which he uses in a unbearably tense scene to murder the protagonist—who, it turns out, was the child of a witch. Dogoman uses his magical powers to control the other characters and subject them to his rule. Gothic elements (the setting of the insane asylum, the ruined detritus on the stage) and stage trickery (the lights grow slowly redder as Dogoman uses his powers) add to the tension and fright felt by the play's viewers.

---

[13] Van Graan, "Die rol van ruimte in Afrikaanse spookstories," 24.

Chapter Seven: The Americas

Argentina

The Gothic continued to be the dominant form of long-form fear literature in Argentina in the mid-century decades, not least because the conditions which gave rise to the Argentine Gothic, the tension between civilization and barbarity and the omnipresence of violence and repressed ghosts, remained constant. One of the foremost practitioners of the Gothic during the mid-century decades was Manuel Mujica Láinez, who began publishing in 1936 and continued publishing as late as 1993, but the majority of whose work was published from 1942 to 1969. Mujica Láinez was a novelist, essayist, translator and art critic, but his Gothics are his best-known work. These novels, especially the quartet of "the Buenos Aires saga" published from 1953 to 1957, are accounts of the decadence of the wealthy class in Buenos Aires. In these and in some of his short stories, Mujica Láinez describes Buenos Aires' history, its gruesome violence and its sinister architecture, its dissolute aristocrats and its individual tragedies.

Meanwhile, mainstream Argentine literature, like most Latin America literature, was still under the sway of the realism movement of the nineteenth century–"realistic and rustic,"[1] as Enrique Anderson Imbert put it. However, a movement was growing, sprung from the antirealist authors of the pre- and post-World War One generations. This movement, which would eventually be labelled "magic realism," began applying, often in a haphazard and partial manner, the changes that would later be part of the definition of magic realism: urban rather than rural, neurotic characters rather than simple ones, the fantastic rather than the real, existentialism rather than realism, poetic prose rather than "realistic" prose, and experimental language rather than ordinary language. A major mover–a founding father--in the Argentine magic realism movement was Enrique Anderson Imbert, who was influenced by the proto-magic realists he read in his youth as well as the modernist techniques of Proust and Joyce. Anderson Imbert would go on to become a novelist, short story writer, literary critic, and academic, but his claim to fame remains the magic realism fiction he wrote, beginning with a 1934 novel but primarily appearing from 1940-1965. Anderson Imbert wrote what he called *"microcuentos,"* short stories which were strongly magic realism or which blended outright fantasy ("lo real maravilloso," "the marvelously real") and magic realism. However, Anderson Imbert's *microcuentos* tend toward outright horror. Not the traditional horror of supernatural curses, creatures, and haunted houses, but horror stories that "undercut readers' expectations and take them by surprise. The characters in the *casos* may be invaded by air and disappear; they may be smoked by a cigarette, turn to flies, or have false teeth stolen by a ghost."[2] More than undercut expectations await readers in Anderson Imbert's stories, however. His stories portray humanity as made up of solitary men (rarely women) who live in a chaotic world where relationships offer little but progressive

---

[1] Enrique Anderson Imbert, "'Magical Realism' in Spanish-American Fiction," *International Fiction Review* 2, no. 1 (1975): 7.

[2] Ludmilla Kapschutschenko, "Enrique Anderson Imbert," in *The Penguin Encyclopedia of Horror and the Supernatural,* ed. Jack Sullivan (New York: Viking, 1986), 5.

disintegration and deliberate betrayal. Pessimistic and bleak about sexuality, friendship, and the human heart, the stories present a universe of emptiness into which intrude menaces against which ordinary humans are neither prepared nor capable of combating.

The most famous of the Argentinian horror writers of the mid-century decades, and in all likelihood the most famous Argentinian author of any time and any genre, is Jorge Luis Borges. Although he began writing in the 1930s, his first collection of short stories was not published until 1941, and he only gained international fame in the 1960s. Critically his best work is viewed as having taken place from 1941 to 1970. One of the writers who defined magic realism, Borges rarely used traditional supernatural creatures or tropes or plot devices in his fiction. Rather, the horror in Borges' stories is conceptual and intellectual, even if the end result is the reader feeling the emotions of unease and fear. Numerically, the majority of Borges' stories are not horror stories; Borges' ultimate goal was to astonish his readers, something he achieved frequently and easily. But Borges' techniques, the magic realism and metafictional aspects that make it difficult in his stories to distinguish between the natural and the "irreal," lent themselves easily to those stories he chose to write whose purpose was to frighten.

> Borges's fictions often have dark and paranoiac textures, like a nightmare, and his world is one haunted with numinous presences, thick with ghosts, yet he largely eschews conventional depictions of the supernatural in favor of a hazy sense of lurking immensities, a creative treatment for which the term "Borgesian" has been coined.[3]

Furthermore, as Ludmila Kapschutschenko writes, "Borges does not convey immediate meanings–only a sense of what lies beneath them–beneath the elegant and cerebral surface, ful of understatement and affirmation by negation, we sense the tension and horror of intimate dreams and nightmares."[4] His stories are elliptical, oblique, full of last-minute plot twists, told with elegance and panache, and full of moments and concepts which derive the most chill from the least amount of words.

After the end of World War Two existentialism became famous thanks to the work of Jean-Paul Sartre, Simone de Beauvoir, Albert Camus and others. Existentialism became influential in Argentina, whose major cities were heavily influenced by European artistic and intellectual movement. One of the foremost Argentine existentialists was Ernesto Sábato, a writer, an essayist, and a critic. Widely read in Argentina for his essays, Sábato's novels were what brought him international fame. Sábato only wrote three novels, in 1948, 1961, and 1974, but the three were acclaimed first nationally, then regionally, then internationally, and award winners besides. All three share certain elements–existential angst, itinerant and psychologically damaged characters, and an enigmatic, sinister universe–so that the three can be seen as a trilogy rather than three separate novels. And all three are horror as well as classics of Argentine

---

[3] Rob Latham, "Jorge Luis Borges," in *Horror Literature Through History*, ed. Matt Cardin (Santa Barbara, CA: ABC-Clio, 2017), 234.

[4] Ludmilla Kapschutschenko, "Jorge Luis Borges," in *The Penguin Encyclopedia of Horror and the Supernatural,* ed. Jack Sullivan (New York: Viking, 1986), 48.

literature. Sábato saw modern civilization as having brought about the loss of pre-existing morals and metaphysics, and as having replaced them with isolation, loneliness, and insanity. Nightmarish recurrent themes of incest, blindness, madness, abnormal psychology, the split personalty of the Argentine people, the impossibility of true communication, the tenuousness of logic, and the terrible rule of military strongman are present in the three novels. Gothic elements can be found, and though Sábato's horror tends to be conceptual rather than visceral, the Gothic elements, the surrealism, the insanity, the madness of every day life under the military tyrants–all add up to nightmarish, disturbing reading experiences. Sábato's work stands in contrast to the magic realism work of Enrique Anderson Imbert and others.

Another existentialist writer, of sorts, was Hector A. Murena, an essayist, poet, short story and novel writer, and translator. He wrote in all genres, usually in parables or using traditional premises. His characters suffer from the existentialist problem of isolation; Murena wrote protagonists who exist in a hostile and desolate world and are horribly alone. This is true of both his novels and his short stories, which are otherwise quite different, though equally horrific. His novels are bitter in their portrayal of the nightmarish conditions of life under the Perón regime, and have "characteristics of existential fiction: characters who are feeling extreme isolation, purposelessness, disorientation, insubstantiality, and a free-floating sense of horror."[5] But Murena's short stories were *fantastika*, not realist, and many of them, especially those gathered in his 1956 collection, are overt, fantastic horror stories. Like his novels, Murena's short stories are possessed of a bitter black humor and a dark and gloomy ethos. But unlike the novels what happens to the protagonists is usually supernatural, whether a man, bent on total isolation, transforming into a cat, or the personification of the "demon rum" disrupting a wake, or a personified butcher's saw malignantly making men into tools of its will. Murena's protagonists in his horror stories suffer from an existentialist malaise, but their malaise leads not to anomie but to unusual, macabre ends.

Jorge Luis Borges was the head of an influential circle of writers in Buenos Aires. His best friend was Adolfo Bioy Casares, who like Borges became internationally known for his *fantastika*. Much less known internationally, although she always had a high reputation in Argentina, was Bioy Casares' wife Silvina Ocampo, who was acclaimed for both her poetry and short stories, although only the latter has seen widespread publication outside of Latin America. Ocampo began writing in 1937 and continued almost to her death in 1993. Her two collections in 1959 and 1961 made her reputation, with collections in 1987 and 1988 broadening her fame. She began by telling relatively conventional stories, with the more uniquely Ocampo-esque stories appearing later, but even in her early work the distinctive Ocampo strangeness is present. Initially her work is influenced by nineteenth century horror; later she goes through a period of formal inventiveness; and during her mature period she perfects the type of story she made uniquely her own: disturbing, fantastical, where everyone's motives are obscured, where mundane suburban reality is overwhelmed by the intrusion of inexplicable and disturbing events, and where the final lesson for the living is that life is cruel. Ocampo's stories are stylized, very imaginative, cryptic,

---

[5]Naomi Lindstrom, "Hector A. Murena," in *Spanish American Authors: The Twentieth Century*, ed. Angel Flores (New York: H.W. Wilson, 1992), 572.

and extremely cruel, though in an innocent and oblique fashion. Her earlier work is full of malicious violence, while her later work is more subdued in its use of violence.

> The distorted, estranged world to which she gives life is dominated by an interest in magical transformations; doubles or other shattered personalities; play with time and space; dreams or nightmares; mad or obsessed characters; the mixture of plant, animal, and human elements; the mixture of animate and inanimate qualities as in machines and automatons, puppets, dolls, and masks; and also what Mikhail Bakhtin calls the lower bodily processes of eating, defecation, and sexual life.[6]

A technique for which she became known was the lack of closure in her stories, something which undercut readers' expectations and added to the disquiet and even horror felt by her readers. Her narrative tone is reminiscent of fairy tales in their calm narration of the most gory horrors, and the occasional moment of humor casts the horrors into relief.

A different kind of writer from Ocampo was Julio Cortázar, who began writing in the forties but whose published short stories (arguably his best work) only began appearing in collections in 1951. He published short stories through the 1950s and switched to writing novels in the 1960s. He continued writing into the 1980s, but a critical consensus has formed that his greatest work came between 1951 and 1973, when he was one of the key writers of the "Latin American boom." In both his short fiction and his novels, Cortázar displayed the influences of Poe, Borges, James Joyce and the modernists as well as the Surrealists, the French *nouveau roman*, and the improvisational aspect of jazz music—but despite all these influences, Cortázar told stories in a voice very much his own. "Cortázar's stories begin disarmingly; they playfully deceive their readers, making them think they are not reading horror tales at all. But before they realize it, they find themselves enveloped in a world of mysteriously changing realities."[7] Many of his stories, though possessed of substantial ambiguity, serious themes, and technical innovations of language and form, are lightened by humor and are ultimately about freeing a character from the prison of their reality in exchange for a greater, expanded freedom and reality. However, many of his stories use ambiguity to suggest that the intrusion of a different reality is merely the appearance of something beyond the protagonist's (and humanity's) perceptive abilities, and that what is liberating the protagonist from our reality is a monster or a series of events whose ultimate effect is to doom them, not liberate them. Adding to the ambiguity are Cortázar's unreliable narrators, who may be lying, hallucinating, or simply insane. Those reading Cortázar's stories and novels can never be sure if what they are reading is true or the product of a damaged mind. Between the ambiguity and the surreal nature of events, the potent symbolism, the dazzling originality of the story's ideas, the vividly luminous nature of the prose, and the unsettling events, a Cortázar story is like no one else's. His later stories are more experimental

---

[6]Patricia Nisbet Klingenberg, *Fantasies of the Feminine: The Short Stories of Silvina Ocampo* (Lewisburg, PA: Bucknell University Press, 1999), 40.

[7]Dominick Finello, "Julio Cortázar," in *The Penguin Encyclopedia of Horror and the Supernatural,* ed. Jack Sullivan (New York: Viking, 1986), 98.

and even metafictional and carry political messages his earlier stories did not possess. Nonetheless, the disquieting horror of events remains potent.

Luisa Mercedes Levinson was a journalist, playwright, short story writer and novelist. Although she is known for her collaborations with Jorge Luis Borges, her best known work is *La casa de los Felipes* (*The House of the Felipes*, 1951), a Gothic novel. *La casa de los Felipes* has, as the genre requires, everything from an incestuous pair of siblings to a dead husband reincarnated as a black dog that follows his former wife around to a mad family haunting a rambling, half-ruined townhouse. "In *La casa de los Felipes* there is a mix of living people and ghosts, of reality and fantasy, where chronological time seems not to exist."[8] Levinson is skilled at evoking and deepening a mysterious and sinister atmosphere (in proper Gothic fashion) as well as critiquing the decadent aristocracy via her protagonists.

During the latter part of the 1960s a right-wing government took and kept power at the same time that there was a rise in science fiction being published in anthologies. The result was that a substantial amount of science fiction was published which allegorically hid their politically or culturally radical messages. Alicia Suárez's "Samantha" (1970), for example, tells the story of a young woman with gaps in her memory whose husband builds a robot–her exact double–to help her with housework and keep her company. At the end of the story, "Leonard and a woman identical to Samantha walk in, he pulls a remote control from his pocket and, with the click of a button, the 'Samantha' we have followed so far in the narrative turns into a servile automaton who can only utter a numb, soulless 'sí, señora.'"[9] "Samantha" is psychologically twisted, poetically told, hauntingly ambiguous, and frightening in its feminist implications: either the Samantha whose viewpoint the reader experienced was a malfunctioning android throughout the entire story, or (and the evidence of the story seems to support this interpretation) "the human Samantha has had her brain modified without her knowledge, thus clouding her memories and judgment until her autonomy is lost and her actions become entirely dictated by Leonard's remote control. Meanwhile, ageless robot Samantha has taken her place, something Leonard had planned from the start."[10]

Barbados

Barbados has a centuries-old traditional of oral storytelling, but written literature by native Barbadians (as opposed to British colonials) got its first real start in 1942 with a literary journal, *Bim*. Frank Collymore was the founding editor of *Bim*, and in that position would showcase first and early works by a large number of Caribbean writers who would go on to

---

[8]Clara H. Becerra, "Levinson, Luisa Mercedes," in *Latin American Women Writers: An Encyclopedia,* eds. María Claudia André and Eva Paulino Bueno (New York: Routledge, 2008), 277.

[9]Grace A. Martin, "For the Love of Robots: Posthumanism in Latin American Science Fiction Between 1960-1999" (PhD diss., University of Kentucky, 2015), 66.

[10]Martin, "For the Love of Robots," 69.

become famous, including Nobel prize winner Derek Walcott. Collymore never achieved the fame of a Walcott, but he was instrumental in the development of West Indian literature thanks to his position with *Bim* and also gained fame in the Caribbean world of letters through his poetry and to a lesser degree his short stories. Not as well known during his lifetime, even in the Caribbean, were his macabre horror stories. Collymore was heavily influenced by Ambrose Bierce and especially by Edgar Allan Poe, and told horror stories in the Poe tradition, albeit leavened with a sense of humor that Poe never included in his horror stories. Collymore struck a balance between telling outright supernatural stories and those involving disturbed personalities. Collymore had a tendency to write trick-ending stories with grotesquely ironic resolutions, arguably in the Poe tradition but which have not aged well and led to them being dismissed in *Publishers Weekly* in 1993 as "penny dreadfuls of the sort that might have graced the pages of a pulp magazine in the '40s"[11]–an uncharitable though unfortunately somewhat accurate judgment.

Far less famous or influential on West Indies literature was the work of Geoffrey Drayton, a white Barbadian whose career was spent as a journalist, magazine editor, and petroleum consultant. Drayton wrote only a few short stories, a collection of poetry, and two novels, *Christopher* (1959) and *Zohara* (1961), which although selling well on publication have been forgotten in recent decades. Of note to horror readers are his short story "Mr. Dombey the Zombie" (1951) and *Zohara*. "Mr. Dombey the Zombie" is more a tale of whimsy than horror, but its story of a zombie's indentured servitude and eventual freedom is full of horror tropes, not least the zombie protagonist. More genuinely frightening is *Zohara*–not because of an intrusion of the supernatural into the real or because of a Poe-esque turn of events, but because of Drayton's accurate depiction of the horrors that superstition can lead humans to. The supernatural in *Zohara*, the supposed witches haunting the Spanish village where the novel takes place, doesn't exist. The prophecy of the village's doom is self-fulfilling and not in the least occult. The atmosphere of terror is purely the creation of the villagers. As Derek Walcott wrote, "Drayton's Gothic novel has the progress of a nightmare in its plot,"[12] and the peasants' superstitions and fear are sharply drawn. "Medicine, the church, education and even charity appear to be powerless against rampant vampire beliefs that suck the life-blood of the hapless young."[13]

Bolivia

Oscar Cerruto was one of the five most important Bolivian writers of the twentieth century, as a poet, novelist, and short story. His collection *Cerco de penumbras* (*Frame of*

---

[11]"The Man Who Loved Attending Funerals and Other Stories," *Publisher's Weekly*, last modified Aug. 2, 1933, https://www.publishersweekly.com/978-0-435-98931-6.

[12]Derek Walcott, *Derek Walcott: The Journeyman Years, Volume 1: Culture, Society, Literature, and Art*, ed. Gordon Collier (New York: Rodopi, 2013), 260.

[13]Roydon Salick, "Drayton, Geoffrey (1924-)," in *Encyclopedia of Post-Colonial Literatures in English*, ed. Eugene Benson and L.W. Conolly (New York: Routledge, 2005), 417.

shadows, 1958) was important in the history of Bolivian literature because it represented a serious departure from the dominant mode of realism.

> *Cerco de penumbras* does not attempt to represent reality but rather to explore the unreal through fictions created in language. The themes of the short stories that form the book are dreams, death, madness, time displacement, and the magic of Indians. As the title of the book suggests, reality seems to be surrounded by shadows....[14]

The result is a book with "an air of mystery pertaining to magical realism: the characters appear to be enveloped in subconscious and supernatural forces, as seen in the themes of love, loneliness, death, hope, and hatred."[15]

Brazil

Brazilian horror literature during the mid-century decades continued to be divided between that appearing in very low literature–*folheto* (the Brazilian equivalent of the dime novel) and cheap paperbacks–and that appearing in respectable high literature. The latter type of horror story or novel tended not toward magic realism or the supernatural but instead toward surrealistic or nightmarish horror fiction. Graciliano Ramos' horror work is a good example of this trend. Ramos is known primarily as a regional writer, one of the "Northeastern writers" of the 1930s and 1940s who focused on the cultural and social problems of northeastern Brazil, including the multiethnic/multiracial component of the population, and the hardships and adversities of life in the area. Ramos is in fact the best known of the Northeast writers. His 1930s work earned him renown in Brazil, and he gained international fame just before and after World War Two. His reputation has grown steadily ever since, to the point where in the twenty-first century he is seen as a member of Brazil's canon of great writers. Ramos writes in a fluid narrative style and writes penetrating social criticism. Much less well known, either inside Brazil or out, are Ramos' horrific stories, what Julio França and Luciano Cabral da Silva call "'fear literature,'–a fictional narrative that produces artistic fear"[16] and what I am choosing to call "High Art Horror." Although Ramos wrote these kinds of horror stories in the 1930s, his best work in the genre was in the 1940s, especially those appearing in his 1947 collection *Insônia* (*Insomnia*). In these stories insomnia or delirium inevitably leads to an irrational nightmare full of unreal and surreal elements. While the nightmare inevitably ends–usually with the protagonist's death–the reader is left with the chills produced by the story and its frightening imagery of returned dead or the figure of Death as a pursuer.

---

[14]Leonardo Garcia Pabón, "Oscar Cerruto (13 June 1912-10 April 1981), *Modern Spanish American Poets: First Series*, ed. Maria A. Salgado, (Detroit, MI: Gale, 2003), 88.

[15]Flores, *Spanish-American Authors,* 191.

[16]Julio França and Luciano Cabral da Silva, "A Preface to a Theory of Art-Fear in Brazilian Literature," *Ilha do Desterro* 62 (Jan/Jun 2012): 341.

Another example of horror fiction in respectable high literature, by a respected author, is José Lins do Rêgo's *Água-mae* (*The water mother*, 1941). A novelist best known for his regionalist work–Lins do Rêgo is regarded as one of the greatest of all Brazilian regionalists–his *Água-mae* is a pessimistic, heavily symbolic ghost story. Although an award winner on publication, *Água-mae* is not well-regarded by critics:

> Lins do Rêgo is at his best in creating mysterious moods and an environment of weird sounds, wild waters, bats, screech owls, and apparitions suitable to the tale. But he has failed to give this novel any serious meaning. And we know from the symbolism of the title that he had a serious intent.[17]

However, purely as a horror narrative, *Água-mae* works well, although it tends to provoke melancholy rather than outright fear.

A third example of horror fiction in respectable high literature, by respected authors, is the work of João Guimarães Rosa. A diplomat, novelist, and short story writer, Guimarães Rosa wrote one novel, *Grande Sertão: Veredas* which became internationally acclaimed. He published three collections of short stories, in 1946, 1956, and 1962, although his tales of *fantastika* and horror date back to the late 1920s. His short stories, like his novel, are largely about rural Brazil, especially northeast Brazil. So too with his horror short stories, which share the magic realism, regionalism, and linguistic invention of his more mainstream work. His horror stories are full of the fantastic, the oneiric, and the surreal whose deployment is toward the end of shocking the reader into experiencing something poetic. Elements of the Gothic, elements of the grotesque, double meaning and mysticism, and eerie ambiguities abound. The stories are influenced by Poe and Hawthorne, and are sophisticated, elegantly-written, psychologically insightful, and macabre.

Jerônimo Monteiro was not a horror writer–he was a journalist who became Brazil's first major science fiction writer during the 1940s, first in his "Dick Peter" detective series, and then in novels. His science fiction narratives began incorporating increasing amounts of horror, so that his *Visitantes do espaço* (*Visitors from space,* 1963) is a full-blown alien invasion epic. But it is Monteiro's *Fuga para parte alguma* (*Escape to nowhere*, 1961) which has the most horrific content of his work. Influenced by both H.G. Wells' "The Empire of the Ants" (1905) and American atomic monster films of the 1950s, *Fuga para parte alguma* is set in the far future and depicts the war of a group of large mutant ants which emerge from the Amazon and devastate the world, eating their way through humanity, all animals, and all crops. Despite the possession of laser weapons which can kill the ants, the humans are defeated by the ants and the protagonist and his family, in a series of harrowing scenes, are forced to flee first to Australia and then out to open sea, where they await their death by drowning or starvation. *Fuga para parte alguma*'s

---

[17]Fred P. Ellison, *Brazil's New Novel: Four Northeastern Masters: José Lins do Rego, Jorge Amado, Graciliano Ramos, Rachel de Queiroz* (Berkeley: University of California Press, 1954), 71-72.

"anti-climactic ending is the antithesis of those found in American science fiction films and novels,"[18] but is a perfect ending for a work of science fictional horror.

Chile

The "Generation of 1938" were a group of socially conscious Chilean writers who sought in their writing to bring the problems of the lower classes and the demands of the middle classes to light and to describe the ways in which twentieth century man was exploited by society. The novelist Carlos Droguett was one of the Generation of 1938, although his best work were his novels published in the late 1950s and 1960s. Droguett's work has entered the Chilean canon and is generally seen as transgressive, vehemently emotional, and furiously critical of Chilean government and society. His work is primarily concerned with the psychological and physical violence perpetrated by those in power against those without. It is also, in his best novels, concerned with the difference between "normal" and "abnormal," a difference which takes on metaphysical proportions. There are intensely grotesque scenes full of horrified emotion in Droguett's work, whose usual setting is a Chilean landscape of cold, rainy weather. These scenes show a great interest on Droguett's part in the psychology of criminals, which is described in stream-of-consciousness monologues. Droguett's narrative voice

> assumes varying temporal dimensions and takes in differing levels of reality–dreams, myth, nightmare, conscious imaginary creation, primitive speculation, delirium, madness–while also adapting itself to each one of the character who, in turn, embody a stream of consciousness that responds easily to the surges of the unconscious. This poetics of excess, fantasy and fright, violence and terror, is at the basis of...Droguett's most important novels.[19]

The cumulative effect is to feel like one has been exposed to a font of madness and horror.

Rafael Maluenda Labarca's fiction, not as sophisticated as Droguett's, nonetheless had high aims. His *Vampiro de trapo* (*The rag vampire*, 1958) is about a ventriloquist's doll that takes control of its ventriloquist and psychically drains the life from him. The novel is an homage to John Polidori's "The Vampyre" (1819)–the doll is named "Polidoro" and there are thematic similarities between *Vampiro del trapo* and "The Vampyre"–and incorporates elements from *Dracula* and *Frankenstein*, but primarily "fits into the thematics of a group of Chilean writers

---

[18]M. Elizabeth Ginway, *Brazilian Science Fiction: Cultural Myths and Nationhood in the Land of the Future* (Lewisburg, PA: Bucknell University Press, 2004), 68.

[19]Rene Jara, "Chile," in *Handbook of Latin American Literature*, ed. David William Foster (New York: Routledge, 1992), 162.

Rene Jara labels as the Generation of 1950,"[20] whose hallmarks were the pessimism about the possibility of a Utopian society and the self-examination for the causes of the guilt and weaknesses that all Chileans were presumed to possess. *Vampiro de trapo* is effective in the way that it creates uneasiness in the reader through the portrayal of the slow possession of the ventriloquist.

Colombia

José Abimael Pinzón's *El Vampiro* (*The vampire*, 1956), about a "vampire" who rapes and murders boy prostitutes, comes close to "producing a representation of the vampire figure that crosses boundaries of popular media"[21] in its use of a historical figure, journalistic reports about him, and commentaries about the journalism, thus "providing a double discourse on what can result from within an atmosphere of political and social violence."[22] An examination of sensationalist journalism and homophobia, *El vampiro* is comparatively brutal in its deployment of violence, and compounds the horror with the statement, in the last paragraph of the novel, that the "vampire" (it's left ambiguous whether or not he is actually a supernatural being) caught by the police and sent to prison was actually innocent.

Inarguably the most famous Colombian writer, and one of the most famous of all Latin American writers, is Gabriel García Márquez. Considered one of the most significant authors of the twentieth century, and one of the best in the Spanish language, García Márquez is famous for his novels, particularly *One Hundred Years of Solitude* (1967). García Márquez did not invent magic realism or introduce it to Latin America, but via *One Hundred Years of Solitude* he helped popularize it. Although his style varies from novel to novel and story to story, the influences of Kafka and Faulkner can be seen in most of his prose, as can his usual lyrical descriptions, the sometimes subtle humor, and the deadpan narration of frightful and unusual things, of myth, absurdity, allegory, satire, fable, and fantasy. However, his early work, specifically the novella and stories collected in *La Hojarasca* (1955), are not well known, even in Latin America, and are little studied by García Márquez scholars, not having been translated into English until 1972. In these stories, an early version of García Márquez—and a different one from the García Márquez of *One Hundred Years of Solitude* and his later novels—can be seen. The novella and stories of *La Hojarasca* display the influences of Kafka and Faulkner to an unusual degree, and are told in a primitive (for García Márquez) style full of mannerisms which he would later lose. As Mario Vargas Llosa wrote, the stories are "cold and humorless,"[22] quite the opposite of García Márquez's later warmth and good humor. Moreover, the version of magic realism in these stories is nightmarish rather than whimsical or related with a straight face. Emotions and thoughts and

---

[20]Gregory A. Clemons, "The Vampire Figure in Contemporary Latin American Narrative Fiction," (PhD diss., University of Florida, 1996), 184.

[21]Clemons, "The Vampire Figure," 39.

[22]Mario Vargas Llosa and Roger Williams, "A Morbid Prehistory (The Early Stories)," *Boooks Abroad* 47, no. 3 (Summer, 1973): 451.

sensations are heightened. Death is a constant concern. The atmosphere of the stories is nightmarish and neurotic, and there are heavy Latin American Gothic elements. As with a number of other Latin American writers of the mid-century decades, García Márquez uses magic realism in these stories to evoke fear rather than an oneiric or joyful state.

Costa Rica

Fantastika came to Costa Rica relatively late. There were examples of it, both novels and short stories, published in the nineteenth century and the first half of the twentieth century (see Chapter Two), but as late as 1966 realism—by that point an anachronistic literary school—was still the predominant literary mode in Costa Rica. Alfredo Cardona Peña helped to change that. Best known as a poet—his critical reputation now is quite high, and he has been described as one of the most relevant and important Central American poets of the twentieth century Cardona Peña also wrote science fiction, fantasy, and horror stories, and in doing so became a pioneer of science fiction and fantasy in Costa Rica. Miguel Ángel Fernández Delgado calls him "the Latin American version of Ray Bradbury."[23] In his *fantastika* Cardona Peña shows great diversity of theme, and in his horror stories he takes a number of approaches toward the end of frightening the reader. His horror stories are brief and intense, filled with irony and a sharp sense of humor. The influence of Borges and Kafka are obvious, although the plots are more traditional and the twist endings ironic in the mode of an O. Henry. In one story four wandering souls discover a loophole which allows them to get back to Earth—but the being manipulating their actions turns out to be the opposite of God. In another story a corpse is conscious and aware of her state of affairs, though paralyzed. She becomes aware that there's a creature in the morgue alongside her, one that sucks the eyeballs out of corpses. In a third story, set in Europe a few centuries previous, a gardener specializes in growing exotic plants, all of which are deadly. She tries to engineer a constant diet of bodies for her plants, only to end up their prey herself.

Cuba

In Cuba, the relative scarcity of novels of the first three decades of the twentieth century gave way to a slowly increasing number, and then a boom in the 1940s and 1950s, when social realism combined with magic realism. This culminated in the great year of 1966, when a number of classics of Cuban literature were published. Esther Díaz Llanillo's *El Castigo* (*The penalty*) is not counted among them. However, *El Castigo* was the first book of Díaz Llanillo's long and distinguished career as a writer, librarian, and essayist. The stories in *El Castigo* are typical of Díaz Llanillo's later work. She writes about God, the relationship between God and humanity, justice, aloneness, and death, in fantasies and stories about protagonists with psychological problems. A general template of Díaz Llanillo's work is a protagonist in a mundane setting, such as a home, a kitchen, or conference room, being exposed to the intrusion of the unexpected and

---

[23]Miguel Ángel Fernández Delgado, "Cardona Peña, Alfredo," *The Encyclopedia of Science Fiction*, last modified Jan. 8, 2017, http://www.sf-encyclopedia.com/entry/cardona_pena_alfredo.

the threatening. The atmosphere of many of these stories is anguish-filled and desperate, much like the haunted, hallucinatory, and menacing atmosphere in Kafka's work (one of Díaz Llanillo's primary influences). The plots are influenced by Poe, and possessed of plot twist and a marked black humor. The major influence on Díaz Llanillo, however, was Borges. In her own words, Díaz Llanillo was influenced by Borges' "style, his predilection for nuanced adjectives, in his contradictory lists, in his search for perfection, and in the intellectualism that I have imbued in some of my short stories."[24] The horror in Díaz Llanillo's work comes not from supernatural elements but from dismaying occurrences happening to the protagonist which usually disrupt their daily routine, and from the dark edge of magic realism, in which reality gives way to the dangerous surreal and irreal.

Ecuador

In Ecuador in the 1930s writers were still largely in thrall to nineteenth century modes and writers. A group of young novelists began writing social realist novels full of political advocacy. One literary group in particular, the Guayaquil Group, which emerged in the mid-1930s and continued for a decade, wrote particularly acute condemnations of the elites and groups in Ecuadorian society who were oppressing poor and the natives. Demetrio Aguilera-Malta was one of the founding members of the Guayaquil Group, and after its demise continued producing socially conscious work, as a newspaper reporter and writer of fiction. Work as a government official interrupted his writing career, and he did not return to writing novels until 1970, when he produced his masterpiece, *Siete lunas y siete serpientes* (*Seven moons and seven snakes*). In his early work with the Guayaquil Group he helped foster a new variety of Ecuadorian prose–blunt, choppy, crude, and realistic–while also writing, in *Don Goyo* (1933), one of the earliest magic realist novels. However, Aguilera-Malta's pre-*Siete lunas* work is largely focused on politics and the plight of the poor, leaving the kind of magic realism relatively benign. That is not the case with *Siete lunas*, which tells a story of good and evil (rather than the traditional magic realism conflict of civilization versus barbarism) in blatantly symbolic terms, with Christ and Satan being speaking characters. *Siete lunas* projects

> Latin American realities (*caciquismo*)...in a light of grotesquerie (*esperpentismo*) or anthropomorphic distortion–a trait that should be linked with his early pioneering use of magic realism. The other common note has to do with linguistic experimentation, with the forging of a style, virtually a metalanguage, that befits the type of novelistic stuff being employed. In this respect a writer usually considered old hat, appears as revolutionary and innovative as a Severo Sarduy or a Fernando del Paso.[25]

---

[24]Esther Díaz Llanillo, "Interview with Esther Díaz Llanillo," interview by Sara E. Cooper, *Cubanabooks*, April 2015, http://www.csuchico.edu/cubanabooks/authors/Interview_Diaz_Llanillo.shtml.

[25]Luis A. Diez, "The Apocalyptic Tropics of Aguilera Malta," *Latin American Literary Review* 10, no. 20 (Spring 1982): 35-36.

Aguilera-Malta's prose in *Siete lunas* is an advance on that of his work in the 1930s and 1940s, being full of skillfully deployed surrealism, characterization, and a generally greatly improved style which verges on lyricism. The horror in *Siete lunas* comes from the actions of the evil characters, whose murders and rapes are described in horrifying detail, and from the ambivalence with which reality and the supernatural are described.

Guyana

The literature of Guyana before the 1940s was predominantly influenced by that of Great Britain. In this environment what popular fiction was written by Guyanese writers was largely the product of British and to a lesser degree American traditions. Typical of these writers was J.A.V. Bourne, a photographer who in 1940 published *Dreams, Devils, Vampires*, a collection of six horror stories. The stories in *Dreams, Devils, Vampires* are in the tradition of Poe, featuring supernatural monsters (a vampire) and items (a cursed chest), and are of mediocre quality.

The 1941 publication of Edgar Austin Mittelholzer's *Corentyne Thunder* changed the situation for writers in Guyana. *Corentyne Thunder* was Mittelholzer's first novel, and the first novel by a native Guyanese to be published. His later work in the 1950s inspired a wave of young writers to imitate him. Mittelholzer was the first West Indian writer to support himself fully by writing, and is generally considered by critics to be the father of the novel in the Anglophone Caribbean. Mittelholzer usually told stories about psychological, cultural, and racial/ethnic tensions and conflicts. He was particularly strong in his descriptions of atmosphere and environment, of sexual obsessions, colonialism, and post-colonialism. In his horror novels and novellas, he put his skills at evoking atmosphere to excellent use, though in very different ways. His novella *The Adding Machine* (1954) is relatively traditional in its story of a greedy estate owner who commits atrocities against villagers in order to gain wealth, only to buy a cursed adding machine which puts physical blemishes on his skin every time he enters the figures of his cruelly-gained wealth. Told in Mittelholzer's usual laconic, succinct style, *The Adding Machine* has a somewhat obvious allegory about the true costs of racism and capitalism on their victims and their perpetrators. The allegories in *A Morning at the Office* (1950) are much thicker and more obscure, leaving critics to debate the true meaning of the novel and its many elements and characters for decades. Frighteningly, though, there is a long scene in which an imaginary monster shows up to haunt a child, who hides her face beneath a pillow as the monster talks to her about himself and his "more dreadful" friend.

Eltonsbrody (1960) is a standout Gothic novel which is nearly perfect in both setting and prose. Unusually, though, Mittelholzer avoids the use of the supernatural to frighten, instead portraying the Gothic mistress as a deeply disturbed and psychologically warped personality. The fear in the novel, for the reader, is the way in which Mittelholzer shows the horrors which a twisted person will commit. *My Bones and My Flute* (1955), generally recognized as Mittelholzer's single best work, drew its inspiration from the works of M.R. James, Edgar Allan Poe, Joseph Conrad, and William Faulkner. In a swift and laconic fashion, using acute characterization and a brilliantly evoked atmosphere and setting, Mittelholzer tells the story of a posthumous curse that haunts all those who touch a certain document. The haunting builds slowly and subtly until a certain point deep in the novel, after which the haunting quickens and becomes more dreadful and remorseless.

Critics, especially those from the Caribbean countries, though acknowledging Mittelholzer's historical importance, have tended to be quite critical of him, both because of his politics (conservative, more so as he grew older) and his studied avoidance of contemporary racial politics, and because, in the view of those critics, Mittelholzer sacrificed art for Mammon. A much differently received author was Wilson Harris,

Wilson Harris began by writing poetry but after 1960 became a novelist and essayist. One of the greatest Caribbean writers, and generally viewed by critics as one of the greatest postcolonial writers in the English language, Harris writes complex, abstruse, and challenging novels. They are abstract and metaphorical, with a range of subject matters and a range of genres in which they fit, from surrealism to magic realism to mysticism to modernism. His fiction can be called experimental, in that he attempts to create new approaches to storytelling and new uses of words. His first novel, *The Palace of the Peacock* (1960), is generally regarded as his masterpiece and is the work by him that is the most commented upon by critics; D.H. Figueredo calls it "cerebral, baroque, oblique and philosophical."[26] A dreamlike allegory of the European invasion and colonization of the jungles of Guyana and South America, *Palace of the Peacock* turns nightmarish in its middle sections, as the characters undergo quantum uncertainty and are exposed to dangerous characters and events out of myth and folklore.

> Not only do outer and inner psychological landscapes coincide and real landscape features spatialize inner states of mind, the concrete and the intangible often overlap as again and again the surface reality is breached to reveal the tormenting obsessions of the crew with power or wealth, with Mariella, the native woman (at once sexual object, symbol of the land and spirit of the place, and ambivalent muse), to reveal also the mixture of terror and beauty they experience in their journey towards death and rebirth.[27]

Although the characters eventually achieve a harmonious, beneficent apotheosis and epiphany—a climactic apotheosis unusual in Harris' work—the trip to get there is frightening both for the characters, who lose their identities and consciousnesses, and for the readers, whose usual identification with the protagonists leads them into ambiguous, atmospheric, nightmarish territories.

"In both of these stories [*My Bones and My Flute* and *Palace of the Peacock*] the ghost—the 'uncanny cannibal'—has a dual function, reasserting the presence of a past (or pasts)

---

[26] D.H. Figueredo, "Palace of the Peacock," in *The Encyclopedia of Caribbean Literature*, ed. D.H. Figueredo (Westport, CT: Greenwood Press, 2005), 603.

[27] Hena Maes-Jelinek, "Wilson Harris: Seeking the Mystery of the 'Universal Imagination,'" in *International Literature in English: The Major Writers*, ed. Robert Ross (New York: Garland, 1991), 450.

that had previously been repressed while estranging that past and converting it into forms that sublimate material exploitation."[28]

Mexico

By the 1940s Mexican literature had separated into three different branches: one influenced by the European modernists, one influenced by the European avant-garde, and one penning realistic novels about Mexican history, culture, and identity. One of the authors to change this situation and to bring experimentalism and magic realism into Mexico was Juan José Arreola, who wrote into the 1970s but whose best work is regarded as that published between 1941 and 1963. A writer of stylistic inventiveness, fecund imagination, and a light-hearted, sophisticated use of language, Arreola was one of the most influential prose stylists in Mexico during his heyday. His smart, witty short pieces, which ranged from biographics to poems to stories to essay-stories to microfictions to bestiaries, were and are essentially unclassifiable; he wrote detailed prose about bizarre things, combining elements of magic realism, satire, and allegory. His work shows the influence of Marcel Schwob, Franz Kafka, and the Italian writer Giovanni Papini–Arreola's primary inspirations–but his stories also show the influence of Poe, Borges, and Baudelaire, among others. The main characteristics of his prose work is it imaginativeness, its conciseness, its irony, and the hybridization of various genres. His *fantastika* were unpredictable stories which often took cliches and put them in unusual environments where their original elements would be highlighted. There was no one type of Juan José Arreola *fantastika* or horror story. Some found horror in the mundane. Some extrapolated science fictional premises to horrific, logical ends. Some were tales of twisted psychologies. Some were Gnostic fear literature. And some were Kafkaesque nightmares. All were told with the highest skill and artistry.

A quiet, mysterious man of a bourgeois background and lifestyle, and a writer whose fame was never that of his one-time neighbor Octavio Paz or the other writers in this chapter, Francisco Tario is nonetheless viewed critically as one of the foremost "explorers of the Mexican fantastic," "the most original contribution by Mexican literature to the genre of the supernatural narrative,"[29] and an important forerunner to the Mexican writers of *fantastika* of the 1950s and 1960s. Tario wrote poetry, short stories, and novels, with his horror work appearing in his 1943 and 1952 collections and in his posthumously published novel *Jardin secreto* (*Secret garden*, 1993). Thematically, his work, both horror and non-horror, is often the limitation of man's senses to perceive the vast reality of the world, with the horror arising from this limitation. But Tario's was not a horror of misdirection, the ambiguous, or the unseen. Tario wrote violent, grotesque, morbid, aggressive horror, horror that was macabre and fantastic, absurd, sensual, even

---

[28]Graham Huggan, "Ghost Stories, Bone Flutes, Cannibal Countermemory," in *Cannibalism and the Colonial World*, eds. by Francis Barker, Peter Hulme, and Margaret Iversen (Cambridge: Cambridge University Press, 1998), 126.

[29]Ross Larson, *Fantasy and Imagination in the Mexican Narrative* (Tempe: Arizona State University Press, 1977), 18.

hallucinatory. Tario's dark sense of humor shines through even in these stories, in which very human ghosts, talking animals, and personalized objects exist side by side, all offering differing perspectives on the gloom of humanity. *Jardin secreto* is about hereditary madness and a crime that lives on after the criminals have passed, but in its final pages it "touches on aspects of the literature of horror (Henry James, Edgar Allan Poe, Walpole) with a final wrenching twist."[30] Tario's style is akin to Borges', but Tario uses magic realism for entirely different purpose: to frighten, to create unease, and to convey the ever-present sense of gloom. If Borges' magic realism is a Latin American tradition, then Tario's is the nightmare version in the European tradition of Charles Nodier.

An acquaintance of Juan José Arreola's, and one whose short stories were compared to his, was Juan Rulfo. For a writer of such prominence, importance, and impact—and Rulfo has all of those things—his total output was small, no more than 250 pages of prose. But thanks to his lone published novel, *Pedro Páramo* (1955), Rulfo made a permanent mark on Mexican literature and provided a model of technique, an introduction to magic realism, and a solid example of experimentalism that the authors of the Latin American boom would later follow. His work is still much read in Mexico and very relevant to young writers. Rulfo wrote two works of *fantastika*, a collection of short stories (*El Llano en llamas* (*The Burning Plain*), 1953) and *Pedro Páramo*. The short stories are those of stark, brutal reality accompanied by horror plots, while *Pedro Páramo* is a work of haunting liminality. Yet stories and novel have things in common. Both are narratives of the haunted, tortured peasants of Jalisco, Rulfo's home region. Both are full of fatalism, resignation, stoicism, lack of free will, solitude, and an obsession with death. Rulfo's themes—misery, desperation, sex, infirmity, hatred, terror, and death—are common in stories and novel. In all his fiction he uses a terse, spare tone, lyrical when it comes to the environment and atmosphere. He is keen in portraying his characters,

His stories are rarely supernatural, instead relying on the arbitrary violence of the Jaliscan environment, the inexorability of death, startling plot twists, and a haunted environment inflicting stoic resignation on its tormented characters to frighten the reader. *Pedro Páramo*, conversely, is about myth, the presence of death in life, a literally ghost-haunted town, an overriding sense of doom and gloom, and the ambiguity of perception to deliver not fright in the reader but a deep unease. *Pedro Páramo* was both a departure from the social realist denunciations of rural injustice that were in vogue for the first half of the twentieth century in Latin America, and a deeply experimental novel. Time, in *Pedro Páramo*, happens all at once, and is narrated in that fashion. The structure of the novel breaks down, voices merge with on another, the stylized folk language becomes frayed, reality becomes surreal, and the reader can never be sure who is speaking or what is going on or if the protagonist himself is not one of the ghosts of the town. As Chris Power writes, "the silences yawn in Rulfo's writing. Its rhythms seem to slow time, and reality's edges fray into a strange gulf."[31]

---

[30]Mariza Aldaco Vidrio, "Francisco Tario," in *Spanish American Authors: The Twentieth Century*, ed. Angel Flores (New York: H.W. Wilson, 1992), 838.

[31]Chris Power, "A brief survey of the short story part 52: Juan Rulfo," *The Guardian*, last modified Aug. 27, 2013, https://www.theguardian.com/books/2013/aug/27/juan-rulfo-brief-

An unjustly forgotten Mexican horror writer is Guadalupe Dueñas, who in her time was a well-respected and widely enjoyed novelist, short story writer, and essayist. The current state of neglect for Dueñas is curious—sexism may be at the root of it, although other women horror writers, like Amparo Dávila, are still remembered and read. Perhaps it is as simple as the relative infrequency of her stories; although she had collections published in 1954, 1976, and 1991, she did not write the dozens of horror stories that other Mexican horror writers did. Whatever the cause, Dueñas is, again, unjustly forgotten, for her stories are on par with any of the other writers' in this chapter. Her career would not have been possible without Juan José Arreola and Juan Rulfo publishing their horror stories, but when her first collection was published it was clear she was staking out new territory and calling it her own—something her later collections would affirm. Her stories are marked by strong characterization, love of detail, and general originality. Dueñas' stories usually begin with portrayals of everyday life, and then through the use of time and perceptual distortions creates an atmosphere of subjectivity, estrangement, dread, and nightmarish horror. Dueñas' stories are death-obsessed, but not without a comic/humorous side, and the macabre is less emphasized (unusually for Mexican horror literature) than psychological acuity and visceral terror. Dueñas was influenced by Poe and especially by Horacio Quiroga, and like them shows an affection for the physical and mental tormenting of her characters. Her stories tend to be concise, evocative, unconventional in her use of the causes of her protagonists' terror, and bizarre and enigmatic, verging on the sublime.

Also debuting in 1954 was Carlos Fuentes, who gained the long-lasting fame denied to Dueñas. In his lifetime Fuentes became Mexico's most celebrated novelist, and the critical consensus, before and after his death, is that he is one of Mexico's two or three greatest novelists. In his early work, beginning with his first short story collection in 1954, he was an important influence on the Latin American boom, virtually introducing the modernist novel to Mexico. In his late work he was as dazzlingly inventive as ever. Although Fuentes was no magic realist, one comparison critics make is to Borges.

> There is something of this encyclopedic impetus paired with a breathtaking heterogeneity in Fuentes's own works, which range in style and content from the traditional 19th century *bildungsroman* style, to the dazzling technical flights of the Latin American "boom" generation's postmodern fancy, to undefinable works written in a subterranean, invisible English, or French, or German, Or Italian.[32]

A mystical writer, but one who injected a political consciousness and his own Marxism into his fiction, Fuentes not only made use of different genres and different modes of expression, he used a multiplicity of voices and awarenesses in his works, an anticipation of postmodern narrative fragmentation. Besides his mainstream work and those novels and stories which mainstream critics see as most typically Fuentesian, there stand a variety of horror narratives.

---

survey-short-story.

[32]Debra A. Castillo, "Carlos Fuentes," in *Spanish American Authors: The Twentieth Century*, ed. Angel Flores (H.W. Wilson, 1992), 322.

One apposite comparison for the Fuentesian horror story is the work of Robert Aickman, which as Peter Straub writes is not full of "dripping revenants but the feeling – composed in part of mystery, fear, stifled eroticism, hopelessness, nostalgia, and the almost violent freedom granted by a suspension of rational rules – which they evoked...."[33] Like Aickman, Fuentes often wrote enigmatic, ambiguous horror stories, dreamlike in their atmosphere, open-ended in its resolution. Not all of his horror stories were like this, of course. Many them, though mysterious and full of the *unheimlich*, conclude in ways that horror fans expect. Some of his horror work is straightforward and traditional. Some are heavily influenced by the Gothics, if not Gothic themselves. Fuentes has certain themes he revisits in most of these stories: the recrudescence of the region's past, pre-Hispanic Mexico as something encoded in the genes of all Mexicans; the interplay of the returned or revived past and the present; the use of pre-Hispanic gods, spirits, and myths to evoke horror; sorcery and witchcraft existing in modern Mexico; reincarnation, immortality, and the transmigration of souls; the merging of myth, fantasy, and reason; the weight that the unspeakable has for those made aware that the dreadful unknown is a part of their own existence. Fuentes' horror stories are macabre, sometimes surreal, and told in a masterfully understated fashion, but always beautifully told.

Amparo Dávila has the fame that Guadalupe Dueñas does not. In Dávila's favor is her increased output—story collections in 1959, 1964, and 1977—and a greater overall readability. However, that readability is a trap, for Dávila conceals her horror in gaps that the unwary fall into. Dueñas' horrors were physical and visceral; Dávila's are ambiguous, living in-between words rather than in them. As Alberto Chimal writes, "her texts...tend to treat what is not seen and what is not said, the imprecise–and unsettling–which is just beyond language and experience."[34] The terror of these things is what drives Dávila's stories, more than the immediate cause of unease or fear. One can almost say that Dávila is resistant, that she deploys her text to distract and hinder the reader.

Her stories have a dark and gloomy atmosphere and blend reality and the imaginary to the point of, and often verging into, psychological horror. She claimed Kafka and D.H. Lawrence as her main influences rather than Poe or Borges. Never one to overtly refer to Mexican politics or Mexico itself, or to draw on Latin American authors for inspiration, she avoids magic realism entirely: "The stories of Dávila pass from the criticism of the provincial *estanco* to the fantastic rupture without stopping in the elaboration of the marvelous real."[35] Stylistically, an apt comparison is to Shirley Jackson, although on a technical level Jackson is Dávila's superior. But both deal with mundane existences whose facades of normality are suddenly shattered by the intrusion of something horrible. Both writers portray female characters, violence, madness, and

---

[33] Peter Straub, introduction to *The Wine-Dark Sea*, by Robert Aickman (New York: Arbor House, 1988), 7.

[34] Alberto Chimal, "El huésped," *Las Historias*, accessed June 19, 2018, http://www.lashistorias.com.mx/index.php/archivo/el-huesped/.

[35] Christopher Domínguez Michael, "Amparo Dávila," *Diccionario crítico de la literatura mexicana (1955-2011)* (Mexico City, Mexico: FCE - Fondo de Cultura Económica, 2012), 94.

death. Dávila's common themes are entrapment and escape, isolation, immobility and insanity. Narratively, her stories are precisely, finely told, often with a sharp twist at their end.

As is fitting for Mexican *fantastika* of the mid-century decades, a novel designed to arouse horror in the reader was published in 1965 that was completely unlike anything that had come before. Salvador Elizondo, a novelist, poet, and playwright of the Mexican avant garde in the 1960s, wrote a cult masterpiece, *Farabeuf*, that was wholly unlike the magic realism then in vogue–and unlike any Latin America *fantastika* of that time or any time previously. *Farabeuf*, ostensibly about the titular French surgeon, a torturer and eroticist, is a work of experimental fiction. It is fractured, disordered, and complex. It shifts in time, perspective, character, location, and time. It is not a work of magic realism or the supernatural. Elizondo rejected local authors, influences, and movements, and chose Europe for inspirations. The work of European writers like Alain Robbe-Grillet and film makers like Sergei Eisenstein can be seen in *Farabeuf*, and while Elizondo is often compared by critics to Pound, Joyce, and Cortázar, the more precise comparisons are to Mallarmé and Valéry, Poe and Baudelaire. While *Farabeuf* is filled with sensuous, poetic prose, it has scenes full of savagery, shocking violence, and horrors. Obscure and impenetrable, with scenes that cut to other scenes like a cinematic montage, *Farabeuf* is a labor to work through, but those who do will find themselves horrified and dismayed and perhaps even shaken.

Québéc

The 1960s were a period of enormous social change in Québéc, with secularization, modernization, and Francization adding up to what was called the "Quiet Revolution." Writers of *fantastika* were affected along with everyone else, with horror writers in particular being influenced by the French interest in the work of H.P. Lovecraft. One major author who produced Lovecraftian narratives was Michel Tremblay. Best known for having revolutionized Québécois theater, Tremblay also produced two collections of cosmic horror in 1966 and 1969, both of which were written as a teenager and which were overtly influenced by Lovecraft's work, recapitulating Lovecraftian themes: "imaginary lands, hybrid creatures, horrible inventions, and…cosmic gods."[36]

Uruguay

The influence of Horacio Quiroga on later Uruguayan writers of fantastical horror was significant, even taking into account the influence of magic realism during the 1960s. One post-Quiroga author who was not influenced by Quiroga, but who was a significant influence on magic realism writers, was Felisberto Hernández. Hernández was not a successful writer during his lifetime, and he's generally seen as a writer's writer rather than a reader's writer, but, like the Velvet Underground, every one of the hundred people who read Hernández went on to become writers themselves, including Gabriel García Márquez, Italo Calvino and Julio Cortázar. Strictly

---

[36] Amy J. Ransom, "Lovecraft in Québéc: Transcultural Fertilization and Esther Rochon's Reevaluation of the Powers of Horror," *Journal of the Fantastic in the Arts* 26, no. 3 (2015): 452.

speaking, Hernández did not write horror fiction. He was a fabulist who wrote surrealistic, oneiric, Kafkaesque stories. But the cumulative effect of his stories, to those who surrender themselves to them, is a deep unease. Hernández tells stories of deranged, obsessed narrators who have injected their obsessions into everyday life. Accompanying these narrators is the subjective use of time–Hernández splits up narratives, reverses the progression of Time's Arrow, portrays its passage subjectively rather than objectively. Much is ambiguous in Hernández's stories, which contributes to the unease readers feel while consuming his work. There is humor and subversiveness as well, and a replication of the Decadents' moods. Reading Hernández's stories, it's easy to see what the magic realists took from him, although his *leitmotif* of conscious, feeling inanimate objects is only a prototype for the lengths the magic realists would go to.

Despite the existence and work of Horacio Quiroga and Felisberto Hernandez, the nineteenth century tradition of descriptive realism and linear narration continued to be the dominant mode of Uruguayan narrative in the mid-century decades of the twentieth century. One writer who challenged this mode and helped pave the way for more writers of experimental fiction and *fantastika* was Armonía Somers, who wrote into the mid-1990s but the majority of whose work was published from 1950-1969. Chronologically Somers is a member of the "Generación del 45," the group of influential Uruguayan writers whose careers began between 1945 and 1950, but Somers' concerns and approaches to her fiction place her more firmly in the successive "Generación del Crisis." A feminist novelist and short story writer, Somers wrote deeply transgressive work which discomforts and unnerves the writer through its postmodernist elements, its male-female role reversals, its obsession with death and sexual violence, and its transformation of the every day into the alien and the uncanny. "What sets Armonía Somers apart is that she combines the charm of the fantastic mode with a more brutal (and implicitly more critical) focus on the cruel–sexual violation, the indifference of god, the visceral reality of human experience. She effects this combination in unapologetically direct language within dense narrative structures."[37] Somers' protagonists are often marginalized or maladjusted individuals trying to make their way through a hostile and uncaring universe; "these characters, both human and animal, provide a sordid, nightmarish view of the world."[38] Her themes of desire escape, rebelliousness, transgression and freedom from the world-system of oppressive norms are deployed in stories thick with macabre atmosphere, violence, and eroticism. In her stories "everything is uncanny, alien, disconcerting, repulsive and yet incredibly fascinating."[39]

Venezuela

---

[37]Rebecca E. Biron, "Armonia Somers' 'El Despojo': Masculine Subjectivity and Fantasies of Domination," *Latin American Literary Review* 21, no. 42 (Jul-Dec 1993): 7.

[38]Nora Erro-Orthmann, "Armonía Somers," in *Spanish American Women Writers: A Bio-bibliographical Source Book*, ed. Diane E. Marting (Westport, CT: Greenwood Press, 1990), 498.

[39]Angel Rama, "La fascinación del horror. La insólita literatura de Somers," *Marcha* 1188 (Dec. 27, 1963), 30.

As with other Latin American countries, Venezuelan literature in the mid-century decades was largely in thrall to the tenets of realism, with *fantastika* not able to set down any sort of roots in the country. One writer who began the process of changing this, and who functionally was the progenitor of magic realism in the country, was Adriano González León. González León is best known for his groundbreaking novel *País Portátil* (1968), still regarded as the best Venezuelan novel of the second half of the twentieth century. Less well known are his 1957 and 1967 collections of short stories, which are not only *fantastika* but also verge on horror. González León wrote, in his short stories, novels, and poetry, fictions of resistance against the oppressive Venezuelan political establishment. His style, however, was neither literary nor typically activist, but instead drew on inspirations ranging from Joyce to Kafka to Faulkner to André Breton, the Comte de Lautreamont, and Arthur Rimbaud. His prose is poetic, but also fragmentary, and González León distorts the progression of time, creating a personal type of magic realism that is both recognizably Latin American and surreal. Too, González León emphasizes the psychologies and inner worlds of his characters, whose fears, obsessions, and dreams or nightmares add to the darker edge of González León's brand of magic realism. The result is stories about cities gone mad and brutal and hurtling toward self-destruction, and about ghostly, surreal fortune-tellers. González León's influence on later Venezuelan writers of *fantastika* was considerable, although it is for *País Portátil* rather than his *fantastika* that he is remembered.

Chapter Eight: Asia

India

The cleavage in Indian ghost stories of the 1920s and 1930s, with the genre splitting into traditional horror stories and those containing heavy and unsubtle political messages, ended with the independence of India in 1947 and the split of India and Pakistan. The incorporation of political messages into ghost stories essentially ceased, and ghost and horror stories became largely politics-free (though by no means social criticism-free). But post-Partition horror stories were no longer bound to colonialist models, nor traditional ones, and began a slow evolution. Ghost and horror stories were not highly regarded by Indian critics or the Indian literary establishment during the mid-century decades, leading to a high degree of ghettoization for the genre and to most talented authors avoiding the genre. Nonetheless, there were a large amount of ghost stories and horror stories produced in Indian during the mid-century decades, with some of the stories being of exceptional quality.

One author who wrote a number of ghost and horror stories during this time period was the poet, novelist, and short story writer Premendra Mitra. Mitra wrote a great many stories and novels, both mainstream and genre. He's known critically as one of the handful of writers in the 1930s who started the movement in Indian letters away from the modes and tendencies of Rabindranath Tagore. In his mainstream work Mitra "experimented with the stylistic nuances of Bengali prose and tried to offer alternative linguistic parameters to the high-class elite prosaic Bengali language."[1] His ghost and horror stories were equally a departure from the norm and from Tagore's work. Mitra wrote a not-inconsiderable amount of *fantastika*, much of it ghost and horror stories, from the late 1930s to the mid-1980s, but the majority of it was published from 1940-1970. Mitra's ghost and horror stories range from the relatively straightforward and traditional ghostly tall tales of his character Ghānāda to chillingly bleak stories of impoverished middle class workers living in expressionistic landscapes full of ghostly mansions and dark roads. Mitra's horror work is largely uninfluenced by Western models (not always the case for Indian horror writers) and shows his skill as a writer: from horror-adventure to neo-existenialist horror, Mitra's ghost and horror stories are imaginative, ingenious, and surprisingly chilling.

A more traditional ghost and horror story writer was Bulchand Jhamatmal Vaswani, a possibly pseudonymous author (nothing is known about him) who in 1945, 1946, and 1947 produced a series of English-language books on a variety of topics. Two of the books were collections of horror short stories, set in wartime India, Burma, China, Sri Lanka, and America. The stories are adequate in most respect, told in a straightforward manner, and ranging from an adaptation of Jacobs' "The Monkey's Paw" to a story of Indian witches to a malign Burmese snake-charmer. While not extraordinary in any way–Vaswani's updating of "The Monkey's Paw" is in no way an improvement on the original--Vaswani's stories are typical of the types of stories appearing in *Indian State Railways Magazine* and other mass interest periodicals of pre-Partition aimed at the lower classes. While not as artistically successful as the work of Tagore or Mitra,

---

[1]Jeff VanderMeer and Ann VanderMeer, "The Discovery of Telenapota," in *The Weird*, eds. Jeff VanderMeer and Ann VanderMeer (New York: Tor Books, 2012), 618.

stories like those of Vaswani were in all likelihood read by an audience that dwarfed that of those better writers.

For the most part, Indian horror fiction during the mid-century decades continued to be something that authors, prominent and otherwise, dipped into and played the tourist in rather than committing themselves to as a full-time author of the genre. No doubt this was because of the literary prejudice shown against horror stories by the Indian literary elite; an author who tried to make a full-time career out of writing genre stories and novels in India during the mid-century decades would be condemning themselves to a lifetime of disrespect, even if their stories and novels sold well.

So famous authors wrote ghost and horror stories which were viewed as respectable despite being genre work. The disrespect shown to the horror genre would begin to disappear only at the end of the century. There continued to be venues for mass market horror stories, akin to the *Indian State Railways Magazine*, but these were scorned (though popular with the lower class and lower caste masses) by the elites and paid too poorly to support someone writing full-time in the genre. One example of these was the children's magazine *Shuktara*, which from the 1950s forward published a wide variety of juvenile and Young Adult ghost stories in both prose and comic strip form. Some of these horror stories were translated from foreign sources, but most were original.

One of the rare authors who made a living by writing genre work was Sharadindu Bandyopadhyay, whose work in the horror genre began in the 1930s but for the most part took place in the 1940s. Although he was and is most famous for his detective character Byomkesh Bakshi, during the 1930s Bandyopadhyay wrote a series of occult detective novels about Baroda "the Ghost Hunter." The following decade Bandyopadhyay wrote a group of non-series horror stories. Bandyopadhyay generally wrote intelligently-plotted ghost stories which were strong in dialogue, in sense of place (usually Kolkata), and in the resolution, which was usually a surprising plot twist of some kind.

Another writer, famous as Sharadindu Bandyopadhyay but known for his social novels, was Bibhutibhushan Bandyopadhyay. Best known for *Pather Panchali*, Bandyopadhyay also wrote a variety of horror stories, including the first two in a series which was later continued by his sown. Bandyopadhyay injects more of a sense of the occult and of a menacing atmosphere into his stories than does Sharadindu Bandyopadhyay, and where Sharadindu Bandyopadhyay's chosen locale for his stories was Kolkata, Bibhutibhushan Bandyopadhyay preferred rural Bengal, with its abundant plant and animal life, as the setting for (and sometimes threats in) his horror stories. Too, unlike Sharadindu Bandyopadhyay's Baroda, whose only weapons against the supernatural are his force of will and his faith in Theosophy, Bibhutibhushan Bandyopadhyay's Taranath Tantrik is a practitioner of the occult and deeply learned in the lore of the supernatural.

Less serious than either of the Bandyopadhyays was Parashuram, Generally regarded as the greatest Bengali humorist of the twentieth century, Parashuram began writing in the 1920s and began incorporating humor into his ghost stories in the 1930s, but the majority of his comic horror work was written in the 1940s and the 1950s. Parashuram's comedy was not without its harder edge, and on occasion Parashuram include social criticism by way of satire in his horror stories, but generally Parashuram's comic horror were light-hearted and intended to raise more smiles than goose bumps.

Another well-known novelist was Manoj Basu, famous for both his prose (non-fiction and fiction) and poetry. Basu's fiction was powerful and emotional, and his horror stories retain those qualities, occasionally veering from emotional into brutal. Basu was known for exploring themes which were new to Indian fiction and in experimenting with narrative techniques, and those, too, were a part of a number of his ghost stories.

Sunil Gangopadhyay was famous for his poetry, but wrote widely in other genres, from travelogues to children's fiction to essays. Gangopadhyay's ghost stories were told in his usual elegant style but tended toward melodrama and a certain over-obvious quality.

From the 1950s forward Lila Majumdar became famous for her children's stories and novels. Less well known were her ghost stories, which were usually written for children. Despite their target audience, adults have also found them to be effective and frightening. Majumdar sometimes wrote stories in which the ghosts were benevolent, friendly, and even impish, but in most of her ghost stories she tells unsentimental stories full of frightening atmosphere, increasing tension, and heartbreaking and horrifying plot twists.

Other well-known mainstream authors only wrote a handful of horror stories, or only one, but that story was well-received enough to become minor classics. From 1910-1912 the Indian philosopher, yogi and guru Sri Aurobindo wrote four horror stories; they were only published posthumously, in 1951. Aurobindo's horror stories are generally well-written, but suffer from the insertion of his religious philosophy. Tarashankar Bandopadhyay was a leading Bengali novelist who was best known for the realism of his works and his portrayal of relationships in them. In 1964 he published "The Witch," which had his trademark realism and familiar psychological portraits but with the addition of a menacing occult figure. Banaphul, a Bengali novelist, short story writer, poet, and playwright, usually wrote humorous fiction, or realist fiction with a humorous tone, but in his few horror and ghost stories there was no humor to be found. Craftsmanship, sharp observations, and frightening occurrences, usually in stories no longer than a few pages, but no humor. And Pramatha Chaudhuri's "Sacrifice by Fire" is conceptual horror rather than visceral horror, told in an urbane and colloquial prose style.

Indonesia

In the mid- and late-1940s, when Indonesia was still a de facto and de jure colony of the Dutch, and when the Indonesian independence movement was still an armed rebellion, literature in Indonesia was largely Dutch-controlled and Dutch-driven:

> Those were the days when "literature" still played a central role in the Netherlands' bookshops and in intellectual life. In the book trade as well as in the educational system, literary work was considered of crucial importance in commercial as well as in cultural terms.[2]

---

[2]M.J. Maier Henk, "Escape from the Green and Gloss of Java: Hella S. Haasse and Indies Literature," *Indonesia* 77 (Apr. 2004): 83.

Fiction written in Indonesia for Indonesian audiences tended to be of lesser quality and more concerned with meeting genre requirements than in producing great literature. Most of those Indonesians who wanted to write literature did so in Dutch, for Dutch publishers and Dutch audiences. The same was true of Dutch colonial writers, who never wrote for native audiences. One writer who made her debut in 1948, a year before Indonesia's independence was recognized by the United Nations, was Hella S. Haasse, who would go on to become known as the "Grand Old Lady" of Dutch Literature thanks to her numerous novels for both children and adults, written from 1948 to 2008. Most of her fiction was what is known as "Dutch Indies literature," dealing with the Indonesia during both the colonial and post-colonial years and with the Dutch relationship with the Indonesian. Unusually for Haasse, her debut novel, *Oeroeg*, has substantial horror elements. *Oeroeg* is a *bildungsroman* that deals with the coming divorce between the Dutch and the Indonesians in a way that was painful for Dutch readers to consume. But in *Oeroeg* the cause of much misery and suffering is Telaga Hiteung, the black lake which

> is pictured as the ultimate source of horror. It is the place where Oeroeg's father meets his end when he tries to save the narrator, his master's son. It is the place of ghosts, the place of spirits and jinns that fill the boys with attraction and repulsion at once. Not to be understood. Oeroeg repeats that horror and, therefore, he is bound to stay in his friend's memory, even after the dissolution of their relationship. Oeroeg is a black lake that torments the narrator and forces him to write a clueless report in order to fill up the experiences of his formative years.[3]

The emotional trauma which the narrator suffers because of the loss of his friendship with Oeroeg is exacerbated by the trauma both the narrator and Oeroeg suffer from their experiences at the black lake.

Naturally, the situation for Indonesian literature changed substantially following independence in 1949, as Indonesian publishers were established and began publishing all genres of work from Indonesian publishers, from mimetic to the fantastic, all intended for a Indonesian audience. However, over the next twenty years the world of Indonesian letters would split into three groups, each demanding that literature voice their own different ideologies: nationalists, Muslims, and communists. In such an environment genre fiction became rare. This was most true of the 1960s; in the 1950s, authors like Rijono Pratikto were still allowed to flourish. Pratikto's peak years of production for his short stories, of which there were many, were 1954-1961. Pratikto specialized in horror fiction with substantial supernatural elements. He became known as the "Edgar Allan Poe of Indonesia," although his work was much more folkloric and made use of local legends much than Poe did. Pratikto created stories filled with mounting tension and frightening witches, ghosts, and monsters.

> *Si Rangka dan Beberapa Tjerita Pendek Lain* (*The Skeleton and Other Short Stories*, 1968), is much more mature, and in it the writer makes a very individual contribution to the corpus of Indonesian *tjeritapendek* literature...these stories do usually contain an

---

[3]Henk, "Escape from the Green and Gloss of Java," 88.

element of horror, or sometimes of the gruesome and sombre. The normal and the occult worlds merge and effects are heightened by the very irony and matter-of-fact-ness of the author's stye. Starting from an everyday situation he uses the simplest of means to build up tension gradually to a climax.[4]

Another author of the 1950s was Kho Ping Hoo, who was the rare Indonesian popular fiction writer to flourish in the 1950s, stop writing in the 1960s, and resume writing and become more popular in the 1970s and 1980s. Kho is best known for his martial arts fiction serials, but in the 1950 he made his name writing romances, mysteries, and ghost stories. Kho's ghost stories were similar to Pratikto, using folklore and local legends as the stuff of his stories.

Japan

The start of World War Two for Japan (as distinct from its invasions of China in 1931 and 1937) transformed Japanese literature, mainstream and genre, in ways that left no room for horror fiction. Similarly, the years of the American Occupation of Japan, 1945-1951, were ones of American censorship of anything questionable by the Japanese, which included genre work. It wasn't until after the American Occupation ended in September, 1951, that genre fiction, including horror fiction, was welcomed by Japanese publishers.

The first great horror writer of the post-Occupation era was Fumiko Enchi, generally regarded by critics as one of Japan's most important women writers. She became famous for her novels and short stories, almost all of which explored sexuality and female psychology and the conflicts between the old ways and new in post-war, post-Occupation Japan, usually to subversive effect. She used subtle symbolism and a precise use of language along with a thorough knowledge of classical Japanese literature to create allegorical and feminist works which conflated reality and fantasy to varying effects, from comforting to unnerving. Fumiko was primarily concerned with women and focused on them, their psychology, and their concerns in her works, and so horror was not the *primum mobile* of her work. But the effects of horror, the arousal of dread and fright through her stories and novels, were important to the stories she wanted to tell, and in several works she uses the supernatural, specifically spirit possession and posthumous vengeance, to scare the reader. She wrote in a sensual style that some critics described as "Gothic;" she found this style useful in creating the otherworldly atmosphere of her stories. A recurring plot in Fumiko's novels and short stories is of an older woman who seeks vengeance for the wasted lifetime and unfulfilled sexuality that her husband (and conservative, repressive Japanese society more generally) inflicted on her. The older woman, either personally or, more often, with the help of a shamaness, summons up a spirit to help her complete her vengeance.

---

[4]A. Teeuw, *Modern Indonesian Literature* (Berlin: Springer-Science+Business Media, R.V., 1967), 246.

Enchi takes the image of the shamaness (miko), and appropriates it for the purpose of critique by forging an unconventional link between the shamaness and the traditional image of the woman possessed by vindictiveness and jealousy. By bringing to consciousness the link between spirit possession and possession by powerful emotions, showing how the latter are inscribed in women's bodies as cultural codes, Enchi harnesses hidden energies and affirms the continuity of women's history.[5]

The effect of the presence of the shamaness and the possession by spirits, combined with Fumiko's prose style, is to insert the frightening supernatural into a well-portrayed everyday and mundane scene. For Japanese readers especially, the scenes in which the older women, who should (according to traditional Japanese mores) be submissive and loving to their husbands, instead take chilling revenge on them, would be both frightening and transgressive.

Abe Kōbō, a writer, dramatist, and photographer, was one of the foremost Japanese Modernists of the mid-century decades, and arguably the most consistent Japanese writer of *fantastika* thanks to his use of avant-garde and surrealist themes. "He could also be termed 'the master of dystopia,' since his visions, although original and fascinating, are almost relentlessly bleak."[6] He frequently places his genericized, displaced characters in strange, anonymous situations of the sort that could occur in an industrialized society, and plays out hopeless scenarios for the characters. "Much of Abe's work in general, can be seen as belonging to the genre of paranoid horror. This genre, significantly coming to the fore in the socially conscious and politically activist 1960s, delineates a world in which the supposedly normal is actually threatening and sinister."[7] Abe generally subverts Japan's consensus ideology, for example parodying "the traditional respect for doctors and [making] the hospital itself a place of further pain rather than healing,"[8] but while doing so he also links women and technology in negative ways, creating horrific stories of women come to bad ends in stories without hopeful resolution.

Kawabata Yasunari, a Nobel Prize winner for his novels and short stories, wrote High Art Horror, novels and stories in which the apparatus of horror was put to use for different ends. "Kawabata's distinctively Japanese writings are characterized by nostalgia, eroticism, and melancholy. He presents these elements with a poetic style sometimes described as a series of linked haiku."[9] But one of Kawabata's influences was Sōseki Natsume, and Kawabata

---

[5]Wayne Pounds, "Enchi Fumiko and the Hidden Energy of the Supernatural," *The Journal of the Association of Teachers of Japanese* 24, no. 2 (Nov. 1990): 167.

[6]Napier, *The Fantastic in Modern Japanese Literature*, 238.

[7]Napier, *The Fantastic in Modern Japanese Literature*, 108.

[8]Napier, *The Fantastic in Modern Japanese Literature*, 76.

[9]"Yasunari Kawabata," *Contemporary Authors Online*, accessed June 19, 2018, http://link.galegroup.com.lscsproxy.lonestar.edu/apps/doc/H1000052623/CA?u=nhmccd_main&sid=CA&xid=01b9b01d.

plays with Sōseki's images of an unseeing woman, death, and passivity to produce works that are both surreal yet somehow frighteningly believable. Unlike Sōseki and more similar to Tanizaki, however, Kawabata was also interested in fictional attempts to control women and to actively create worlds of escape. His fantasies problematize escape, suggesting that wish-fulfillment fantasies are no longer believable in a postwar world.[10]

Kawabata's particular touch is the construction of gothic spaces, as in *Nemureru Bijo* (*House of the Sleeping Beauties*, 1961) and "Kataude" ("One Arm," 1963), which are sinister, shadowy, and disturbing, and which force their inhabitants into a series of unpleasant recollections. Worse, however, is the situation that the women are relegated to, as objects without agency, existing to be preyed upon by older men desperate for an infusion of youth.

Japanese comic books, known as *manga*, draw upon a long tradition of illustrated storytelling in Japan. After the end of World War Two Japanese artists began expressing themselves in the form of *manga*, which unlike prose was not subject to the Allied Occupation's censorship policies (with the exception of any *manga* glorifying war or Japanese militarism). Manga began to grow almost immediately after the end of the war, with Machiko Hasegawa's *Sazae-san* (1946) proving to be an immediate success and Osamu Tezuka's *Tetsuwan Atomu* (1951) (popularized in the United States as "Astro Boy") even more successful. While *manga* was growing in popularity a number of future *manga* artists were getting experience illustrating *kamishibai* ("paper theater") boards. *Kamishibai* is a form of street theater in which storytellers entertain audiences using specially illustrated boards to accompany the narration. "In the second half of the 1940s, up to 10,000 storytellers earned their living in that way, and some future stars of the manga world — including the jidai mono (historical manga) master Shirato Sampei and the horror master Mizuki Shigeru, whose famous character Gegege no Kitarô was first created for the paper theater — started their career by drawing boards for *kamishibai*."[11]

Manga was generally lighter-hearted and focused either on domestic or science fictional stories through most of the 1950s, but in 1957 a new style of *manga* developed: *gekiga* ("dramatic pictures). "The *gekiga* movement began in 1957 and was a reaction against how early post-war manga were mostly kids' stories and light humor. *Gekiga* authors focused on dark, dramatic, suspenseful stories which developed slowly, using lots of pages of dialog-free atmospheric and action sequences to establish mood and tension."[12]

Given Japan's long history of telling horror stories through art, it was a natural progression for *gekiga* artists, along with their *kamishibai* counterparts, to begin telling horror in

---

[10]Napier, *The Fantastic in Modern Japanese Literature,* 61.

[11]Jean-Marie Bouissou, "Manga: A Historical Overview," in *Manga: An Anthology of Global and Cultural Perspectives*, ed. Toni Johnson-Woods (New York: Continuum, 2010), 26.

[12]Ada Palmer, "Japan's Manga Contributions to Weird Horror Short Stories," *Tor.com* last modified Feb. 18, 2014, https://www.tor.com/2014/02/18/japans-manga-contributions-to-weird-horror-short-stories/.

manga form. While there were individual horror stories in the anthology *manga* in the immediate wake of *gekiga*'s appearance, in 1959 the first horror *manga* appeared. Written and drawn by Shigeru Mizuki, *GeGeGe no Kitaro*, the story of the titular young boy *yokai* (spirit-monster) and his interactions with both humans and *yokai* and his interventions when there are conflicts between the two groups. Shigeru would become a specialist in *yokai* stories, which thanks to his encyclopedia knowledge of traditional *yokai* legends and stories and his expressionist art were made menacing rather than whimsical. Kitaro, the protagonist of *GeGeGe no Kitaro*, eventually became a charming and benevolent hero, but in his early years he is edgily mischievous with a pronounced lack of empathy for humans, which combined with his greed leads him to act in a horrific manner, even leading humans deceptively to Hell.

The second major horror *manga* creator was Kazuo Umezu, who began his horror work in 1962 and almost immediately became popular. Umezu eventually became known as, variously, "the grandmaster of horror manga," "the grandfather of gore," and "the Stephen King of *manga*." He earned these titles through a very detailed art style coupled with stories of graphic body violation. Influenced by childhood readings of the Grimm brothers' fairy tales as well as by traditional Japanese horror stories, Umezu told stories of warped worlds in which psychologically complex characters endure viscerally horrific fates. Before Umezu, horror *manga* was *kaiki* (abnormal, grotesque, enigmatic); after Umezu, horror *manga* became *kyoufu* (terror and fear).

Malaysia

Malaysia, like the Philippines and like Indonesia, was not a welcoming place for genre fiction, at least as far as the Malaysian literary elite were concerned. The masses consumed horror in the form of oral folktales and legends, but there was little in print during the post-war years and after independence in 1963. What was in print appeared primarily between 1952 and 1956, when two men, Yusof bin Ishak (future President of Singapore) and Othman Wok (future Cabinet Minister in Singapore) were working for a Malay-language newspaper in Malaysia, bin Ishak as editor and Wok as a journalist. Bin Ishak asked Wok to write a horror story for the newspaper's Sunday edition. Circulation skyrocketed thanks to the readers' love of being frightened, and Wok continued writing horror stories for the next four years. Wok's horror is a combination of a modern setting with traditional creatures from Malay legends and other cultures, from the vampiric *penanggalan* to the disembodied feet of an Indian woman, Chinese ghosts, and a Dayak mummy.

Pakistan

Pakistan achieved independence in 1947, the same year that India did, but Pakistani letters did not experience overwhelming success in the 1947-1970 years the same way that Indian letters did. During these years the national language of Pakistan was Urdu, while the official language was English. Mainstream writers in Urdu during the 1947-1970 years flourished, producing dynamic and challenging work. But mainstream writers in English were not so productive. English's ties to officialdom and the previous colonial regime made it a language that the newly patriotic Pakistani scorned to write in, leaving English-language novels in Pakistan in the 1950s moribund. The 1958 publication of Zaib-un-Nissa Hamidullah's *The Young Wife and Other Stories* therefore came as a revelation, and it was quickly viewed as the most significant English-language book in Pakistan. Hamidullah was a journalist and writer who was a pioneer of feminism in Pakistan and a crusading political journalist. Her short story collection was a surprise to her readers, who were used to reading her journalism. The stories in *The Young Wife* are generally of high quality and show the influence of Poe and de Maupassant. There are significant elements of Gothic romances in them, accompanied by O. Henry plot twists. Not all the stories in *The Young Wife* are horror, but those that are make effective use of the techniques of Hamidullah's influences.

Philippines

Literature in the Philippines after World War Two and the declaration of independence from the United States was much like that of Pakistan and Indonesia: mainstream literature of a fairly restrictive variety was honored, and genre fiction was seen as trash. Mateo Cruz Cornelio's *Doktor Satan* (*Doctor Satan*, 1945) didn't exactly change this situation, but it did introduce science fiction to the Filipino masses as well as provide them with a new kind of horror story to enjoy. (A literate work, *Doktor Satan* is quite unlike the horror ballads and dime novel horror stories Filipinos had been consuming before the war). Cruz Cornelio was a successful novelist before and after the war, writing both mainstream and genre work, but *Doktor Satan* was his first science fiction-horror novel, and it proved to be quite popular. In the novel, a mad scientist who drinks a formula of a wonder medicine. Unfortunately, the formula gives him a split personality, with the alternate personality, "Satan," being evil, *Doktor Satan* bears the obvious influence of both Mary Shelley's *Frankenstein* and Robert Louis Stevenson's *Dr. Jekyll and Mr. Hyde*, but is told in a straightforward way that even the semi-literate were able to enjoy. The horror segments, in which "Satan" goes on murderous rampages, are unsubtle and even obvious, but enjoyable enough and frightening to those not experienced in reading horror literature.

In the 1950s Nemesio E. Caravana was one of the leading Filipino directors of genre films, including science fiction. He was also an actor and, as a sidelight, wrote fiction, including horror fiction. In 1956 he wrote the serial "Exzur," from which a film of the same name was produced the same year. The serial and film were about the alien invasion of the Philippines by an armada of flying saucers and the mass destruction they spread, including the destruction by explosion of Manila's City Hall and Bureau of Posts and the Quezon bridge. "Exzur" will never be mistaken for high-quality horror fiction–Caravana wrote for the masses and generally produced straightforward prose, uncomplicated concepts, and horror scenes thick with obvious events and frights and thin with sophisticated emotions, motives, or nuances–but "Exzur" has a certain relish in its freewheeling destruction of the landmarks of the Philippines and the widespread devastation caused by the aliens. "Exzur" is horror in much the same way that the American alien invasion films of the 1950s were horror: science fictional and focused on explosions and mass destruction, with horror a (welcome) byproduct of the plot rather than the intended result of the plot.

Clodualdo del Mundo, Sr. was a prolific novelist, playwright, screenwriter, and critic who turned out not only a large number of literary pieces but numerous genre works, including *fantastika*. His first known horror work was *Tuko sa Madre Kakaw* (*Geko on the Madre de Cacao Tree*, 1958), which was later filmed under the same name. *Tuko sa Madre Kakaw*, written under the obvious influence of H.G. Wells' *The Island of Dr. Moreau*, is about a tormented, psychologically-unstable scientist who creates a formula for increasing the size of any animal to enormous proportions. In the depths of his insanity he plots to destroy humanity, so he tests the formula on a gecko, which is transformed into a gigantic creature, hungry for flesh and happy to destroy anything that gets in its way, including buildings and entire towns. Like Nemesio Caravana's "Exzur," *Tuko sa Madre Kakaw* is anything but subtle in its horrors, but the rampant destruction caused by the gecko are portrayed with an infectious glee.

In 1959 Caravana took a chance and wrote a novel, *Ang Puso ni Mathilde* (*The Heart of Mathilde*), which focused on a concept that his usual audience might not understand: cross-species heart transplantation. *Ang Puso ni Mathilde* is about Dr. Lino Romasanta, whose girlfriend goes crazy and has a heart attack after being raped. Dr. Romasanta takes the heart from his loyal bulldog, Mathilde, and puts it into Angela, his wife. The result is that Angela survives, but her behavior changes and she begins acting more like a wild animal than a human being. Angela kills her rapist and displays other feral behavior before Dr. Romasanta can bring her back to herself. *Ang Puso ni Mathilde* is a more sophisticated novel than most of what Caravana wrote, dealing as it did with the science fictional extrapolation of a theoretical medical procedure. Likewise, the horrors are dealt with in a more subtle manner than in "Exzur:" "This was a dark and brooding story reminiscent of Mary Shelley's Frankenstein but with a touch of Alfred Hitchcock and H.P. Lovecraft."[13]

Bienvenido N. Santos was a prose, poetry, and non-fiction writer who spent many years in the United States. While much of his work was humorous, his 1965 novel, *Villa Magdalena*, is a full-blown Gothic novel–a "tropical Gothic," as Filipino writer Nick Joaquin describes such work. *Villa Magdalena*, what Caroline S. Hau calls a "hothouse tale of greed, forbidden passion, decadence, and madness,"[14] is about an aristocratic family, beautiful, proud, and doomed, and the dark, demonic, ambitious, and sexually voracious man who marries into the family and brings about its demise. *Villa Magdalena* is a good example of the tropical Gothic:

> The tropical gothic novel has been one of the genres that Filipino writers have productively used to explore issues of economic and social inequalities, violence and injustice, the situation of women, and the social and political upheavals that have made Philippine society what it is today. They have marshaled an army of motifs, devices, and conceits—familiar to readers of literature produced, for example, in the American South,

---

[13] Victor Fernando R. Ocampo, "A Short and Incomplete History of Philippine Science Fiction," *The Infinite Library and Other Stories*, last modified May 5, 2014, https://vrocampo.com/2014/05/05/a-short-and-incomplete-history-of-philippine-science-fiction/.

[14] Caroline S. Hau, "Tropical Gothic," *The Manila Review* 6 (Mar. 2015), accessed June 19, 2018, http://themanilareview.com/issues/view/tropical-gothic.

in Latin America, and in Europe over the past two or more centuries—to hold up a mirror to the country's so-called best and brightest, to show them what the Philippines has come to, who have been the authors of its plight, and why things need to change.

Tropical gothic novels offer invitations to the Philippine nightmare. They explore all kinds of anxieties experienced by people in the cusp of change without necessarily issuing wake-up calls. Nonetheless, as with any decent tale of terror, tropical gothic is engrossing, and people come to the end of the story with a sense of release not unlike the feeling of having survived a dark, stormy night in September.[15]

---

[15]Hau, "Tropical Gothic."

Chapter Nine: Europe

Belgium

Writers of *l'ecole belge de l'etrange,* begun in the 1920s, continued to be the primary generators of Belgian horror during the mid-century decades. Although Belgium had comics and magazines publishing short fiction, those venues, which in other countries with a powerful literary establishment published horror fiction for the masses, did not publish horror fiction. What horror fiction there was appeared in the novels and short story collections of the writers of *l'ecole belge de l'etrange.*

Michel de Ghelderode was a Belgian playwright. An avant-garde dramatist, Ghelderode's work, though dark and obsessed with death, cruelty, and corruption, was performed often and was critically acclaimed, earning praise even from Jean Cocteau. Less well known than his plays are the thirteen *fantastika* short stories he wrote, published in a 1941 collection. Ghelderode's *fantastika* is as obsessed with death, the devil, masks, and the notion that society is as bitter farce as his plays, and are as hallucinatory and gloomy as the best of his stage work. The stories share protagonists who are filled with anomie and a soul malaise, who wander through supernaturally-haunted urban streets, searching for distraction from their own lonely, unmoored lives. "The ennui that pervades 'The Devil in London' and 'The Collector of Relics' evokes the sense that this corporeal existence is simply not the one we were meant to inhabit, a sentiment that will strike many readers as sharing a kinship with the modern author Thomas Ligotti."[1] Ghelderode tells his stories in vivid, bold, and intense sentences, with transgressive characters, an uncaring (and often malevolent) universe. The horror felt is conceptual rather than visceral, but Ghelderode's prose style and the unceasing cruelty of the stories make for well-crafted, chilling stories.

A much different writer from Ghelderode was Thomas Owen, a lawyer, plant manager, and art critic who became interested in writing following a meeting with detective writer Stanislas-André Steeman. From 1941-1943 Owen wrote detective novels, but in 1942, inspired by and perhaps jealous of the success of his friend Jean Ray, Owen began writing *fantastika*, primarily horror of *l'ecole belge de l'etrange* variety. In his lifetime Owen would write two dozen novels and over 300 short stories, most of which were *fantastika*. Owen would become (with Jean Ray) the most important Belgian writer of *fantastika* and horror, and arguably its best writer and stylist. Jean Ray never produced Art (and never bothered to try), while Owen routinely achieved it. Owen had obsessions distinctive to himself: morbid eroticism, perversity, and the animalistic. And Owen's characters were usually present to create the effect of horror in the reader rather than existing as sympathetic beings. But Owen's style—evocative, precise, restrained, clear and cold—overwhelmed these flaws, and the doomed atmosphere, erotically macabre imagery, and general existential dread Owen generates in the stories make them

---

[1] Christopher Burke, "Review: Spells by Michel de Ghelderode," *Weird Fiction Review*, last modified Jun. 27, 2017, http://weirdfictionreview.com/2017/06/review-spells-michel-de-ghelderode/.

memorably frightening. Owen's brand of terror has been called "intimate horror," as it focuses closely on ordinary lives rent by the moral and emotional ambiguities of life to the point that Owen's protagonists are vulnerable to supernatural assault. "Owen refined the tale of supernatural horror to an almost anachronistic degree of economy and purity…his unsettling work has been compared to that of Poe and Buzzati."[2]

The third major writer of *l'ecole belge de l'etrange* during the 1941-1970 time period was Gérard Prévot, who wrote horror novels throughout the period and into the mid-1970s. Like the other members of *l'ecole*, Prévot's work contains, in the words of a French critic, "rupture irrémédiable, l'irruption du surnaturel, une logique narrative, une ambiguïté."[3] Prévot is the subtlest of the trio of Ghelderode, Owen, and himself. The horrors in his work are subtle disturbances brought about by themes being pushed to the limit and characters and events working in slight—though disquieting—fashion. Too, in his shorter works Prévot, unlike Ghelderode or Owen, tends toward experimentation with form and with creating a sense of wonder rather than dismay and fear in his readers.

The foremost woman writer of *l'ecole belge de l'etrange* is Anne Richter, whose debut story collection, written when she was only fifteen, appeared in 1954. She went on to become a prominent Belgian author, editor, and critic and scholar of *fantastika*, publishing both short story collections and important critical anthologies and histories. Her style (predictably) changed as she grew older; her younger work has a more assured, even precocious narrative voice, while her older work "is far more hesitant, the structures and conclusions more conventional. If middle age visits upon us all a dark wood, then these stories are written from the gloom."[4] But throughout all the stories the traits of Richter persist: the swift and smooth entry into the supernatural, the sensitive observation, the perceptive characterization, the discomfiting intelligence, and the portrayal of the world as callous and full of sudden misfortune and death.

Jehanne Jean-Charles began publishing horror stories in the late 1950s, but it was her two story collections in 1962 and 1964 which brought her fame; although she continued writing into the 1980s, her early 1960s stories were the stories most often read and remembered. A gleefully malicious writer of barbed and twisted short stories, Jean-Charles' narratives depict a universe in which bad things happen to good people, often inexplicably but always stylishly told:

> if influence or affinity her style betrays, it's with the silken menace of Saki, though readers have claimed for her kinship with Matheson, Bradbury, and Dahl…though her sense of mischief approaches John Collier's, her prose isn't quite as fancy. The forthrightness of Jehanne's style and her choice of theme owe much more to Anglophone

---

[2]Edward Gauvin, "An Accounting by Thomas Owen," *Weird Fiction Review*, last modified Sept. 17., 2012, http://weirdfictionreview.com/2012/09/an-accounting/.

[3]Jean-Baptiste Baronian, *La Belgique fantastique Avant et après Jean Ray* (Paris: Editions Jacques Antoine, 1984), 17.

[4]Edward Gauvin, "Two by Anne Richter," *Weird Fiction Review*, last modified Sept. 3, 2012, http://weirdfictionreview.com/2012/09/two-by-anne-richter/.

traditions of the fantastic than to the Surrealism that tainted many of her French contemporaries, although in sensibility she descends from the conte cruel, in which conventional morality is subverted and puffery punished.[5]

Marcel Thiry was primarily a poet, but wrote several novels and short story collections. One typical story from them is "Un Plan Simple" ("A Simple Plan") (1958), a surrealist story that is part of the *fantastique reel* aspect of *l'ecole belge de l'etrange*. Thiry liked to use a very realistic middle class setting and atmosphere in his *fantastika*, and then, as in "Un Plan Simple," introduce the one bizarre or surrealist element which disrupts normalcy and propels the plot or the characters.

Czech Republic

The communist party ruling Czechoslovakia from 1948-1970 was disinclined to favor the publication of non-mainstream, non-communist literature, with even the healthy pre-war Czech science fiction community being pressured into silence. Horror was more harshly repressed by the Czech Communist Party as it was felt–as in the Soviet Union–that horror fiction was particularly Western and decadent. There was a brief liberalization of this attitude toward both science fiction and horror literature in the mid-1960s, resulting in a spate of science fiction and two important works of horror. The Czech novelist Ladislav Fuks generally wrote psychological mainstream books which were both autobiographical and which metaphorically or literally dealt with the plight of the Jews and the Czechs under the German occupation during the war. Even his mainstream works are on the bizarre and grotesque side, with Fuks' obsession with death quickly becoming clear.

Fuks wrote two works that neatly fall into the horror category. *Spalovač mrtvol* (*The Cremator*, 1967), the less well-known of the two, is about a worker in a crematorium who grows increasingly demented under the influence of Asian philosophies and Nazi propaganda and murders his half-Jewish wife and children–to "cleanse them"–before finally becoming an operator in the Nazi death camps. A purely psychological horror story, *Spalovač mrtvol* shows both the deterioration of the protagonist's mind as well as the deteriorating social atmosphere in the pre-war years. *Spalovač mrtvol* uses grotesqueness and the protagonist's insanity and obsession with death to increase the reader's horror. *Variace pro temnou strunu* (*Variations for a Dark String*, 1966) is generally seen as Fuks' best novel. Set in Czechoslovakia in the weeks before the German occupation, the novel tells the story of a boy, unloved by his parents, who has schizophrenic conversations with inanimate objects and for whom the walls of reality breakdown under the onslaught of fairy tales, stories, and rumors told to him by a family servant, leading him to see hints of vampires and werewolves everywhere. The novel is

> a balladic composition based on a vague and lurking horror, a premonition of the disasters of Hitler's coming to power. It is not so much a book of the deeds of men as a

---

[5]Edward Gauvin, "Jehanne Jean-Charles," *Weird Fiction Review*, last modified Oct. 1, 2012, http://weirdfictionreview.com/2012/10/jehanne-jean-charles/.

book about an atmosphere—the typically Central European atmosphere of terror, which is unknown, I think, to this American corner of the civilized world. The terror of a people jailed by the frontiers of their small country, surrounded by a powerful enemy, the perpetrator of an almost metaphysical evil."[6]

France

After a brief economic and artistic lull caused by the war, the *fantastique populaire* thrived again in the postwar period, following in the footsteps of the now-classic tradition established by the Grand-Guignol theater...in the literary field, the popular *fantastique* was more than ever synonymous with horror, and was primarily meant to thrill, entertain and shock the readers, not offer them a subtle, sophisticated, literary experience. Its niche existed between the thriller genre, especially when it involved gory or surreal crimes, and the popular adventure/science fiction literature developed in the 1920s and 1930s.[7]

The most artistically accomplished of the *fantastique populaire* authors of the 1950s was Jean-Louis Bouquet, a novelist and scriptwriter. Bouquet was not an innovator in the horror genre so much as a writer dedicated to putting a new gloss on old favorites: "in his works, Bouquet gave a new lease on life to such classic themes as witches' curses, reincarnation and spells enabling men to enter occult realms."[8] Another popular author to rehabilitate older concepts like demons, ghosts, and ghouls was Raoul de Warren, who published a number of novels with titles like *L'Énigme du Mort Vivant* (*The Mystery of the Living Dead*), *Rue du Mort-qui-Trompe* (*Street of the Cheating Dead*), and *La Bête de l'Apocalypse* (*The Beast of the Apocalypse*) from the late 1940s to the late 1950s.

During the 1950s a number of popular paperback imprints devoted to horror novels emerged, similar to the adventure and science fiction lines of publishers like Tallandier and Ferenczi. Most of these imprints were short-lived, but one, Fleuve Noir's *Angoisse*, lasted from 1954 to 1974. The best of *Angoisse*'s authors was Kurt Steiner, whose was one of the best French science fiction writers of the 1950s and 1960s. Steiner's horror work for *Angoisse*, twenty-two novels from 1953 to 1960, used both old themes and creatures and new, ranging from zombies to occult dimensions to modernized vampires to witchcraft, haunted castles, pacts with the Devil, and murderous split personalities. "Perhaps because of Steiner's medical background, the strength of his novels lay in their detailed, almost clinical, atmosphere of heavy, oppressive, bludgeoning horror, which anticipated the stronger, gorier books of the next decade."[9]

---

[6] Josef Skvorecký, "Some Contemporary Czech Prose Writers," *NOVEL: A Forum on Fiction* 4, no. 1 (Autumn, 1970): 9-10.

[7] Lofficier and Lofficier, *French Science Fiction*, 387.

[8] Lofficier and Lofficier, *French Science Fiction*, 387.

[9] Lofficier and Lofficier, *French Science Fiction*, 388.

B.R. Bruss, a very popular author for *Angoisse*, wrote nine novels from 1955 to 1971, with subjects ranging from cursed Egyptian talismans to carnivorous beasts hunting the residents of an isolated rural village to homicidal telepaths to hereditary curses.

> Like Belgian author Jean Ray, Bruss liked to depict strange and pathetic characters, moving in mundane, yet suffocating environments. The horrific elements were introduced slowly, but implacably, in a clear and colorful style. In his novels, men were usually the predestined victims of unspeakable Lovecraftian-like forces. The Bruss horror novels have few equals in their spellbinding atmosphere of oppressive horror.[10]

The most prolific of the *Angoisse* novelists, and one of the line's best and most respected writers, was Marc Agapit, who wrote forty-three novels for the imprint between 1958 and 1974.

> Unlike Steiner and Bruss, Agapit used the supernatural sparsely, his catalog of horrors being somewhat more akin to a Ruth Rendell rewritten by the Grand-Guignol. Agapit delighted in throwing a light on the perversity of the human soul, showing sordid, lonely, ordinary people ravaged by time, sinking slowly into madness. They exhibited an unhealthy sexuality and may even have had physical handicaps...Agapit's protagonists were often young boys who became natural prey for decrepit, evil females, or innocently trafficked with the most monstrous, unnatural creatures.[11]

Between 1945 and 1965 there were also a handful of French horror writers producing high-quality work. However, these writers wrote sophisticated horror stories and novels influenced by the Surrealists or by other avant-garde movements; these works abjured the tropes and motifs and apparatus of popular culture, both foreign and French, and wrote works that ordinary readers sometimes found difficult.

Best and most typical of these "difficult" authors was Julien Gracq, a novelist, playwright, poet, essayist, and geography teacher. Gracq's writing career began in 1938, but the majority of his work appeared during the mid-century decades. Gracq's work was generally known for an abstract, dreamlike environment, an elegant, refined prose style, and an advanced vocabulary. He avoided realism in his work, concentrating on the creation of a surrealist and usually menacing atmosphere. "In many ways, Gracq's work is the antithesis of Jean-Paul Sartre's. While Sartre accepts as literature only what is realistic and engagé, Gracq vigorously refuses realism and naturalism and praises, above all, disinvolvement with politics and other practical aims."[12]

---

[10]Lofficier and Lofficier, *French Science Fiction,* 389.

[11]Lofficier and Lofficier, *French Science Fiction,* 389.

[12]Pierre Brodin, "Gracq, Julien," in *Columbia Dictionary of Modern European Literature,* eds. Jean-Albert Bédé and William B. Edgerton (New York: Columbia University Press, 1980), 322.

Although all of Gracq's work has an obsession with the attraction of death and the inexorability of tragedy, two of his works stand out for their horror content. *Au château d'Argol* (*The Castle of Argol*) (1938) is perhaps the most famous and most successful work of Gothic surrealism. Influenced by both the late German Romantics and the surrealist work of André Breton, *Au château d'Argol* is a dark, disturbing, and violent story in which a brooding atmosphere of close menace, densely textured imagery, and general otherworldliness brought on by the plentiful use of surreality combine to create a novel whose readers grow increasingly disquieted the further into the novel they go. Short and relentless, *Au château d'Argol* is abstract; readers expecting direct or indirect discourse will be disappointed. But those willing to indulge heavy symbolism and abstract philosophizing will be rewarded with lush, sensuous prose and a growing atmosphere of expectancy and menace.

Gracq's other outstanding horror novel, *Un beau ténébreux* (*A dark stranger*) (1945), is a psychological thriller wedded to baroque and poetic prose. Critics have traditionally been split on *Un beau ténébreux*, some seeing its careful pace and inexorable, merciless unfolding of events as tedious and too slow. But even the book's harshest critics admit that the prose is wonderful and the plot complex, and for those readers open to reading *Un beau ténébreux* on its own terms, the novel is chilling in the heightening of tension and fear that doing so creates.

An author who shared little in common with Gracq apart from being French and writing stories and novels that frighten is Claude Seignolle. Seignolle's fiction is a very long way from Gracq's, being based on French regional folk tales and legends of French monsters rather than abstract intellectual concepts. Seignolle's fiction–very popular in France, largely unknown outside of it–appears simple and earthy, combining the pragmatic perspective of a commoner with elements of the supernatural. But Seignolle is a clever, even ironic writer, and his stories have an emotional impact not usually found in folk tales. His stories range from merely unlucky and inexplicable events to O. Henry-style plot twists to the overt intrusion, at exactly the wrong time, of unknown and malevolent intelligences. Seignolle uses monsters from traditional French folklore, including the Devil, werewolves, vampires, and revenants, but these monsters are usually representative and symbolic of more than just themselves, and Seignolle describes them with a blend of poetry, irony, and mystery. Seignolle's longer work emphasizes the characters of the peasants and leaves the supernatural implicit rather than explicit, but the protagonists continue to be victimized, this time by the actions of mobs rather than supernatural creatures. Essentially, Seignolle is the French Manly Wade Wellman, only a far better writer, and critics inside France and outside are in consensus that Seignolle is one of the true masters of the macabre.

Much closer to Gracq than Seignolle was Pierre Gascar, a journalist, critic, writer, essayist and screenwriter who was much-lauded in France and the recipient of highly-sought-after literary awards. Gascar, a veteran and survivor of German P.O.W. camps, was much affected by the war and by the Holocaust–influenced by it but not inspired by it–and both are recurring backdrops and looming, unspoken influences in his fiction. Gascar's horror fiction is not supernatural in the slightest, instead relying on the reader's knowledge of the war and the Holocaust for conceptual horror and for Gascar's recreation of the Kafka atmosphere for the more emotional horror. "It is the world of Kafka born anew: strange, somber, mysterious, irrational, eternally menacing."[13] Gascar relates his horrific stories in a de Maupassant-like deadpan realism in stories that often begin with the mundane and inexorably bring both reader and protagonist down into the depths of human barbarity. What allegories there are, are delivered with a helping of surrealism, creating "a Kafkaesque dream-like haze envelops the impotent animals and anguished humans, overlying the world of reality and lending an air of timelessness to their tragic situation."[14] Gascar was an original, versatile writer, but his horrors tend to be somber and deeply sad.

Roland Topor was best-known as an avant-garde artist, but he also wrote two novels with horrific content. *Le Locataire chimérique* (*The Tenant*, 1964) is the most famous of the two novels. It is about an apartment tenant who becomes consumed by the spirit of the previous tenant, who committed suicide in the apartment. Topor, whose usual publications were books of drawings, adroitly maintains the ambiguity of the situation, so that the reader can't be sure if the tenant is simply going mad or whether the spirit of the suicide actually exists. There are echoes of Kafka and Poe in *Le Locataire chimérique*, which is both psychologically acute and a bleak study of alienation, guilt, paranoia, and sexual obsession. Topor maintains a certain detachment from the proceedings, telling the events in a sparing, almost clinical style. Topor's second novel, *Joko fête son anniversaire* (*Joko's Anniversary*, 1969), is the better of the two. Again about alienation and loss of identity, *Joko fête son anniversaire* also has substantial amounts of surrealism of the Sadean sort. It's a particularly acidic fable about sociopolitical concerns, full of a cold fury and Kafka's themes. A complex novel with a grisly denouement, *Joko fête son anniversaire* is ultimately a raging indictment of modern society. The horror in *Joko fête son anniversaire* is less than that in *Le Locataire chimérique*, but more philosophical and contemplative.

Michel Bernanos, son of the French writer Georges Bernanos, wrote poetry and fantasy novels under a pseudonym so as not to ride the coattails of his famous father's reputation. Little read now, Michel's major work, *La montagne morte de la vie* (*The Other Side of the Mountain*) appeared in 1967, four years after he committed suicide. A nightmarish work influenced in part by Poe's *The Narrative of Arthur Gordon Pym*, *La montagne morte de la vie* is split into two halves: the first, about a sea voyage gone terribly wrong, has great similarities with the work of William Hope Hodgson; the second, about the survivors of the sea voyage, who find themselves on a very strange island in a reality that is different from ours. The first half of the novel is full of visceral horrors, including cannibalism; the second half of the novel is a surreal fantasy which conveys greater horror than the first half of the novel, because the surreality contains symbolic horrors and leads to a powerful, devastating ending. *La montagne morte de la vie* goes beyond the Lovecraftian uncaring universe and posits that reality–at least the reality of the island–is actively hostile to humanity. Reality, in Bernanos' novel, is intelligent, alien, and out to get us, and the characters on the island suffer greatly because of this. Told in a spare, methodical style, the novel has superior horrific imagery, but the true horror is conceptual, in the growing, dismaying discovery that humanity means nothing to the universe except as a foe to be

---

[13]Chester W. Obuchowski, "The Concentrationary World of Pierre Gascar," *The French Review* 34, no. 4 (Feb. 1961): 327.

[14]Obuchowski, "The Concentrationary World of Pierre Gascar," 327-328.

brutalized. "In Bernanos' scheme, man is the measure of nothing; he is a millimeter, and his struggles the busy quarrels of ants beside the extent of swift, casual natural destruction. Sin is a desperate act of self-importance. Forgiveness is a matter of supreme impersonality."[15]

Germany

Literature under the Nazis was heavily censored, with the result that from 1941-1945 there was nothing produced that qualified as horror literature. After the end of the war, Allied censorship all printing was subject to Allied approval, and any content the Allies deemed unacceptable–which included horror fiction–was denied permission to print. Until 1949, there was no horror fiction published in West Germany. After 1949, and for two decades, German social constraints prevented horror fiction from being published. As a general rule, German *fantastika* was discouraged in Germany from 1949-1970, with only the most literary of writers being able to get away with including elements of *fantastika* in their work.

There were two exceptions to this, however. The first was in the German dime novels, or *heftromane*, which flourished through the 1950s and provided the German reading audience with cheaply produced, sensationalist genre fiction, including horror. Although the horror was usually of the most unsubtle and elementary sort, quite unlike the classics of pre-war German and English horror that the German reading audience was used to, the *heftromane* was at least something that horror loving Germans could read during the otherwise lean years.

The second exception came in 1969, a time when German literary mores were changing and German society was more open to *fantastika* of all sorts, as would be seen in the 1970s. The renowned poet Marie Luise Kaschnitz put the short story "Vogel Rock" at the head of her 1969 short story collection. A work of magic realism, about a woman whose household is invaded by a very large and hostile bird, "Vogel Rock" is a rare venture into the unnatural by Kaschnitz, who tells the story with a sober, matter-of-fact narration combined with a tight focus on the emotions, especially the fear the protagonist feels because of its presence and its unshakeable determination to stay in the protagonist's apartment.

Italy

Italy was in much the same situation as Germany during World War Two and during the Allied occupation of Italy through 1947: government censorship prevented horror fiction from being published. However, unlike Germany, newly independent Italy rapidly embraced *fantastika*, especially the Gothic, as a means by which to oppose realism in narrative fiction and as a way to voice opposition to repressive political and cultural forces.

The two major Italian horror writers of the mid-century decades were Dino Buzzati and Tommaso Landolfi. Buzzati was a novelist, short story writer, painter, poet, and journalist who

---

[15]Edward Gauvin, "Michel Bernanos' "The Other Side of the Mountain": Sin, Destruction, and Forgiveness," *Weird Fiction Review*, last modified Nov. 21, 2011, http://weirdfictionreview.com/2011/11/michel-bernanos-the-other-side-of-the-mountain-sin-destruction-and-forgiveness/.

was best known in his lifetime for his existentialist work, but among connoisseurs of horror Buzzati is known and acclaimed for his horror stories, which are imbued with his existentialism but go beyond that into the surreal and the weird. Buzzati began writing in 1933, but the great majority of his stories were published from 1940 to 1967. Critics have reached for a number of comparisons and inspirations for Buzzati's work, comparing them with the work of Kafka and Stefan Grabinski and arguing for the influence of Italo Calvino and Primo Levi. These critics further charge that Buzzati's work lacks the grandiose imagination of Calvino and the profundity borne of life experience of Levi. But Buzzati's work, though undoubtedly influenced by those writers, was uniquely his own. Buzzati's stories are fabular, lacking in supernatural elements but filled with weird dreads of no apparent or explicable cause. The horror in them comes from their angst, bleak pessimism, and sense of futility, their paranoia and feeling of impending catastrophe, their *contes cruel* endings, from the way in which ordinary institutions become menacing and destructive monsters. Buzzati's style journalistic realism, which he thought the best manner in which to present the fantastic–adds to the horror in its matter-of-fact narration. His stories are terse and slickly told, narratively dextrous, emotional in the way of the best *contes cruel*, and effective in their argument that life is futile and that all dreams of achievement come to nothing in the end.

Tommaso Landolfi was a writer, translator, and critic whose work was primarily *fantastika*, much of it grotesque and horrible. Although he began publishing in 1938 and ended in the late 1970s, the majority of his work was published between 1940 and 1970. His work, which tends toward the surreal, magical, and grotesque, is usually told in an elegant narrative style whose graceful, complex vocabulary is jarringly at odds with the stories' subject matter and his frequent use of nonlinear or fragmented narratives. Though Landolfi frequently made use of supernatural devices, much of his work is psychological, with Landolfi bringing the reader into the mind of either a victim of some incomprehensible ontological transgression, or into the mind of someone unbalanced and violent. His horror is modern horror–no Gothics or traditional ghost stories for Landolfi, rather stories that are set in spaceships, that build on the works of earlier horror writers, from Poe to Gogol to Kafka, that incorporate existentialist attitudes toward society. In Landolfi's stories horror can never be controlled, conquered, or exorcized; humans are small next to whatever terrorizes them, "abandoned, each on their own in a narrative of fear without resolution."[16]

Portugal

While much literature was censored or heavily controlled during the Salazar dictatorship of 1932-1968, some literature with elements of *fantastika* slipped through or were allowed to be published.

Domingos Monteiro, a lawyer, poet, and novelist, primarily wrote Realist fiction, but in a number of his short stories, published in the 1940s and 1950, he embraced horror. Monteiro's horror ranges from the supernatural (the ghost of a father murdered by his sons avenges itself on

---

[16]Keala Jewell, "Tommaso Landolfi," in *Encyclopedia of Italian Literary Studies*, ed. Gaetana Marrone (New York: Routledge, 2007), 997.

them) to the grimly, bleakly mundane (murderers grapple with the consequences of their actions, those dying of disease describe the possibly-metaphorical visit of Death to their ward).

José Régio was one of the foremost Portuguese Modernists of the twentieth century. Régio published novels, plays, poetry, and criticism, mostly of the Modernist variety, but in *Há Mais Mundos* (*There Are More Worlds*, 1963) he wrote a series of fantastic stories which contained horror, whether direct (as in the story of half-man half-beast who terrorizes a mountain village) or more ambiguous (as in the proto-metafictional "Os Alicerces da Realidade" ("The Foundations of Reality") where the insane protagonist threatens to wake the audience out of its dreams).

Spain

Fantastika in Spain during the mid-century decades suffered for two central reasons: the first being the Francoist regime's disapproval of genre fiction, and the second being the strong tradition of Spanish realism, which led the entire Spanish literary establishment to strongly look down upon those writers who dared to write *fantastika*. "During these years, the government placed a strong emphasis on religion and tradition by censoring any criticism of Catholicism or the normative Spanish society."[17]

Science fiction was a partial exception to this–still looked down upon, but enjoying a minor publishing boom in the 1950s. Horror was more the norm for Spanish *fantastika* during these years, being rare and published only in a very limited fashion. There were three exceptions to this, both women authors who wrote horror not (just) to horrify the reader but to make social statements and express criticism of the Francoist government and the repressive aspects of Spanish society.

Carmen Laforet was an important Spanish author. Best known for her first novel, *Nada* (1945), Laforet wrote a number of other novels which were, for the time period and culture, relatively open about feminism and the mystical variety of Catholicism while also expressing the author's existentialism. *Nada* was a critical sensation when it first appeared and has since become a part of the Spanish canon, being called Spain's answer to *Catcher in the Rye*. *Nada* is also a kind of Spanish Gothic, emphasizing a grim atmosphere in a sprawling house. The house has gloomy halls and rooms which go beyond gloom into insanity and perhaps the supernatural:

> It looked like a witch house, that bathroom. The soiled walls retained the imprint of hooked hands, of cries of despair. Everywhere, chipped open, their toothless mouths, moisture oozing. On the mirror, because it could not fit anywhere else, they had placed a macabre still life of pale breams and onions on a black background. The madness smiled in the twisted taps.[18]

---

[17]Pallejá-López, "Houses and Horror," 156.

[18]Carmen Laforet, *Nada* (Barcelona: Destino, 1995), 19.

Additionally, the house is said to have "devilish" furniture and to whisper and grunt to itself, and those who live in it seem ghostly and half-real. *Nada* also has a Gothic cathedral, an infernal-seeming Chinatown, a street foul with rotten odors, a young, pure and innocent woman as protagonist, a tyrant (unusually, a woman), night journeys, and a general element of fear.

Isabel Calvo de Aguilar, a novelist and radio scriptwriter, was a popular rather than serious writer, and wrote several novels that "combine fantastic adventures, Gothic elements, exotic settings and love interest with intrigue or crime."[19] Although she was known as the "Agatha Christie española" because of her emphasis on crimes and mysteries in her writing, she also produced novels with substantial horror elements. *Doce sarcófagos de oro* (*Twelve gold sarcophagi*, 1951) is about a wicked sociopath who meets a beautiful woman during his travels in Asia and then kills and embalms her. Similarly necrophiliac was *La danzarina inmóvil* (*The motionless dancer*, 1954), in which an artist transforms his ballerina wife into a statue. Calvo's writing was as mentioned popular rather than serious, including her use of horror elements and scenes, whose purpose was to frighten readers more than it was to make a feminist point.

By contrast, Mercè Rodoreda is the very definition of a canonical author in Spain. Her novel *La plaça del diamant* (1962) is generally acknowledged to be the most critically acclaimed novel in Catalan of all time, and Rodoreda is seen as the most important Catalan novelist of the postwar years. A skilled writer of enchanting prose who combined a keen observational eye with humor and emotion, Rodoreda was seen as important enough in her lifetime to have a literary prize named after her. Less noticed than her novels are her short stories, which were gathered together in four collections. Two of them, in 1967 and 1979, contain substantial horror work. The horror is not limited to her short stories, of course; her *La mort I la primavera* (*Death and spring*, 1986) presents a town with weird and sinister customs, and her *Del que hom no pot fugir* (*What One Cannot Flee*, 1934) portrays the female protagonist's descent into madness in ways similar to Gilman's "The Yellow Wallpaper." But it is in Rodoreda's short stories that she most makes use of horror. Drawing inspiration from writers such as Poe and Lovecraft as well as Borges and Cortázar, Rodoreda used horror both to terrorize the reader and to allegorically refer to the horrors of how men treat women and the horrors of war, especially the horrors suffered by civilians during the Spanish Civil War. Rodoreda sometimes told magic realist horror stories, sometimes more traditional horror stories about spookily possessed animals, sometimes Gothics, and sometimes psychological horror. In all her stories she uses her knack for observation to create realistic emotions, character psychologies, and believable settings before introducing the horror elements.

---

[19]Noël M. Vallis, "Calvo de Aguilar, Isabel," in *Dictionary of the Literature of the Iberian Peninsula*, eds. Germán Bleiberg, Maureen Ihrie, and Janet Pérez (Westport, CT: Greenwood Press, 1993), 276.

Chapter Ten: The Middle East

Israel

Yiddish *shund* (lit.: "trash") literature, much of which was in serial form as a version of dime novels, was published from the late nineteenth century through the late 1930s in Europe and the United States, and gave way to Hebrew-language pulps, which appeared from the 1930s into the late 1970s. The great majority of these pulps, unlike Hebrew belles-lettres, "usually focused on the personal, the melodramatic, and the sensational–and at times the erotic; they employed distinct language and recycled story lines; they were neither planned by central literary publishing houses nor signed by recognized authors; and they were not listed or individually reviewed in official channels."[1] The genres in these pulps ranged from mysteries to pornography to superheroes, with horror only appearing in two pulps, *Mivhar sipure pahad* (*Suspense and Tremors*) #1-8 (1963) and *Sidrat ha-emim* (*The Series of Horrors*) #1-6 (1971-1982). The pseudonymously-signed horror stories were standard pulp horror stories, told with gusto if not with apparent skill.

Syria

While the mid-century decades were years in which the novel and short story in their Western forms reached maturity in the Middle East, they were not years in which the literary elite or the publishers of the various Middle Eastern countries were welcoming to horror fiction. Various forms of *fantastika* would appear in these countries but horror, with a few exceptions, did not. Perhaps the most prominent of these exceptions was George Sālim, a Syrian novelist, short story writer, critic, and high school teacher. Generally considered as one of the avant-garde Syrian writers of the 1960s and 1970s, Sālim addresses contemporary themes in his work: the loneliness of the individual, the futility of effort and striving, the inexorability of death and annihilation. But "the literary tools with which George Sālim seeks to probe the deepest questions of existence are the fantastic, the bizarre, the inexplicable."[2] Notable is the fact that these tools often verge on horror. He tells ghost stories, magic realism with substantial horrific symbolism, and even realistic fiction turned nightmarish because of the intrusion of the terrifying into an otherwise mundane story. Sālim tells these stories with a poet's grace and imagery, but does not scant on the frightening elements and qualities of his stories.

Turkey

---

[1] Rachel Leket-Mor, "IsraPulp, The Israeli Popular Literature Collection at Arizona State University," *Judaica Librarianship* no. 16/17 (2011): 1-2.

[2] M.J.L. Young, "The Short Stories of George Sālim," *Journal of Arabic Literature* 8 (1977): 123.

1950 was a significant transitional year in the history of Turkish society, as the government of Adnan Menderes begins its ten year rule, during which time the transition from peasantry to the middle class reached its height, and during which restrictions on Islam were relaxed and the economy boomed. By the latter half of the 1950s, however, the economy was faltering and the Menderes government introduced censorship laws designed to limit dissent.

It was in this environment that Kerime Nadir, a popular romance novelist, published *Dehşet Gecesi* (*Night of Terror,* 1958), a *Dracula*-influenced Gothic romance. Full of a frightening atmosphere and a number of traditional Gothic touches, including a two-hundred-year-old ghost who drinks human blood to survive, *Dehşet Gecesi* also contains, allegorically and symbolically, all the fear and the anxiety of the Turkish people, from the location of the novel's castle (Hakkari, where in real life foreign oil investment was starting and already becoming troublesome to the Turks) to the effects of the Marshall Plan.

Part Three: 1971-2000

Chapter Eleven: Africa

The effect of liberation from colonization was remarkable on many levels for the African countries, but in the fields of popular literature liberation did not automatically result in the creation of original, genuinely local popular literature. Most African writers of popular literature, in the years and decades after liberation, wrote stories and novels which, as in the days before liberation, were influenced, whether lightly or heavily, by the European models which the writers had been educated in and which had been the sole or great majority of what had been available to read before liberation. It wasn't until the 1990s that African popular literature became genuinely African and genuinely local and specific to each country. This is true of horror literature as well as other popular literature genres. The African horror literature of the 1970s is markedly different from the African horror literature at the end of the century, as we'll see. Moreover, the distribution of horror literature on the continent was, by the year 2000, even: of 43 stories from four post-2000 English language anthologies in African literature, six were horror, coming from the North (Mauritania), the South (South Africa), the East (Kenya, Uganda), and the West (Cameroon, Nigeria).[1] Horror is a universal concept, and in the new century and millennia it is and will continue to be written by people of many more nations than it has in the past.

Congo

Paul Lomami-Tshibamba (see Chapter Six) continued to publish allegorical work about the effects of colonization on the colonized after Congo achieved liberation in 1960. In 1972 he published *La Récompense de la Cruauté* (*The Award for Cruelty*) (although it had been written during the colonial period). Like *Ngando le crocodile*, *La Récompense de la Cruauté* addresses social and political issues through allegory published as popular literature. In the case of *La Récompense*, the popular literature is about a gigantic wild beast with the body of a dinosaur and the head of a human, topped by the crest of an iguanodon. In the novel, which is set early in the eighteenth century, at the time of Congo's colonization, the creature lives in the forest of Kilimani, near what will later become Kinshasa, and is known as the "Belzebuth de Kilimani."[2] The local Catholic missionaries push the local colonial administrator to kill what they view as a demon, so administrator organizes an expedition composed of scientists and troops. After a long trip into the wilderness, they find the creature and shoot it dead, but as it dies it expels poisonous gas which agonizingly kills the entire expedition. *La Récompense*, written during Lomami Tshibamba's *cycle du merveilleux*, is as mentioned an allegory about colonized and colonizer,

---

[1] E. Dawson, "Emerging Writing From Four African Countries: Genres and Englishes, Beyond The Postcolonial, " *African Identities* 10, no. 1 (2012): 24.

[2] Paul Lomami Tshibamba, *La Récompense de la Cruauté* (Paris: Editions du Mont noir, 1972), 10.

with the expedition representing not just the Belgians but those Africans who have allied themselves with the Belgians–what Susanne Gehrmann calls "representatives of the colonial order"³–and the creature representing native Congolese, who, just as the creature did, will pay back the murderous colonizers with a cruelty of their own. As Susanne Gehrmann notes, like *Ngando*, *La Récompense* starts

> with a realistic description of daily life in a colonial society, only to quickly turn into a fantastical mode of narration; to a universe of the magic, ruled by monsters and sorcerers, a universe grounded in popular beliefs familiar to the Congolese reader through oral storytelling. The realism of the modern world is touched by the magical-fantastical elements of a timeless time, out of space.⁴

The horror of *La Récompense* comes not through the presence of the creature–it has an expressive human head (albeit one the size of four or five normal human heads)–but through what is done to it by the merciless Europeans and their African troops, what happens when the creature dies ("the sun which was radiant at this moment, veiled itself entirely, as if blown off: suddenly night fell down, taking everybody into a surprising darkness"⁵)–what is done to the troops as the creature dies, and the implicit cruelty of the colonial order itself.

Sylvain Bemba was a Congolese journalist, novelist, playwright and musician. In 1976 he published his stage drama *Tarentelle noir et diable blanc* (*Black tarantella and white devil*), on the surface a story of a native, Faustin Moudouma N'Goyi, who on the orders of his sinister master, Faustino, buys the African souls from two generations of a Congolese family. Allegorically, of course, the play is about the painful price that the colonized pay because of the colonizers. The play and the stage directions are full of animals used as metaphors, with colonialism and its representatives appearing in the image of the tarantella spider, whose webs are inescapable. Faustino is a figure of horror, Faustin is gruesomely executed after he dares to question Faustino's orders, and the violence of the colonial order is hyperbolically portrayed, further heightening the effect on the viewer.

Sony Lab'ou Tansi was a novelist, short story writer, playwright, and poet. A prolific writer, he is one of the most internationally renowned authors of "New African Writing."⁶ His style is baroque, satiric, and filled with black humor and a disrespect for conventions of genre or what African writers were supposed to write about. Tansi's first play, *Conscience de tracteur*

---

³Susanne Gehrmann, "Remembering Colonial Violence: Inter/textual Strategies of Congolese Authors," *Tydskrif vir Letterkunde* 46, no. 1 (2009): 18.

⁴Gehrmann, "Remembering Colonial Violence," 16.

⁵Lomami Tshibamba, *La Récompense de la Cruauté*, 38.

⁶Lucy Stone McNeece, "Black Baroque: Sony Lab'ou Tansi (1947-1995)," *The Journal of Twentieth-Century/Contemporary French Studies revue d'études français* 3, no. 1 (Spring, 1999): 127.

(*The Awareness of a Tractor*, 1973), is set in the future year of 1995, on the eve of the 35th anniversary of the founding of the Republic of Coldora, somewhere in Central Africa. An old scientist, known as "Le Vieux" (The Ancient One), who considers himself a modern Noah, believes that a new "Cosmocide" is necessary, to wipe out humanity and rid the world of mankind's vices and sins. Le Vieux begins to carry out his plan to save humanity through genocide and selective rebirth, using six androids whose mission is to kill everyone on Earth except a select few thousand, who will be brought to Le Vieux's underground city and kept safe for the nine years necessary for the Earth to recover from Le Vieux's light-based doomsday device. Unfortunately, Le Vieux's "Rational Revolution" is stopped by Leiso, the General-President of Coldora who wants to hold on to his power above all else. *Conscience de tracteur* works on several levels: as a trial of science, which "appears as the apprentice magician of whom Karl Marx and Friedrich Engels spoke in *The Communist Manifesto*: it can no longer control the forces it has triggered;"[7] as a plaint against the West, whose reliance on science has come, in Tansi's view, at the cost of the human heart; and as a horror narrative, in which the stage devices, the portrayal of Le Vieux as a mad scientist gone genocidal in his partial senility, and the portrayed examples of science not being able to stop dictatorships, much less the collective madness science has spawned, are all aimed at and succeed at making the play's viewer deeply uneasy, if not outright frightened.

Six years later Tansi published his first novel, *La vie et demie* (*The half life*, 1979), a leading part of the "epistemological rupture"[8] in African francophone letters, as it was seen to herald in a new generation of francophone sub-Saharan African writers. Set in the vast, imaginary African country of Katamalanasie, *La vie et demie* is about the tyranny of its dictatorship–an obvious commentary by Tansi on the Zairean dictatorship of Mobutu Sese Seko–and the resistance to the dictator, the "Providential Guide," which includes Martial, a dead man who refuses to die and who takes refuge in the body of his daughter, and thirty of Martial's grandchildren. *La vie et demie* is generally viewed as a prime example of francophone African magic realism, although the second half of the novel, as Lydie Moudileno argues, is much more science fictional than magic realism.[9] *La vie et demie*, which cannily makes selective use of the usual African stereotypes, has all the usual horrors of a tinpot African dictatorship, including ritualized cannibalism, torture, assassination, and rape, but adds to it science fictional horrors, including stinging mutant insects and radio-controlled ray-gun-wielding drones in the shape of insects. More broadly, in *La vie et demie* Tansi

---

[7]Fernand Nouwligbeto, "Les Dramaturges Africains Francophones Face Aux Enjeux Scientifiques," *Ethiopiques* no. 96 (Spring, 2016), accessed June 20, 2018, http://ethiopiques.refer.sn/spip.php?article1977.

[8]Lydie Moudileno, "Magical Realism: 'Arme miraculeuse' for the African Novel?" *Research in African Literatures* 37, no. 1 (Spring, 2006): 29.

[9]Moudileno, "Magical Realism," 33-34.

resorts to the usage of the fantastic, gigantic, and horrible chaos and non-realistic dimensions to conjure up the morbid, cast out the putrid, exorcise said chaos and injustice in African political life...[Tansi's novels] take place in settings dominated by political violence, devious sexuality, human cowardice, ugliness, corruption, silence, and death.[10]

Thematically quite similar to *La vie et demie* was Pius Ngandu Nkashama's *Yakouta* (1995). Ngandu, an expatriate (exiled) Congolese academic who wrote *Yakouta* while in Paris, created, in *Yakouta*, a horror novel that nonetheless contains an ultimately hopeful note. The titular woman has seen her father assassinated by a group of witches on the orders of the cruel tyrant of a nameless country where the action takes place. Yakouta herself has been tortured, raped, and mutilated. But she rises to become a messianic figure to her people and ultimately overthrows the despot. *Yakouta* is "representative of what I call fragmented narration, a style that overturns realistic writing through disruptions and uses language as a marker of unspeakable experiences, uncured ills and unforgettable violence throughout Congolese history."[11] Ngandu does not avoid detailing the horrors done to Yakouta, describing them in language that almost becomes poetic at times, and does not allow the reader to look away from the cruelty and terror of the "mad tyrant," creating a novel who, despite the happy ending–a rare hopeful, future-looking finale for Congolese novels–drags the reader into the territory of fear literature from almost the first page.

Ghana

The surge in publishing following independence in 1957 produced a range of fiction both serious and commercial in the 1960s and 1970s, ranging from conspiracy thrillers to science fiction (J.O. Eshun's *Adventures of the Kapapa* (1976)) to horror. A leading example of the latter was Nii Yemoh Ofoli's *The Messenger of Death* (1979). A husband and wife are preyed upon by a witch, who kills off the couple's children, and the couple must discover the identity of the witch before all their children die. An entertaining mix of 1970s narrative style and traditional Ghanian folklore, *The Messenger of Death* is horrifying both because of its content and because of the description of the scenes involving the witch.

Guinea

Alioum Fantouré, a prize-winning author for his novels and plays, is known critically for being one of the first sub-Saharan authors to shift the focus of his criticism away from colonialism and on to the local dictatorships which arose in the wake of the departure of the colonial powers. Fantouré's *Le récit du cirque* (*The story of the circus*, 1976) does not use–or need to use–supernatural elements to terrify its readers. Instead, Fantouré simply shows the more

---

[10]Anthere Nzabatsinda, "Sony Labou Tansi," in *The Encyclopedia of African Literature*, ed. Simon Gikandi (London: Routledge, 2003), 704.

[11]Gehrmann, "Remembering Colonial Violence," 15.

extreme examples by which African dictatorships oppress and terrify their citizens, and uses them to educate–and frighten–his readers.

> A captive audience locked literally into a theatre become gradually involved in the devastating spectacle being acted out on stage, a "circus" of horror and suffering in an African dictatorship complete with political trials and concentration camps. There is no final curtain, only newsreel shots being projected onto a screen as the actors turn to watch the panic-stricken spectators seek an exit which is not there.[12]

Kenya

After Kenya achieved independence, in 1964, its literature, especially its popular literature, went through a long period in which its writers grappled with the long-term effects of colonialism. The greatest influences on Kenyan writers during this period were Achebe's *Things Fall Apart* and the Mau Mau Rebellion of 1952-1964. The greatest influence on Kenyan authors of popular literature were Nigerian models, including Onitsha marketplace literature, and Western models. David G. Maillu is a prime example of the latter. A writer, publisher, painter, musician, Maillu is best known for his dozens of popular novels. *Kadosa* (1979) is about a Kenyan scholar who is visited by an extraterrestrial ghost, a *femme fatale* named Kadosa who has superhuman powers.

> Kadosa possesses immense powers, including the ability to transform herself at will into anything visible or invisible. She treats Mutava to terrifying displays of her total control over the bodies and minds of human beings, injuring and even killing those who annoy her. She also rules Mutava's imagination, filling his dreams and other unconscious moments with horrific sights that nearly drive him mad.[13]

A love affair of sorts develops between Mutava and Kadosa, but she is ultimately called back to her home planet and ends the affair. *Kadosa* is, like much of Maillu's work, a page-turner, very competently told with strong (if somewhat broad) characterization, though most academic critics find it "undisciplined, unrefined, uncouth, and outrageously excessive,"[14] and of course beneath serious consideration due to its generic self-identification. But as horror, *Kadosa* works exceptionally well. Maillu describes Mutava's hallucinations and dreams in intense and vividly-described terms. "Maillu, in delving so deeply into morbid zones of the imagination, was

---

[12]"*Le récit due cirque*," in *A New Reader's Guide to African Literature*, eds. Hans M. Zell, Carol Bundy, and Virginia Coulon (New York: Holmes & Meier Publishers, 1983), 244.

[13]Bernth Lindfors, "The new David Maillu," *Kunapipi* 4, no. 1 (1982): 140.

[14]Lindfors, "The new David Maillu," 142.

breaking new ground in African fiction. Kadosa was the first Kenyan novel to explore the surreal mysteries of the occult."[15]

Karanja we Kang'ethe is an academic. In 1989 he wrote *Mission to Gehenna*, in which the protagonists, Kimuri and Keega, are (without explanation) transported to Gehenna, the domain of "Satan Lucifer," where they have a series of terrifying encounters. Gehenna is an allegory for Kenya in the late 1980s, and its central village, Ahera (Hades), is quite similar to Nairobi. "Satan is dictator in a land where cheating, corruption, and killing are commonplace; politicians are greedy, slums abound; religion is corrupt; and there are epidemic diseases (including AIDS) and employment problems."[16] *Mission to Gehenna* works as a straightforward horror narrative and as an allegory for contemporary Kenya, but as Anna Petkova-Mwangi notes, the novel also works as a Gothic: *Mission to Gehenna* has a Gothic setting (Satan Lucifer's very Gothically described castle-cum-palace-cum-mausoleum-cum-domicile), a Gothic atmosphere of mystery and suspense (described in Gothic terms), supernatural and mysteriously inexplicable events, overwrought emotions, two women modeled on the vampire women from *Dracula*, and even an intercalated poem.[17]

Libya

After the military coup which brought Muammar Gaddafi to power in 1969, authors were legally required to write in support of the government, with those who refused being imprisoned, deported, or forced to emigrate. This situation lasted until the early 1990s, when the censorship laws were loosened, allowing for a measure of literary renewal in Libya. Ibrahim Kuni is one of the best known of Libyan novelists, although his fame is limited to the Arab world. In 1990 he published *The Bleeding of the Stone*. A novel in which the desert is lovingly described and is as much a character as the protagonist, *The Bleeding of the Stone* is about Asouf, a Bedouin Muslim herdsman in the mountain desert of southern Libya. His parents both dead, Asouf lives alone, tending to his goats and avoiding other humans because of their capability for evil. Unfortunately, two Arab and one American hunters intrude on his world, eventually torturing him to find out where the sacred *waddan* (mouflon sheep) is hiding. Asouf becomes one with the *waddan*, transforming into it, and is slaughtered by the hunters. This killing fulfills an apocalyptic Tuareg prophesy about the end of the world: "I, the High Priest of Matkhandoush, prophesy, for the generations to come, that redemption will be at hand when the sacred waddan bleeds and the blood issues from the stone. It is then that the miracle will be born; that the earth

---

[15]Lindfors, "The new David Maillu," 141.

[16]John Roberts Kurtz, *Urban Obsessions, Urban Fears: The Postcolonial Kenyan Novel* (Trenton, NJ: Africa World Press, 1998), 102.

[17]Anna Petkova-Mwangi, "The Gothic Novel as an Avenue in Disguise for Political Protest: A Fresh Look at the Gothic From Its Origins to Its Appearance in Kenya," *The Nairobi Journal of Literature*, no. 7 (July 2013): 36-39.

will be cleansed and the deluge cover the desert."[18] One of the foremost works of Arab-language magic realism of the 1990s, *The Bleeding of the Stone* "intertwines the lives of Tuaregs (Tawariqs), jinn, and animals;"[19] its relevance to this work lies in the number of gruesomely violent scenes, including the crucifixion of Asouf, in the general degradation that outsiders, especially Westerners, bring to the desert and creatures that Asouf loves, and in the aforementioned apocalyptic ending. The finale of *The Bleeding of the Stone*, when Asouf is murdered by one of the Arabs (whose name is "Cain"), begins with the wailing of the female jinn and a darkness across the world as the sun is abruptly eclipsed. That the blood of Asouf transforms this finale into one of hope, as the prophesied, redeeming deluge finally arrives, does not diminish the power of the frightening aspects of the finale or the general tone of diminishment and degradation that pervades the novel.

Mauritania

Mauritania, under the rule of *juntas* and despots for the great majority of the 1970-2000 time period, had a low literacy rate and a literature which was controlled by the government and restricted by law. Nonetheless, the Arabic tradition of storytelling continued to manifest itself in a few Mauritanian authors. Moussa Ould Ebnou is one of those, his work in the 1990s establishing him as one of the most innovative writers in the world of Arabic letters. His *Barzakh (City of Winds*, 1993) features a protagonist, Vara, who is trapped in a cycle of death and rebirth, always finding himself in a new and different but still misery-laden situation. In each cycle there is a Westerner or Westerners who try to exploit and despoil the virgin land or a virgin planet, in the future using advanced technology as a means of slavery and evil.

> In the author's philosophy, humanity is unable to free itself from an inborn egocentric cruelty and a relentless will to acquire hegemony, riches, and power at the expense of the weaker majority. Even the introduction of the fantastic, in the figure of a beautiful jinn who strives to save the hero, provides no permanent solution and, in the end, cannot save the novel's protagonist.[20]

As Salma Khadra Jayyusi writes, *Barzakh* is a "potent satire on the assault of technology on a virgin African world and an elegy on the innocence of man soiled by greed and mighty technocratic powers. A symbolic novel engaging the fantastic, it relates the history of human avarice, corruption, injustice, violence, sinister technological hegemony, and above all the story

---

[18]Ibraham Kuni, *The Bleeding of the Stone* (Northampton, MA: Interlink Publishing Group, 2002), 135.

[19]Miriam Cooke, "Magical Realism in Libya," *Journal of Arabic Literature* 41, no. 1/2 (2010): 12.

[20]Salma Khadra Jayyusi, "Moussa Wuld Ibno: *City of Winds*," in *Modern Arabic Fiction*, ed. Salma Khadra Jayyusi (New York: Columbia University Press, 2005), 922.

of the death of the heart."[21] Moussa Ould Ebnou is a writer of great sophistication and style who deftly handles the more fantastic and science fictional moments while also emphasizing the horrific aspects of the novel and how the Westerners act upon indigenous peoples.

Mauritius

After independence in 1968, Mauritian literature went through a long phase in which the major concerns of Mauritian writers were topics like multiracialism, miscegenation, exoticism, racial and social conflicts, and coolitude. Mauritian popular literature during this time period, which ran more or less unabated to the end of the century, suffered, with the traditional Western divide between "high" and "low" literature becoming pronounced, and the contempt shown by "high" literature writers and publishers negative affecting the critical view of "low" novels and stories. "Low" Mauritian literature (a.k.a. popular Mauritian literature) demonstrated a mix of indigenous culture along with east African, Indian, and Chinese cultures. One example of popular Mauritian literature was C.S. Mahadoo's collection of five horror short stories, *Twilight Escapism* (1974). Mahadoo, a writer about whom nothing is known, wrote horror stories with titles like "The Lady of the Coffin," "The Grave-Diggers," and "Baboo Blagueur" (Baboo the Joker). The stories make use of indigenous, east African, and Indian myths to tell straightforward stories of horror that would not have been out of place in *Weird Tales*. *Twilight Escapism* did not spawn any sequels but did sell well, relative to Mauritian popular literature, and presumably was both an expression of local popular culture and influential on later Mauritian popular literature writers.

Nigeria

With independence in 1960 came the opportunity for Nigerian authors to write in Hausa and Igbo rather than just English, and to address issues such as corruption, racism, and imperialism/colonialism, rather than to write folklore-influenced narratives. The tendency, therefore, in Nigerian literature after independence and for most of the 1971-2000 period, was for Nigerian authors to write mimetic, realistic stories and novels rather than those taking part in *fantastika*. Nonetheless, there were some authors who mixed *fantastika* into their realistic writing, and created fear literature.

Elechi Amadi was a member of the Nigerian Army, an academic, and a writer of mimetic and genre fiction. Amadi's *The Great Ponds* (1973) is about a pair of eastern Nigerian villages who conduct a war over the fishing rights to the titular ponds. Decimated by their physical battles, they agree to abide by the judgment of the gods: if the great Chiolu warrior Olumba is alive at the end of the six months, the ponds will belong to the Chiolu; if Olumba dies, the ponds will belong to the Aliakoro. The war between the two villages becomes psychic and supernatural, with Olumba barely surviving but a dreadful sickness–the byproduct, everyone thinks, of the supernatural war–spreads through both villages and even to those villages several days' walk away. The Africans call this sickness "the wrath of Ogbunabuli," but Westerners know it as the

---

[21]Jayyusi, "Moussa Wuld Ibno," 31.

Influenza epidemic of 1918. Amadi's purpose in writing *The Great Ponds* was to demonstrate how "primitive" man dealt with a natural disaster, with herbs and magic and a strong attitude in the face of ignorance—much in the same way that Western medicine, with its prescriptions and medicine, dealt with it.

> In no other African novel has the reader the feeling of being so completely immersed in an ancient utterly non-European world. But it is Amadi's distinctive gift that his objective manner of telling the story without attempting to superimpose modern rationalizations, gives an air of inevitability, verisimilitude and even matter-of-factness to the characters' uncanny experiences, to their involvement with supernatural forces. Whatever the reader's own beliefs, Amadi's novels seem neither implausible, nor extraordinary nor even unrealistic—at least no more so than *Wuthering Heights* or *Moby Dick*.[22]

The horror in *The Great Ponds* comes from two sources: the physical and supernatural harms done to various characters by the war, which are eloquently described by Amadi, and by the mounting knowledge that the war is damaging everyone, so that there will be no easy recovery from it—and then the realization that the influenza epidemic is occurring, and the knowledge of just how many will die because of it.

Dillibe Onyeama is a Nigerian author of popular literature. Although he is perhaps best known for *Nigger at Eton* (1972), his autobiographical expose of the shocking racism at Eton in the 1960s, Onyeama also wrote a variety of occult and supernatural horror novels during the 1970s and 1980s, with titles like *Juju* (1976), *Secret Society* (1978), *Revenge of the Medicine Man* (1980), and *Godfathers of Voodoo* (1985). Onyeama's work will never be confused with art, but it succeeds finely at being readable and suitably frightening. His narratives are Nigeria-centric and incorporate substantial amounts of Igbo folklore and mythology, so that *Juju* is about a witch whose wicked nature and evil supernatural behavior manifest in her son, so that the witch's tormenting of the Igbo community lasts for over seventy years. *Secret Society* is about the secret society of the Leopard Men, who specialized in brutal attacks on the British colonizers as a means to protect the traditional Igbo way of life; they emerge in the 1970s in London to avenge the death of a young Igbo woman at the hands of a British hunter. *Revenge of the Medicine Man* depicts what happens when the titular magic-worker is crossed, and *Godfathers of Voodoo* explores in fictional form the ties between voodoo and Igbo beliefs and religion. Onyeama can be described as the Nigerian Dennis Wheatley—both tell tales of the occult, both were quite popular with Nigerian audiences, and both were moderately successful in writing entertaining fear literature.

Adaora Lily Ulasi was a journalist and writer best known for writing detective novels in English–a hitherto unknown tongue for Nigerian detective authors to write in. (Ulasi also–controversially for the time–used pidgin in her novels). Her *Who is Jonah?* (1978) is a hybrid detective/horror novel about the eponymous master thief, who uses black magic to commit

---

[22] Juliet Okonkwo, "Popular Urban Fiction and Cyprian Ekwensi," in *European-language Writing in Sub-Saharan Africa*, ed. Albert Gérard (Philadelphia, PA: John Benjamins Publishing, 1986), 713.

crimes and then to murder an ally who was about to inform on him. Jonah ultimately escapes capture and conviction through the invocation of supernatural powers. Jonah is the novel's anti-hero, but the scenes with the supernatural are frightening rather than reassuring.

Buchi Emechata was a writer who was best known for her works on the role of women in traditional African societies and in expatriate/immigrant societies, and for exploring the tensions between modernity and tradition. *The Rape of Shavi* (1983) is by critical consensus seen as her strongest work. *The Rape of Shavi* is about a group of Europeans whose plane crashes in an undiscovered African village on the edge of the Sahara, and the deleterious effects that the Europeans' presence and knowledge has on the residents of Shavi and Shavi itself. Shavi is an isolated, self-sufficient European utopia, but the Europeans perform literal and figurative rape in Shavi, and Shavi's prince flies to England and eventually returns with jeeps and guns and hitherto unseen aggressive plans to war on Shavi's neighbors. "The Fabian-socialist fabric of Shavi (an extended series of intertextual allusions to Shaw) collapses into militarism, aid-induced dependence, ecological disaster, and the wholesale rape of a culture. By the close the Shavians have seen enough of Western civilization to last forever, and retire into isolation."[23] While there is no supernatural material in *The Rape of Shavi*, the story of a utopia's degradation and destruction is horrific enough, and well-described by the author.

Ben Okri is a poet and novelist, generally considered one of Nigeria's foremost postmodernists and magic realists. He is best known for *The Famished Road* (1991), which won the Booker Prize. *The Famished Road* is about Azaro, an *abiku* or "spirit child" who has ties to the world of the supernatural. He has "boiling hallucinations" and can see the grotesque and invisible demons and witches who prey on his family and neighbors in their Nigerian ghetto community. Besides the residents of the phantasmagoric supernatural world, Azaro also sees the corruption, violence, and greed that possess the humans who wield power and influence over his community, and the squalor and violence that occur in his community. In *The Famished Road* Azaro's community, like mankind itself, is doomed to repeat the errors and mistakes of their past and to fight corruption and evil in each generation without ever achieving the moral and spiritual progress necessary to redeem the world. *The Famished Road* is magic realism (a label Okri himself objects to) of a distinctive sort, African in vocabulary, structure, humor, and lore rather than Central or South American. The novel is energetic, with potent imagery and a slowly mounting momentum. The novel is also disquieting and even horrific, not only because of the residents of the world of the supernatural, but because of the frightening violence and conditions of Azaro's ghetto.

Rwanda

Rwanda does not have a strong literary culture, but individual Rwandan writers began to make a name for themselves as writers in the years immediately before and after the genocide against the Tutsi in 1994. One such writer was Antoine M. Ruti, who in 1992 wrote *Affamez-les,*

---

[23] Judie Newman, "The Colonial Voice in the Motherland," in *Postcolonial Discourse and Changing Cultural Contexts: Theory and Criticism*, eds. Gita Rajan and Radhika Mohanram (Westport, CT: Greenwood, 1995), 53.

ils vous adoreront (*Starve them, they will adore you*), a dark, surrealistic, allegorical narrative of far-future science fiction. Set in the year 47947, in a peaceful civilization of mice and rats ruled by the universal muscat Macromyx XCVI the Elegant, *Affamez-les* describes (via its journalist rat narrator) the political and scientific issues of the past. In describing the past, the narrator describes the world of the humans, and portrays that world and the technological horrors it spawned in explicit, horrifying terms. *Affamez-les* features a "surrealist and anachronistic juxtaposition of historical facts and fictional elements"[24] along with a deliberately confused spatial universe (Babylon is on the edge of the Red Square in Moscow) and an almost gleeful portrayal of horrific technological actions and achievements.

Senegal

The revival of interest among Senegalese writers in the short story form led to a rise in Senegalese *fantastika*, usually in the form of narratives inspired by traditional myths and legends. Historian Amadou N'Diaye's *Assoka, ou les derniers jours de Koumbi* (*Assoka, or The Last Days of Koumbi*, 1973) is

> an elaborate epicohistorical novel with a complex action and a large cast, based on the legend of the serpent-fetish Wagadu. There is a splendidly horrific setting of sacred woods, witches' caves, hoaxed supernatural effects, melodramatic episodes of kidnapping, attempted rape, last-minute rescues, violent deaths, gladiatorial contests, and even an African version of the Trojan horse....[25]

In 1979 poet and novelist Nabil Ali Haïdar published *Silence cimetière!* (*Silence cemetery!*), a collection of short stories influenced by Edgar Allan Poe. The narratives have titles like "Mort d'une Femme" ("Death of a Woman"), "L'enfer, vous connaisez?" ("Hell, you understand?"), "La maison du diable" ("The House of the Devil"), and "La fête des morts" ("Party of the Corpses"), and are able combinations of Poe-like plot structures and writing style and Senegalese/west African environments.

Sierra Leone

Until the 1980s Sierra Leone's progress in the field of creative writing was slow compared to other West African countries. But during the 1980s Sierra Leonean authors began producing respectable works of fiction. One such was R. Sarif Easmon, a doctor, political agitator, and writer who in 1981 published *The Feud*, a collection of short stories with contemporary African and European settings and supernatural themes and elements. Story titles

---

[24] Désiré K. Wa Kabwe-Segatti, *Écriture de la jeunesse: mutations et syncrétismes (1990-1996)* (Paris: Éditions Publibook, 2011), 230.

[25] Blair, *Senegalese Literature*, 124-125.

include "The black Madonna," "The mad woman," and "Disenchantment," and are told in a contemporary European style with no other intent but to frighten the reader.

South Africa

Alone among the African nations covered in this work, South Africa was never colonized and never had to go through a decolonizing phase. However, the end of apartheid in 1991 led to the first universal suffrage elections in 1994, which resulted in a government of blacks rather than whites and a fundamental change in South African society. This change was reflected in the literature of South Africa, which quickly became more friendly to Zulu, Xhosa, and other native South African authors. However, the traditional South African literary contempt for popular literature remained in place, with works that smacked of genre being scorned. Despite this, South African writers, white and black, produced traditional South African horror, of the sort written by Leipoldt and Marais (see Chapter One), throughout the 1971-2000 period.

Anna M. Louw's *Vos* (1999) was a rare exception to the disdain by *literateurs* for genre work, as it was both shortlisted for the M-Net Prize and a Gothic modeled on the myth of Faust. *Vos* is about Hendrik Vos (an Afrikaans version of Heinrich Faust), a churchgoer and farmer in a drought-stricken part of northwest South Africa. Prayers for rain don't work, so Vos tells God that unless He sends rain, Vos will take matters into his own hands. He does so by making a deal with the devil ("Grootbass," the "Prince of this World") via a Bushman rainmaker. The rains come, but only for the area in which Vos has his farm, and though he is initially prosperous Vos suffers through a series of defeats, from his wife and son leaving him to disasters and plagues besetting the farm. Vos dies with less than he had before he made the deal with the Grootbass. The combination of Gothic elements (the harsh, wasted setting that functions as a character, the deal-with-the-devil), the Faust myth, and the indigenous elements combine to make *Vos* disquieting and thoroughly Afrikaans Gothic.

Chapter Twelve: The Americas

Argentina

Argentine literature went through a very dark period during the 1970s and early 1980s, as the "Dirty War," which began in 1974 and did not end until 1983, pitted the junta running the country against students, militants, trade union members, journalists, artists, and anyone suspected of having left-wing beliefs. Many Argentine writers went into exile or disappeared, others were forced to shield their opinions in allegorical terms. It was not until the 1990s that Argentine letters began to fully recover from the trauma of the Dirty War. During that decade Argentine writers continued to write works influenced by both previous Argentine writers and Continental writers like Sartre and Camus, and to emphasize urban and social disarray as a primary concern. Argentine horror of the period continued to be incorporated into works of High literature, with horror effects being vehicles for conveying emotions and themes rather than being the point of the narratives, as in Low literature.

Luisa Valenzuela was a journalist, short story writer, and novelist best known for her experimental style and the feminist themes in her work. Another recurring theme in her work is fear, specifically the "subtle transition from individual fear (forged from archetypal childhood fears, vacillating, ambiguously, between fear and cowardice) to collective terror, lived out like a nightmare."[1] This transition, which is always expressed in disquieting and unsettling terms, is a leitmotif throughout much of Valenzuela's work. *El gato eficaz* (*The effective cat*, 1972), in which the female narrator, Pandora-like, allows all the evils of the world, in the form of "black cats of death," to escape from confinement, while she expresses a strong protest against the waste and corruption of the male-center world. In narratives like "Aqui pasan cosas raras" ("Weird things happen here," 1975) and *Realidad nacional desde la cama* (*National reality from the bed*, 1990) fear, and the "dark forces of violence," are constant companions to the narrators in Buenos Aires and New York City. In *Cola de lagartija* (*The lizard's tail*, 1983), "a kind of double allegory on the obsessive, egocentric empire of Jose López Rega, the influential welfare minister of Isabel Peron's government,"[2] the protagonist Sorcerer becomes psychopathic in the wielding of his power, just like López Rega did, with the resulting devastation of the people, expressed in surrealistic terms.

Ernesto Sabato's *Abbadón, el exterminador* (1974) is an experimental novel, partially autobiographical, with a fragmented plot and a circular structure. Roughly, it is about a writer named Sabato who in 1973 Buenos Aires interacts with various characters from previous novels by Sabato and who becomes a four foot tall bat, which may or may not be the titular "Angel of Darkness." *Abbadón* is thematically about the struggle between good and evil, and has an apocalyptic tone. Horror elements include Sabato's increasing paranoia, witchcraft, torture, demons, Kafkaesque transformations, and the secret society the Sect of the Blind who persecute

---

[1]Fernando Ainsa and Djelal Kadir, "Journey to Luisa Valenzuela's Land of Fear," *World Literature Today*, 69, no. 4 (Autumn, 1995): 683.

[2]Ainsa and Kadir, "Journey to Luisa Valenzuela's Land of Fear," 686.

Sabato. Generally, *Abbadón* is a nightmarish, haunting, phantasmagoric narrative filled with horrifying imagery and events. "If this destabilizing experience is intended to engage the hapless reader in an...infernal phantasmagoria that also seems to be...Sabato's only possible response to what was by 1974 the ever-darkening tunnel of Argentine reality, it succeeds very well."[3]

Mempo Giardinelli was an academic and author of novels, short story collections, and essay collections. Giardinelli's *Luna Caliente* (1983) is ostensibly a thriller about a young Argentine man who becomes obsessed with the thirteen-year-old daughter of a friend. The man, Ramiro, rapes and then kills the daughter and later kills her father, but when the police investigate the father's murder the daughter, Araceli, appears, both alive and willing to provide an alibi for Ramiro. Later, Ramiro kills Araceli again, on account of her brazen sexuality, and flees to Paraguay. The novel ends when the hotel desk clerk calls to inform him that Araceli, come back from the dead yet again, is looking for him. Though initially marketed as a thriller, and a best-seller on its initial release, *Luna Caliente* is in fact several different types of novel: an allegory of the Argentine political climate during the Dirty War; a *novela negra*, or hard-boiled crime novel; a *noir* mystery; a Gothic; and a political thriller. Giardinelli is a skilled storyteller, a master of prose, and *Luna Caliente* is, in the advertising phrase, a "page-turner," but it is also a work of increasing paranoia and mental instability with a mounting sense of doom and a *noir* undercurrent of the inescapability of the protagonist's fate. "*Luna Caliente*, in its use of devices such as melodrama, coincidence, suspense and the supernatural derived from narratives of popular culture, is a good example of the more immediate appeal of the post-Boom novel as distinct from its rather erudite forbear, the Boom novel."[4]

Humberto Constantini was a Jewish Argentine writer, poet, and dramatist, who in the 1970s and 1980s was known critically as one of Latin America's most important contemporary writers. In 1979, in exile in Mexico, he published *De dioses, hombrecitos y policias* (*Of gods, little men, and the police*), and 1985, finally back in Argentina, he published *La larga noche de Francisco Sanctis* (*The long night of Francisco Sanctis*). *La larga noche de Francisco Sanctis* is about the titular protagonist being faced with a choice: he receives a message that two men will be taken by government agents and become *desaparecidos* ("the disappeared"), Sanctis—a former revolutionary, now a comfortable burgher—must decide if it's worth it to do the moral, and very dangerous, thing and warn the men. *De dioses, hombrecitos y policias* is about a poetry club (of poetasters) targeted for death by a right-wing Argentine government death squad. The would-be poets are saved by the intervention of the Olympian gods, and twelve other innocents are massacred instead. Both works address recent Argentine history and the Dirty War, and each narrative is full of tension and terror, albeit in quite different ways. *La larga noche* lacks any *fantastika* or supernatural elements, and is simply about a moral choice that Francisco Sanctis is forced to make, with extremely dire consequences for him if he does the moral and good thing. Any Argentine, and anyone who has ever lived in fear of authorities, would be chilled thinking

---

[3] Allen Josephs, "Abbadón, el exterminador," *New York Times Book Review*, Dec. 29, 1991, 13.

[4] Stephen M. Hart, *A Companion to Latin American Literature* (Rochester, NY: Tamesis, 2007), 254.

about the consequences of Sanctis' choice—either the two men are kidnapped and killed by the government agents, or Sanctis puts himself at risk of being their replacement. *De dioses*, conversely, has a baseline of horror—the same prospect of becoming *desaparecidos*—but adds *fantastika* to the novel, in the form of the Greek gods, who add elements of black comedy while also demonstrating themselves, frighteningly, to be helpless in the face of what the government is doing. *La larga noche* is tragicomic, but earnest in depicting the moral decision Sanctis has to make and finally does. *De dioses* is ironic, subtle, formally inventive, and chilling in its depiction of evil being not intentional malice but ill-will allowed to grow to monstrous size.

Brazil

The 1970s saw a change in Brazilian literature, with a shift away from narratives about rural life and toward narratives about urban life and contemporary issues, including racism, the environment, political corruption, and urban violence and crime. Brazilian horror literature continued to be produced as High Art, in which the horror effect was not the primary goal of the writer, and as Low Art, in Gothics (usually written by women) and in *cordel* literature, the Brazilian equivalent of dime novels and pulps.

Lya Luft is a writer, translator, and academic, and from the 1980s forward was seen by critics as one of Brazil's most important contemporary writers. Most of her work is in the Gothic vein—her narratives often have an "atmosphere of sexual fear and uncertainty surrounding her protagonists, whose dramas unfold in the claustrophobic space of the patriarchal home."[5] Her narratives have restrictive spaces and time frames, and her protagonists are usually haunted by an "other" presence, whether a ghost, a grandmother in the attic, or a dwarf gnome. Luft's narratives have multiple levels of reality, open-ending and ambiguous or circular endings which lack resolution and do not answer the questions the story prompts from the readers. As Giovanni Pontiero, translator of Luft's *The Red House*, puts it, in a statement that applies to most of Luft's work, "Morbid realities and humiliating discoveries are expressed with disarming honesty and vigor. Lya Luft's perceptions about existence and its traumas are articulated with chilling frankness."[6] When the supernatural arises in her novels, it is dealt with in a casual and offhand way, allowing Luft to foreground her female protagonists' struggle for self-definition.

A writer who was often compared with Luft was Lygia Fagundes Telles, a novelist and short story writer who began publishing in the 1950s but reached her maturity as a writer in the 1970s.

In both Telles's and Luft's fiction the reader often finds a gap between the expected, common logic and the characters' actual lives, and feels, along with the characters, the

---

[5]Darlene J. Sadlier, "Lya Luft," in *One Hundred Years After Tomorrow: Brazilian Women's Fiction of the 20th Century*, ed. Darlene J. Sadlier (Bloomington, IN: Indiana University Press, 1992), 215.

[6]Giovanni Pontiero, "Translator's Note," in *The Red House* (Manchester, UK: Carcanet Publishing, 1994), iv.

ambiguity caused by the merging of two worlds–'that of the real and that of the fantastic' (Todorov 26) Their novelistic works are characterized by a probing into the lives of middle-class women, constituting a study of the female subject in her relations with the Other within the context of Brazilian society–a society that continues to be inherently patriarchal, in spite of some relative freedoms that women from the upper classes have achieved…a recurrent theme in Telles's and in Luft's novels is precisely the decadence of the bourgeois order and, within it, the decadence of the family institutions. It is the conflict between the characters' desires and aspirations, on one hand, and the demands and obstacles still imposed by the social order, on the other hand, that originates the ambiguity and absurdity highlighted by the use of the fantastic and the gothic, or metaphorized through the use of the grotesque. The fantastic, the gothic and the grotesque constitute thus strategies of estrangement which will lead to the revelation, in the lives of these otherwise ordinary women, the ruling of a different logic, or the lack of any logic altogether. In this respect, their novels can be seen as Kafkaesque narratives, in that the everyday, ordinary middle-class lives of the protagonists are revealed to obey an absurd order.[7]

Telles is primarily a writer of psychological stories, emphasizing the personalities of her female protagonists and their relationships with their families. Her characters are usually alone, and experience misunderstanding, conflict, disillusionment, deceit, fear, death, and fantasy, with conflicts not being happily resolved and the narrative tension not being relieved. It is in her short stories that she most makes use of the supernatural and the surreal, with shifting realities being a norm. Occasionally she uses surreal elements as an allegory against the oppressive Brazilian government. Often the atmosphere of her short stories is dreamlike, nightmarish, or hallucinatory.

Murilo Rubião, by day a government employee, was a writer who restricted himself entirely to short fiction. He is commonly credited with having introduced magic realism into Brazilian literature. Although he began writing in the 1940s, it wasn't until the 1970s that he achieved fame and prominence in the world of Brazilian letters. Rubião's work was notable for its magic realism, in which the fantastic does not break from reality but instead peacefully co-exists with realist narrative elements. A political writer, his narratives worked on both the literal and the allegorical level and are often pointed commentaries on the state of the Brazilian government and contemporary life in Brazil. His stories, from the 1940s through to his death in 1991, used magic realism as well as elements from science fiction and absurdist fiction. Whether focusing on human abnormalities and madness, as in some of his earliest work, or on more fantastic elements like werewolves, dragons, magic, and magicians, Rubião skillfully mixed reality and the supernatural and fantastic, creating *contes cruel* and weird tales with equal aplomb. Rubião was often more intent on dazzling his readers than in frightening them, but his stories deal with real human emotions and are often baffling and unnerving.

---

[7]Cristina Ferreira-Pinto, "The Fantastic, the Gothic, and the Grotesque in Contemporary Brazilian Women's Novels," *Chasqui* 25, no. 2 (1996): 72-73

Ignácio de Loyola Brandão was a journalist, scriptwriter, and mainstream novelist who is nonetheless best known for his dystopias *Zero* (1974), *Não Verás País Nenhum* (*No country*, 1981), and *And Still the Earth* (1981). Although the novels themselves have experimental elements and structurally are playfully postmodern, their content is grim and chilling. In *Zero*, which Brandão set in a nameless country in "Latindia America," is about an ordinary man whose life becomes a nightmare thanks to the police, who torture him, and thanks to a witch-led group of cannibals, who kill the protagonist's wife in a cannibalistic rite held in the middle of a *macumba*. In *Não Verás País Nenhum* the protagonist, an average man who works as a clerk, abruptly loses all his rights and is thrown from his ordinary urban life into "the unstable world of the underclasses, that include mutants and homeless people, wandering in an environmentally damaged world."[8] In *And Still the Earth* São Paulo is an overpopulated city wracked by constant battles between criminals and police, in which the protagonist, a blacklisted former history professor, describes the devastated natural environment and Orwellian government for the reader. *Zero* is "overwhelming in its relentless description of how the police, the army and the special repressive forces collaborate to torture, rape, castrate or kill anyone foolish enough to denounce or oppose them."[9] *Não Verás País Nenhum* coldly describes "some side effects of the dictatorship— the rising of that technocratic class, police brutality, bureaucratic arbitrary acts,"[10] and so on. *And Still the Earth* is a

> terribly intimate image of Brazil in the not-so-distant future...our receptive good will is pummeled by a vision of mental and physical deprivation. We learn that we are glimpsing the aftermath of the "Corte Final," the highly-publicized felling of the last tree in the Amazon forest and the consequent depletion of the water table. Streams and rivers have dried up, and the Amazon has become a desert where the jet-set spends weekends dressed as Arabs. The sea is polluted, the beaches fenced off. Under the "Regime de Poupança para Evitar Recessão," Souza and his wife are assigned a "Dia de Consumação" (the Sabbath?) on which they must spend a specific amount of money or have their food and water rations suspended.[11]

---

[8] Roberto de Sousa Causo, "Science Fiction During the Brazilian Dictatorship," *Extrapolation* 39, no. 4 (1998): 317.

[9] E. Rodríguez Monegal, "Writing Fiction Under the Censor's Eye," *World Literature Today* 53, no. 1 (Winter, 1979): 20.

[10] De Sousa Causo, "Science Fiction During the Brazilian Dictatorship," 317.

[11] Kenneth Krabbenhoft, "Ignácio de Loyola Brandão and the Fiction of Cognitive Estrangement," *Luso-Brazilian Review* 24, no. 1 (Summer, 1987): 37.

The cumulative effect of the novels is not just cognitive estrangement but a horror–as a critic wrote of *And Still the Earth* in the *New York Times*, "the conditions he describes and the grim future he foresees for his city may also await Lagos, Calcutta, Shanghai and Mexico City."[12]

> In this refiguration in pieces, in agony, of characters, portraits and narrators in recent Brazilian cultural production, there seems to be a combination of dialog with the corporeal fragmentation characteristic of modern art, and with one of its artistic pastiches, the Guignol; with the torture, executions, banishment and political experience of the 1970s, and with the increase of violent crime, including that committed by public security forces in Brazil during the 1980s and 1990s. Attention must, however, be paid to the fact that, in these attempts at bloody identification of fictional subjects, the exposure of these subjects is not anchored to subjective idealizations, to cohesive corporeal images, that the very process of figuration and subjectivization involves a kind of non-disposable awareness of instability, an obligatory concomitant impulse for defiguration, for the guignolization.[13]

For example, Nelson de Oliveira's short stories, such as in his collection *Naquela época tínhamos um gato* (*At that time we had a cat*, 1998), are

> full of "animals from the strangest places", "imprisoned creatures", haunted figures, people "moving against their own feet", sleepwalkers, cannibals, "primitive-mannered and malformed" people, "more beast than man", monsters at times hideous which, however, devote themselves to the most trivial of things - to telephone calls, checks, accounting, everyday things. In a kind of particularly perverse hybridization between everyday life and the bestial, between perversity and victimization, paralysis and annihilation.[14]

More popular and commercial horror was not necessarily as artistically successful. A typical work of this sort was Carlos Orsi Martinho and Miguel Carqueija's *Medo, mistério e morte* (*Fear, mystery, and death*, 1996), a collection of Lovecraftian pastiches. There are the usual ancient races, cosmic horrors, mysterious old books capable of raising the dead, and spells to summon unfathomable monsters. But Martinho and Carqueija are "able to convert the Lovecraftian excesses to the Brazilian reality, surrounding them with indigenous allusions or

---

[12]Larry Rohter, "Paperbacks; Life Under the Militechs," *New York Times,* Sept. 29, 1985, A38.

[13]Flora Süssekind, "Deterritorialization and Literary Form: Brazilian Contemporary Literature and Urban Experience," Working Paper Series, University of Oxford Centre for Brazilian Studies, June, 2002, 12.

[14]Süssekind, "Deterritorialization and Literary Form," 13.

football or New Age cults, but almost always their language sounds out of tune and their effects cheap."[15]

The "Brazilian Anne Rice" is Heloisa Seixas, who debuted in 1995 and in 1996 published her first novel, *A porta* (*The door*). The man character, Helena, meets a mysterious man during an orgy in Rio de Janeiro. He's a vampire, and he lures her into a world of sexual domination and eschatology. "As with most of the short fiction of Seixas, the themes of female submissiveness and sexual slavery are important. Prosy and pompous, full of convoluted phrases of ambitious images that are exhausted in some obliterated metaphor."[16]

Chile

Chilean literature during the 1971-2000 era was largely influenced by the dictatorship of General Augusto Pinochet (1973-1990), both during and afterwards. During the dictatorship most writers chose exile, and wrote and published in other countries, usually attempting raise awareness of the plight of Chile. After the dictatorship Chilean writers attempted to process the trauma of the dictatorship through the act of writing. What horror was published appeared either before Pinochet seized power, as with José Donoso's *El obsceno pájaro de la noche* (see below), or from abroad, as with the work of Isabel Allende.

Donoso was a short story writer and novelist who was best known for *El obsceno pájaro de la noche* (*The Obscene Bird of Night*, 1970). *El obsceno pájaro* is about an unsuccessful writer who is hired to be the tutor of the only child of a decaying aristocratic family. The child is deformed and is surrounded by those also deformed or suffering from birth defects. Eventually the writer flees to a convent, where he undergoes a series of transformations before being burned to ashes. A nightmarish magic realist novel that incorporates Chilean myth, including that of the magically warped infant known as the *invunche*, *El obsceno pájaro* was initially viewed as an indescribable masterpiece, with one critic asking, "How do you review a dream?"[17] As time passed *El obsceno pájaro* became viewed by critics as one of the best novels of the "Latin American Boom." As a reading experience *El obsceno pájaro* is a deeply disquieting one–because of the way past and present recklessly intermingle, because of the numerous transformations, and because of the increasing sense the reader gets that the novel is the narrative of a schizophrenic mind slowly retreating from reality into a world in which his perceptions are ones of fantasy, fears, and resentments–as Wolfgang Luchting writes, "the whole novel strikes

---

[15]De Sousa Causo, *Ficção científica*, 110.

[16]De Sousa Causo, *Ficção científica*, 112.

[17]Wolfgang Luchting, "Review: *El obsceno pájaro de la noche*," *Books Abroad* 46, no. 1 (Winter, 1972): 82.

one as the delirium of a physical and metaphysical hypochondriac, almost a schizophrenic."[18] Indeed, as Michael Ryan wrote, reading *El obsceno pájaro* is a "descent into hell."[19]

Colombia

Colombian authors contributed significantly to the "Latin American Boom," but once the boom ended a new generation of authors arose, the "Disillusioned Generation," so-called because of the failure of the National Front regime (1958-1974) and the violence that followed it.

The foremost Colombian author of the Disillusioned Generation–and according to critical consensus the foremost author in the history of the country–was Gabriel García Márquez. Although best known for magic realism works–he popularized the genre worldwide via *Cien anos de soledad* (*One Hundred Years of Solitude*, 1967)–he occasionally wrote works with horror elements or which were entirely horror, as in "Espantos de Agosto" ("The Ghosts of August," 1992). "Espantos de Agosto" is about a family of four who make the mistake of staying overnight in a castle reportedly haunted by the builder of the castle–the family discovers to their terror that the ghost is in fact real. The story has no tension, relying upon the sudden change of pace and tone in the last paragraph to shock and frighten the reader. In a sense the story is not far from the stories of M.R. James, with a mundane reality abruptly intruded upon by the supernatural, although James was the superior of the two at writing ghost stories; García Márquez, perhaps because of his extensive experience writing magic realist narratives, is good at description but not so much at adding the ingredients that make up great fear literature.

Fanny Buitrago was an award-winning playwright and author of prolific output and a high level of quality. Her work is generally apolitical but addresses themes like broken homes and disrupted families, elements which can be metaphorically applied to Colombia as a whole. Her *La otre gente* (*Other people*, 1973) is a collection of short stories featuring ghosts, family curses, abused and abandoned children, and mistreated wives. As Teresa Arrington says, despite the seriousness of the subject matter, "many of the selections in *La otre gente* could be classified as horror stories,"[20] for the appearance of ghosts inevitably foretells doom and narratives about mothers and children devolve into the mother viewing her daughter as a demonic entity sent to intrude on the mother's shaky marriage.

Costa Rica

Rafael Ángel Herra is in some ways representative of Costa Rican popular authors of the 1971-2000 period. Ángel Herra, an academic, novelist, short story writer, poet, and essayist, has

---

[18]Luchting, "Review," 83.

[19]Michael Ryan, "Circuses and Mythologies: Latin American Fiction," *The North American Review* 258, no. 3 (Fall, 1973): 75.

[20]Teresa R. Arrington, "Fanny Buitrago," in *Spanish American Women Writers: A Bio-Bibliograpical Source Book*, ed. Diane E. Marting (Westport, CT: Greenwood Press, 1990), 67.

made the monster one of the central figures of both his fiction and his non-fiction. Like other Costa Rican horror writers of the period, he samples freely from all manner of frightening creatures: "golems, superhumans, personifications of evil, genetic codes, chemical inventions or runaway artificial brains, aliens and alien invaders."[21] But unlike most other Costa Rican writers of fear literature, Ángel Herra writes from a psychoanalytical basis, "which sees the monster, not as an external creation to its creator, less as something with its own existence, but as a kind of projection."[22] He writes in a variety of modes. His short stories range from traditional horror to postmodern horror-humor, while his *La guerra prodigiosa* (1986) is an allegory, full of *fantastika* elements, in which wandering anchorites struggle with ethical and philosophical dilemmas, including the Devil itself.

Cuba

Despite the presence of a dictatorship and the economic privation brought about by the American economic isolation of Cuba, Cuban literature during the 1971-2000 period was rich, with numerous authors producing outstanding work, including genre narratives.

Jose Sanchez-Boudy wrote prolifically, in a variety of genres, including reference books, becoming one of the best known Cuban exile authors. In 1971 he published *Cuentos a luna llena*, the third of three volumes of short stories which had nothing to do with the Cuban Revolution or exile, but rather was a collection of horror stories modeled on the work of Edgar Allan Poe. The stories usually rely on twist endings and protagonists with aberrant psychologies, and are well-told and short, usually not more than three to five pages in length.

Antonio Benitez-Rojo was a novelist, short story writer, and essayist who became an academic in exile, won awards for his novels and stories, and eventually became regarded by critics as the most significant Cuban author of his time. His stories fall into two categories: one dealing with the history of the Caribbean countries, and second dealing addressing the crumbling position of the bourgeoisie in the aftermath of the Cuban Revolution. The former stories have their own kinds of horror, from slave trading to invasions to mutinies and murders, but it is in the latter stories that he wrote *fantastika*, usually under the influence of Poe, Hearn, Quiroga, Borges, or Cortázar, but also, in his earlier work, under the influence of magic realist authors. Benitez-Rojo was a vivid writer who wrote potent stories of the bourgeoisie simultaneously tormented by realistic (social and economic) pressures and by supernatural pressures, including malign voodoo *loa* and cursed inheritances. At times absurd or comical in their depiction of bumbling members of the middle class, Benitez-Rojo's stories usually have an underlying darkness from which disquiet and horror spring.

Daina Chaviano is a writer of both *fantastika* and mainstream literature. Before 1991, the great majority of her work was science fiction and fantasy. As a science fiction writer she

---

[21]Néstor Braunstein, "Palabras Preliminares," in *Lo monstruoso y lo bello*, ed. Rafael Ángel Herra (San Pedro, Costa Rica: Editorial de la Universidad de Costa Rica, 1988), 12.

[22]José Ricardo Chaves, "Monstruos Fantásticos en la Literatura Costarricense," *Filología y Lingüística* 42 (2016): 87.

established herself as one of the three most important female science fiction writers in all of the Spanish-speaking countries of the Americas. However, after 1991, when she emigrated to the United States, she began writing mainstream literature. In 1998 and 1999, though, she wrote a tetralogy, *La Habana oculta* (*The occult side of Havana*), in which Havana serves as the point of departure for trips into other dimensions. The second novel in the series, *Casa de Juegos* (*House of Games*, 1998), is about a young woman, Gaia, who is led by a mysterious woman into a mansion where everything, matter and energy, is in a state of constant movement and change.

> Feeling that she must embrace this frightening environment as a path to self-knowledge, she returns again and again to this world of bewildering rituals where gods appear in human form and humans assume temporarily the guise of deities. The fantastic, supernatural element in this book is provided by the orishas, the spirits of the Afro-Cuban practice of Santeria. With its underlying foundation of fantasy and imagery drawn from virtual reality scenarios, the *House of Games* functions as a post-modernist version of the archetypal narrative of the search for the self.[23]

In the description of the house the influence of Poe and Lovecraft—two of Chaviano's favorite authors—can be seen.

Esther Díaz Llanillo was a writer, essayist, and librarian, most of whose work deals with the fantastic in one form or another. Her *Cuentos antes y después del sueño* (*Tales before and after sleep*, 1999) was a collection of short stories which, in the style of M.R. James, creates normal environments and routines for the stories' protagonists, only to have the uncanny and sinister intrude on those environments and routines, changing them utterly. Her stories can be Kafkaesque or *contes cruel*, and often emphasize environment over plot, but they are psychologically acute, filled with gallows humor and cruelty and strong symbolism.

Ecuador

Ecuadorian literature in the 1971-2000 time period featured a new generation of authors, post-Guayaquil Group, who brought new, more contemporary concerns to the Ecuadorian novel, but also showed some element of self-referentiality as well as the effect of the oil boom and the rise in the numbers of the urban poor. Toward the end of the century authors began moving away from social realism toward *fantastika*, although many of those works were allegories or addressed political and ecological concerns.

Demetrio Aguilera Malta played many roles in his lifetime: writer, playwright, film director, teacher, painter, diplomat, and war correspondent during the Spanish Civil War. He was a member of the Guayaquil Group, but it was in the 1970-2000 time period that he published his best work, beginning with *Siete lunas y seite serpientes* (see Chapter Seven). His post-*Siete lunas* work returned to the Guayas River region of western Ecuador, but accompanying the island milieu and the poverty-stricken *cholos* were substantial elements of magic realism. Aguilera

---

[23]Lizabeth Paravisini-Gebert, "Unchained Tales: Women Prose Writers from the Hispanic Caribbean in the 1990s," *Bulletin of Latin American Research* 22, no. 4 (Oct. 2003): 449.

Malta's narratives became about clashes between good and evil, with the forces of good represented by liberation theology Christianity, scientific enlightenment, and nostalgia for a possibly fictional pre-Conquest paradise, and the forces of good being portrayed by the military, politicians, the oligarchy, and the Church. His post-1970 novels are "stylistically sophisticated and structurally complex,"[24] and "influenced by the technical innovations and success of the writers of the Boom in Latin American fiction."[25] Horror elements come from the evoking of sinister environments, omen-laden atmospheres, and sometimes-cartoonish horror elements, such as the robot dictator of *El secuestro del general* (1973) who has an army of gorillas who he uses to crush any opposition to his reign.

El Salvador

The 1971-2000 period were largely ones of stagnancy and danger for the world of El Salvadoran letters, as the lethargy of the 1970s was replaced by peril and instability during the Salvadoran Civil War (1979-1992), when the military dictatorship targeted a number of leftist writers and forced others to flee the country.

Roberto Armijo was a lyrical poet, considered by critics to be the "voice of Chalatenango," the rural province in which he was born, and to be one of the foremost Salvadoran poets of the 1960s and 1970s. In 1970 he published a play, *Jugando a la gallina ciega* (*Playing the blind hen*), a horror narrative about two couples, one old and one young. The young couple set out to try to rebel against a decadent society and its Orwellian government and are ultimately destroyed by it, emphasizing the theme of the play, that life is only a game in society and that playing the game is the only way that one can survive. The old couple, both men, watch the young couple on behalf of the government and resort to increasingly outlandish and grotesque games of imagination and fantasy as a way to survive their guilt at what they do. *Jugando a la gallina ciega* is ultimately a pessimistic and horrifying play–pessimistic about the role of the individual in modern society, and horrifying for the way that the government goes about destroying the young couple.

The writer, poet, academic, and painter known as "Salarrué" produced the largest and most complex corpus of work in Salvadoran literature. He is best known for his academic essays and his short stories, both those for children, which tend to portray life in rural El Salvador in idealized and romanticized fashion, and for adults, whose elements of *fantastika* anticipate aspects of magic realism. His final novel, *Catleya luna* (1974), addresses the events of the Salvadoran government's "anti-communist" purge of 1932, which resulted in the massacre of between 10,000 and 40,000 indigenous peasants. *Catleya luna*, like Salarrué's earlier collection of stories, *Cuentos de Barro* (*Stories of mud*, 1933), is told in a unique style and an inventive use of language—popular speech mixed with *nahuatismos* (the vocabulary of the Nahua natives of El Salvador)—so as to escape the government censors. Its horror lies in its use of numerous occult

---

[24] C. Michael Waag, "Demetrio Aguilera Malta 1909-1981," in *Encyclopedia of Latin American Literature*, ed. Verity Smith (Chicago, IL: Fitzroy Dearborn, 1997), 26.

[25] Waag, "Demetrio Aguilera Malta," 27.

elements, in peasant ritual dances and elsewhere, and in the unblinking description of the slaughtering of the native peasants.

Manlio Argueta was a novelist and critic. His third novel, *Un dia en la vida* (*A day in the life*, 1980), deals–like Salarrué's *Catleya luna*–with the 1932 peasant massacre. Argueta, however, chooses a more straightforward narrative style in which to tell the tale, letting the voice of the native peasants carry the story. At the same time, though, *Un die en la vida* is a magic realist novel with substantial horror elements:

> as the peasants' ancestral gods fill the sky with bloody wounds in angry response to the bloodbath in the countryside below. Ghosts and gremlins materialise before Lupe's eyes and a mixture of pagan and Catholic superstition shapes her vision of life. In this case, however, the spirit of magic is overwhelmed by the sheer horror of human reality as conveyed by such images of children eaten from within by worms that have been expelled through their noses and mouths, and a naked priest lying on a road with a stick up his anus.[26]

Published not long before the civil war of the 1980s was to begin, *Un dia en la vida* "can now be interpreted as a lugubrious prophesy of the orgy of violence that was soon to descend upon the country."[27]

Guatemala

The long Guatemalan civil war (1960-1996) affected all levels of Guatemalan society, including the world of Guatemalan letters. Guatemalan writers created two new modes of expression to deal with the violence, torture, and fear in Guatemala during war: the *testimonio*, first- and second-hand accounts of the torture and violence perpetrated by the government forces, and the "new novel," intelligently postmodern novels which employ diverse narrative techniques and discourses. Guatemalan popular literature was largely absent, and what existed was strictly controlled by the government.

Rodrigo Rey Rosa was one of the most prolific and acclaimed Guatemalan novelists of the 1971-2000 time period. His *El cuchillo del mendigo* (*The beggar's knife*, 1985) is a collection of short stories, most of which deal with the supernatural—ghosts and witchcraft and supernatural assassins and the like. *El cuchillo* reads like horror fiction told in simple and unadorned prose, but part of Rey Rosa's skill is his ability to conceal gravely serious subject matters beneath conventional plots and language. In the case of *El cuchillo*, the stories address the ever-present fear in Guatemalan society during the civil war. *El cuchillo* is horror fiction in which the supernatural is used to create an aura of the sinister and the uncertain; "destabilizing the boundaries between the real and the unreal, the certain and the uncertain, Rey Rosa is able to

---

[26] Roy C. Boland, "Manlio Argueta 1935-," in *Encyclopedia of Latin American Literature*, ed. Verity Smith (London: Fitzroy Dearborn, 1997), 128.

[27] Boland, "Manlio Argueta," 128.

repeat—to recreate—the spectral fear of torture."[28] Influenced by his mentor Paul Bowles and by a close reading of the work of Borges, Rey Rosa creates in *El cuchillo* intense, sinister, and macabre tales based on indigenous folklore.

Rey Rosa's tales seemed eager to capture "the possible activity of the unconscious", in the author's own words, uncanny events that occurred on the boundary between dreams and reality. However, given Guatemala's sociopolitical reality at the time, the tales were plagued by acts of vengeance, threats of parricide, nightmares and violent deaths. The narratives, "like the tricks of a magician", were a mixture of the magical and the perverse.[29]

Guyana

As in a number of other Central and Southern American nations during the 1971-2000 period, an autocratic government and its negative effects on the Guyanese economy and culture left Guyanese letters in a fragile state for much of the time period, although there were a number of notable and productive Guyanese writers, both at home and abroad.

Roy A.K. Heath was probably the most internationally famous Guyanese writer of the time period. His work won awards, and his *The Shadow Bride* (1991) was short-listed for the Booker Prize. His work is a combination of traditional social realism with local folklore and myths, including native religion and *obeah*, emphasizing and dramatizing the mundane, every day lives of the Guyanese poor and the lower middle class. While characterization was never one of Heath's strengths, and his style only developed a vitality and effectiveness later in his career, Heath was good at describing the perspectives of his characters, the diversity of Guyanese life, and the local environment and social milieu. Heath's narratives are not celebrations of Guyanese life and peoples, however; they are more concerned with the inadequacies and failures of his characters and the communities he portrays. Many of his protagonists are "diminished characters, derided and victimized by large, anonymous forces that they do not understand."[30] The horror in his work comes from the cruel circumstances, societal or familial or matrimonial, in which his characters are stuck, the psychologically disturbed personalities which emerge from those circumstances, and from the Edgar Mittelholzer-like use of the supernatural, creating sinister environments in which sorcery and curses have ill effects. Heath's novels *Kwaku* (1982) and *The Ministry of Hope* (1996) are altogether lighter in their use of the supernatural, telling the story of an Ananse-like trickster's adventures and ultimate self-knowledge and redemption.

---

[28]William Jarrod Brown, "Specters of the Unspeakable: The Rhetoric of Torture in Guatemalan Literature, 1975-1985" (PhD diss., University of Kentucky, 2012), 190.

[29]Ronald Flores, "The Enigmatic Drifter," *Latin American Review of Books*, last modified March 29, 2008, http://www.latamrob.com/the-enigmatic-drifter/.

[30]Mark McWatt, "Heath, Roy A.K. (1926--)," in *The Encyclopedia of Post-Colonial Literatures in English*, eds. Eugene Benson and L.W. Conolly (London: Routledge, 2005), 642.

Mexico

Mexican literature during the 1971-2000 period was largely dominated by the surrealism and existentialism of Octavio Paz and the literary magazine he founded and published, *Vuelta*. But the world of Mexican letters was a productive and energetic one during those years, with a number of works of High Art horror emerging during the time period. It was not until the late 1990s that genre horror began appearing in Mexican novels.

Carlos Montemayor was a novelist, poet, critic, and promoter of contemporary indigenous literature. His *Las llaves de Urgell* (*The keys of Urgell*, 1971) is an experimental novel consisting of nineteen stories and prose-poems. *Las llaves'* narratives are unconnected but share certain themes in common: dead or hallucinating narrators; the metaphysical wedded to the mundane; a laconic, understated narrative style; a fixation on death; surrealistic worlds, but psychological realism; and urban environments portrayed as ominous, destroyed, littered with corpses and overrun by vampires or other cursed beings. *Las llaves* is a disjointed collection, but Montemayor was a skilled writer who took great pains in choosing his words and who creates in his stories collections of vivid, timeless images rather than plot-oriented narratives–although the images, and the narratives more generally, tend to the nightmarish rather than the lyrically beautiful. Critics have compared various stories in the collection to the work of Cortázar, Arreola, and even Borges.

Although born in England, artist and novelist Leonora Carrington spent most of her adult life in Mexico, a country she loved, and is generally considered as a Mexican creator. Best known for her Surrealist art and sculpture, Carrington also wrote a number of novels and short story collections. Although she began writing in the late 1930s, it is in her mature work in the 1970s and 1980s that her substantial talent as a writer is best displayed. Always a writer of fierce intelligence and a vivid imagination, Carrington's best novels, *Le Cornet acoustique* (*The hearing trumpet*, 1974) and *La Porte de pierre* (*The stone door*, 1976), bring together the alienated sensibility and fabulous monsters of her early stories and novels and add to them black humor, romantic fantasy, surreal worlds, and a potent combination of terror and wonder. *Le Cornet acoustique*, set in a sinister nursing home, has occult secrets, mythical identities, a feminist uprising, poisonings, and a quest for the Holy Grail, all in a text filled with (but not over-filled with) meaningful symbols. *La Porte de pierre*, generally seen by critics as not quite reaching the heights of *Le Cornet acoustique*, is a blackly humorous fantasy romance involving the zodiac, Qabalah, Transylvania, and the Stone Door of Kecske. In both novels, Carrington grounds the frightening and the marvelous in a dry and witty style, and smoothly portrays the triumph of the feminine principle over the male principle.

Inés Arredondo was a writer, critic, and academic who is best known for her short stories. She published three collections: *La señal* (*The signal*, 1965), *Río subterráneo* (*The underground river*, 1979), and *Los Espejos* (*The mirrors*, 1988). In them she tells stories of the female spirit and female fears, addressing subjects that the male-dominated world Mexican literature hadn't taken on before, subjects like women's lust, rape, and the death of babies. Arredondo's approach to doing so was to focus on the subjectivity of women and other marginalized characters, including adolescents and gay men, and to place her protagonists in strange and often grotesque families in her native Sinaloa, thus creating the "Sinaloa Gothic." (Arredondo was among the first Mexican women of her era to write Gothic stories; previously the Mexican Gothic had been the province of men). Critics have compared Arredondo's work to that of Carson McCullers and Flannery O'Connor; like theirs, Arredondo's stories are dark and disturbing, full of sexual and moral predators and victimized innocents. She makes skillful use of Gothic elements—the confinement of women, wicked clergy, symbolic incest, abhuman monsters, monstrous father figures, transgressive relationships, violent and grotesque sexuality, castle-like mansions, and so on—to create a modern version of the traditional Gothic, one which utilizes the Gothic aesthetic and creates a Gothic atmosphere while still emphasizing modern psychology. "In Arredondo's writings, horror is not of supernatural but of (all too) human origin, and it is narrated in a prose where the exquisite and the uncanny meet in shuddering complicity."[31]

Humberto Guzmán was a Mexican writer and journalist whose stories and novels have won a number of awards. His work in the 1970s, especially in *Manuscrito anónimo llamado consigna idiota* (*The anonymous manuscript called idiotic*, 1975), is of the High Art Horror variety, being experimental and written for purposes beyond the mere production of the fear effect. Guzmán's narratives de-emphasize plot in favor of creating an atmosphere which depending on the story can be dreamlike or nightmarish. Guzmán is a skilled writer who precisely describes the details and settings of his stories, but he rejects logic in favor of magic and imagination, which can be wondrous or terrible or both. His central theme in a majority of his stories is transformation, but Guzmán shows transformation at work in grotesque fantasies fueled by his macabre imagination. His work is usually dramatic and is always interesting, but as time passed he de-emphasized the role of feeling in his work. In *Manuscrito* the theme of transformation becomes one of metamorphosis and decomposition, the previous eroticism and wild fantasy of earlier stories giving way to a "macabre, nightmarish world of desolation" whose atmosphere has strong similarities to the work of Samuel Beckett.[32] The cumulative effect is one of physical revulsion, alienation, and schizophrenia.

José-Emilio Pacheco was a poet, essayist, novelist and short story writer, generally regarded as one of the major Mexican poets of the second half of the twentieth century. He also wrote novels and short stories, with his *El principio del placer* (*The pleasure principle*, 1972) generally being seen as his best collection. The stories in *El principio del placer* are experimental and elaborate, Pacheco deliberately blurring the borders between the narrator and the (dead) protagonist, between the living and the dead more generally, between the past and the present, between fantasy and reality, between ambiguity and the nakedly supernatural. Despite the presence of the supernatural, such as ghosts, Pacheco's emphasis is on the psychological aspects of the events the characters experience; Pacheco uses the supernatural not to directly frighten but to scar his protagonists, whose damaged psyches are what is directly frightening to the reader. Despite the formal experimentation of the stories Pacheco tells them in a straightforward style;

---

[31] Aurora Piñeiro, "'No vengas al país de los ríos': la escritura de Inés Arredondo y la estética de la oscuridad," *Badebec* 3, no. 6 (Mar. 2014): 254.

[32] J. Ann Duncan, *Voices, Visions, and a New Reality: Mexican Fiction Since 1970* (Pittsburgh: University of Pittsburgh, 1986), 101.

his strongest skill as a horror writer is the creation of an oppressive atmosphere and the depiction of the psychological injuries his characters undergo.

Alberto Huerta was a writer, playwright, and academic best known for his short stories and anthologies. His *Ojalá estuvieras aquí* (*Wish you were here*, 1977), a collection of short stories, follows a trend among a certain group of progressive Mexican writers in the 1970s and early 1980s, a "fascination with the sinister and unexpected possibilities lurking beneath apparently normal and anodyne situations, so that the dividing line between hallucination and observed reality is unstable, a source of ecstasy or anguish."[33] In *Ojalá estuvieras aquí* Huerta's protagonists face grim realities—sexual frustration, prison, or death—and conjure up imaginary presences to lead them out of those realities. These presences are so real and vital, for both the protagonist and the reader, that the line between fantasy and reality becomes blurred and ambiguous. "These are no stream-of-consciousness texts; the style…is precise, even factual in its presentation, so that past and present, dream and action have equal validity."[34] But the "imaginary" presence is not wholly or even mostly beneficial. The stories generally follow the same pattern: a mundane, if unpleasant situation turns horrible or occasionally wonderful and the real becomes strange, even bizarre. "The partial restoration of 'normality' at the end, and the hint of a logical explanation, do nothing to dissipate our unease. On the contrary, they often clinch it, since fantasy was the only way out of an untenable situation, whose reality is then affirmed."[35] *Ojalá estuvieras aquí* has elements of the surreal in it and seems somewhat inspired by the work of both Samuel Beckett and the rock band Pink Floyd, whose song "Wish You Were Here" gave Huerta's collection its title.

Antonio Delgado was a writer and poet whose work has been recognized internationally. His *La hora de los unicornios* (*The hour of the unicorns*, 1979) consists of a series of prose poems. In each the familiar world of mundane reality increasingly becomes hazy, sinister, and nightmarish as the characters fall prey to their psychological problems, their fears and hatred and doubts. The characters begin to doubt their own identities, hallucinate, and undergo paranoid delusions of persecution. Told in a poetically lyrical style, *La hora de los unicornios* leaves the reader with a continuous sensation of the ominous and the threatening seemingly everywhere.

Guillermo Samperio was a novelist, essayist, poet, and critic. His *Textos extraños* (*Strange stories*, 1981) is a collection of stories about the failing borders between the imaginary and the real, for both Samperio's characters and for Samperio's readers. Written at a time when Samperio himself was feeling an essential disconnection and alienation from reality, the stories in *Textos extraños* feature hallucinations, transformations, and invasions from one reality to another. The themes of the stories are loneliness, obsession, and a sense of being haunted, with characters transforming, Kafka-esque, into a book, or turn green and begin to attract dragon-men. Samperio anticipates postmodern metafictional narratives in one story in which the flies which

---

[33] Duncan, *Voices, Visions, and a New Reality*, 195.

[34] Duncan, *Voices, Visions, and a New Reality*, 195.

[35] Duncan, *Voices, Visions, and a New Reality*, 195.

are the protagonist's main subject assault Samperio and convince him that the drawings from *Textos extraños* have come alive.

Homero Aridjis was a poet, novelist, academic, journalist and diplomat best known for his lyric poetry. His *La leyenda de los soles* (*The legend of the suns*, 1993), set in Mexico City in 2027, is a genre-leaping apocalyptic work which encompasses both fantasy and science fiction, fantastic structures and Gothic atmospheres. In *La leyenda* humans in Mexico City are struggling to survive in an environment of death and rot; the world is dying of pollution, disease, and political and social corruption. For their own political and self-interests humans have allowed the forests to be cut down, the animals slain, and the rivers, lakes, and oceans to be drained dry. Though set in the near-future and underpinned by scientific and ecological thinking, *La leyenda* partakes of fantasy as well: the end of the world in the novel coincides with the beginning of the New World and the death of the Fifth Sun in Aztec mythology. This cycle of death and rebirth takes places, with the moral and ecological apocalypse accompanied by the presence of the sinister ghosts of the *conquistadores*, the *cihuateteo* (mothers who died giving birth), and the *tzitzimime* (demons of darkness), who begin attacking civilians. These legendary beings become Gothic reminders of the past, even as the apocalypse hints at a better future for all. The horror elements of *La leyenda* are many: the ecological catastrophe, the moral decadence of the Mexican government, the presence and attacks of the ghosts of the *conquistadors* and the *cihuateteo* and the *tzitzimime,* and the wickednesses perpetrated by the President, José Huitzilipochtli, and the Police Chief, Carlos Tezcatlipoca, both incarnations of Aztec gods of darkness, temptation, corruption, and bloodthirstiness.

Luis G. Abbadie is a writer who specializes in horror and fantasy short stories—arguably the first Mexican writer to successfully specialize in those genres. Beginning with his 1995 novel *El último relato de Ambrose Bierce* (*The last story of Ambrose Bierce*), he wrote a wide range of stories about Lovecraft and the Cthulhu Mythos, utilizing characters ranging from Ambrose Bierce to Jorge Luis Borges to Sir Thomas Raffles. The stories are told in Abbadie's own style, or in attempts to imitate the styles of other writers; Abbadie does not merely ape Lovecraft's style, but attempts to update it for the late twentieth century and for a Mexican environment and audience. The terror of the stories, however, derives from much the same elements that it does in Lovecraft's stories—the knowledge which is too much for men's minds, the incursion of horrific creatures into our reality, etc.

Jose Luis Zárate is a writer best known for and associated with the genre of science fiction, although he has written several works in other genres, from horror to fantasy. His *Xanto: Novelucha libre* (1994) is a tribute to the Mexican *lucha libre* El Santo, with a meek protagonist becoming aware that Lovecraftian "Beings of Great Darkness" are about to invade the world, beginning in the prim Mexican city of Puebla; the protagonist decides that only El Santo (dubbed here "Xanto") can fight and defeat them. Zárate's *La ruta del hielo y la sal* (*The route of ice and salt*, 1998) is a retelling of the portion of Bram Stoker's *Dracula* in which Dracula makes his way to England via a sea voyage on the ship *Demeter*. *La ruta* emphasizes the horror of the captain at the strange events that take place on the *Demeter* (exactly matching those mentioned in *Dracula*) and the slow disappearance of his crew members. *Xanto* is Lovecraftian horror mixed with the existentialism of the *roman noir*, while *La ruta* is closer to classic horror, as an unseen force slowly eliminates the protagonist's associates.

Puerto Rico

The "Nuyorican" literary movement of the 1970s leant a great deal of impetus to expatriate Puerto Ricans in the United States, encouraging them to maintain their cultural identity while in the U.S. The movement would energize these writers and eventually spill over into the writing of Puerto Rican authors in Puerto Rico itself.

Jaime Martínez Tolentino was a writer and academic whose fiction was primarily *fantastika*, usually supernatural in nature. Beginning in 1970 and continuing through to the end of the century, he wrote a large number of horror and ghost stories whose influences range from Balzac to Henry James to Poe. There is no typical Martínez Tolentino story; their plots range from drowned sailors come back to haunt the innocent to evil amulets to magic realist stories about the death of an old woman to mimetic stories about the terrors of race hatred to surrealist stories in which the terrible and fantastic appear side-by-side, unexplained. While not strikingly innovative or original on the plot level, Martínez Tolentino was an absorbing stylist and story-teller, and was more than capable of arousing fear even from well-worn story paths.

Arguably foremost among the Puerto Rican women writers of the 1970s and 1980s was Rosario Ferré, whose first book, in 1976, is seen by critics as beginning the feminist movement in Puerto Rico. Ferré became one of the most important feminist writers in Spanish America over the next twenty-four years, influencing and inspiring many Puerto Rican women to become authors and to write their own realities. Ferré is the leader among what critics call the "magic feminists." "By combining classical mythology with indigenous folktales that usurp the traditional actions of female characters, Ferré has interpreted, translated, and rewritten a more active and satisfying myth of Puerto Rican women."[36] One of Ferré's chosen genres in which to write is horror, although Ferré's horror is almost always feminist and/or full of political allegories. Ferré's horror fiction, much of which is in the myth or fairy tale genres, makes use of hyperbole, subjective viewpoints, and fantastic, grotesque, and allegorical elements to violate traditional norms of realism. What takes their place is a tense, phantasmagoric, and often nightmarish atmosphere in which time is dislocated and disjoined, personalities become multiplied and schizophrenic, and points of view shift without warning. Occasionally Ferré's work is more folkloric than fabular; in these stories Gothic atmospheres and elements become pronounced, and the narratives' climaxes become inevitable rather than predictable. Ferré is an intelligent and thoughtful writer who deploys horror tropes and motifs and plot twists in a skilled manner, simultaneously evoking fear in her readers as well as an understanding of the oppression of women and the poor delivered through Ferré's allegories. Even in her most horrific of stories there are still moments of lyricism to be found, and a strong poetic strain is evident in most of her writing.

Mayra Montero is arguably the most innovative of the Puerto Rican writers who came of age in the late 1980s and 1990s. Montero ranges widely in her stories and novels, bringing in elements of Caribbean folklore, such as Afro-Caribbean cults and zombies, as well as Gothic conventions, in stories that work both as horror and as allegories about the nature of romance and

---

[36]Carmen S. Rivera, "Rosario Ferré (28 July 1942-)," *Modern Latin-American Fiction Writers: Second Series* 145 (1994): 130-131.

marriage, Caribbean history, feminism, imperialism/colonialism, and contemporary politics. "Montero is, of all contemporary Caribbean writers, the most indebted to the Euro-American Gothic tradition, which she has made her own, transforming the familiar conventions through her deep knowledge of Caribbean magico-religious traditions and her concerns for social justice."[37] In one novel Montero applies the Gothic genre to the Duvalier regime of Haiti, portraying Vodou priests as heroes in the armed struggle against agents and militia of the Duvaliers. In another novel the Gothic features as a backdrop to the struggle between the leaders of two rival Vodou societies; allegorically the novel depicts the vicious and corrupt politics of Haiti and the Dominican Republic. In a third novel an American herpetologist in search of a nearly-extinct frog ventures into a supernatural "heart of darkness" on a vast mountain in Haiti. Montero writes in a beautifully poetic style, which renders the violence, terror, and shocking events of her narratives all the more jarring to the reader.

Québec

Following the decades of introspection of the 1930s, 1940s, and 1950s, Québécois literature underwent a number of drastic changes during the 1960s and the 1971-2000 time period. Surrealism, linguistic experimentation, and a concern with form and structure become common, as were borrowings from and influences of contemporary French literature. This coincided with the beginning of widespread production of *fantastika* in Québec literature. Science fiction and fantasy were foremost, with horror a distant third or fourth. This began to change, however, in the 1990s.

One of the earliest of the Québécois horror writers was Natasha Beaulieu, who began writing horror stories in the early 1990s but who came to wider attention with *L'Ange écarlate* in 2000. Beaulieu's work tends toward the Gothic and erotic end of contemporary horror, with the production of a fetishistic frisson sometimes taking the place of the evocation of fear. But Beaulieu's characterization is strong, with well-realized protagonists and antagonists, and her style lush, and she usually strikes an adequate balance between the horrific and the erotic in her narratives.

Patrick Senécal began writing horror novels in 1994 and quickly became a success, as there was nothing like his work available at the time in Québec. Senécal is usually compared with Stephen King, both because of the success of his novels and because of the content of the novels and his storytelling approach. His *5150 rues des Ormes* (*5150 Ormes Street*, 1994) is about a young man held hostage by a family of religious fanatics; *Le Passager* (*The passenger*, 1995) is about an amnesiac who picks up a hitchhiker who knew the amnesiac during his lost years; and *Sur le Seuil* (*On the doorstep*, 1998) is about a horror writer who is mutilated and left catatonic by a brush with something monstrous. Senécal uses King's approach–realistic characters placed in a realistic world in which the intrusion of supernatural/unnatural evil frightens both because of its innately monstrous nature and because of its existence in an otherwise realistic world–but adeptly makes use of Québec, and Montreal, as settings.

---

[37]Paravisini-Gebert, "Unchained Tales," 459.

Similarly King-styled were the horror works of Joel Champetier, first appearing in 1994. *La Mémoire du lac* (*The lake memory*, 1994) is about a man whose two children drowned in a lake, and a Native American curse. *La Peau Blanche* (*White skin*, 1997) is a novel about the forbidden love of a man for a vampire woman. And *L'Aile du Papillon* (*The butterfly wing*, 1999) is about a patient in a psychiatric asylum who psychically spreads delusions among the other patients and staff.

Arguably the most skilled horrorist of the Québécois authors of fear literature is Claude Bolduc, a Young Adult writer who began penning horror stories in 1993 and published his first collection, *Les yeux troubles et autres contes de la lune noire* (*The troubled eyes and other tales of the black moon*) in 1998. Bolduc is equally skilled at telling traditional ghost stories and contemporary horror stories. Bolduc, like Joel Champetier and Patrick Senécal, is influenced by Stephen King in the manner in which Bolduc portrays real life as an assemblage of quotidian detail. But unlike Champetier, Senécal, or King, Bolduc often plays with subjectivity and insanity in his stories in addition to more objective-seeming narratives. His work features "delicious horrors, skillfully narrated to build suspense, often leading up to a climactic moment of sublime but abject horror that permanently marks his French-Canadian protagonists."[38]

Venezuela

Venezuelan literature, like Venezuela itself, suffered cruelly under the 1950s dictatorship of Marcos Perez Jimenez, but recovered quickly in the 1960s and received a significant boost in the late 1960s and 1970s thanks to the new freedom of speech and publishing and to the establishment of the Monte Avila Editores and its encouragement to new and old writers alike.

Most Venezuelan literature was of the High Art variety, serious-minded and intent on discussing and purveying serious artistic, social, and political themes and topics. The dominant form of Venezuelan popular literature during the 1971-2000 time period was the romance, and no writer was more responsible for this than Salvador Garmendia, an award-winning author who wrote in a variety of genres, including children's literature, but who will always be remembered for popularizing the *telenovela*. Less well known are Garmendia's novels and stories of *fantastika*, particularly those in which he uses the vampire symbolically, usually to represent disorder on a personal, familial, or social scale. In Garmendia's stories mundane reality is full of monsters, from dictators to policemen, but it is the irruption of the unreal, in the person of the vampire, that disorders the protagonists. Garmendia makes good use of horror tropes—the invisible monster, the being that is only visible in a mirror—but the real horror comes from the way in which the protagonists are forced to deal with their previously ordered lives being turned upside down and left in shambles.

---

[38] Amy J. Ransom, "Popular Fiction in Québec: National Identity and 'American' Genres," in *New Directions in Popular Fiction: Genre, Distribution, Reproduction*, ed. Ken Gelder (London: Palgrave Macmillan, 2016), 251.

Chapter Thirteen: Asia

Bangladesh

Bangladesh, as an Islamic nation, has a complex relationship with horror fiction. It shares with most other Muslim nations a religion-based bias against horror fiction, but culturally, as a nation of Bengalis, it has a long tradition of folklore and popular myths with horror elements. Consequently, while there was a dearth of High Art Horror, there was a substantial amount of it in cheap popular magazines during the 1971-2000 period. One exception to this was the author Humayun Ahmed, a critically acclaimed writer as well as a bestseller. Among his other novels were two series which often made use of horror tropes: the first starred Misir Ali, a professor of parapsychology who solves a variety of baffling cases which often involve the paranormal; the second starred Himu, who has supernatural abilities and is haunted by the ghost of his father, who advises and guides Himu so that he will become a modern-day saint. Additionally, Ahmed wrote a variety of traditional ghost stories for both adults and children. Ahmed's work is influenced by his Bengali predecessors, especially Rabindranath Tagore and Bibhutibhushan Bandyopadhyay, but Ahmed wrote contemporary, late twentieth-century horror. Ahmed added humor to some of his horror stories and novels as well as his personal political and pro-establishment politics, but never at the expense of making his narratives frightening.

Muhammed Zafar Iqbal is best known as the foremost Bangladeshi author of science fiction. He began writing sf for adults in the mid-1970s and for children in the mid-1980s. Iqbal also wrote a horror novel, *Pret* (1983) and a short story collection, *Pishachini* (1992), during the 1971-2000 time period. Iqbal's approach as a horror writer departs from his approach as a science fiction writer, in that Iqbal uses popular horror motifs, such as ghosts or possessed women and children, and a straightforward narrative style, but adds to them allegorical messages about the malign influence of foreign (Western) cultures on Bangladeshi society. Iqbal's allegory does not become preaching, but it is less than subtle in execution.

China

Zong Pu, a writer and scholar equally fluent in English, French, and Chinese, and an expert in classical Chinese and classical Western literature, was generally a highbrow, High Art, Modernist writer. On occasion she allowed elements of *fantastika* and even horror to enter her stories. Her "Wo shi shei?" ("Who Am I?," 1979), set during the Cultural Revolution, is about a female scientist who returns from work overseas to serve the new regime, but instead is distrusted and viciously condemned. The story portrays her fragmented thoughts and disconnected emotions in the hours and minutes before she commits suicide. "Wo shi shei?" combines the degrading horror of the Cultural Revolution with the fraught atmosphere of a Kafkaesque government of unfeeling bureaucrats. "Woju" ("The Shelled People," 1981) is an allegorical fable. The story

> takes the reader to a nightmarish realm to demonstrate how political oppression leads to extreme dehumanization. The process of people growing snail-shaped backs echoes

Kafka's *Metamorphosis*. More ironic and tragic is that Zong Pu's characters symbolically use their own saliva (words) to grow their shells for protection, and, because of their inherent weaknesses (such as betrayal), the hacks of the deified leader (the authority) can shrink them to the size of a snail at their whim.[1]

Liang Xiaosheng was one of the foremost representatives of fiction written by *Zhiqing* youth (the urban youths sent to the countryside by Mao during the "Up to the Mountains and Down to the Countryside Movement" of the late 1960s and early 1970s). Both a social critic and a fiction writer, Liang Xiaosheng's narratives usually concern the *Zhiqing* (lit.: "sent down youth") and what he sees as the moral degeneration of modern Chinese society. The great majority of his work is non-*fantastika*, but in his "Zheshi yipian shenqi de tudi" ("A Land of Wonder and Mystery," 1982) he uses horror elements for didactic purposes. The story is about a group of *Zhiqing* who are sent to the rural "Ghost Swamp" to cultivate it and turn it into new land. However, Ghost Swamp lives up to its name:

> The eerie atmosphere is immediately conjured up with images of bear skeletons, hunting guns, and abandoned tractors. It is further compounded by "ghost fire," strange cries of birds, horrifying "nine-headed evil dragons," and the rumor that a group of Japanese soldiers had gone there but never returned.[2]

A series of untimely deaths follow, including one member of the *Zhiqing* who is eaten by wolves. But the story ends on the protagonist's vow that the surviving *Zhiqing* will stay and eventually conquer the Swamp.

Liang Xiaosheng's *Foucheng* (*Floating City*, 1992) is a satire of early 1990s Chinese society—with he sees as "contaminated with excessive material greed, sexual debauchery, and violence"[3]--accompanied by an apocalyptic backdrop. An unnamed city in China drifts away from the mainland and out to sea, causing the people to panic through many scenes of prolonged tension. The horror high point of *Foucheng* comes from a massed seagull attack on the people of the city, in a scene undoubtedly influenced by Alfred Hitchcock's *The Birds*.

Chinese popular literature did not entirely recover from the reign of Mao Zedong and the Anti-Spiritual Pollution Campaign until after the Tiananmen Square massacre in 1989 and the commencement of China's market reforms. However, from the early 1980s forward there were a number of Chinese writers who made use of elements of horror fiction in their own narratives—a departure from the Mao years, but a continuation of earlier trends.

---

[1] Laifong Leung, *Contemporary Chinese Fiction Writers: Biography, Bibliography, and Critical Assessment* (New York: Routledge, 2017), 344.

[2] Laifong, *Contemporary Chinese Fiction Writers*, 133.

[3] Laifong, *Contemporary Chinese Fiction Writers*, 135.

This emergence, or reemergence, of a modern Chinese literature of the fantastic is an evident departure from the predominantly realist aspirations or pretensions of the previous decades, and can be seen largely as inspired by, or in imitation of, translated writers such as Borges, Márquez, Kafka, and others. Viewing the modernity of Chinese literature in the twentieth century in terms of one long negotiation with Western influence, interrupted only by the years dominated by the Mao regime, has been the common view held by not only Western scholars but also Chinese writers and critics.[4]

Zhu Lin is known for many things: for her novels about Chinese women; for her novels for children and young adults, which have substantial science fictional elements; for her social and cultural criticism; and for being the first Chinese writer to discuss the dark side of Mao's "Rustication Movement." In her *Nu Wu* (*Woman Shaman*, 1993) she uses *fantastika* to frighten readers while also criticizing aspects of modern Chinese society. In the novel the woman of a rural village are raped and made pregnant by the ruling cadre of elites. One of those woman, with no way to express her griefs, goes to a woman shaman so that she can vent her anger in a mystical trance. Fearful events follow, including the appearance of a ghost nun who was raped and then drowned in life, and the appearance of a cursed notebook containing all the sins of the village. Then the protagonist gives birth to a malformed, cursed embryo.

> The grotesque embryo, or, for that matter, cultural inbreeding, will continue to harm the community in its various manifestations…many writers have written about rural evil; Zhu Lin transcends the topic by raising a metaphysical issues: that a confined, corrupt environment will suffocate culturally unless it cleanses itself and opens its doors to the outside world.[5]

Bei Cun is an avant-garde writer and an openly-practicing Christian who often incorporates religious themes in his work, making him doubly unusual in the world of Chinese letters. Bei Cun's avant-garde fiction collapses the reader's expectations, whether of an emphasis on realistic character depiction or through "labyrinthine plotting and insistent repetition of scenarios within the same story…[which] play havoc with the conventions of realist fiction…his is a fictional fabric pron to sudden and unexplained irruptions of the supernatural and the sordid."[6] Bei Cun's *Shixi de he* (*The Baptismal River*, 1993), set in the Republican period, is an allegorical novel about humanity's capability for evil and the prospect of hope and redemption through conversion to Christianity. *Shixi de he* has, as would be expected, a hopeful ending, but before that point the protagonist has become an opium dealer and married his rival's wife.

---

[4]Wedell-Wedellsborg, "Haunted Fiction."

[5]Laifong, *Contemporary Chinese Fiction Writers,* 338.

[6]Kirk A. Denton, "Avant-Garde Fiction in China," in *The Columbia Companion to Modern East Asian Literature*, ed. Joshua Mostow (New York: Columbia University, 2012), 558.

Liu Lang has become a monster. He even orders the killing of his young brother, who, by mistake, has gone to Ma Da's camp. He tortures his subordinates according to his whims. He mistreats his wife and locks up his concubine until the latter becomes insane. After becoming addicted to opium, he deteriorates physically and mentally. By building a grave-like mansion in which to store his fortune and live, he has metaphorically turned into a half-human, half-demon. His double, Ma Da, is no better. Both have turned the city into hell, reminiscent of the evil cities of Sodom and Gomorrah.[7]

But the great majority of Chinese horror literature in the 1980s and for most of the 1990s was not strictly horror—rather, it was *fantastika* containing horror elements used for purposes other than or in addition to frightening the reader. Can Xue, for example—one of the first and leading modern advocates for the Chinese avant-garde—wrote stories, first published in 1985 and continuing through the decade, influenced by Borges and Kafka. Her work is

variably called "gothic," "surrealistic," and "absurd"…focusing on the subconscious of the human mind, Can Xue has created a world that is invariably irrational, fragmented, and nightmarish, with no clear definition of time, space, and identity.[8]

Liu Suola, primarily known as a composer and singer, also wrote a handful of novels and stories, one of which, "The Quest for the King of Singers" (1985), fits neatly into the Gothic category. Ostensibly about the search by a singer and a composer for a being called the "King of Singers," the story is actually about the search for the sublime, which in this case takes the form of music. Told in "Gothic hints and flashbacks, lit by an uncertain gleam and illustrated by snatches of half-heard music,"[9] "The Quest for the King of Singers" has as an environment a set of Gothic mountains and the very Gothic vengeance of the natural world for the sins of the characters' ancestors.

A number of other author authors, while not removing the frightening aspects of the horror tropes in their stories, used "ghosts and the strange to represent psychological/mental phenomena…in many stories otherwise taking place in realistic contemporary surroundings."[10] Wang Shuo, for example, an author, director, and actor, whose work is otherwise of the "hooligan" or "spiritual pollutant" genre of modern, confrontational, "street" literature, uses supernatural and horror elements in works like *Wanr de jiushi xintiao* (*Playing for Thrills*, 1989) to emphasize a protagonist's loosening or fractured grasp of reality, and to represent repressed emotions and hidden attachments.

---

[7]Laifong, *Contemporary Chinese Fiction Writers*, 23.

[8]Li-hua, *Historical Dictionary of Modern Chinese Literature*, 14.

[9]David Punter, *Gothic Pathologies* (London: Macmillan Press, 1998), 181.

[10]Wedell-Wedellsborg, "Haunted Fiction."

Chinese High Art authors, too, make use of this dynamic. Nobel prize-winner Gao Xingjian, in *Lingshan* (*Soul Mountain,* 1990), uses a metafictional structure with a story-telling protagonist to convey a number of stories in traditional form about ghosts, shamans, and legendary figures. The framing narrative of *Lingshan* contains realistic descriptions of mundane life in 1980s China, but the fantastic narratives counterpoint the realism with powerful emotions and adventure-filled deeds, lending the protagonist, a detached and observing-rather-than-doing modern personality, a poignant air.

Nobel laureate Mo Yan's *Jiuguó* (*Wine Country,* 1992) is similarly metafictional, being both a satire of detective novels as well as a series of letters from Mo Yan to a fan and three short stories written by the fan. Inside the nested narratives are cannibals, a monster child, and a demonic, cannibalistic mother-in-law. These creatures frighten in the original context of the embedded stories, but their purpose, in *Jiuguó* as a whole, is to "underscore and upset conventional concepts of fictionality and authorial command."[11]

Some Chinese authors, however, do not use horror tropes and motifs and creatures for purposes other than to unnerve and disquiet the reader. Ge Fei, one of the foremost experimental writers in China during the late 1980s and 1990s, uses the stuff of horror, both folklorish creatures and ominous atmospheres, to create mysterious and sinister stories that create the effect of fear while never quite overtly portraying the horrific. Realistic environments, in Ge Fei's narratives, become blurred by the intrusion of the fantastic, resulting in situations which could be supernatural or could merely be the product of a disturbed mind. "Ge Fei's texts are loaded with ambiguity and produce hesitation in both reader and characters, thus creating an enigmatic atmosphere even when nothing manifestly supernatural is around."[12]

Yu Hua's work straddles the two types of horror. Yu Hua, an avant-garde writer in the 1980s, uses the traditional *zhiguai* (lit.: "recording the abnormal") form to satirize and pastiche traditional genres as well as to tell metafictional narratives. In his work he combines the Chinese version of the postmodern narrative style with bizarre events and improbable coincidences and traditionally Chinese fantastic motifs ranging from ghosts to magical swords to fatal coincidences.

> Like the majority of traditional *zhiguai*, Yu Hua's texts are two-dimensional in the psychological description of characters, and they also resemble traditional narratives in their matter-of-fact depiction of blood and violence. In keeping with "the conventions governing the *zhiguai* genre, according to which the text is taken as a report and the author as a recorder of actual events," the style is, at least on the surface, detached and laconic.[13]

---

[11] Wedell-Wedellsborg, "Haunted Fiction."

[12] Wedell-Wedellsborg, "Haunted Fiction."

[13] Wedell-Wedellsborg, "Haunted Fiction."

A significant change took place in Chinese horror fiction in the late 1990s. The first Chinese translations of Edgar Allan Poe and Stephen King were published in 1997, at roughly the same time as a marked upsurge in the amount of commercialized horror fiction. At the end of the century the primary influences on Chinese horror writers were no longer traditional forms like the *zhiguai* or High Art authors like Borges and Kafka, but rather Low Art, American authors like Poe and King.

India

During the 1971-2000 time period Indian horror and ghost stories continued to evolve in the direction that it had developed in during the 1941-1970 time period. Indian horror stories continued to be disregarded and held in contempt by literary critics or the Indian literary establishment, despite the horror fiction of esteemed creators like Satyajit Ray. Ghettoization was the rule for most Indian horror fiction during the time period. Nonetheless, despite its presence in the literary ghetto, Indian horror fiction continued to sell well and be popular with the reading audience.

Perhaps the foremost Indian venue for horror literature during the 1971-2000 time period was the same venue available to and popular with the average middle- and lower-class reader during the 1901-1940 and 1941-1970 time periods: railway literature, the Indian version of the dime novel or pulp magazine. The best and most popular authors of railway literature write hundreds of "novels" and can sell in the millions of copies, but few of their names are well-known or remembered, and certainly not given academic or critical attention. Railway (and later bus station) "novels" feature a variety of genres, from action/adventure to detective to romance to spy, and horror is prominent among them. The horror literature of the railway "novels" is often vivid and colorful, if not of great literary quality. Tabish Khair's definition of pulp fiction–"fiction that uses largely fixed generic features to satisfy the largely fixed reading expectations of as large a market as possible"[14]–certainly applies to these stories, which are designed to appeal to the largest audience possible and to meet their demands. The stories, while again not written to the highest aesthetic standard, make use of a variety of Indian and Western horror tropes and fulfill the minimum expectation for horror: that they frighten the reader. Murder, family curses, murderous robots, mad scientists, bloodthirsty lycanthropes, and other horror plots, devices, and creatures are common in railway horror "novels," and if these narratives do not stand comparison with more mainstream works of horror they are nonetheless remarkably popular, and as a medium remarkably long-lasting.

Originally, in the 1960s, Narayan Dharap made a name for himself as an author of science fiction as well as a proponent of it. While this gained him a number of fans in the Indian science fiction community, it also earned him the scorn of the Indian literary establishment, who had no use for science fiction, especially of the local variety. Frustrated by the ongoing lack of appreciation for his work, Dharap in the late 1960s began writing horror and supernatural novels, which he continued to do for three decades and nearly one hundred novels. Like many popular

---

[14]Tabish Khair, "Indian Pulp Fiction in English: A Preliminary Overview from Dutt to Dé," *Journal of Commonwealth Literature* 43, no. 3 (Sept. 2008): 61.

Indian authors, Dharap's wrote several series, each with their own set of recurring heroes. Dharap's heroes were usually possessors of superhuman abilities, which they used to fight evil supernatural powers, evil men and women possessed of superhuman abilities, and the men and women who assist the evil superhuman powers. In plot Dharap's work has been compared to that of Stephen King, but his characters and environment are thoroughly Indian. Moreover, unlike King, Dharap's narratives, though frightening, lack gore, references to sex, explicit violence, or anything that might be considered in poor taste. His work, though, doesn't need those elements to be frightening. Dharap creates ominous atmospheres and palpable terrors in the minds of his characters, and his work usually has a surprising or even shocking twist late in the plot.

Satyajit Ray is best known as India's greatest film maker, and one of the twentieth century's greatest film makers. Ray was additionally a scriptwriter, graphic artist, composer of music, and an author. Like Narayan Dharap, Ray began writing his horror stories in the 1960s but wrote the majority of them in the 1970s and 1980s. Unlike Dharap, the majority of Ray's horror stories do not feature series characters, although several of Ray's "Tarini khuro" (lit.: "respected uncle Tarini") stories are horror or horror-adjacent. Ray's horror stories–many of which are aimed at young adults–were, like Dharap's, both frightening and restrained. Ray exercised his imagination in creating fearful scenarios and vividly-described monsters, but Ray never made use of explicitly-described violence or gore, much less anything with sexual implications or references. Among the horror tropes Ray made use of were ghost-haunted castles, cursed bungalows, cursed treasure, men transformed into snakes after killing snakes, de-evolution, doppelgängers, the murderous insane, the helplessly obsessed, evil surgeons, possessed dolls, the dead using the telephone, and so on. Like Dharap, Ray was skilled at evoking a sinister atmosphere and often made use of fear-inducing plot twists.

A third author who began writing in the 1960s but published the majority of his horror stories in the 1971-2000 time period was Syed Mustafa Siraj, an award-winning author of hundreds of stories and novels. Best-known for his detective character Colonel Niadri, Siraj also created a much different series character, Muraru Babu. Babu is an anxious, innocent Kolkatan hobbyist who enjoys buying antique furniture. But inevitably Babu is drawn into encounters with the paranormal and the supernatural, whether because the old furniture he has just purchased is cursed, because a friend or furniture seller is involved with the supernatural, or sheerly through bad luck. Like Dharap and Ray, Siraj avoided explicit gore in his narratives, preferring to evoke fear through atmosphere, mood, plot twists, and the presence of ghosts and other supernatural creatures.

In 1980 Yandamuri Veerendranath published *Tulasi Dalam*, first as a magazine serial and then as a best-selling paperback. Partially inspired by the 1973 film version of Blatty's *The Exorcist* (1971), *Tulasi Dalam* is a thrilling mishmash of Western parapsychology and Indian occult practices, witchcraft, and demonology lore, the sort of novel for which the phrase "too much is too much, but way too much is just enough" was invented. Told in simple but expressive terms, with vivid enough emotions and occurrences that the reading audience got a surfeit of both familial love and fear, *Tulasi Dalam* was successful enough to spawn a mini-boom in novels about witchcraft in India. None of these imitations were as successful as *Tulasi Dalam*, financially or aesthetically, and *Tulasi Dalam* remains alone in the Indian canon of horror as the witchcraft novel.

The increasing globalization of horror literature in the 1980s and 1990s led to a wide range of American and British horror authors being translated into Indian languages and published in India for the first time: Stoker's *Dracula* in 1978, Poe in 1985, King in the early 1990s. The result was a surge in Indian horror novels. Often these were imitations of Western models, such as the wave of Stephen King-like horror novels in India in the late 1990s, but others reacted differently to the increasing presence of American and English horror novels, creating distinctly Indian horror novels with distinctly Indian characters, milieu, and monsters. One such was the anonymously-written *Pishacho ki Mallika* (1997), about a black magic-practicing witch and her quest to become immortal, which involves constantly eating the flesh of young men. While *Pishacho ki Mallika* takes its narrative and stylistic cues from King and other modern Western horror novels, in content it is thoroughly Indian.

By the late 1990s Indian horror fiction had developed a thriving hybrid form, written by Indians and making use of Indian environments, characters, and monsters, but told in a form close to that of Western horror fiction, published in English, and sold both in India and (thanks to the burgeoning Internet and online book brokers like Amazon.com) in the West. Two works typical of this "new Indian horror" were Namita Gokhale's novel *The Book of Shadows* (1999) and Ruskin Bond's story collection *A Season of Ghosts* (1999). *The Book of Shadows*, about a university lecturer who is badly scarred in an acid attack and retreats to her childhood home in the foothills of the Himalayas, only to encounter the ghosts of the people who used to live in the house and the ghost of the house itself, is part ghost story and part erotic romance, narrated in a very contemporary and Western style but with an Indian ethos. The stories in *A Season of Ghosts* are pure ghost and horror story, making use of the looming Gothic presence of the Himalayas and traditional Indian folklore figures like ghosts, witches, and rakshashas. Bond, like Gokhale, chooses to tell the stories in a Western narrative style and with a Western approach to producing fear in the readers.

Indonesia

As in India, the majority of Indonesian horror literature appeared historically in dime novel form. The Indonesian variety, the *sastra picisan* (lit.: "popular novel"), began in the 1920s while Indonesia was still under Dutch rule and contained a wide variety of genres, from romance to martial arts, much of it a combination of native Indonesian and foreign (usually Indian and Chinese) influences. The horror stories which appeared in the *sastra picisan* were similarly hybrids, making use of local folklore, Indian and Chinese folklore, and the Western horror forms, specifically nineteenth century ghost stories. The *sastra picisan* remained popular with Indonesian readers throughout the twentieth century, but became more widely read in the 1980s and 1990s and began incorporating more modern influences in its horror fiction.

A step above the *sastra picisan* were the cheap paperbacks sold in railway and bus stations and local airports. Like the *sastra picisan* these paperbacks told a variety of stories from a variety of genres, usually in a formulaic fashion and relying on then-popular characters and story formulae, like James Bond and the spy novel. In horror, the best-selling novelist was Abdullah Harahap, who began writing horror in 1975 and published around 70 novels until he ceased writing in the 1990s. Abdullah's horror is in the traditional hybrid vein, mixing action and adventure, Gothic environments and atmospheres, and stock horror antagonists; sample titles of his work include *Werewolves, Redeeming the Sins of Derivation, The Mystery of Satan's Children, Demonic Dances,* and *Hell Calls.* What distinguished Abdullah from his many competitors and led to his being the top-selling Indonesian horror novelist of his time and the single greatest influence on later Indonesian horror writers were his style, which was slick and modern and easily readable, his emphasis on evoking fear in the reader (though at the expense of in-depth characterization and sometimes logic), and his depiction of a contemporary Indonesia under the rule of the Suharto "New Order" government. Abdullah was equally unsparing in his portrayal of supernatural horrors and more mundane violence perpetrated by corrupt policemen, soldiers, and government officials, and a common interpretation of his work during the 1970s and 1980s was that it was subtly critical of the Suharto government.

The popularity of Abdullah's work, as well as the increase in popularity and frequency of horror films, led to a mainstreaming of what might be called the vocabulary of horror literature, the tropes and motifs and creatures which are commonly used in horror narratives. Mainstream, respected writers in the 1980s began using this vocabulary in stories that belonged in the horror genre but whose intention was more than just to frighten the reader. Seno Gumira Ajidarma's "The Mysterious Shooter Trilogy" (1985, 1987, published as a collection in 1993) is one of these. Ostensibly about a series of killings in Jakarta, both political and criminal, the trilogy culminates in the hundreds of assassinated criminals rising from the dead and overwhelming the city in a massive wave of zombie attacks. But beneath its violent and horror-filled surfaces "The Mysterious Shooter Trilogy" is actually a commentary on the police murdering suspected criminals in the 1980s and the government's complicity in those murders.

Japan

The growth of urban Japan in the late 1970s and 1980s sparked a boom in popular literature in both prose and manga form. High Art literature continued to prosper, and horror narratives appeared in both modes.

One of the most popular Low Art Horror novels of the 1971-2000 time period was published at the start of the period, in 1971: Ryō Hanmura's *Ishi no ketsumyaku* (*Bloodlines of stones*). A landmark among Japanese horror novels, *Ishi no ketsumyaku* was a bestseller despite or perhaps because of its mishmash of elements: "in addition to vampires and werewolves, it contains a mixture from different genres, such as the legend of Atlantis, worldwide megalithic monuments, a legendary cult of assassins, and the sexual esotericism of ancient religions, and it describes long conflicts between the privileged minority and the exploited majority in human society."[15] Published during a politically fraught period in Japan, *Ishi no ketsumyaku* was popular not only because it touched on seemingly every popular horror trope of the period, but also because it strongly espouses a Marxist philosophy, with the beautiful and extremely rich

---

[15] Masaya Shimokusu, "A Cultural Dynasty of Beautiful Vampires: Japan's Acceptance, Modifications, and Adaptations of Vampires," in *The Universal Vampire : Origins and Evolution of a Legend*, eds. Barbara Brodman, and James E. Doan (Madison, NJ: Fairleigh Dickinson University Press, 2013), 187.

vampires preying on and being hunted by the proletariat. Too, the vampire virus which the protagonist carries within its body is a potent symbol of "the ambivalence toward foreign culture embraced by most Japanese men who were witness to World War II,"[16] a symbol that resonated with the male Japanese audience.

One of the High Art Horror writers of the 1970s was Kanai Mieko, a prize-winning poet, postmodern fiction author, and eminent critic. Kanai's horror narratives have been compared by critics to the work of Borges (one of her admitted influences) and Kafka; she writes complex, experimental novels and short stories which confound and sometimes shock readers. Her strength is her poetic orientation; her short stories are lyrical but at the same time dreamlike and often nightmarish, with bizarre occurrences and an often deadpan delivery. These contribute to a disquieting and eerie atmosphere where the characters discover that little is as it seems. Her early work was quick, intense, and "full of scenes of blood, cannibalism, dismemberment, incest,"[17] while her longer later work, focusing on the metafictional theme of writing, did away with the graphic violence of her earlier stories in favor of the transgression of narrative, plot, and readerly comfort. "We find boxed structures made up of internal and external narratives, and stories whose metafictional qualities are heightened by nameless, allegorical characters and settings, by wordplay, and by rich allusions to fables and children's stories,"[18] but the cumulative effect on the reader is not respect for the skill Kanai displayed in crafting the story, but rather a deep unease as mundane logic and the safety of realism are entirely done away with.

Another writer of High Art Horror from the 1970s through the 1990s was Nakagami Kenji, the first and only Japanese writer to identify himself as a *Burakumin*, one of the lowest of the castes in the Japanese social system. Nakagami was best known for his works set in *buraku* and other outcaste districts, which stressed gritty realism, Japanese prejudice against the *Burakumin*, and what Mark Morris described as "the rough end of the economic miracle,"[19] but Nakagami also made use of the legends and myths of the Kumano region of southwest Japan. In those stories, which Nakagami told in his usual blunt and provocative style, legends become unsettlingly complex, Nakagami's heroes are

> angry, violent, untamed, and unrepentant, either outlaws escaping the jurisdiction of society or self-imposed outcasts who cannot fit into the mainstream world. Often this generic "man" roams the mountain of Kumano, encountering a mysterious realm

---

[16]Mari, "Techno-Gothic Japan," 191.

[17]Sharalyn Orbaugh, "Arguing with the Real: Kanai Mieko," in *Ōe and Beyond : Fiction in Contemporary Japan*, eds. Stephen Snyder and Philip Gabriel (Honolulu: University of Hawaii, 1999), 246.

[18]Mary A. Knighton, "Kanai Mieko," in *The Columbia Companion to Modern East Asia Literature*, ed. Joshua S. Mostow (New York: Columbia University, 2003), 243.

[19]Mark Morris, "The Untouchables," *New York Times*, Oct. 24, 1999, 7, 23:1.

occupied by unquiet spirits of fallen noble warriors and half-human, half-demonic creatures.[20]

These stories range in setting from medieval to contemporary to mythic time, and emphasize the violence and demonic nature of both heroes and monsters.

A third High Art Horror author of the 1971-2000 time period—although she began writing in the 1960s—was Kurahashi Yumiko. Kurahashi is best known for her sexually transgressive fiction, which uses themes like incest, sex with aliens and robots, wife- and husband-swapping, and sexually active homicidal women to challenge Japanese ideas about women, sexuality, and moral and social norms. But Kurahashi also wrote a substantial amount of supernatural fiction. These stories were erotic, as is much of Kurahashi's work, but also emphasized the grotesque and were cruel and violent. Too, Kurahashi's use of irruptive evil and monsters violated reader expectations of her fantasies being playful and benign. Much of her supernatural fiction is a revisionist reworking of traditional Japanese fairy tales and folk tales. "Kurahashi's fairy tales are...based on reason rather than emotion; they are *cruel*, she wrote, because they are governed by standards of retributive justice and didactic morals; and *for adults* because their erotic nature might be considered too poisonous for children."[21]

Although Ōba Minako was best known for as a mainstream writer, in which guise she was one of the most well-known women writers of the 1971-2000 time period, in the 1970s and 1980s she wrote a number of stories inspired by traditional Japanese folklore and legends. These stories, which usually have female protagonists and contain feminist themes, are disquieting more conceptually than narratively. In "Yamanba no bisho" ("Yamanba's popularity," 1976) a stereotypical housewife, self-sacrificing and meek, is revealed to have an interior life akin to the titular, terrifying mountain witch (a character type who often appears in Ōba's work). In *Urashimaso* (1977), a novel similar to the Japanese folktale about Urashima Tarō, who visits the undersea palace of the Dragon King and on returning home finds that three hundred years have passed, the protagonist discovers that her ten years in America have wrought radical changes on both her family and Japanese society. "Awakening to the realities of her native country, Yukie is forced to confront a troubling mix of horror, memory, and family trauma resulting both from the war and from the binding of women to an uncompromising patriarchal system."[22] While Ōba's female characters are usually sympathetic figures of resistance to Japanese patriarchy—even Ōba's mountain witch and demon women characters—their resistance can become a vengeance terrifying in its excessiveness.

---

[20]Faye Yuan Kleeman, "Nakagami Kenji," in *Japanese Fiction Writers Since World War II*, ed. Van C. Gessell (Detroit: Gale, 1997), 149.

[21]Marc Sebastian-Jones, "Kurahashi Yumiko (1935-2005)," in *The Greenwood Encyclopedia of Folktales and Fairy Tales*, ed. Donald Haase (Westport, CT: Greenwood Press, 2008), 549.

[22]Janice Brown, "Ōba Minako," in *The Columbia Companion to Modern East Asian Literature*, ed. Joshua Mostow (New York: Columbia University, 2003), 232.

Beginning in 1971 and continuing through to the end of the century, manga writer/artist Hino Hideshi produced a long series of distinctive horror narratives. Of the two types of horror manga, *kaiki* (abnormal, enigmatic, grotesque) and *kyoufu* (terrifying, fear-inducing), Hino is known for producing *kaiki*, featuring rotting corpses, misshapen monsters, and deviant murderers, although Hino and his predecessor Kazuo Umezu helped to merge *kaiki* and *kyoufu* into a single, broader genre of horror manga. Inspired by the work of Ray Bradbury as well as by the German *märchen* (fairy tales), Hino uses both explicitly-drawn gore and grotesqueries for ends both horrifying and moving.

Hino's body of work is dedicated to chronicling psychosis, pestilence, and the supernatural, everything rendered in a distinct 'blood blown from the brush' style of draftsmanship. For lack of a better term, he is one very sick fuck. And yet, by wading into the extremes of madness and gore, he offers a genuine catharsis both to himself and his readers.[23]

Takahashi Takako was known for her novels, which were primarily psychological in focus, and for her short fantasies, many of which had substantial erotic content in them. A number of these stories, however, were horror or horror-adjacent. Like a number of other women authors of the 1970s and 1980s, Takahashi used Gothic motifs and conventions, surrealist techniques, and dark themes to challenge Japanese social ideals of motherhood, femininity, and women's writing. A recurring dynamic in her stories is the female protagonist preoccupied with delusions and personal fantasies of sado-masochism, murder of husbands and children, and dismemberment. The frightening aspect of her stories comes not so much from the Gothic or surrealist elements as the continuing revelation that women's interior lives are so full of subversive, violent, and terrifying qualities. As well, she "makes effective use of both fantasy and the fantastic to unsettle distinctions maintained by ordinary modes of cognition and standards of behavior. Her fiction deploys boundary transgression on thematic and textual levels as a trope for social defiance and personal transformation."[24]

Manga writer/artist Morohoshi Daijiro began regular work in the manga industry in 1974 and continued writing and drawing horror stories until the end of the century. Many of his stories incorporate revisionist and secret histories as well as Japanese folklore and myth, while others show the influence of H.P. Lovecraft. Uniquely for manga, however, Morohoshi's artistic style is nor entirely or even primarily derived from or influenced by preceding or contemporary manga artists. Morohoshi's style draws equally upon *gekiga* (lit.: "dramatic pictures"), the realistic art style of Japanese cartoonists who did not want their works to be identified with *manga*, and upon

---

[23]Patrick Macias, "Hino Hideshi," in *Fresh Pulp: Dispatches from the Japanese Popular Culture*, eds. Nobuhide Hamada, Patrick Macias, and Yuki Oniji (San Francisco: Viz Media, 1999), 80.

[24]Maryellen Toman Mori, "The Subversive Role of Fantasy in the Fiction of Takahashi Takako," *Journal of the Association of the Teachers of Japanese* 28, no. 1 (Apr. 1994): 30.

the shadow- and crosshatch-heavy work of Western artists like Goya, John Tenniel, and Edward Gorey.

Hideyuki Kikuchi began publishing novels in 1982, and soon moved on to manga and then short stories. Kikuchi's horror narratives are a mishmash of a variety of elements, from Atlantis and similar Western myths and legends to traditional Japanese folklore to H.P. Lovecraft and Western cosmic horrorists. Hideyuki's horror narratives are told in a plain, terse style akin to a manga script. The horror of Hideyuki's work is sensationalist in nature, violent and gory; subtlety is not one of Hideyuki's strengths.

Mariko Koike's career as a novelist of mystery/horror stories was short, less than a decade, beginning in 1985 and ending in the mid-1990s, after which she transitioned to writing romances in the style of Yukio Mishima. But during those years she produced a series of very popular horror narratives, both at novel-length and in shorter work. In Koike's stories there are psychological as well as supernatural causes for terror, even in works that are ostensibly romantic or poignant. Haunted apartments and vengeful ghosts, told in Koike's engaging and suspenseful style, chill even when the latter are welcome by the living and the former is inhabited by unlikable protagonists.

Ken Asamatsu was involved in horror from the beginning in 1986, whether as a publisher of Lovecraft in translation or as a writer of occult horror novels. His fiction tends toward cosmic horror, specifically Lovecraftian/Cthulhu Mythos, as in *The Queen of K'n-Yan* (1999), or historical horror, as in *The 47 Demonic Ronin* (1995).

Although Ito Junji only began writing and drawing horror manga in 1987, by the end of the century he was widely regarded as the successor to Kazuo Umezu. Ito's work draws on Kazuo's, but other influences that Ito has acknowledged include Hino Hideshi, science fiction writer Yasutaka Tsutsui, and H.P. Lovecraft. Ito's horror is bleak; his universe is cruel, random, and capricious, with protagonists being victimized by unnatural or supernatural beings and events either randomly or for some minor violation of social norms. Much of his horror is body horror, with Ito almost gleefully showing the ways in which the human body can be distorted or violated. Recurring motifs and tropes in his work include irrational compulsions, societal breakdown, deep sea organisms, beautiful women being disfigured or turned into grotesqueries, black humor, and the inevitability of cruel fate. Ito's art, detailed and impressionistic, enhances the horror of Ito's stories.

Koji Suzuki's first published work was a fantasy novel in 1990, and his first published horror novel appeared in 1991. But that horror novel was *Ringu*, which was an immediate smash hit, spawning two sequels (1995, 1998), manga, and both Japanese and American movies. Koji went on to write a number of horror short stories and novels in the 1990s, earning him the informal title of "the Stephen King of Japan." Rather than using the supernatural, as was traditional in Japanese horror, Koji used technology and science as the vector for his frights; this shift was widely copied by Japanese horror writers. Koji's style emphasizes the psychological aspect of horror and works hard to evoke dread rather than terror in his readers. But Koji is not a good writer; his prose is awkward, his characterization poor and inconsistent, and his style inept. Koji is an example of a writer whose concepts are so strong that no amount of bad writing can prevent them from becoming bestsellers.

Murakami Ryu is best-known as a mainstream author, but his mainstream novels are dark, full of disillusioned people, drug addicts, surrealism, and murder and this darkness naturally led Murakami to write horror novels and short stories in addition to his mainstream work. Murakami's horror narratives are primarily psychological rather than supernatural. Told in a simple, candid narrative style, albeit with vividly-written images, his works of horror emphasize the terror which an unbalanced or deluded person can inflict on others. Subtlety is not Murakami's strength, although his works display a sound knowledge of the extent to which sexism and classism exist and can damage people. What Murakami shines at is the portrayal and evocation of dread and terror, the ways in which the mind preys on itself, and in the explicitly-described scenes of gore, sex, and general violence.

Malaysia

The economic growth of Malaysia during the 1970s and 1980s, along with greatly increased government attention to and involvement with Malaysian literature, led to a great increase in the amount of both High Art and popular literature. A significant portion of Malaysian literature was horror literature, spurred forward to a large degree by both Malaysian folklore and the widespread consumption of Western supernatural fiction. A common mode of Malaysian horror in the 1971-2000 time period was the Gothic:

> Fantasy and the supernatural are everyday expressions of the imaginative experiences of Malaysian and Singaporean women writers who use the Gothic to explore and expose the contradictions within their societies, constraints upon people's lives, and most specifically, women's roles...through the gaps and fissures of colonial homes and those of grand Chinese or Malay families leak tales of repression and silencing legitimated by cultural, economic and gendered differences. The repressed return, as they do in all good Gothic tales, to bring cultural and personal discrepancies to the notice of the living.[25]

One such female writer is Shirley Lim, who though an expatriate in America for forty years was still considered by critics to be a Malaysian writer. Lim was better known for her scholarly work, but she wrote a number of short stories that fit more or less neatly into the category of the postcolonial Gothic. Of the two types of Gothic, "male" and "female"—male Gothics having a male protagonist and being about a quest to regain patriarchy, and female Gothics having a female protagonist and being about a challenge to patriarchy and its cultural assumptions—Lim's work falls into the female Gothic category. Of one of Lim's stories, "Haunting," Andrew Hock-Soon Ng writes that

> despite foregrounding domestic issues and centering on a female protagonist, [it] cannot be comfortably read as a female Gothic plot. Instead, the story works on a powerful level of irony which invites contrasting interpretations. Rehearsing certain patriarchal

---

[25]Gina Wisker, "Showers of Stars: South East Asian Women's Postcolonial Gothic," *Gothic Studies* 5, no. 2 (Nov. 2003): 64.

assumptions about the family and femininity, "Haunting" seems to reinforce them by demonstrating women's collusion with them. In the story, a woman is haunted not by some revenant but by the house itself. This suggests a metonymical implication of the domestic ideology that entraps, in the form of housing, the female victim. Yet, it is not clear if the story, in the vein of the male Gothic plot, is implying women's acceptance of their fate, or if it is a female Gothic story that reveals the terrible interpellative power of patriarchy in entrapping women without their being aware.[26]

"Haunting" in particular is comparable to Gilman's "The Yellow Wallpaper" in its treatment of the way that the haunted woman eventually embraces her hauntedness:

Like "The Yellow Wallpaper," Lim's story palpably suggests that the domestic ideology haunts women with the shadow self of patriarchal femininity. Women who are interpellated by such an ideology cannot consider a differentiated vantage point because they are thoroughly immersed in their construction. Any inclination for escape is quickly arrested, leaving the woman with merely a vestige of the subject that she can possibly become, but will never attain. That the narrative ends with such a "comforting" scene only belies its deeply menacing ideology. Not only has the house successfully domesticated another potentially dissenting woman, it has even appointed her as the next guardian of patriarchal tradition, thus disguising her entrapment as privilege.[27]

If not as outright terrifying as "The Yellow Wallpaper," "Haunting," and other Gothic stories by Lim, remain menacing and frightening for the way in which the female protagonists are eventually broken by the spirits that haunt them.

Beth Yahp was an award-winning author of fiction and non-fiction as well as an academic. Yahp's novel *The Crocodile Fury* is a Malaysian Gothic novel, about (in proper Gothic form) the recrudescence of the past in the present and the exposure of a great sin.

Beth Yahp's Malaysian Gothic...rewrites and revalues space and stories, landscapes, lives and houses. She exposes the appropriation of wealth and resources and the disempowerment of women, each seen as objects of ownership. Yahp's *The Crocodile Fury* parallels and interrelates the mythic figure of a jungle bandit in crocodile form, one who invades property and upsets enforced imported rules, with that of a shape-shifting sea creature, a crocodile figure of the lover of the great imperialist landowner who built on Malaysian land and imported and stole precious artefacts with which to fill his imposing house. The crocodile bandit and the now long dead lover are figures of otherness representing refusal of the oppression of colonial rule, and their spirit enters the

---

[26] Andrew Hock-Soon Ng, "Malaysian Gothic: the Motif of Haunting in K.S. Maniam's 'Haunting the Tiger' and Shirley Lim's 'Haunting,'" *Mosaic: A journal for the interdisciplinary study of literature*, 39, no. 2 (June 2006): 76.

[27] Hock-Soon Ng, "Malaysian Gothic," 82.

child whose story we follow, granddaughter of a bondmaid who suffered at the hands of the great imperialist landowner, who owned her labour, and her body.[28]

The Crocodile Fury is frightening because of the presence of the jungle, which is inhabited by predatory bandits as well as wild animals, by the presence of ghosts and spirits, and especially by the presence of the carnivorous and sexualized crocodiles, but ultimately *The Crocodile Fury* ends on a revolutionary and liberatory note. As Gina Wisker writes, "The Crocodile fury of the title is [. . .] something wielded as a threat by those who would control girls, women, the colonised, but something recognised as empowering; alternative, wild energies leaking through imposed gender, linguistic and colonial controls for others."[29]

K.S. Maniam was a Malaysian writer and academic of Indian descent. The majority of Malaysian Gothics are written by women, which makes Maniam's work of special interest. His Gothic novels, with their male protagonists and thematic concerns with nationalism and gender, seem ostensibly to be traditional male Gothics. But as Andrew Hock-Soon Ng argues, Maniam's *Haunting the Tiger* (1990), typical of Maniam's work, is actually a female Gothic

> in its emphasis on symbolic castration by an otherwise feminized landscape that resists the protagonist's desire for belonging. The narrative insinuates an oedipal struggle disguised as cultural identity formation. The protagonist, Muthu, attempts, but fails, to "possess" the land (figuratively represented by the tiger) as his strategy for belonging. In this sense, the story questions the very masculinist agenda of nationalism and assimilation, and demonstrates that such an agenda is often ruptured by an attending fear of failing to live up to such objectives, resulting in the subject suffering a metaphorical form of emasculation.[30]

Maniam's strong sense of place–in the jungle and in his fictional town of Kedah–"approaches a kind of Malaysian 'gothic,' giving an extra dimension to the exploration of the theme of inward-looking lives in a society felt to be evermore stifling and sick."[31]

One of the rare Malaysian writers of the 1990s to attempt Western-style horror was Tunku Halim, who though he had only published one short story collection (*The Rape Of Martha Teoh and Other Chilling Tales* (1997)) and two novels (*Dark Demon Rising* (1997), *Vermillion Eye* (2000)) by the end of the century was still viewed at the time as Malaysia's best horror

---

[28]Gina Wisker, *Contemporary Women's Gothic Fiction: Carnival, Hauntings and Vampire Kisses* (London: Palgrave Gothic, 2016), 127.

[29]Wisker, "Showers of Stars," 75.

[30]Hock-Soon Ng, "Malaysian Gothic," 76.

[31]Margaret Yong and Shanthini Pillai, "Maniam, K.S. (Subramaniam Krishnan) (1942-), in *The Encyclopedia of Post-Colonial Literatures in English*, eds. Eugene Benson and L.W. Conolly (London: Routledge, 2005), 954.

writer. Halim's work straddles the line between dark fantasy and outright horror, mixing Malaysian horror tropes and creatures with Western approaches to horror writing. Vampires, shamans, rape, child abuse, murder, and ghosts are common in his stories, which tend more toward shocks and plot twists than the slow mounting of dread or a sinister atmosphere. Halim is a self-avowed enormous fan of Stephen King, and Halim's style, which emphasizes the mundane as a counterpoint to the appearance of the supernatural or the mundane dreadful, can be compared to King's. But Halim lacks King's ability to evoke actual terror, and instead creates it at an arm's length.

Pakistan

The 1971-2000 time period was a difficult one for Pakistani horror fans and writers. The left-wing democracy of the Bhutto government (1971-1977) was hostile to Western culture, particular American popular culture, and the successive military dictatorship (1977-1988), though friendly to the aims of the U.S. government, was stridently Islamic and hostile to parts of Western culture seen as "decadent," which included horror fiction. It was not until the 1988-1999 democratic era that Western popular culture made significant inroads into Pakistani culture, and inspired Pakistanis to write horror literature.

However, as in other Muslim countries, there were exceptions to the religious rules against horror fiction. The Pakistani equivalent of the pulps were the "digests," small booklets typically priced at 50 rupees (roughly $0.75) and selling widely at markets and at train and bus stations.

> Each digest is devoted to a particular genre, from detective or science-fiction to love and horror stories. Charmingly idiosyncratic and often ending with deus ex machina figures, their colloquial style entertains a wide Urdu audience, and print runs number from 10,000 to 30,000 copies per month.

> One particularly intriguing sub-branch of this genre features tales of horror published in magazines such as *Dar Digest* (*The Fear Compendium*), which often combine classical gothic motifs with South Asian mythology. Scenes of dissatisfied jinns (spirits) terrorising their kin, evil snake-demons pretending to be innocent virgins, or haunted house situations (out of which many dear protagonists do not emerge alive) all feature.[32]

Horror digests of this sort began appearing in the late 1980 and early 1990s, and are popular with readers; a 30,000 copy print run is over a quarter of the print run of the largest English-language newspaper in Pakistan. The closer to the century that horror digests drew, the more the digests included non-Gothic, non-South Asian mythological creatures. By the end of the century the horror creatures included mad scientists and wicked surgeons alongside witches,

---

[32] Jürgen Schaflechner, "Why does Pakistan's horror pulp fiction stereotype 'the Hindu'?" *The Conversation*, last modified March 14, 2017, https://theconversation.com/why-does-pakistans-horror-pulp-fiction-stereotype-the-hindu-73885.

ghosts, and demons. Typically Hindus are the villains, wedding ancient folklore and mythology to modern stereotypes.[33]

Abdur Rashid Tabassum wrote widely on topics ranging from diction and rhetoric to poetry, working by day as a journalist and editor of a news magazine. His *A Window to the East* (1981), an award-winning collection of short stories, contained "The Man With Dusty Shoes," about the surprise appearance of a relative who is a dead man mysteriously returned to life. Like Tabassum's other stories, "The Man With Dusty Shoes" is colorful, even vivid, with some obvious inspiration from Poe and with the abrupt narrative twist being reminiscent of some of O. Henry's stories. Both Poe and Henry (first translated into Urdu and published in Pakistan in 1958) were influential on Pakistani horror and suspense writers during the 1971-2000 time period.

Adam Zameenzad is a writer of novels, two of which were long listed for the Man Booker Prize. Zameenzad's *The Thirteenth Hour* (1987), one of those Booker-long listed novels and Zameenzad's first novel, is ostensibly about an unlucky, poverty-stricken protagonist whose life is filled with chaos and dismay, and whose luck, when it finally appears to have changed for the better, quickly reverts back to bad, crushing his hopes and ultimately resulting in tragedy. On the surface, *The Thirteenth Hour* is a dreary novel, but the plight of the protagonist and his family becomes moving—and political in its description of the arbitrary and wicked political forces that can and often do crush the lives of men, women, and children in developing countries. Zameenzad's universe is an absurd, even existentialist one, in which all moral values are the products of human beings, and nothing is God-given, for God does not exist.

M.A. Rahat was a popular writer of suspense and crime stories and novels. In some of his novels, however, he made use of horror tropes. His *Kalu Jahad* (1995) is in some ways similar of Rahat's crime and suspense work, being published in a cheap paperback form and told in a hasty manner. In the case of *Kalu Jahad*, Rahat uses crude shocks and colorfully primitive descriptions to tell the story of a man seeking to gain great wealth through the use of black magic. Muslim in a sort of pro forma way, with a Muslim character and the power of Islam defeating the villain and saving the day, *Kalu Jahad* was popular, as all of Rahat's work, but like the horror digests was cheaply sold, poorly written, and frightening only in the most basic of ways.

Philippines

The prevailing trend of the 1941-1970 time period—that horror fiction was produced by "popular" authors and aesthetically was Low Art rather than High Art—continued through the 1971-2000 time period, as Filipino horror literature, with a few exceptions, appeared in low art forms such as comic books and dime novels.

One notable exception to this was Nick Joaquin, arguably the foremost Filipino writer in English of his generation. Joaquin's work was usually magic realist, full of fatalistic humor,

---

[33] Jürgen Schaflechner, " The Hindu " in Recent Urdu Horror Stories from Pakistan (2016)," *Academia.edu*, accessed June 19, 2018, https://www.academia.edu/27523878/_The_Hindu_in_Recent_Urdu_Horror_Stories_from_Pakistan_2016_.

surreal imagery, complex characterization, and lush, poetic prose. But on occasion, as in his 1972 short story collection *Tropical Gothic*, magic realism verged into dark territories:

> Gothic elements are in full flower here. Lush prose. Check (and check out the opening and final paragraphs of "May Day Eve"). Melodramatic situations. Check. Folklore and centuries-old Catholic rites. Check and check. The Spanish colonial past in all its baroque splendor and excess. Check, check.

> Stock characters such as madmen; beautiful, entrapped women; tyrants of the state, the church, and the house; Byronic heroes; heretics ("The Order of Melkizedek"); and magicians (the magus Mateo Maestro in "The Mass of Saint Sylvestre) populate these pages. Even animated skeletons, props much favored by Gothic horror, execute their dances of death.[34]

Singapore

A writer of little distinction and attention during his lifetime, and who was forgotten about within a generation before being rediscovered in 2013, was Gregory Nalpon, who worked at everything from being a disc jockey to a journalist to a trade unionist, but whose primary output was his writing. Nalpon's work was more horror-adjacent than horror, although there is substantial Malay supernatural imagery in his work (which was written from the 1950s through to his death in 1978, but generally only published in the 1970s), and his work can be regarded as "examples of an early postcolonial Singapore gothic,"[35] although Ng Yi-Sheng sees a greater similarity with magic realism:

> They are dark and full of shadows, and yet illuminated by unexpected beauty. Running through all this is a vein of magic, both horrific and transcendent. One encounters vicious black dog spirits in mango trees, or else discovers God in a square parcel wrapped in brown paper — a phenomenon Whitehead calls a 'Singaporean Gothic', but which I also find resonates with the magical realism of the Latin American Boom.[36]

The history of Singaporean literature did not begin in earnest until some years after Singapore gained independence from Malaysia in 1965. Short stories flourished before and after independence, but the first true Singaporean novel is viewed by critics to be Goh Poh Seng's *If We Dream Too Long*, published in 1972.

---

[34]Hau, "Tropical Gothic."

[35]Angus Whitehead, "Introduction," in *The Wayang at Eight Milestone: Stories & Essays by Gregory Nalpon* by Gregory Nalpon (Singapore: Epigram Books, 2013), xvi.

[36]Ng Yi-sheng, "Illusions of Memory," *Quarterly Literary Review of Singapore* 13, no. 2 (Apr, 2014), accessed June 19, 2018, http://www.qlrs.com/critique.asp?id=1104.

One of the most widely read authors of the time was Catherine Lim, who gained renown as the author of social realist short stories in the 1970s and feminist novels in the 1980s. But Lim also wrote horror, beginning with her 1980 short story collection *Or Else the Lightning God and Other Stories*. Although later horror writers do not cite Lim as an influence, she prepared the way for them, and is critically considered to be the mother of Singaporean horror. Lim's horror is primarily about the influence of the Chinese spiritual and supernatural world on the psyches of modern Singaporeans; in her work, creatures and evil magic from Chinese folklore and myth irrupt into the world of modern Singapore. "This helped to lay the groundwork for the rebirth of our horror culture, and its transformation from a specifically Malay milieu to a multiethnic one."[37] Lim's horror novels, written in the 1980s and 1990s, shift to the Gothic mode, focusing on the physical changes in Singapore that eradicate evidence of the past. "Singaporean Gothic tropes…reflect local preoccupations with development-projects, with submerged or newly conceptualised heritage, and most pointedly, with suppressed aspects of turbulent histories, both on a national and an individual level,"[38] and Lim makes full use of these tropes, including the ghosts of Singaporeans killed by the Japanese during World War Two.

A more conventional horror writer was Nicky Moey, who began publishing horror short stories in 1986. Moey's horror primarily appears in short story collections and anthologies, the mode in which most Singaporean horror writers of the 1980s and 1990s published their horror. Moey is representative of the typical Singaporean horror writer. Moey's horror stories are largely variations on traditional Singaporean myths and legends, but set in the modern world and with scaffoldings or framing devices averring that the story told is a true one.

> Truth is a primary obsession in Singaporean horror fiction…if horror, in the words of Gillian Beer, "takes space, and it is this usurpation of space by the immaterial which is one of the deepest terrors released by the ghost story," then such a device becomes the ultimate in the provocation of fear, where fantasies come to life, crossing the threshold of rational order into reality. Limits of sanity are hence eroded when ghosts become "true." Such an assumption would explain the relatively tame response to openly fictional horror works. In comparison, those writings that proclaim actual paranormal testimonies attain a greater success. Fictional horror, admitting to an imagination at work, is apparently delegated a secondary position in terms of Singaporean popularity.[39]

---

[37] Ng Yi-Sheng, "A History of Singapore Horror," *biblioasia*, accessed June 19, 2018, http://www.nlb.gov.sg/biblioasia/2017/07/03/a-history-of-singapore-horror/#sthash.B2xEGBwO.Jv3oY9LT.dpbs.

[38] Tamara S. Wagner, "Ghosts of a Demolished Cityscape: Gothic Experiments in Singaporean Fiction," in *Asian Gothic: Essays on Literature, Film and Anime*, ed. Andrew Hock-Soon Ng (Jefferson, NC: McFarland, 2008), 47.

[39] Joash Moo, "Horror Fiction (Singapore)," in *The Encyclopedia of Post-Colonial Literatures in English*, ed. Eugene Benson and L.W. Conolly (London: Routledge, 2005), 1146.

The primary example of the popularity of these "paranormal testimonies" is the work of Russell Lee, whose *Almost Complete Collection of True Singapore Ghost Stories* (1989) is reputed to be the best-selling short story collection in Singapore's history, and which spawned a series of twenty-six sequels, all written by Lee. From the title of the collections to Lee's statements within them, everything about Lee's stories is supposed to be true. Lee's style cannot be said to be the reason for their popularity (and Lee is far and away the most popular horror writer in Singapore's history); his work is simple in plot and plainly written. But his work is famously popular, both because of their supposed truthfulness and because he draws upon the myth and popular and religious folklore of all the residents of Singapore, from Muslim to Christian to Hindu to Buddhist to pre-Islam.

Of Moey and Lee's popularity, Mary Loh and Teri Shaffer Yamada write:

> Perhaps the only way to account for the popularity of the horror genre is to argue that it is an extension of the gothic mode in Singaporean literature. It may be true to say that, just as the gothic genre was a reaction to the strictures of Victorian society, the perception of entrapment fostered the growth of the Singaporean gothic. The opposite of materialism is a strong belief in a spirit world, the world of the uncanny and inexplicable, the source of all superstition.[40]

However, beginning in 1990, a different strain of horror emerged in Singapore, striking out beyond the "truthful" mode. One such work is Z.Y. Moo's *The Weird Diary of Walter Woo* (1990), which is set in a satirically-portrayed English university and whose protagonist, a student at the university, falls prey to a series of strange events. While satirizing the university and the dual forces of anarchy and order, and displaying the influences of Lewis Carroll and Bram Stoker, *The Weird Diary of Walter Woo* also "locates its subversions and symbols of unease within a contemporary network, breaking away from the ghost-story format drawn from historical folklore. It creates a new fantastic alternative entrenched within Singapore's gradually evolving society."[41]

Arguably the most talented and skilled of the Singaporean horror writers of the 1980s and 1990s was Damien Sin, who wrote for Russell Lee before publishing the four volume *Classic Singapore Horror Stories* (1992-2003) series. A poet, Sin added a certain lyricism to the grotesque and horrible events in his stories. Sin's plots and characterization were notably strong compared to his counterparts, but his strength lay in his vivid, visceral descriptions, both of the creatures and curses he portrays and in his descriptions of the sordid, grimy, desperate and crime-ridden side of Singapore.

South Korea

---

[40] Mary Loh and Teri Shaffer Yamada, "Conflict and Change: The Singapore Short Story," in *Modern Short Fiction of Southeast Asia: A Literary History*, ed. Teri Shaffer Yamada (Ann Arbor, MI: Association for Asian Studies, 2009), 228.

[41] Moo, "Horror Fiction (Singapore)," 1146.

South Korean popular literature did not flourish until the despotic Chun regime gave way to the Sixth Republic in 1987. Mass market genres, ranging from suspense to mystery to science fiction, quickly dominated the literature market, a situation that remained in place through the end of the century. Horror was one of those genres, although it was much more frequent in film than in prose. Much more frequent in popular literature than mainstream literature (which made use of horror tropes like ghosts and supernatural beings but for purposes other than to frighten the reader), horror of the South Korea variety tended to mix traditional Korean folklore with contemporary situations and milieu. Typical of this approach, although far better selling than the norm, was Lee Woo-hyuk's *Toemarok*, which began life as a novel on a computerized bulletin board in 1993 before being published later that year. Four sequels, consisting of nineteen volumes, were published between 1994 and 2001. *Toemarok* and its sequels are about a trio of exorcists ("soul guardians") who fight off demonic and supernatural creatures and intrusions into modern Korea, both Seoul and more rural locations. Gory, dark, and action-filled, *Toemarok* was never mistaken for high art but supplied both entertainment and frights for its readers.

Taiwan

Horror stories and novels make up a significant fraction of Taiwanese popular literature. Taiwan's horror literature did not come into its own until the 1970s, however, as the autocratic government strictly controlled the media. Two authors early in the 1971-2000 time period published mainstream work with supernatural elements, though, and laid the groundwork for the popular horror writers of the 1990s.

Zhong Ling, a fiction writer, essayist, and poet, began publishing short stories in 1970. Through the 1970s and 1980s she published short stories which used ghosts and characters from fantasy and traditional Chinese folklore. In her narratives, these figures and supernatural beings represent psychological and mental disturbances. Zhong Ling's main themes are female sexuality, social oppression, and personal liberation, and while most of her stories have uplifting or happy endings, the appearance of ghosts *et al.* are frightening, as are Zhong Ling's portrayals of mental illness.

Shi Shuqing, an avant-garde novelist and short story writer, wrote more thoroughly horrific stories. Her narratives "are teeming with characters who are physically and psychologically disfigured and whose world is rampant with madness, psychosis, morbidity and death. With these gothic stories, Shi was recognized as [a]…writer interested in exploring the alienating effects of modern society on the lives of the individual."[42] Shi's style is variously absurd, surreal, and Gothic, playing with the reality of the stories in order to unnerve and disquiet the reader.

Thailand

---

[42] Li-hua, *Historical Dictionary of Modern Chinese Literature*, 167.

Thai literature during the 1971-2000 period was similar to that of other Southeast Asian countries: a mix of traditional High Art and commercial fiction, with the latter growing increasingly popular in the 1980s and 1990s. What horror fiction there was in Thailand was a mixture of folklore-influenced and foreign-influenced.

Perhaps the foremost Thai writer of horror or horror-adjacent material during the period was Chart Korbjitti, an award-winning novelist and writer of short stories. While several of his works are sharp-edged satire–a quality Korbjitti is known for–a number of his other works, beginning with *Chon Trok* (*No Way Out*, 1980) and *Khamphiphaksa* (*The Judgment*, 1981), his second and third novels, were Gothics. While Korbjitti's works do fall under the rubric of the Asian Gothic, there is nothing supernatural in his Gothic narratives. Korbjitti's Gothic works focus on the ways in which the people of Thailand are marginalized, economically and politically oppressed, and rendered primitive. Korbjitti particularly uses the grotesque as the means to discuss madness, disease, degeneration, corruption, perverse sexuality, and social disorder.

Another Thai Gothic writer of the period was Pira Sudham, although like Korbjitti Sudham is a political writer who does not use the supernatural to horrify. Sudham's narratives "abound in Gothic tropes employed to demonize the oppressors and invoke the reader's sympathy for the plight of the rural poor, who continue to be taken advantage of."[43]

---

[43]Katarzyna Ancuta, "Asian Gothic," in *A New Companion to the Gothic*, ed. David Punter (Chichester, West Sussex: Blackwell Publishing, 2012), 437.

Chapter Fourteen: Europe

Austria

As a general rule Austrian popular literature suffered during the 1971-2000 period, with both authors and readers focusing on sober, serious-minded High Art literature. Authors like Walter Brandorff were rarities. Brandorff, a figure of some biographical mystery, three novels and two short story collections between 1989 and 1995. Brandorff was a writer of some ability, and his horror narratives are of varied sorts; some are conventional horror stories told with a subtle malice, others are visceral and explicit splatterpunk or pornography. A recurring theme in his works, however, is of the imponderability of grotesque fates which await Brandorff's characters, who exist in a unjust universe in which grim fates such as being carried away on midnight trains can happen to even the best of people. The style in which Brandorff tells the stories varies according to their content—some subtly and even delicately told, others as blunt as a hammer to the back of the head.

Most of the horror that did appear in Austria during the 1971-2000 period was of the High Art variety, such as Elfriede Jelinek's *Der Kinder der Toten* (*The children of the dead*, 1995). Jelinek, a Nobel Prize-winning novelist and playwright, wrote *Der Kinder der Toten* as an examination of the Austrian memory of, and suppression of the memory of, the Holocaust. *Der Kinder der Toten* has a large cast of characters, multiple plot threads, and a number of cross-references and allusions; it also has constant punning, linguistic invention, looping scenes and plot lines, and numerous different types of texts inserted into the novel. The effect of the novel is the disruption of linearity and a destabilization of the reading experience, making *Der Kinder der Toten* a postmodern horror novel. All the characters are zombies, mute, flesh-eating, sex-obsessed, and rotting. *Der Kinder der Toten* features a purgatory for the main characters (for life as a zombie is significantly unpleasant), cannibalism, castration, and vampires, told in a flat style with characters separated from the world of the living. The novel works as both a Gothic novel and a parody of the Gothic novel, but the horror comes not from Gothic devices, but primarily from the metaphorical way in which Jelinek invokes the Jewish victims of the Holocaust:

> Parallels are drawn between the reader and the Jewish victims, only to be undermined by linkages to the Nazis, as well as to the undead, implicating the reader in the suppression of the memory of the Jewish dead. No critical distance vis-a-vis the Austrian past can be maintained nor can the reader opt for an empathetic identification with the victims, as her depiction of the Jewish dead, like those of most of Jelinek's victims, is far from sympathetic. She does not resurrect the dead so that some easy emotional connection might be forged that could ease our collective conscience. Rather, we are violently called to remember.[1]

Belgium

---

[1] Hillary Hope, *Vienna Is Different: Jewish Writers in Austria from the Fin-de-Siècle to the Present* (New York: Berghahn Books, 2011), 264.

The boom in *fantastika* publishing in Belgium of the mid-century decades did not last long past 1980, and by the end of the century publishers of *fantastika* were selling in the same (low) numbers as they had in the 1960s. What Belgian horror writers there were of the 1971-2000 time period fell into two categories.

The first is a hybrid of science fiction and horror. The standout example of this sort of horror fiction is Eddy C. Bertin. Bertin began publishing in 1969, but is best known for his linked series of "Membrane Universe" stories, begun in 1976 and published in three collections (1976, 1981, 1983). The stories chart the future history of the human race, from 1970 to 3666. Modernist in inclusion of non-standard texts (song lyrics, fake documents, timetables, etc) into the main texts of stories, the Membrane Universe narratives are relatively standard in plot, but show a depth of character that is rare in horror (or science fiction). The stories are a combination of supernatural and psychological horror with science fiction heavily influenced by the work of H.P. Lovecraft, so that the end result is psychological cosmic horror when it is not straight psychological horror or horror-noir. Bertin is a skilled stylist with a firm grasp of both his material and the best ways in which to frighten his reader.

The second category of 1971-2000 Belgian horror was that of *l'ecole belge de l'etrange* variety, and there was no better practitioner of it during the last three decades of the twentieth century than Thomas Owen, whose mid-century work was outstanding but who actually improved upon it during the 1971-2000 time period. A writer of "intimate" horror—what Thomas Ligotti, in a pull-quote for a Eddie Angerhuber story collection in which he compared Angerhuber to Stefan Grabinski, Dino Buzzati, and Owen, described as "the nightmare of being alive"—Owen tells sad and even tragic stories of ordinary men and women whose lives are degraded by moral and emotional ambiguities to the point where they are vulnerable to supernatural assault. Owen's characters are trapped in meaningless lives and by story's end have no chance of achieving their expectations or hoped-for accomplishments. The stories are solemn, sardonic, morbid, and splendidly, gracefully told. Owen's style is sparse, although his imagery is saturated with a poetic, macabre, eroticism and Owen includes a substantial amount of dark humor. "If Owen's tales sometimes read like throwbacks now, it should be noted that they read like throwbacks even in their day: that his project was to make them so, to strip them of time and place until they addressed some essential, eternal condition."[2] Unsettling, disquieting, and subtly horrific, Owen's horror stories are among the best not only of *l'ecole belge de l'etrange* but of the Continent itself.

Czech Republic

Government censorship under Communist rule meant that there was little that could be considered as horror literature in Czechoslovakia in the 1970s and 1980s. The exceptions to the no-horror rule under the Communists–not officially endorsed, but allowed to be published–were social and political satire and humor. Miloslav Švandrlík, a writer and humorist, published a

---

[2]Edward Gauvin, "100 Years of Unease," *Small Beer Press*, last modified Jan. 20, 2011, http://smallbeerpress.com/not-a-journal/2011/01/20/100-years-of-unease/.

work of comic horror, *Černí Baroni* (*Black Barons*, 1969). Ostensibly about Švandrlík's time in the Czech army after World War Two, the novel humorously deals with soldiers' lives in and around a castle, and features vampires, werewolves, and corpses both animate and inanimate, though always treated in comic fashion.

It was not until the "Velvet Revolution" of 1989, when the Czech Communist government stepped down in the face of protests, that freedom of the press returned to Czechoslovakia, which was split into the Czech Republic and Slovakia. Like many other genres, horror experienced a surge of popularity, an explosion of writers and books and stories that continued through the end of the century.

Vladimír Medek was an economist and translator of English, Spanish, and Portuguese literature into English. In 1992 he took advantage of the new liberty granted to Czech writers to begin publishing his own fiction in Czech. His story collection, *Krev na Maltézkém náměstí* (*Blood on Maltese Square*, 1992), is about ordinary men and women encountering the supernatural in the form of haunted houses, werewolf wives, cursed fates, blind painters, vampires, and zombies. Intelligently written, by someone with an obvious knowledge of the standard tropes of the genre, the stories in *Krev na Maltézkém náměstí* are entertaining and suitably frightening, if not landmark but for being the first Czech collection of conventional horror short stories.

Jiří Kulhánek is a writer of science fiction and fantasy, much of which has horror elements. His *Vládci strachu* (*Lords of Fear*, 1995) is a neo-cyberpunk sf/horror novel set in 2023 in Bohemia and environs. *Vládci strachu* is about the struggle between a group of heroic vampires and a group of human Hunters who are dedicated to wiping out the vampires, who have co-existed alongside humans for centuries. *Vládci strachu* is heavy on violence, blood and gore, and sensationalist thrills, told in a plain prose leavened only by black humor. Kulhánek will never be mistaken for Anne Rice, Stephen King, or even the writers behind the tv show *Buffy the Vampire* and the *Blade* movies, but his work is imaginative and moderately entertaining.

Jana Moravcová is an author, translator, and editor who wrote books for children as well as poetry, mysteries, and science fiction. Shortly after the formation of the Czech Republic she published the first in a quartet of novels about vampire. *Nemrtvý* (*Undead*, 1994) was followed by *Dračí krev* (*Dragon Blood*, 1995) and *Trůn pro mrtvého* (*A Throne for a Dead*, 2000). Moravcová's novels about Dracula focus on both the life of the historical Vlad Tepes the Impaler and on his posthumous existence as a vampire. Heavily researched and smoothly told, Moravcová emphasizes the historical atmosphere as much as she does the individual moments of terror that both the living and the undead Vlad Tepes created. Too, Moravcová emphasizes the loves of Vlad Tepes' life, lending both the historical figure and the vampire three dimensional characterization and even a bit of pathos.

Lastly, in 1999 Daniela Mičanová published *Modrá krev: O upírech a lidech* (*Blue Blood: About Vampires and People*). Mičanová, a translator and author, is primarily known for *Modrá krev* and its post-2000 sequels, novels which have led to her being known as the "Czech Anne Rice." *Modrá krev*'s debt to *Interview with the Vampire* is obvious and at times nearly overwhelming, although Mičanová matured into an independent writer in the later vampire novels. Mičanová's style is somewhat archaic and makes for difficult reading, but she does not scant on the horror, as the two human protagonists discover to their terror that the new American they have just met at a vampirological congress is an actual vampire, and a long-lived, deadly one at that.

Denmark

Danish popular literature in the 1971-2000 time period tended to be primarily non-fantastic, with an emphasis on thrillers and mysteries/detective novels rather than science fiction, fantasy, or horror. The foremost member of the small group of Danish horror writers of that period is Steen Langstrup, an author, cartoonist, and publisher. He published seven horror novels and story collections from 1995 to 2000, ranging in subject matter from evil revenant cats to vampires to pyromaniacs to non-*fantastika* Russian Mafia to haunted houses to sewer monsters. Although Langstrup manipulates language and plot masterfully, his style is, in his own words, short, minimalistic, and dark, lacking happy endings or anything typical of conventional horror fiction.

Finland

Like many of the countries of northern Europe and Scandinavia, Finland during the 1971-1980 had a flourishing market for genre literature, although (as usual) the greater respect was given to the many authors writing mainstream, serious works of mimetic fiction. However, as with Denmark, the emphasis was on non-*fantastika*, especially not horror.

One of the few exceptions to this, and one of the few Finnish authors who repeatedly wrote horror with any degree of success, was Kari Nenonen, a prolific paperback writer who wrote in genres ranging from romance to detective to horror. Nenonen wrote two horror novels (1988, 1991) and one collection of horror stories (1989). Nenonen's stated influence is Mika Waltari, but Nenonen is a more subtle stylist than Waltari ever was, though Waltari was stronger in creating inventive plots. Nenonen involve the appearance of supernatural evil in modern settings, such as *Ken kuolleita kutsuu* (*Ken's Dead Call*, 1991), in which the development of a computer game through which one ask questions of the dead leads to surprisingly coherent, and very disturbing, answers. The stories in *Noitarovio* (*The witch Rovio*, 1989) feature vampires, zombies, and witchcraft, but in contemporary Finnish settings. Nenonen's strength is his ability to evoke a sinister and frightening atmosphere.

A much different sort of horror appears in the short stories of S. Albert Kivinen, an author and academic. Kivinen's short horror stories, appearing in the late 1980s and gathered together in an edition of his collected work in 1990, are Lovecraftian pastiches. Inconsistently successful—to paraphrase Mark Twain, Kivinen knows the notes but not the music—Kivinen's Lovecraftian horror too often are mere pastiche, aping Lovecraft and nakedly imitating his plot structures and vocabulary. The best of his Lovecraftian work, "Keskiyön Mato Ikaalisissa" ("The Midnight Worm in Ikaalinen," 1987), successfully attempts to transplant Lovecraft's horror to the Finnish landscape, using Finnish folklore to augment and add to the Cthulhu Mythos. Generally, though, Kivinen's Lovecraftian horror, with its attempt to create a Finnish version of Dunwich, are not successful.

Jyrki Vainonen is a translator, academic, and author. In 1999 he published *Tutkimusmatkailija ja muita tarinoita (The Explorer and Other Stories)*, a short story collection. Vainonen's style is cool and calm, almost detached, but like Saki, to whom Vainonen has been compared by critics, Vainonen's laconic style and black humor conceal wonders and (more often) terrors, ranging from paranoid medical patients to a husband who disappears on an expedition into his wife's thigh to fly-cursed biologists to mysterious animals. Vainonen's stories tend to be more literally fantastic than Saki's work, and are leavened with what might be called a Finnish humor and outlook, but otherwise the apposite comparison for Vainonen is Saki.

France

French horror literature of the 1971-2000 time period can be divided into the work of the 1970s and the work of the 1980s and 1990s. French horror literature of the 1970s came out of traditional French literature, which mixed High Art and Low Art elements and tended toward authorial seriousness and the deployment of horror tropes, motifs, and creatures for purpose beyond mere fear and entertainment. This began to change in the late 1970s and early 1980s, when foreign horror films (*Halloween* (1979), *Scanners* (1981), *Dawn of the Dead* (1983), and various Italian versions of popular American horror films) and translations of American and British horror writers (including Dean Koontz from 1974, Stephen King from 1976, Clive Barker from 1987) began flooding the French literary and cinematic markets, and drawing great numbers of French movie watchers and readers. In the mid- and late-1980s and 1990s French horror authors began working in imitation of American and English horror writers, moving away from French traditions and toward English-language traditions. This new breed of French horror writer was popular with readers but less original and inventive than their predecessors, and moved away from the French *fantastique* and toward a more American conception of horror. Edward Gauvin writes,

> the French *fantastique* as a genre is bound up with the word *étrange* of whose supernatural suggestion our "strange" retains but an attenuated echo ("estrangement" preserves some of the alienating force, though not its vector). And so *étrange* in this context is generally rendered as "uncanny," both of which are standard for the German *unheimlich*—literally, "unhomely."[3]

But it was exactly this uncanniness and unhomeliness which is lost in the American- and English-influenced French horror fiction of the 1980s and 1990s; straightforward shocks and scares, violence and terror replaced unease and disquiet.

Robert Clauzel, a doctor, wrote thirty science fiction novels from 1970-1984 that were largely a hybrid of science fiction and horror. Clauzel's horror narratives were Lovecraftian in conception, with extra-dimensional horrors impinging on our universe and threatening humanity, but with added elements of the Dean Koontzian horror-thriller. Clauzel's style is not

---

[3] Edward Gauvin, "Unhomed," *World Literature Today*, last modified May 2018, https://www.worldliteraturetoday.org/2018/may/unhomed-edward-gauvin.

Lovecraftian, being altogether more conventional, and on occasion Clauzel over-indulges in nostalgia for 1930s pulp science fiction or 1950s "Golden Age" science fiction.

Jeanne Champion, a painter and historical novelist, is usually considered to be a mainstream writer. But a number of her historical novels include horror elements. *Vautour-en-Privilège* (1973) includes a variety of malign supernatural events occurring in the titular rural French village which is torn by superstition and rivalries. In *Dans les jardins d'Esther* (*In the garden of Esther*, 1975), a young actor/director is nightmarishly killed one night when statues and figures from paintings come alive. In *Les Gisants* (*The recumbent*, 1977), a murder mystery in a monastery assumes Gothic proportions. Champion is a surrealist painter and a bitter writer, with recurring themes of violence and mutilation.

Joe Houssin is an author of science fiction, fantasy, and crime novels. His first novel, *Locomotive Rictus* (1975), is science fictional horror, viscerally-told, about a future apocalypse in which a virus causes a revolt of the animals. The novel features a murderous panther spirit possessing humans, a monstrous gestalt of handicapped children, and a new synthetic biological organism which infects people and makes them murder and cannibalize.

Pierre Kast was best known as a screenwriter and director of film and television, but in 1975 he wrote a horror novel, *Les Vampires d'Alfama* (*The vampires of Alfama*). An anticipation by one year of Anne Rice's *Interview with the Vampire*, *Les Vampires d'Alfama* features heroic vampires at work in a secret quarter of Lisbon in the 18th century, fighting to save mortals from death and from the wiles of the Catholic Church. A neo-Gothic novel full of horror story tropes, motifs, character types and stereotypes, *Les Vampires d'Alfama* is well-written, grotesque and erotic, full of literary Satanism and a rewritten vampire mythology of the sort that Rice and Chelsea Quinn Yarbro would later popularize in the United States.

Perhaps the best-known and most respected French horror writer of the 1980s and 1990s—albeit one whose influences are primarily Anglophone rather than French—was Serge Brussolo, called by critics "France's answer to Stephen King" and "the French Clive Barker." A consistent bestseller in France, and an author whose output sometimes reached six novels published per year, Brussolo began publishing in 1982 and continued nonstop through the end of the century, writing in every major genre but concentrating in horror. The influence of Barker is notable on Brussolo's post-1985 work; Brussolo began writing morbid, powerful narratives displaying a Barker-like fascination with the manipulation and violation of flesh and a Barker-like obsession with portraying the extremes of pain and biological/body horror. Among the plot devices Brussolo uses are radical organ transplants, living symbiotic tattoos, werewolves, mad sculptors, flesh-eating monkeys, and carnivorous micro-organisms.

> Brussolo is most noted for his violent originality, the seemingly bottomless fecundity of his imagination, and the breathless sense of dread, a visceral fatalism, that pervades the worlds he creates…among his recurrent themes are the decay of social order, the illusory consolation of religion, imprisonment, and madness. His prose is marked by a density of

playful neologisms, and an energy from feverish riffing on images and ideas that concretizes dreamscapes.[4]

Germany

The world of German letters in the 1971-2000 time period had, until the 1990s, little time for horror literature, classifying it as *schund und schmutzliteratur* (lit.: "rubbish and dirty literature") in much the same way that the German *heftromane* (dime novels) of the 1920s and 1930s were dismissed by the German literary establishment. Until the 1990s German horror fell into one of two categories: pulp/dime novel, and High Art Horror.

The German *heftromane* industry dates back to the early part of the twentieth century, but the *heftromane* industry never went through a horror phase the way that the American pulp industry did, and it was not until 1968 that the first horror *heftromane* was published. A number of horror *heftromane* followed, none more popular or archetypal of horror *heftromane* than the *Geisterjäger John Sinclair* (*Ghosthunter John Sinclair*) series, which began publishing in 1973 and continued appearing through the end of the century. *Geisterjäger John Sinclair* is about the eponymous character, a Scotland Yard inspector who fights the forces of darkness, including but not limited to vampires, werewolves, zombies, witches, necromancers, and so on. The creator of John Sinclair and the author of all the *Geisterjäger John Sinclair* novels from 1973 onward was Helmut Rellergerd, a professional writer whose output was one novel a week, every month. Rellergerd will never be mistaken for a genius, and the comparison that over-enthusiastic German fans and critics make to Arthur Conan Doyle is mistaken. But Rellergerd's work displays a powerful imagination, an engaging, colloquial style, a skill at vivid horror descriptions, an awareness of how and when to best deploy horror elements, and an ability at evoking the maximum amount of fright with the minimum amount of words. Rellergerd's horror is of the blunt, hammering variety; there's nothing subtle about the *Geisterjäger John Sinclair* novels. But within the confines of the *heftromane* medium Rellergerd is the best of the authors of horror narratives.

A typical High Art Horror novel of the 1980s—typical not in sales but in approach—was Patrick Süskind's *Das Parfum* (*Perfume*, 1985). Süskind, a screenwriter and mainstream author, created in *Das Parfum* an international bestseller and story that, if not horror, is at the last horror-adjacent. About an orphaned boy with a superhuman sense of smell who becomes the most skilled perfumer in the world and commits murders to preserve the unworldly scents of his young female victims, *Das Parfum* is lushly-told, inventive and unpredictable. The plot and main characters are provocative, with the murderer meant to be both sympathetic and repellant and the mass of humanity portrayed in misanthropic fashion. *Das Parfum* is evocative, detailed, and haunting.

German horror began to change in the early 1990s, with horror authors creating works that were outright horror rather than High Art but were more literary and subtle than pulp horror.

---

[4]Edward Gauvin, "Weird France and Belgium: A Best Of," *Weird Fiction Review*, last modified Oct. 30, 2014, http://weirdfictionreview.com/2014/10/weird-france-and-belgium-a-best-of/.

Foremost among the new crop of horror writers was Michael Siefener, a translator and author of both historical and fantastic fiction. Siefener's first published work of horror was his 1993 story collection, which immediately marked him as different from previous German horror authors. His horror work through the end of the century confirmed his status as Germany's leading horror and weird dark fiction author. Siefener occasionally uses Lovecraftian imagery, but his horror narratives are more traditional, in the vein of M.R. James or even Ramsey Campbell. However, unlike Campbell, Siefener does not write bleak, hopeless stories, instead preferring "what Thomas Ligotti called 'the consolations of horror.'"[5] Siefener's stories can be somber and even grim, but rarely are they depressing. Siefener writes intensely emotional stories, dealing with loneliness and social anxieties in addition to stories about obsessions and occult books. His strengths are his general sophistication as a writer, his adroit use of language, and his evocation of a sinister, horrific atmosphere.

Debuting the same year as Michael Siefener was Malte Schulz-Sembten. While a lifelong admirer of Poe, Lovecraft, and Robert E. Howard, Schulz-Sembten's horror was altogether different from theirs. Schulz-Sembten's horror stories are dark, full of terror, pain, remorse, perverse sexuality, described far more graphically and at times brutally and gore-filled than Poe, Lovecraft, or Howard were ever allowed to write. Schulz-Sembten's stories are structurally sound, with a wide range of characters and more than occasional subtle uses of language and horror tropes and motifs. His plots often surprise readers, as they contain "ironic and original twists...[which] also strike deep and tragic notes."[6]

One of the most skilled German practitioners of horror in the mid- and late-1990s was Monika "Eddie" Angerhuber, who took her male nickname from Edgar Allan Poe, who Angerhuber is a fan of. Little-known in Germany, and that only as a translator and proponent of the work of Thomas Ligotti, Angerhuber is a writer of sophisticated horror stories, subtly-told and narratively rich. "Never condescending to cheap formulaic writing, most of her stories are experiments in language, style and mood derived from a highly developed aestheticism that nevertheless does not neglect questions of character and plot."[7] Her stories tend toward darkness and sadness, leaving the reader by turns horrified and melancholy, emotions aided by her writing style, which can be either oneiric or nightmarish depending on her purposes in a story. Prominent themes in her work are loneliness, death, decay, and the dehumanization of humanity because of increased industrialization and mechanization of society.

Another skilled German female horror writer who debuted 1996 was Christiane Neudecker. Better known as a director of performing arts, Neudecker's short stories range from the weird dark to the overtly horrific. Neudecker is equally skilled at portraying psychological

---

[5]Marco Frenschkowski, "Siefener, Michael," in *Supernatural Literature of the World*, eds. S.T. Joshi and Stefan Dziemianowicz, (Westport, CT: Greenwood Press, 2005), 1024.

[6]Marco Frenschkowski, "Schulz-Sembten, Malte," in *Supernatural Literature of the World*, eds. S.T. Joshi and Stefan Dziemianowicz, (Westport, CT: Greenwood Press, 2005), 986.

[7]Marco Frenschkowski, "Angerhuber, Eddie," in *Supernatural Literature of the World*, eds. S.T. Joshi and Stefan Dziemianowicz, (Westport, CT: Greenwood Press, 2005), 34.

disturbances, delusions, and mind-born fears, and at telling stories in which original plots, tropes, motifs, and creatures (haunted pianos, living shadows, a demonic boxer, a game of chess with the dead) are deployed. Neudecker, whose influences include E.T.A. Hoffmann and Daphne Du Maurier, is strong at evoking an ominous atmosphere and mounting tension, at linguistic innovation, and at frightening readers conceptually and viscerally.

Italy

Italy has in fact never had a solid tradition of horror, science or detective fiction because of the Fascist cultural protectionist policies which came into effect shortly after the introduction to the Italian market of a series devoted to crime stories (*I Libri Gialli*, 1929). After the Second World War, Italian intellectuals devoted themselves to recounting first the catastrophic social and existential conditions after the conflict, then the dark side of progress and urbanization, but following a format that had little in common with the classic detective fiction.[8]

Despite the existence of the work of Dino Buzzati and Tommaso Landolfi, not to mention the pre-World War Two Italian writers of horror, the preceding quote is equally true of horror fiction as it is of detective fiction. Buzzati, Landolfi, *et al.* had their adherents, but Italy cannot be said to have had any sort of continuity of horror literature, much less a flourishing market for it, before the 1990s. Those significant writers of horror who did appear did so more or less in generic isolation or under the guise of other fictional modes.

One significant novel of horror, published in 1977, left little impact at the time and was forgotten about until reprinted in 2017. Giorgio De Maria's *Le venti giornate di Torino* (*The hundred days of Turin*) became a cult favorite among Italian fans of horror and dark weird fiction, but otherwise did not inspire imitations or influence other authors. This is regrettable, as *Le venti giornate* is superior horror literature. *Le venti giornate* is a mix of magic realism and cosmic horror: Borges ala Lovecraft, though some critics have only half-accurately called it "the novel you get when you cross the demonical complexities of Poe with the malignant banalities of Kafka."[9] Too, *Le venti giornate* has the additional element of an uncannily accurate–and menacing–prediction of the future in its portrayal of a version of social media as a social net negative. Stylistically, the novel moves with the pace and logic of a dream or nightmare; events and personalities are indirect, allusive, ambiguous, surreal, and ultimately capricious and ominous. Whether De Maria knew it or not, *Le venti giornate* worked as future horror to his contemporary audience and as disquietingly accurate predictive horror to the audience of the twenty-first century. "It's a book steeped in the idiosyncratic culture of Turin that speaks to psychic elements of crises now gripping much of the world. *The Twenty Days of Turin* depicts

---

[8]Virginia Agostinelli, "Mass Media, Mass Culture and Contemporary Italian Fiction," (PhD diss., University of Washington, 2012), 7-8.

[9]William Giraldi, "Holy Horror," *Commonweal Magazine*, last modified Feb. 1, 2017, https://www.commonwealmagazine.org/holy-horror.

how the past overflows the feeble efforts of the present to make its own future; in that, it may be the novel that foreshadows our moment more accurately than any number of speculative fictions."[10]

Anna Maria Ortese was an author of novels, stories, poetry, and travel narratives. Although she is best-known for her "Romantic fable" *L'Iguana* (1965) and her realistic depictions of Naples, in her stories and novels of the 1980s and 1990s she struck distinctly horrific tones. In those stories Ortese's usual well-honed poetic style is put to use in describing a sort of psychopathological dark magic realism, hallucinatory and featuring altered states of mind or psychologically disturbed protagonists.

> Her entire oeuvre, indeed, can be considered one extended variation on the theme of the uncanny, the "strange" lying as it does at the center of her world vision in its most diverse forms: dreams and visions...along with angels, linnets, sprites, and spirits, imaginary fathers, sons, and lovers, lost brothers and other "memories of the unreal life," beasts, monsters, and all manner of strange creatures.[11]

Italian comics have long featured horror strips, but Tiziano Sclavi's *Dylan Dog*, first published in 1986, was exceptional. By the mid-1990s *Dylan Dog* was selling over 1.2 million copies a month (from a total Italian population of 56.9 million), making it the best-selling Italian comic of all time. *Dylan Dog* is about the eponymous private detective, an *indagatore dell'incubo* (nightmare investigator), whose cases are supernatural or science fictional in nature, and range from mad scientists to invisible men to aliens to the usual array of traditional monsters. *Dylan Dog* is supernatural *noir*, told with a greater sophistication than most horror comics; its visual style is "clearly influenced by the language of film, are further enhanced by a marked propensity for postmodern pastiche and citation. Frequent inter-textual allusions to everything from Hitchcock films to Umberto Eco contribute a higher cultural and literary dimension for the benefit of more educated readers."[12]

The political and social troubles of Italy in the 1990s influenced the world of Italian letters as they did every other part of Italian society. Although mainstream and High Art authors continued to produce serious literature, Italian readers chose "entertainment literature," including horror fiction, as the preferred genre, and contemporary texts over works from the near- or

---

[10]Peter Berard, ""Foul, Small-Minded Deities": On Giorgio De Maria's "The Twenty Days of Turin,"" *Los Angeles Review of Books*, last modified Feb. 7, 2017, https://lareviewofbooks.org/article/foul-small-minded-deities-giorgio-de-maria/#!.

[11]Monica Farnetti, "Anxiety-free: Rereadings of the Freudian 'Uncanny,'" in *The Italian Gothic and Fantastic: Encounters and Rewritings of Narrative Traditions*, eds. Francesa Billiani and Gigliola Sulis (Madison, WI: Fairleigh Dickinson University, 2007), 47.

[12]Gino Moliterno, "Dylan Dog," in *Encyclopedia of Contemporary Italian Culture*, ed. Gino Moliterno (New York: Routledge, 2000), 261.

distant-past.[13] Translated horror novels from American and English authors flooded the Italian market, and the Italian audience responded favorably, with Stephen King becoming a particular favorite among both readers and younger writers. Another heavy influence on writers was the style, verve, and casual violence of Quentin Tarantino's 1994 film *Pulp Fiction*. A 1996 symposium, "Narrating after *Pulp Fiction*," debated not whether Tarantino's work was influential, but to what degree. A group of writers, influenced by King, by Tarantino, and by a desire to separate themselves from the "soft" horror fiction of Italy's past, came together under the umbrella of "pulp" and called themselves *Cannibali* (lit.: "cannibals"). "The Tarantino connection...was fuel for the *Cannibali* writers who saw more notoriety at the end of this cinematographic-literary convention [the 1996 symposium] on styles and new modes of narrative expression."[14] The *Cannibali* were practitioners of "extreme horror," which was also the title of their first, 1996, anthology of stories. The *Cannibali* displayed a fascination with American mass culture, especially its pulp paperbacks and splatter horror fiction. The *Cannibali*'s horror stories used graphic violence set against ominous postindustrial urban and suburban landscapes; the stories as well emphasized alienation and nihilistic action as the result of modern, soulless Italian society. Stylistically the *Cannibali* writers were brutal and direct, challenging the "arcane literary 'mannerism' which they believed had entrenched itself in accepted 'serious' Italian literature subsequent to Italo Calvino's death in the mid-1980s."[15]

One of the superior works of the *Cannibali* group was Simona Vinci's *Dei bambini non si sa niente* (*Nothing is known about children*, 1997). Vinci, one of the female members of the *Cannibali*, produced an unnerving novel about five children between the ages of 10 and 15 experiencing their sexual awakening and engaging in sex, violence, and reading pornography. Powerfully told in a straightforward, almost simple style, *Dei bambini* brings the reader into the children's world and shows the reader the world as seen through the children's eyes, which makes their adult behavior and cruelty all the more disquieting. Her style is "dry, paratactic...evil in Vinci's work is expressed almost aseptically,"[16] with violence being described with gory details and sex being described in pornographic terms.

Latvia

---

[13] Agostinelli, "Mass Media," 62.

[14] Filippo la Porta, "The Horror Picture Show and the Very Real Horrors: About the Italian Pulp," in *Italian Pulp Fiction: The New Narrative of the Giovanni Cannibali Writers*, ed. Stefania Lucamante (Madison, WI: Fairleigh Dickinson University, 2001), 59.

[15] Stefania Lucamante, "Introduction: 'Pulp,' Splatter, and More: The New Italian Narrative of the Giovani Cannibali Writers," in *Italian Pulp Fiction: The New Narrative of the Giovanni Cannibali Writers*, ed. Stefania Lucamante (Madison, WI: Fairleigh Dickinson University, 2001), 13.

[16] Giorgio Bertellini, "Simona Vinci (1970-)," in *Encyclopedia of Italian Literary Studies*, ed. Gaetana Marrone (New York: Routledge, 2007), 1993.

While traditional, pre-twentieth century Latvian folklore and oral literature feature ghost stories and frightening occurrences, twentieth century Latvian writers (with the exception of poets) were slow to make use of horror motifs and elements in their work. During the 1901-1939 period Latvian horror narratives almost entirely were of the rationalized variety, and during the 1941-1970 period Latvian horror disappeared, as it was unacceptable to the ruling Soviet regime. It was not until the 1970s and 1980s that horror began to appear in Latvian narratives, and following independence in 1990 Latvian writers began openly writing horror novels.

The father of modern Latvian horror was Vladimirs Kaijaks, whose work is described by Latvian critics as "Modern Gothic."[17] Kaijaks, a professional writer, published a landmark collection of stories in 1973 and a novel in 1987, both of which reflect the realities and fears of the 1970s and 1980s rather than being set in the past.

> The finest of Kaijaks' prose exhibits the specific poetry of horror, where the text is based on a terrifying, supernatural or maybe just elegantly paradoxical metaphor. In some cases there is truly apocalyptic terror, while in other cases it is quite individualised: a person's fear of their own shadow. Certainly, all the motifs utilised by Kaijaks are very contemporary.[18]

Kaijaks' stories include material like a Victor Frankenstein-like scientist in a world approaching the apocalypse, an enormous bloodthirsty spider, a near-future story about a voice-operated car falling in love with its driver, a cursed cat and strangling hair.

A notable horror novel to follow in the wake of Kaijaks' 1970s horror work was Jānis Mauliņš' *Ragana* (*Witch*, 1981). Mauliņš, a professional writer under the Soviets and after independence, usually wrote mimetic literature about everyday Latvian life. In *Ragana* Mauliņš takes the keen observation of daily life and mundane detail and uses it as the framework for a story about a scientist investigating the reality behind the legend about a line of witches, stretching back into the middle ages, whose husbands always die soon after they wed the witches. Mauliņš' characters are scientists and doctors who apply up-to-date science to the problem but never reach an answer, and the scientist, who falls in love with a young witch, only escapes death at the last moment.

In 1988, only two years before independence, Dagnija Zigmonte, a professional writer, published a story collection, *Gausīgais Nazis* (*Dead knife*). In the collection she adapted in story form a variety of folklore legends from northern Latvia, using poetic language to transform ghosts, revenants, the cursed "black book," and so on into frighteningly possible objects in stories in which a sinister atmosphere and subtle terrors are the norm. The legendary creatures

---

[17]Simsone, "A Cloud of Vapour," 312.

[18]Guntis Berelis, *Latviešu literatūras vēsture* (Rīga: Zvaigzne ABC, 1999), 214.

"lose their folkloristic 'once upon a time' quality and instead obtain a very specific definition in the 'here and now', which gives the desired effect."[19]

Latvian horror after independence fell under the influence of Western horror writers and horror movies, with the result that much of the horror literature published began to display a 1990s-style mixing of genres.

Andris Puriņš', a popular horror novelist of the 1990s, tends toward the pulpish end of horror, telling stories with a vivid combination of horror elements whose summaries are more entertaining than the reading of the novels. A rare political note appears in Puriņš' *Ar skatienu augšup jeb Vampīru sazvērestība* (*Looking up or Vampire Conviction*, 1992), an otherwise archetypal work of pulp horror:

> The element of horror obtains such a grotesque form in this work as to border on the absurd: giant bats with the heads of diehard communists fly over fields in a remote district of Latvia and enter at night via the chimney to attack the 'good guys', sucking their blood, whereas during the day the monsters are transformed into people who meet in the appropriately named house "The Red Maples" and plot a conspiracy against the independence of the Baltic States.[20]

Another popular horror novelist, Jānis Ivars Stradiņš, wrote *Dēmonu villa* (*Demon's villa*, 1993), a hybrid thriller-cum-detective-cum-horror novel. "A real conspiracy of the Devil's henchmen is plotted in a strange little house hidden away in a courtyard behind the high-rise buildings of Ģertrūdes Street in the city of Riga: it begins with the use of charmed 'ritual masks' to bring about the death of particular individuals and ends with plans for world domination."[21] Unfortunately for the readers, Stradiņš' use of stereotypes and cliches, especially of the antagonists, negates the moments of terror and revulsion.

Poland

Like most other Iron Curtain nations, Poland's transition to capitalism and democracy was, in relative terms, abrupt, and Poland's writers were in some ways slow to adapt. The market, however, was not, and within six months of the declaration of independence there were Polish translations of Stephen King available. Further translations of Anglophone horror writers followed and were eagerly consumed by the Polish public, which displayed a heretofore hidden taste for commercial horror of the King/Koontz variety.

Polish writers responded by imitating popular Western writers, but only partially. As horror writer Łukasz Orbitowski put it, "our demonology is different, if only because of the Catholic traditions of our country. Americans, English, Protestants in general experience religion

---

[19] Simsone, "A Cloud of Vapour," 314.

[20] Simsone, "A Cloud of Vapour," 315.

[21] Simsone, "A Cloud of Vapour," 315.

differently, others have demonic status, and at the same time Protestantism is more puritanical."[22] Polish horror became a mix of Anglophone motifs and Polish and Catholic mythology. Orbitowski, who would become the "King of Polish Horror" in the 2000s, published his first collection of horror stories, *Złe Wybrzeża* (*Bad coast*), in 1999. A relatively inauspicious debut for Orbitowski, the three stories in *Złe Wybrzeża* are told with intelligence and strong prose, but the concepts–a good man decides to commit an evil act just to see if he could do so, the horrific transformation of a secret policeman, and the posthumous adventures of a famous clairvoyant–are not exploited to their fullest potential.

Portugal

The end of the Salazar dictatorship in 1974 allowed for a wave of Portuguese authors to begin writing again, and for Portuguese expatriate writers to return home. However, for the next twenty years the primary type of literature that the Portuguese market was given was serious, High Art fiction. The Portuguese literary market was still developing, but the publishers emphasized award-nominated and award-winning books, books by accomplished, established authors, and books given good reviews by literary critics. If there was a hunger for popular literature and genre literature among Portuguese readers, it was ignored by the literary establishment. This situation did not change until 1994, after which point Portuguese genre authors began being published and the importation of translations of Anglophone authors, including horror authors, began in earnest.

What horror there was in Portuguese letters in the 1971-1994 time period was of the High Art Horror variety. José Saramago's *Ensaio sobre a cegueira* (*Blindness*, 1995) was perhaps the best of these serious horror novels, and was singled out by the Nobel Prize for Literature committee for praise when the committee awarded Saramago the prize in 1998. *Ensaio sobre a cegueira*, about a wave of blindness that overtakes an unnamed city and the social breakdown that follows it, is *fantastika* only insofar as the blindness' arrival, cause, and departure are all unexplained. Otherwise *Ensaio sobre a cegueira* is a very sober–and frightening–look at what might happen when laws and social norms disappear. Hygiene and living conditions rapidly deteriorate, food becomes limited and rationed, leading to starvation, those soldiers sent by the government to contain both the blindness and the blinded act brutally, outsiders rape and murder the blinded, and despair overtakes all of those afflicted. Told in Saramago's usual breathless and elongated style, *Ensaio sobre a cegueira* is both horrifying viscerally and conceptually, neither scanting on the descriptions of violence and rape nor avoiding the devastating emotional impact of the blindness and the degradation of society and humans which follows it.

As mentioned, the post-1994 situation for genre authors was quite different from the pre-1994 situation. One such genre writer who published a significant amount horror post-1994 was

---

[22]M@rio, "Wywiad z Łukaszem Orbitowskim," *Horror Online*, last modified June 10, 2009, http://horror.com.pl/wywiady/wywiad.php?id=32.

Ana Teresa Pereira, who wrote "gothic horror and vampire stories with strong intertextual links to the world of film and fairy tales."[23]

Russia

The long arm of the Soviet government largely forbade the writing and publication of genres which were counter to the goals and ideals of the Soviet Union. Horror fiction was one of these forbidden genres, with the result that only a minimal number of authors succeeded in publishing horror during the 1971-1991 period. After the dissolution of the Soviet Union and the establishment of the Russian Federation, authors slowly began writing in previously banned genres, and within two years Russian translations of Anglophone authors like Stephen King were appearing on Russian bookshelves. The true surge in and renaissance of Russian horror fiction, however, only began in the twenty-first century, outside the remit of this work.

The most significant Russian horror author before the mid-1990s was Ljudmila Petruševskaja, who is best known as a dramatist and short story writer of bleak mimetic fiction. However, Petruševskaja published *fantastika* both pre-*glasnost* and post-1991: "Indeed, all throughout the 'invisible years' in the 1970s and the 1980s pre-glasnost, Petrushevskaia had been able to publish tales for children, and sympathetic editors had managed to slip occasional 'grown-up' stories past the censors under the label of *skazki*."[24] Petruševskaja's horror stories are primarily in the urban legend mode, and are narratives about ghosts visiting upon their victims "the spiritual violation and suffering that are Petrushevskaia's ruling concern."[25]

> The ghost stories of *Songs of the Eastern Slavs* use the supernatural as another indirect mode through which to express this psychic devastation: the supernatural "incidents" create a stark, laconic, heightened representation of the fears which can be identified in many of Petrushevskaia's "realistic" stories.[26]

Petruševskaja's style is standard and literary, reflecting her traditional background; slang and colloquialisms are entirely absent.

A very different type of horror emerged in the late-1990s, typified by Oleg Divov's *The Dog Master* (1997). Divov, who would go on to become a full-time writer of horror and

---

[23] Isabel Cardigos, "Portuguese Tales," *The Greenwood Encyclopedia of Folktales and Fairy Tales*, ed. Donald Haase (Westport, CT: Greenwood, 2008), 761.

[24] Lesley Milne, "Ghosts and Dolls: Popular Urban Culture and the Supernatural in Liudmila Petrushevskaia's *Songs of the Eastern Slavs* and The Little Sorceress," *The Russian Review* 59, no. 2 (Apr. 2000): 269.

[25] Helena Goscilo, "Speaking Bodies," in *Fruits of her Plume. Essays in Contemporary Russian Women's Culture*, ed. Helena Goscilo (New York, 1993), 142.

[26] Milne, "Ghosts and Dolls," 273.

fantastika in the twenty-first century, began publishing with *The Dog Master*, a novel about a paramilitary organization whose specially-equipped soldiers and their faithful hound companions try to kill off all the zombies in their region. *The Dog Master* is in some ways the opposite of Petruševskaja's work, being conversationally told with contemporary words and phrases, and showing the influence not of traditional Russian folklore or urban legends but of contemporary Western horror fiction trends.

Serbia

The troubled history of Serbia–first as a subject state of communist Yugoslavia and then as one of two parts of the Federal Republic of Yugoslavia during the Yugoslav Wars (1990-1999)–did not prevent Serbian authors from creating works of literary seriousness, some of which had horror elements. But Serbian commercial fiction was in short supply, including horror literature.

Milorad Pavić, a poet, academic, literary historian, and writer of novels and short stories, was perhaps the best-known Serbian writer of the 1971-2000 time period. His work is largely *fantastika*, with mimetic realism playing a subservient role. Pavić's novels are complex which play with riddles and puzzles and feature allegory, satire, and thanatopsis. Horrific, haunted and Gothic episodes appear in the novels, but the purpose of the novels is not to frighten but to mystify and entertain. In Pavić's short stories his protagonists are human-shaped monsters based on the folktales and myths of Serbia and the Balkans. Pavić's style is modern and colloquial; his "vernacular speech is only the starting point of his highly extravagant style, which defamiliarizes the language of the common people with a surreal sense of word and phrase choice."[27]

Spain

While it is true that Spanish fiction, High Art or commercial, contains relatively little horror fiction compared to the Anglophone countries, this does not mean that the Spanish reader has no taste for horror fiction. The popularity of foreign authors in translation, from Poe to King, argues against this theory, as does the existence of the Spanish Gothic. Institutional, governmental, religious, and social prohibitions of horror prevented the genre from becoming widespread until the fall of the Franco regime in 1975, and even after that, for much of the 1971-2000 time period, Spanish horror authors were few compared to their authors' European counterparts, despite the influx of Anglophone horror authors beginning in 1980 and 1981. This situation, however, changed in the 1990s with the advent of the Internet and the globalization of the book market, so that in the twenty-first century horror was a respectable if not flourishing genre in Spain.

Juan Benet is today viewed by critics as one of the greatest Spanish authors of the twentieth century. Compared to William Faulkner because of his unique narrative voice and style and because of his use of a fictitious part of Spain similar to Faulkner's fictional Yoknapatawpha

---

[27]Tomislav Z. Longinović, "Milorad Pavić (15 October 1929-)," in *South Slavic Writers Since World War II*, ed. Vasa D. Mihailovich (Detroit, MI: Gale, 1997), 218.

County, Benet wrote award-nominated and award-winning work from 1961 to his death in 1993. In 1971 he wrote the collection *Una Tumba* (*A grave*), which like many of Benet's short stories shows "the influence of the dead and of the spirit world on the vulnerable living."[28] Benet's earlier *Volveras a Región* (*Back to Región*, 1967) had been horrific in its way, containing haunting stories of the terrible effects of the Civil War, but the stories in *Una Tumba* were overtly *fantastika*, using ghosts and the Gothic mode, homaging or parodying Poe and Dostoevsky, among others. Benet's style is, as mentioned, Faulknerian, being more difficult than the norm because of the prolonged sentences and the regional narrative voice, and he often uses horror elements as support for other narrative purposes but Benet's superior skill as a writer makes his frightening moments truly terrifying.

Marina Mayoral, a writer and journalist, is a High Art writer, but in a number of her works of the time period she "writes especially of Galicia with its well-known atmosphere of superstition, legend, mystery, and witchcraft, repeatedly depicting a region where reality is semi-gothic, even before focusing on crumbling mansions and dark family secrets."[29] Her work varies from Gothic to what Janet Pérez calls "para-gothic, containing many ingredients found in gothicism without crossing completely into the paranormal."[30]

The poet Elena Andrés wrote, in 1980, a collection of poems, *Trance de la vigilia colmada* (*Trance of a fulfilled vigil*), which was a departure from her previous work, which were largely about the search for transcendent meaning and the significance of the human condition. *Trance de la vigilia colmada* is full of existential despair, exploring "a strange and sinister universe, expressing once more the poet's existential anguish through depiction of nightmarish surroundings and revealing a kind of identity crisis involving her multiple selves, her authentic internal self versus what (or who) others perceive, as well as the conflicts introduced by the need to be more than one self at once."[31]

Cristina Fernández Cubas was a lawyer and journalist, but her first love was fiction. She began publishing her short stories–her primary mode of fiction–in 1980, and from the beginning she updated the Gothic tradition, and in large part was responsible for introducing the native Gothic to the modern Spanish audience. Her stories focused on unreliable narrators whose psychologies were often disturbed or warped in stories which were either traditional ghostly or haunted house narratives or deconstructive metafiction. Fernández Cubas' work continued to reinvent the Gothic through the end of the century and beyond. Her work

---

[28]Margaret E.W. Jones, "Juan Benet," in *Dictionary of the Literature of the Iberian Peninsula*, eds. Germán Bleiberg, Maureen Ihrie, and Janet Pérez (Westport, CT: Greenwood, 1993), 188.

[29]Janet Pérez, "Contemporary Spanish Women Writers and the Feminine Neo- Gothic," *Romance Quarterly* 51, no. 2 (2004): 131.

[30]Pérez, "Contemporary Spanish Women Writers," 132.

[31]Janet Pérez, "Elena Andrés," in *The Feminist Encyclopedia of Spanish Literature*, eds. Janet Pérez and Maureen Ihrie (Westport, CT: Greenwood, 2002), 26.

abounds in ambiguity, abnormal and alcoholic characters, mirror symbols and incomprehensible passages (others must be read through a mirror). Time...is fluid, unreal, and many perceptions seem inside out or backwards. The title tale creates unresolvable doubt as to the main characters' sanity, and many others raise similar questions....oneiric atmosphere, the interweaving of marvelous and fantastic elements with the normal or realistic, and the problems of communication and perception.[32]

Pilar Pedraza, a writer and academic, began publishing novels and short story collections in 1984 and quickly become "la dama del gotico español," the best-known female writer of the contemporary Spanish Gothic. Pedraza's fiction displays a thorough familiarity with the American and European Gothic traditions, and falls into the "female Gothic" category, "not because Pedraza is a woman...but because her fiction shows a thorough engagement with the position of women in society and their desires, either rewriting Gothic myths or developing a modern Spanish version of them."[33] Her work is a veritable catalogue of Gothic devices: among the other Gothic tropes and motifs and creatures appearing in her work are Frankenstein's monster, vampires, the undead, werewolves, ruins and cemeteries, haunted houses, sanctuaries and places of religious adoration, Hell in various iterations, evil women (especially witches), animal hybrids, and mad scientists. Too, Pedraza, like Angela Carter, "championed erotic-sadistic models of femininity that...often challenge tradition and patriarchy."[34]

Adelaida García Morales was a Spanish writer who achieved fame in 1985 with the publication of her novel *El sur seguido de Bene* (*The south followed by Bene*). *El sur*, like her succeeding novels, was a Gothic, the mode in which García Morales was most comfortable with. As with the traditional Gothic, the past returns to haunt the present in García Morales' work. In fact, García Morales' narratives are a catalogue of Gothic devices: ghosts, physical and moral decay, the sublime, vampires, ghosts, haunted buildings, fear of the Other in the person of women, and guilty secrets hidden, sought-for, and discovered. The supernatural intrudes upon the present in her stories, and the lines and limits between reality and fantasy blur.

Javier García Sánchez is a journalist and writer, one of the new wave of Spanish writers of the 1980s. An ambitious writer who worked in a variety of genres, his *El mecanógrafo* (*The typist*, 1989) and *Los otros* (*The others*, 1998) are notable for their use of obsession and disintegrating personalities as the means to evoke disquiet in the reader. The world, in these novels, is terrifying and evil, and the desperate, lonely obsessives who are García Sánchez's protagonists fall prey to it until their only defense is to shoot love ones in a spasm of insane violence.

---

[32]Janet Pérez, "Cristina Fernández Cubas," in *Dictionary of the Literature of the Iberian Peninsula*, eds. Germán Bleiberg, Maureen Ihrie, and Janet Pérez (Westport, CT: Greenwood, 1993), 591.

[33]Reyes, *Spanish Gothic,* 167.

[34]Reyes, *Spanish Gothic,* 167.

Sweden

Like the other Scandinavian countries during the 1971-2000 period, Sweden had a flourishing market for both serious and commercial fiction. But horror literature—and *fantastika* in general—were not highly regarded by the world of Swedish letters nor produced in any great number by Swedish authors of popular fiction, who instead concentrated on mysteries and romances.

The primary exception to this was the Gothic. There is a long tradition of Gothics in Sweden, as in the rest of Scandinavia, dating back to the eighteenth century.

> The stories are located in Scandinavia, and the Gothic castle or haunted house is replaced by the Nordic wilderness, the vast dark forest, the snow-covered Nordic mountains, or the icy stormy sea. Regional folklore and local traditions are used to enhance the Gothic atmosphere, and the protagonist's dark side is often bound to and triggered by the wilderness and the pagan past of the region.[35]

More common in the twenty-first century than the twentieth, undoubtedly due to the internationalization of the book market and the increasing cross-genre nature and intertextuality of mass culture, the Swedish Gothic, like the Scandinavian Gothic, is more traditional than many other modern Gothics. A typical Swedish Gothic of the 1971-2000 period is Kristoffer Leandoer's "De Svarta Svanarna" ("The black swans," 1994), about a couple in southern Sweden whose marriage is disrupted by a pair of black swans. The wife becomes entranced to the black swans, and the male swans makes love to her, eventually leading to the wife giving birth to a snakelike creature. During pagan times, black swans were representative of an "uncanny connection to the wilderness, forbidden love, uncontrollable hatred and murder."[36] The wife eventually becomes a hybrid creature, human by day and a black swan by night. "The meeting with the black swans, the link to the past, makes chronological time dissolve in a way that is typical of Scandinavian horror. Past, present and future lose their chronological and historical sequence and tend towards an eternal present."[37]

Switzerland

Although the history of Swiss literature is a lengthy one, it does not include much popular literature, whether in the nineteenth or the twentieth centuries. Swiss literature is largely serious

---

[35] Yvonne Leffler, "Scandinavian Gothic," in *The Encyclopedia of the Gothic*, eds. William Hughes, David Punter, and Andrew Smith (Chichester, West Sussex: John Wiley & Sons, 2016), 587.

[36] Yvonne Leffler, "The Gothic Topography in Scandinavian Horror Fiction," in *The Domination of Fear*, ed. Mikko Canini (Amsterdam: Editions Rodopi B.V., 2010), 48.

[37] Leffler, "The Gothic Topography," 48.

literature, and what little horror there is in it appears as High Art Horror. Perhaps the best Swiss writer of High Art Horror was Friedrich Dürrenmatt, a playwright and novelist. Although Dürrenmatt is best known for his works in the "epic theatre" mode, he also wrote novels with substantial horror elements in them. Dürrenmatt did not make use of the supernatural in his works, instead evoking the dark fantastic and the dark weird without resorting to ghost and vampires and zombies. He does, however, succeed in frightening the reader as if he had used supernatural devices. In his *Der Verdacht* (*Suspicion*, 1953) a cancer-stricken detective enters a clinic whose nihilistic, torturing owner convinces his dying patients that their only chance for survival is to undergo horrific operations without anesthesia. *Die Panne* (*The breakdown*, 1956) is a Kafkaesque nightmare of political judgment and identity confusion. In Dürrenmatt's *Der Auftrag* (*The order*, 1986) he makes use of substantial horrific imagery and symbols, from the Fenris Wolf (standing in for modern technological horrors), the gnostic "blind idiot god," and a climax in which a female photographer is hunted by a mindless human beast who is the incarnation of the blind idiot god.

Ukraine

Ukraine gained its independence from the Soviet Union in 1991, and immediately began publishing works that Soviet censorship had forbidden, by authors the Soviets had banned. Horror fiction—against Soviet ideals—was one of the genres of fiction that was popular with the Ukrainian reading audience. Perhaps the best of the Ukrainian horror writers of the 1990s was Andrey Dashkov, who began publishing in 1993. His work is dark fantasy as much as it is outright horror, with occasional added elements of mysticism and dystopia. His works have titles like *The Servant of Werewolves* (1996), *Necromancers' Wars* (1997), and *The Pale Horseman, Black Jack* (1998).

Chapter Fifteen: The Middle East

Middle Eastern literature was largely serious during the 1971-2000 time period, dealing with issues ranging from racism to classism to totalitarianism to Israel, and what popular literature there was was largely of the action/adventure, romance, and detective genres. This began to change in the 1990s, with the globalization of the book market and the advent of the Internet, and horror and horror elements began creeping into Middle Eastern literature, both serious and commercial. In the twenty-first century this would result in a number of authors who specialized in horror fiction, but in the 1990s there were still only a handful of writers who used horror elements or wrote horror fiction.

Egypt

Arguably the father of modern Middle Eastern horror was the Egyptian author Ahmed Khaled Tawfik, who was the first commercial writer of horror and science fiction in the Middle East as well as the first Middle Eastern author to write medical thrillers, and who before his death in 2018 influenced a large number of young Egyptian authors. Tawfik began writing explicitly horrific books in 1993 with *Ma Waraa Al Tabiaa* (*Metaphysics*). Tawfik wrote in a less formal style than serious Egyptian authors, and a number of his novels were set in Egypt, which gave his work a special appeal for an Egyptian audience relatively unschooled in the ways of the horror literature. His horror relied largely on traditional Egyptian and Muslim supernatural tropes and creatures, but his first novel starred involved a group of scientists resurrecting Count Dracula, much to their eventual dismay and fear.

Israel

The Israeli reading market has always had room for the Israeli equivalent of dime novels, pulps, and pulpish paperbacks, whose authors and publishers covered every genre, including horror, although horror stories often appeared under other guises: "many Hebrew science fiction and horror stories in the 1960s were actually published under the superhero genre featuring the character of Tarzan."[1] However, in "respectable" literature horror was shunned by Israeli readers, writers, and publishers before 1970. As Danielle Gurevitch notes, the Israeli world of letters tends to dislike *fantastika*. The emphasis in Israeli literature has always been on the "true to life," with any departure from the mimetic consensus frowned upon by readers and the critical establishment alike.[2]

This situation began to change in the 1971-2000 time period, not least because of the influence of Hollywood films, global postmodernism, and the new generations of Israelis

---

[1] Leket-Mor, "IsraPulp," 47.

[2] Danielle Gurevitch, "What is Fantasy," in *With Both Feet in the Clouds: Fantasy in Israeli Literature*, eds. Danielle Gurevitch, Elana Gomel, and Rani Graff (Brighton, MA: Academic Studies Press, 2012), 23.

developing more cosmopolitan tastes than their predecessors. Arguably the mother of Israeli horror fiction, the poet Nurit Zarchi, began publishing after the 1967 war and continued through the end of the century. Interestingly, however, Zarchi's horror appeared primarily in her books for children and young adults. Zarchi's horror narratives are largely either portal fantasies (trips to other worlds—in Zarchi's case, worlds of fear) or stories in which otherworldly beings intrude upon our world. Although told to children, the Zurchi's horror stories depict a grey, ambiguous world in which pleasure and humor are the only defense, and in which witches and other frightening monsters are common. Her horror narratives are allusive and smart, and tend to be demanding reads for children.

Jordan

Though larger, more populous, and longer-established than Kuwait, the situation in Jordan as far as the horror genre is concerned is much the same as Kuwait. Jordan did not have a Qasim Khadir Qasim to pioneer the writing of horror in the 1970s, and it was not until 1985, when Ibrāhīm Nasrallāh, a Jordanian-Palestinian poet, novelist, academic and journalist, published *Barārī al-hummā* (*Prairies of Fever*) that a substantial work of horror appeared in Jordanian literature. *Barārī al-hummā* is High Art Horror, and works superbly as an allegory for Arabs wrenched out of their traditional locations and societies and forced to make do in strange or aberrant circumstances. But purely on a narrative level *Barārī al-hummā* is a "nightmarish experiment in stopped time,"[3] a story about a flight into fever or madness being the only logical escape route for a man trapped in a hellish situation. Chronology and linear sequence are ignored, reality and dream and fact and fantasy are fused together, and the reader ends up being stuck with an existential dilemma expressed in lyrical terms, resulting in a nightmarish reading experience.

Kuwait

Modern Kuwaiti literature is a fragmented thing; although there are several prominent Kuwaiti writers of the 1971-2000 time period, they tend to be of the English and French school or of a more generalized Arabic school. Kuwaiti literature, which only truly began in the 1940s, has not had enough time or writers to cohere into a unified genre or gain widespread traits unique to itself.

The general distaste of the Muslim world for horror narratives meant that Kuwaiti authors of the Arabic school of literature tended to avoid horror. To a lesser degree the same was true of Kuwaiti authors of the English and French school. However, there was one prominent exception: Qasim Khadir Qasim, a professional writer who in London in the late 1960s discovered the work of Poe and Lovecraft, neither of whom had been translated into Arabic at that point in time. In 1978 Qasim published a collection of short stories, *Madinatt Al-Reyaah wa Qissas Okh' ra ann Al-Ar'waah wa' Al- Ash'baah* (*The City of Winds and other Stories of the Ghosts and Spirits*).

---

[3]Salma Khadra Jayyusi, "Introduction," in *Modern Arabic Fiction: An Anthology*, ed. Salma Khadra Jayyusi (New York: Columbia University Press, 2005), 44.

In general, Qasim uses techniques similar to Gothic writers (such as setting the stories in the past and in mysterious places). In particular, the influence of Edgar Allen Poe, Howard Phillips Lovecraft, William Shakespeare, and other Western writers can be seen in Qasim's work (especially in terms of evoking horror, making use of folkloric motifs, and using grotesque images). Moreover, Qasim uses internationally recognized folkloric motifs within his work, such as the motif of personified winds, a painting corning to life, and people returning from the dead to reveal murder or to demand a proper burial.[4]

Syria

The political situation in Syria in the post-1948 years has meant that Syrian literature has been almost entirely serious and High Art: the social realism "literature of political commitment" from 1948-1967, the gloomy "literature of defeat," after the 1967 Six-Day War, and general censorship by the ruling party following the 1966 coup.

The best of the few Syrian authors to include horror elements in their work was Ghāda al-Sammān, a novelist and journalist. Al-Sammān's *Beirut Nightmares* (1977), written in the early stage of the devastating Lebanese Civil War, is partly a factual description of the horrors of the war in Beirut and partly a collection of dreams which, while containing realistic descriptions, also contain hallucinations and the elements of nightmares. *Beirut Nightmares* has a strong element of fantasy, an unnerving melding of reality and dream, and generally disquieting descriptions, as is fitting for nightmares. Al-Sammān's *al-Qamar al-Murabba'* (*The Square Moon*, 1994), a collection of short stories, is dark magic realism, ghost stories that "rely on the characteristic paraphernalia of the Gothic with its dark, stifling interiors, labyrinthine passages, supernatural events, and psychological disturbances. Intertwined with the Gothic are Romantic traditions that emphasize the fantastic and celebrate beauty in strangeness and strangeness in beauty."[5]

Turkey

Like other Muslim countries, Turkey has not had a great deal of horror fiction in its literature, whether traditional or modern. While there has been a great deal of Turkish popular literature in the twentieth century, nearly of it falls into the categories of romance, police fiction, mystery fiction, or action/adventure. This situation began to change in the 1990s, when Levent Aslan, the pioneer of Turkish horror literature, published the novel *Karanliğin Gozleri* (*Goals of darkness*, 1991) and the story collection *Geceyarisi Kabuslari* (*Midnight nightmare*, 1994), both of which were explicitly in the horror genre. *Karanliğin Gozleri* is a hybrid detective/horror novel about a string of murders committed by a secret underground organization, while the

---

[4]Sabah H. Alsowaifan, "Qasim's Short Stories: An Example of Arabic Supernatural/Ghost/Horror Story" (PhD diss., University of Alberta, 2001), 5.

[5]Fadia Suyofie, "Magical Realism in Ghādah al-Sammān's 'The Square Moon,'" *Journal of Arabic Literature* 40, no. 2 (2009): 183-84.

stories in *Geceyarisi Kabuslari* vary in content but rely on shocking plot twists which bring the stories to an end on grisly down notes.

Bibliography

Agostinelli, Virginia. "Mass Media, Mass Culture and Contemporary Italian Fiction." PhD diss., University of Washington, 2012.
Ainsa, Fernando and Djelal Kadir. "Journey to Luisa Valenzuela's Land of Fear." *World Literature Today*, 69, no. 4 (Autumn, 1995): 683-690.
Alsowaifan, Sabah H. "Qasim's Short Stories: An Example of Arabic Supernatural/Ghost/Horror Story." PhD diss., University of Alberta, 2001.
Ancuta, Katarzyna. "Asian Gothic." In *A New Companion to the Gothic*, edited by David Punter, 428-453. Chichester, West Sussex: Blackwell Publishing, 2012.
Anderson Imbert, Enrique. "'Magical Realism' in Spanish-American Fiction." *International Fiction Review* 2.1 (1975): 1-8.
Andrzejewski, B. W., S. Pilaszewicz, W. Tyloch, eds. *Literatures in African Languages: Theoretical Issues and Sample Surveys*. Cambridge, UK: Cambridge University Press, 1985.
Anisimova, Irina. "The Terrors of History: Revolutionary Gothic in 'Mother Earth' by Boris Pilniak." *The Slavic and East European Journal* 55, no. 3 (Fall 2011): 376-395.
Angles, Jeffrey. "Seeking the Strange: 'Ryōki' and the Navigation of Normality in Interwar Japan." *Monumenta Nipponica* 63, no. 1 (Spring 2008): 101-141.
Bacarisse, Pamela. "Sá-Carneiro and the Conte Fantastique." *Luso-Brazilian Review* 12, no. 1 (Summer 1975): 65-79.
Baronian, Jean-Baptiste. *La Belgique fantastique Avant et après Jean Ray*. Paris: Editions Jacques Antoine, 1984.
Barron, Neil, ed. *Fantasy and Horror*. Lanham, MD: Scarecrow Press, 2000.
Bašić, Sonja. "Edgar Allan Poe in Croatian and Serbian Literature." *Studia romanica et anglica zagrabiensia* 22 (1966): 305-319.
Becerra, Clara H. "Levinson, Luisa Mercedes." In *Latin American Women Writers: An Encyclopedia*, edited by María Claudia André and Eva Paulino Bueno, 276-285. New York: Routledge, 2008.
Bédé, Jean Albert, and William Benbow Edgerton, eds. *Columbia Dictionary of Modern European Literature*. New York: Columbia University Press, 1980.
Benbow, Jerry L. "Grotesque Elements in Eduardo Barrios." *Hispania* 51, no. 1 (Mar. 1968): 86-91.
Benson, Eugene and L.W. Conolly, eds. *Encyclopedia of Post-Colonial Literatures in English*. New York: Routledge, 2005.
Berard, Peter. "'Foul, Small-Minded Deities': On Giorgio De Maria's 'The Twenty Days of Turin.'" *Los Angeles Review of Books*. Last modified Feb. 7, 2017. https://lareviewofbooks.org/article/foul-small-minded-deities-giorgio-de-maria/#!.
Berelis, Guntis. *Latviešu literatūras vēsture*. Rīga: Zvaigzne ABC, 1999.
Bhattacharya, Sumangala. "Between Worlds: The Haunted Babu in Rabindranath Tagore's 'Kankal' and 'Nishite.'" *Nineteenth-Century Gender Studies* 6, no. 1 (Spring 2010). Accessed May 23, 2017. http://www.ncgsjournal.com/issue61/bhattacharya.htm.
Bicakci, Tugce. "The origins of Turkish Gothic: The adaptations of Stoker's Dracula

in Turkish literature and film." *Studies in Gothic Fiction* 4, no. 1/2 (2015): 57-69.

Billiani, Francesca. "The Italian Gothic and Fantastic: An Inquiry into the Notions of Literary and Cultural Traditions (1869-1997)." In *The Italian Gothic and Fantastic. Encounters and Rewritings of Narrative Traditions*, edited by Francesca Billiani and Gigliola Sulis, 15-31. Cranbury, NJ: Rosemont Publishing and Printing Corp., 2007.

Biron, Rebecca E. "Armonia Somers' 'El Despojo': Masculine Subjectivity and Fantasies of Domination." *Latin American Literary Review* 21, no. 42 (Jul-Dec 1993): 7-20.

Blair, Dorothy S. *African Literature in French: A History of Creative Writing in French from West and Equatorial Africa*. Cambridge, UK: Cambridge University Press, 1976.

Blair, Dorothy S. *Senegalese Literature: A Critical History*. Boston: Twayne Publishers, 1984.

Bouissou, Jean-Marie. "Manga: A Historical Overview." In *Manga: An Anthology of Global and Cultural Perspectives*, edited by Toni Johnson-Woods, 17-33. New York: Continuum, 2010.

Braham, Persephone. *From Amazons to Zombies: Monsters in Latin America*. Lewisburg, PA: Bucknell University Press, 2015.

Braunstein, Néstor. "Palabras Preliminares." In *Lo monstruoso y lo bello*, edited by Rafael Ángel Herra (San Pedro, Costa Rica: Editorial de la Universidad de Costa Rica, 1988), 11-15.

Brown, William Jarrod. "Specters of the Unspeakable: The Rhetoric of Torture in Guatemalan Literature, 1975-1985. PhD diss., University of Kentucky, 2012.

Burke, Christopher. "Review: Spells by Michel de Ghelderode," *Weird Fiction Review*. Last modified Jun. 27, 2017. http://weirdfictionreview.com/2017/06/review-spells-michel-de-ghelderode/.

Burness, Donald. "Literature and Ethnography: The Case of O Segredo da Morta and Uanga." *Research in African Literatures* 13, no. 3 (Autumn 1982): 359-365.

Cardin, Matt, ed. *Horror Literature Through History*. Santa Barbara, CA: ABC-Clio, 2017.

Casanova-Vizcaino, Sandra M. "Monstruous, Maniobras y Mundos: Lo Fantástico en la Narrativa Cubana, 1910-2010." PhD diss., University of Pennsylvania, 2012.

Chaudhuri, Runa Das. "The Interplay of the 'Uncanny' and the 'Everyday': Towards a Sociology of 'Ghost Stories' Written for Children in Bangla Between 1940 and 1980." Thesis, Jadavpur University, 2011.

Chaves, José Ricardo. "Monstruos Fantásticos en la Literatura Costarricense." *Filología y Lingüística* 42 (2016): 77-89.

Chimal, Alberto. "El huésped." *Las Historias*. Accessed June 19, 2018. http://www.lashistorias.com.mx/index.php/archivo/el-huesped/.

Chiyoko Kawakami. "The Metropolitan Uncanny in the Works of Izumi Kyōka: A Counter-Discourse on Japan's Modernization." *Harvard Journal of Asiatic Studies* 59, no. 2 (Dec. 1999): 559-583.

Clemons, Gregory A. "The Vampire Figure in Contemporary Latin American Narrative

Fiction." PhD diss., University of Florida, 1996.
Clute, John, and John Grant, eds. *The Encyclopedia of Fantasy*. New York: St. Martin's Press, 1997.
Clute, John, and Peter Nicholls, eds. *The Encyclopedia of Science Fiction*. Accessed June 20, 2018. http://www.sf-encyclopedia.com/.
Connell, Kim, ed. *The Belgian School of the Bizarre*. Cranbury, NJ: Associated University Presses, 1998.
Cooke, Miriam. "Magical Realism in Libya." *Journal of Arabic Literature* 41, no. 1/2 (2010): 9-21.
Dathorne, O.R. *The Black Mind. A History of African Literature*. Minneapolis, MN: University of Minnesota, 1974.
Dawson, E. "Emerging Writing From Four African Countries: Genres and Englishes, Beyond The Postcolonial." *African Identities* 10, no. 1 (2012): 17-31.
De Morais, Aline Pires. "João do Rio e o medo no espaço da cidade." Anais do CENA 2, no. 1 (2016). Accessed June 19, 2018, http://www.ileel.ufu.br/anaisdocena/wp-content/uploads/2016/01/Aline-Pires-de-Morais.pdf.
De Sherbinin, Julie W. "'Haunting the Center': Russia's Madwomen and Zinaida Gippius's 'Madwoman.'" *The Slavic and East European Journal* 46, no. 4 (Winter 2002): 727-742.
De Sousa Causo, Roberto. *Ficçãa científica, fantasia e horror no Brasil 1875 a 1950*. Belo Horizonte: Editora UFMG, 2003.
De Sousa Causo, Roberto. "Science Fiction During the Brazilian Dictatorship." *Extrapolation* 39, no. 4 (1998): 314-323.
De Villiers, J,B. *Agter die somber gordyn: 'n onthullende studie oor die vergete geskiedenis van die Afrikaanse spiritisme*. Kaapstad: Griffel Media, 2011.
Della Coletta, Cristina. "Fantastic." In *The Feminist Encyclopedia of Italian Literature*, edited by Rinaldina Russell, 85-86. Westport, CT: Greenwood Press, 1997.
Díaz Llanillo, Esther. "Interview with Esther Díaz Llanillo." Interview by Sara E. Cooper. *Cubanabooks*. Last modified April 2015. http://www.csuchico.edu/cubanabooks/authors/Interview_Diaz_Llanillo.shtml.
Diez, Luis A. "The Apocalyptic Tropics of Aguilera Malta." *Latin American Literary Review* 10, no. 20 (Spring 1982): 31-40.
Domínguez Michael, Christopher. *Diccionario crítico de la literatura mexicana (1955-2011)*. Mexico City, Mexico: FCE - Fondo de Cultura Económica, 2012.
Dos Reis Sampaio, Gabriela. "De *Uanga* a O *feiticerio*." In *Tecendo histórias; espaço, política e identidade*, edited by Antonio L. Negro, Evergton Sales Souza, and Ligia Bellini, 45-64. Salvador: SciELO - EDUFBA, 2009.
Duncan, J. Ann. *Voices, Visions, and a New Reality: Mexican Fiction Since 1970*. Pittsburgh: University of Pittsburgh, 1986.
Ellison, Fred P. *Brazil's New Novel*. Berkeley: University of California Press, 1954.
Evans, Arthur B. "The Fantastic Science Fiction of Maurice Renard." *Science Fiction Studies* 21 (1994): 380-396.
Fanning, Ursula. "From Domestic to Dramatic: Matilde Serao's Use of the Gothic." In *The

Italian Gothic and Fantastic. Encounters and Rewritings of Narrative Traditions, edited by Francesca Billiani and Gigliola Sulis, 119-140. Cranbury, NJ: Rosemont Publishing and Printing Corp., 2007.

Farnetti, Monica. "Anxiety-free: Rereadings of the Freudian 'Uncanny.'" In *The Italian Gothic and Fantastic: Encounters and Rewritings of Narrative Traditions*, edited by Francesa Billiani and Gigliola Sulis, 46-57. Madison, WI: Fairleigh Dickinson University, 2007.

Ferraro, Diana. "The Argentine Gothic." The Continental Blog. Last modified Nov. 17, 2017. http://dianaferraroenglish.blogspot.com/2007/11/argentine-gothic.html.

Ferreira-Pinto, Cristina. "The Fantastic, the Gothic, and the Grotesque in Contemporary Brazilian Women's Novels." *Chasqui* 25, no. 2 (1996): 71-80.

Figueredo, D.H. *The Encyclopedia of Caribbean Literature*. Westport, CT: Greenwood Press, 2005.

Flores, Angel. "Magical Realism in Spanish American Fiction." *Hispania* 38, no. 2 (May 1955): 187-192.

Flores, Angel. *Spanish American Authors: The Twentieth Century*. New York: H.W. Wilson and Co., 1992.

Flores, Ronald. "The Enigmatic Drifter." *Latin American Review of Books*. Last modified March 29, 2008, http://www.latamrob.com/the-enigmatic-drifter/.

Foster, David William, ed. *Handbook of Latin American Literature*. New York: Routledge, 1992.

França, Julio, and Luciano Cabral da Silva. "A Preface to a Theory of Art-Fear in Brazilian Literature." *Ilha do Desterro* 62 (Jan/Jun 2012): 341-356.

Garcia Pabón, Leonardo. "Oscar Cerruto (13 June 1912-10 April 1981)." In *Modern Spanish American Poets: First Series*, edited by Maria A. Salgado, 86-91. Detroit, MI: Gale, 2003.

Gauvin, Edward. "An Accounting by Thomas Owen." *Weird Fiction Review*. Last modified Sept. 17, 2012. http://weirdfictionreview.com/2012/09/an-accounting/.

Gauvin, Edward. "Jehanne Jean-Charles." *Weird Fiction Review*. Last modified Oct. 1, 2012. http://weirdfictionreview.com/2012/10/jehanne-jean-charles/.

Gauvin, Edward. "Michel Bernanos' "The Other Side of the Mountain": Sin, Destruction, and Forgiveness." *Weird Fiction Review*. Last modified Nov. 21, 2011. http://weirdfictionreview.com/2011/11/michel-bernanos-the-other-side-of-the-mountain-sin-destruction-and-forgiveness/.

Gauvin, Edward. "Two by Anne Richter." *Weird Fiction Review*. Last modified Sept. 3, 2012. http://weirdfictionreview.com/2012/09/two-by-anne-richter/.

Gauvin, Edward. "Unhomed." *World Literature Today*. Last modified May 2018. https://www.worldliteraturetoday.org/2018/may/unhomed-edward-gauvin.

Gauvin, Edward. "Weird France and Belgium: A Best Of." *Weird Fiction Review*. Last modified Oct. 30, 2014. http://weirdfictionreview.com/2014/10/weird-france-and-belgium-a-best-of/.

Gauvin, Edward. "100 Years of Unease." *Small Beer Press*. Last modified Jan. 20, 2011. http://smallbeerpress.com/not-a-journal/2011/01/20/100-years-of-unease/.

Gehrig, Elizabeth Tedford. "Dark spaces, horrifying places: Gothic mode in 19th- and early

20th-century Latin American fiction." PhD diss. Philadelphia, PA: Temple University, 2005.
Gehrmann, Susanne. "Remembering Colonial Violence: Inter/textual Strategies of Congolese Authors." *Tydskrif vir Letterkunde* 46, no. 1 (2009): 11-27.
George, Olakunle. "Compound of Spells: The Predicament of D.O. Fagunwa (1903-1963)." *Research in African Literatures* 28, no. 1 (Spring 1997): 78-97.
Gérard, Albert S., ed. *European Language Writing in Sub-Saharan Africa*. Philadelphia: John Benjamins Publishing Company, 1986.
Gérard, Albert S. *Four African Literatures: Xhosa, Sotho, Zulu, Amharic*. Berkeley, CA: University of California Press, 1971.
Ginway, M. Elizabeth. *Brazilian Science Fiction: Cultural Myths and Nationhood in the Land of the Future*. Lewisburg, PA: Bucknell University Press, 2004.
Giraldi, William. "Holy Horror," *Commonweal Magazine*. Last modified Feb. 1, 2017. https://www.commonwealmagazine.org/holy-horror.
Goldbert-Estepa, Ana Victoria. "Modalidad gótica y tácticas de lo cotidiano en la narrativa de Carmen Laforet, Carmen Martín Gaite y Cristina Fernández Cubas." PhD diss., University of California at Santa Barbara, 2007.
Gordon, Joan, and Veronica Hollinger, eds. *Blood Read: The Vampire as Metaphor in Contemporary Culture*. Philadelphia: University of Pennsylvania Press, 1997.
Goscilo, Helena. "Speaking Bodies." In *Fruits of her Plume. Essays in Contemporary Russian Women's Culture*, edited by Helena Goscilo, 135-164. New York, 1993.
Groberg, Kristi. "'The Shade of Lucifer's Dark Wing'; Satanism in Silver Age Russia." In *The Occult in Russian and Soviet Culture*, edited by Bernice Glatzer Rosenthal. Ithaca, NY: Cornell University Press, 1997.
Gurevitch, Danielle. "What is Fantasy." In *With Both Feet In the Clouds: Fantasy in Israeli Literature*, edited by Danielle Gurevich, Elana Gomel, and Rani Graff, 13-28. Brighton, MA: Academic Studies Press, 2012.
Gutiérrez, Maria Elena. "Alberto Savinio." In *Italian Prose Writers, 1900-1945*, edited by Luca Somigli and Rocco Capozzi, 272-88. Farmington Hills, MI: Gale, 2002.
Haase, Donald, ed. *The Greenwood Encyclopedia of Folktales and Fairy Tales*. Westport, CT: Greenwood, 2008.
Hamilton, Russell G. *Voices from an Empire: A History of Afro-Portuguese Literature*. Minneapolis, MN: University of Minnesota Press, 1975.
Hart, Stephen M. *A Companion to Latin American Literature*. Rochester, NY: Tamesis, 2007.
Hau, Caroline S. "Tropical Gothic." *The Manila Review* no. 6 (Mar. 2015). Accessed June 19, 2018. http://themanilareview.com/issues/view/tropical-gothic.
Hazuchová, Adéla. "Romány Tří Mágů Jiřího Karáska Ze Lvovic." PhD diss., Univerzita Palackého V Olomouci, 2013.
Henk, M.J. Maier. "Escape from the Green and Gloss of Java: Hella S. Haasse and Indies Literature." *Indonesia* 77 (Apr. 2004): 79-107.
Hope, Hillary. *Vienna Is Different: Jewish Writers in Austria from the Fin-de-Siècle to the Present*. New York: Berghahn Books, 2011.
Huggan, Graham. "Ghost Stories, Bone Flutes, Cannibal Countermemory." In *Cannibalism and*

the Colonial World, edited by Francis Barker, Peter Hulme, and Margaret Iversen, 126-141. Cambridge: Cambridge University Press, 1998.

Hughes, Henry J. "Familiarity of the Strange: Japan's Gothic Tradition." *Criticism* 42, no. 1 (Winter 2000): 59-89.

Hughes, William, David Punter, and Andrew Smith, eds. *The Encyclopedia of the Gothic*. Chichester: John Wiley and Sons, 2016.

Jayyusi, Salma Khadra. "Introduction." In *Modern Arabic Fiction: An Anthology*, edited by Salma Khadra Jayyusi, 1-71. New York: Columbia University Press, 2005.

Jayyusi, Salma Khadra. "Moussa Wuld Ibno: *City of Winds*." In *Modern Arabic Fiction*, edited by Salma Khadra Jayyusi, New York: Columbia University Press, 2005), 921-22.

Jing Cao and Linda Dryden. "Comparison of Gothic Genre in both English and Chinese Fictions." *International Journal of Social Science and Humanities* 1, no. 1 (April 2012): 18-25.

Johnson-Woods, Toni, ed. *Manga. An Anthology of Global and Cultural Perspectives.* New York: Continuum, 2010.

Jones, Jordan B. and James R. Krause. "The *Femme Fragile* and *Femme Fatale* in the Fantastic Fiction of Machado de Assis." *Revista Abusões* 1, no. 1 (2001): 51-97.

Jones, Julie. "Paulo Barreto's 'O bebê de tarlatana rosa': A Carnival Adventure." *Luso-Brazilian Review* 24, no. 1 (Summer, 1987): 27-33.

Josephs, Allen. "Abbadón, el exterminador." *New York Times Book Review*, Dec. 29, 1991, 13.

Joshi, S.T. "Introduction." In *Thirty Hours with a Corpse; and Other Tales of the Grand Guignol*, edited by S.T. Joshi, v-ix. Mineola, NY: Dover Publications, 2016.

Joshi, S.T. *Unutterable Horror: A History of Supernatural Fiction*. New York: Hippocampus Press, 2014.

Joshi, S.T., and Stefan Dziemianowicz, eds. *Supernatural Literature of the World*. Westport, CT: Greenwood Press, 2005.

Kellman, Steven G. *The Translingual Imagination*. Lincoln, NE: University of Nebraska Press, 2000.

Khair, Tabish. "Indian Pulp Fiction in English: A Preliminary Overview from Dutt to Dé." *Journal of Commonwealth Literature* 43, no. 3 (Sept. 2008): 59-74.

Kleeman, Faye Yuan. "Nakagami Kenji." In *Japanese Fiction Writers Since World War II*, edited by Van C. Gessell, 143-153. Detroit: Gale, 1997.

Klingenberg, Patricia Nisbet. *Fantasies of the Feminine: The Short Stories of Silvina Ocampo*. Lewisburg, PA: Bucknell University Press, 1999.

Knap, Jakub. "Niesamowitość i groza w literaturze polskiej dwudziestolecia międzywojennego: (rekonesans badawczy)." *Annales Universitatis Paedagogicae Cracoviensis. Studia Historicolitteraria* 8 (2008): 44-55.

Kohlenbach, Margarete. "Transformations of German Romanticism 1830-2000." In *The Cambridge Companion to German Romanticism*, edited by Nicholas Saul, 257-280. Cambridge: Cambridge University Press, 2009.

Košňar, Martin. "Vývoj Hororu a Spřízněných Žánrů Vpróze 19.a 20.století." Thesis, Západočeská Univerzita V Plzni, 2013.

Kotani, Mari. "Techno-Gothic Japan: From Seishi Yokomizo's *The Death's-Head Stranger* to

Mariko Ohara's *Ephemera the Vampire*." In *Blood Read*, edited by Joan Gordon and Veronica Hollinger, 189-198. Philadelphia: University of Pennsylvania Press, 1997.

Krabbenhoft, Kenneth. "Ignácio de Loyola Brandão and the Fiction of Cognitive Estrangement." *Luso-Brazilian Review* 24, no. 1 (Summer, 1987): 35-45.

Kuni, Ibraham. *The Bleeding of the Stone*. Northampton, MA: Interlink Publishing Group, 2002.

Kurtz, John Roberts. *Urban Obsessions, Urban Fears: The Postcolonial Kenyan Novel*. Trenton, NJ: Africa World Press, 1998.

Laforet, Carmen. *Nada*. Barcelona: Destino, 1995.

Laifong Leung. *Contemporary Chinese Fiction Writers: Biography, Bibliography, and Critical Assessment*. New York: Routledge, 2017.

Larson, Charles R. "Patterns of African Fiction." PhD diss., Indiana University, 1970.

Larson, Ross. *Fantasy and Imagination in the Mexican Narrative*. Tempe: Arizona State University Press, 1977.

Lăsconi, Elisabeta. "Taina Romanului Gotic." *Viaţa Românească*. Accessed June 19, 2018. http://www.viataromaneasca.eu/arhiva/70_via-a-romaneasca-1-2-2011/53_carti-paralele/798_taina-romanului-gotic.html.

Lee, Archie C.C. "The Bible in Chinese Christianity: Its Reception and Appropriation in China." *The Ecumenical Review*, 67, no. 1 (March 2015): 96-106.

Lee Oufan Lee. *Voices from the Iron House: A Study of Lu Xun*. Bloomington, IN: Indiana University Press, 1987.

Leffler, Yvonne. "The Gothic Topography in Scandinavian Horror Fiction." In *The Domination of Fear*, edited by Mikko Canini, 43-52. Amsterdam: Editions Rodopi B.V., 2010.

Leket-Mor, Rachel. "IsraPulp, The Israeli Popular Literature Collection at Arizona State University." *Judaica Librarianship* no. 16/17 (2011): 1-53.

Li-hua Ying. *Historical Dictionary of Modern Chinese Literature*. Lanham, MD: Scarecrow Press, 2009.

Lidoff, Joan. *Christina Stead*. New York: Ungar, 1982.

Lin Wang. "Celebration of the Strange: *Youyang Zazu* and its Horror Stories." PhD diss., University of Georgia, 2012.

Lindfors, Bernth. "The new David Maillu." *Kunapipi* 4, no. 1 (1982): 130-143.

Lifshey, Adam. *Subversions of the American Century*. Ann Arbor: University of Michigan Press, 2016.

Lofficier, Jean-Marc, and Randy Lofficier. *French Science Fiction, Fantasy, Horror and Pulp Fiction*. Jefferson, NC: McFarland, 2000.

Loh, Mary and Teri Shaffer Yamada. "Conflict and Change: The Singapore Short Story." In *Modern Short Fiction of Southeast Asia: A Literary History*, edited by Teri Shaffer Yamada, 213-233. Ann Arbor, MI: Association for Asian Studies, 2009.

Lomami Tshibamba, Paul. *La Récompense de la Cruauté*. Paris: Editions du Mont noir, 1972.

Longinović, Tomislav Z. "Milorad Pavić (15 October 1929-)." In *South Slavic Writers Since World War II*, edited Vasa D. Mihailovich, 215-21. Detroit, MI: Gale, 1997.

Lucamante, Stefania, ed. *Italian Pulp Fiction: The New Narrative of the Giovanni Cannibali Writers*. Madison, WI: Fairleigh Dickinson University, 2001.

Luchting, Wolfgang. "Review: *El obsceno pájaro de la noche*." *Books Abroad* 46, no. 1 (Winter,

1972): 82.

Lusky, Mary H. "The Function of Fantasy: Creativity and Isolation as Related Themes in the Fiction of Enrique Anderson Imbert." *Latin American Literary Review* 7.14 (Spring, 1979): 28-39.

MacGaffey, Wyatt. "The Black Loincloth and the Son of Nzambi Mpungu." *Research in African Literatures* 5, no. 1 (Spring, 1974): 23-30.

Machado de Sousa, Maria Leonor. *O <<horror>> na literatura portuguesa*. Amadora, Portugal: Instituto de Cultura Portuguesa, 1979.

Macias, Patrick. "Hino Hideshi." In *Fresh Pulp: Dispatches from the Japanese Popular Culture*, edited by Nobuhide Hamada, Patrick Macias, and Yuki Oniji, 80-81. San Francisco: Viz Media, 1999.

Maes-Jelinek, Hena. "Wilson Harris: Seeking the Mystery of the 'Universal Imagination.'" In *International Literature in English: The Major Writers*, edited by Robert Ross, 447-459. New York: Garland, 1991.

Maguire, Muireann. *Stalin's Ghosts: Gothic Themes in Early Soviet Literature*. New York: Peter Lang, 2012.

Marrone, Gaetana, ed. *The Encyclopedia of Italian Literary Studies*. New York: Routledge, 2007.

Martin, Grace A. "For the Love of Robots: Posthumanism in Latin American Science Fiction Between 1960-1999." PhD diss., University of Kentucky, 2015.

Marting, Diane E., ed. *Spanish American Women Writers. A Bio-Bibliographical Source Book*. Westport, CT: Greenwood, 1990.

Maseia, Josh R. "Southern Sotho Literature." In *Literatures in African Languages: Theoretical Issues and Sample Surveys*, edited by B. W. Andrzejewski, S. Pilaszewicz, W. Tyloch, 610-634. Cambridge, UK: Cambridge University Press, 1985.

Mayer, Paola, and Ruediger Mueller. "Fascism as Dehumanization: Alexander Moritz Frey's Political Fables." *Oxford German Studies* 46 (2017): 58-74.

McNeece, Lucy Stone. "Black Baroque: Sony Lab'ou Tansi (1947-1995)." *The Journal of Twentieth-Century/Contemporary French Studies revue d'études français* 3, no. 1 (Spring, 1999): 127-132.

Miéville, China. "Trainspotting." *The Guardian*. Accessed June 8, 2017. https://www.theguardian.com/books/2003/feb/08/featuresreviews.guardianreview20.

Milne, Lesley. "Ghosts and Dolls: Popular Urban Culture and the Supernatural in Liudmila Petrushevskaia's *Songs of the Eastern Slavs* and The Little Sorceress." *The Russian Review* 59, no. 2 (Apr. 2000): 269-284.

Miri Nakamura. "Horror and Machines in Prewar Japan: The Mechanical Uncanny in Yumeno Kyûsaku's Dogura magura." *Science Fiction Studies* 29, no. 3 (Nov. 2002): 364-381.

Mori, Maryellen Toman. "The Subversive Role of Fantasy in the Fiction of Takahashi Takako." *Journal of the Association of the Teachers of Japanese* 28, no. 1 (Apr. 1994): 29-56.

Morris, Mark. "The Untouchables." *New York Times*, Oct. 24, 1999, 7, 23:1.

Mostow, Joshua, ed. *The Columbia Companion to Modern East Asian Literature*. New York: Columbia University, 2012.

Moudileno, Lydie. "Magical Realism: 'Arme miraculeuse' for the African Novel?" *Research in*

African Literatures 37, no. 1 (Spring, 2006): 28-41.
M@rio. "Wywiad z Łukaszem Orbitowskim." *Horror Online*. Last modified June 10, 2009. http://horror.com.pl/wywiady/wywiad.php?id=32.
Napier, Susan. *The Fantastic in Modern Japanese Literature: The Subversion of Modernity.* London: Routledge, 1996.
Newman, Judie. "The Colonial Voice in the Motherland." In *Postcolonial Discourse and Changing Cultural Contexts: Theory and Criticism*, edited by Gita Rajan and Radhika Mohanram, 47-57. Westport, CT: Greenwood, 1995.
Ng, Andrew Hock-Soon. "Malaysian Gothic: the Motif of Haunting in K.S. Maniam's 'Haunting the Tiger' and Shirley Lim's 'Haunting.'" *Mosaic: A journal for the interdisciplinary study of literature*, 39, no. 2 (June 2006): 75-87.
Ng, Andrew Hock-soon. "South Asia." In *The Ashgate Encyclopedia of Literary and Cinematic Monsters*, edited by Jeffrey Andrew Weinstock, 269-70. Burlington, VT: Ashgate, 2014.
Ng Yi-Sheng. "A History of Singapore Horror." *biblioasia*. Accessed June 19, 2018. http://www.nlb.gov.sg/biblioasia/2017/07/03/a-history-of-singapore-horror/#sthash.B2xEGBwO.Jv3oY9LT.dpbs.
Ng Yi-sheng. "Illusions of Memory." *Quarterly Literary Review of Singapore* 13, no. 2 (Apr, 2014). Accessed June 19, 2018, http://www.qlrs.com/critique.asp?id=1104.
Nouwligbeto, Fernand. "Les Dramaturges Africains Francophones Face Aux Enjeux Scientifiques." *Ethiopiques* no. 96 (Spring, 2016). Accessed June 20, 2018. http://ethiopiques.refer.sn/spip.php?article1977.
Nzabatsinda, Anthere. "Sony Labou Tansi." In *The Encyclopedia of African Literature*, edited by Simon Gikandi, 704-06. London: Routledge, 2003.
Nzuji Mukala, Kadima. *La littérature zaïroise de langue française: 1945-1965*. Paris: Éditions Karthala, 1984.
Obuchowski, Chester W. "The Concentrationary World of Pierre Gascar." *The French Review* 34, no. 4 (Feb. 1961): 327-35.
Ocampo, Victor Fernando R. "A Short and Incomplete History of Philippine Science Fiction." The Infinite Library and Other Stories. Last modified May 5, 2014. https://vrocampo.com/2014/05/05/a-short-and-incomplete-history-of-philippine-science-fiction/.
Odber de Baubeta, Patricia Anne. "Quiroga, Horacio, 1878-1937." In *Concise Encyclopedia of Latin American Literature*, edited by Verity Smith, 525-29. New York: Routledge, 2000.
Oppelt, Riaan N. "C. Louis Leipoldt and the Making of a South African Modernism." PhD diss., Stellenbosch University, 2013.
Orbaugh, Sharalyn. "Arguing with the Real: Kanai Mieko." In *Ōe and Beyond : Fiction in Contemporary Japan*, edited by Stephen Snyder and Philip Gabriel, 245-277. Honolulu: University of Hawaii, 1999.
Pallejá-López, Clara. "Houses and Horror: A Sociocultural Study of Spanish and American Women Writers." Thesis, University of Auckland, 2010.
Palmer, Ada. "Japan's Manga Contributions to Weird Horror Short Stories." *Tor.com*. Accessed June 20, 2018.

https://www.tor.com/2014/02/18/japans-manga-contributions-to-weird-horror-short-stories/.

Paravisni-Gebert, Lizabeth. "Colonial and Postcolonial Gothic: the Caribbean." In *The Cambridge Companion to Gothic Fiction*, edited by Jerrold E. Hogle, 229-257. Cambridge: Cambridge University Press, 2012.

Paravisini-Gebert, Lizabeth. "Unchained Tales: Women Prose Writers from the Hispanic Caribbean in the 1990s," *Bulletin of Latin American Research* 22, no. 4 (Oct. 2003): 445-464.

Peña, Karen. "Violence and Difference in Gabriela Mistral's Short Stories (1904-1911)." *Latin American Research Review* 40, no. 3 (2005): 68-96.

Pérez, Janet. "Contemporary Spanish Women Writers and the Feminine Neo-Gothic." *Romance Quarterly* 51, no. 2 (2004): 125-40.

Pérez, Janet. "Cristina Fernández Cubas." In *Dictionary of the Literature of the Iberian Peninsula*, edited by Germán Bleiberg, Maureen Ihrie, and Janet Pérez, 591-592. Westport, CT: Greenwood, 1993.

Pérez, Janet. "Elena Andrés." In *The Feminist Encyclopedia of Spanish Literature*, edited by Janet Pérez and Maureen Ihrie, 24-26. Westport, CT: Greenwood, 2002.

Petkova-Mwangi, Anna. "The Gothic Novel as an Avenue in Disguise for Political Protest: A Fresh Look at the Gothic From Its Origins to Its Appearance in Kenya." *The Nairobi Journal of Literature*, no. 7 (July 2013): 36-39.

Piñeiro, Aurora. "'No vengas al país de los ríos': la escritura de Inés Arredondo y la estética de la oscuridad." *Badebec* 3, no. 6 (Mar. 2014): 254-278.

Pontiero, Giovanni. Translator's Note to *The Red House*, by Lya Luft, i-vi. Manchester, UK: Carcanet Publishing, 1994.

Pounds, Wayne. "Enchi Fumiko and the Hidden Energy of the Supernatural." *The Journal of the Association of Teachers of Japanese* 24, no. 2 (Nov. 1990): 167-183.

Power, Chris. "A brief survey of the short story part 52: Juan Rulfo." *The Guardian*. Last modified Aug. 27, 2013, https://www.theguardian.com/books/2013/aug/27/juan-rulfo-brief-survey-short-story.

Pringle, David, ed. *St. James Guide to Horror, Ghost & Gothic Writers*. Detroit: St. James Press, 1998.

Punter, David. *Gothic Pathologies*. London: Macmillan Press, 1998.

Punter, David. *The Literature of Terror: Volume 2: The Modern Gothic*. New York: Routledge, 1996.

Rama, Angel. "La fascinación del horror. La insólita literatura de Somers." *Marcha* no. 1188 Dec. 27, 1963: 28-30.

Ransom, Amy J. "Lovecraft in Québéc: Transcultural Fertilization and Esther Rochon's Reevaluation of the Powers of Horror." *Journal of the Fantastic in the Arts* 26, no. 3 (2015): 451-468.

Reichert, Jim. "Deviance and Social Darwinism in Edogawa Rampo's Erotic-Grotesque Thriller 'Kotō no oni.'" *The Journal of Japanese Studies* 27, no. 1 (Winter 2001): 113-141.

Reyes, Xavier Aldana. *Spanish Gothic. National Identity, Collaboration and Cultural Adaptation*. Manchester, UK: Palgrave Macmillan, 2017.

Reyes, Xavier Aldana, ed. *Horror: A Literary History*. London: The British Library, 2016.
Ribas-Casasayas, Alberto, and Amanda L. Petersen, eds. *Espectros: Ghostly Hauntings in Contemporary Transhispanic Narratives*. Lewisburg, PA: Bucknell University Press, 2016.
Riva, Silvia. *Nouvelle histoire de la littérature du Congo-Kinshasa*. Paris: L'Harmattan, 2006.
Rivera, Carmen S. "Rosario Ferré (28 July 1942-)." *Modern Latin-American Fiction Writers: Second Series* 145 (1994): 130-137.
Rodríguez Monegal, E. "Writing Fiction Under the Censor's Eye." *World Literature Today* 53, no. 1 (Winter, 1979): 19-22.
Rohter, Larry. "Paperbacks; Life Under the Militechs." *New York Times,* Sept. 29, 1985, A38.
Rosenthal, Eric. *They Walk By Night.* Cape Town: Timmins, 1951.
Rubin, Jay, ed. *Modern Japanese Writers* New York: Charles Scribner's Sons, 2001.
Ryan, Michael. "Circuses and Mythologies: Latin American Fiction." *The North American Review* 258, no. 3 (Fall, 1973): 73-77.
Sá, Daniel. "Tropical Gothic I." *The Gothic Imagination*. Accessed May 31, 2017. http://www.gothic.stir.ac.uk/guestblog/tropical-gothic-i/.
Sadlier, Darlene J. "Lya Luft." In *One Hundred Years After Tomorrow: Brazilian Women's Fiction of the 20th Century*, edited by Darlene J. Sadlier, 215. Bloomington, IN: Indiana University Press, 1992.
Salmonson, Jessica Amanda. "Some Ghostly Tales from South America." Web Archive. Accessed June 1, 2017. https://web.archive.org/web/20130629032050/http://www.violetbooks.com/magic-realist.html.
Sari Kawana. "Mad Scientists and Their Prey: Bioethics, Murder, and Fiction in Interwar Japan." *The Journal of Japanese Studies* 31, no. 1 (Winter, 2005): 89-120.
Schaefer, William. "Kumarajiva's Foreign Tongue: Shi Zhecun's Modernist Historical Fiction." *Modern Chinese Literature* 10, no. 1/2 (Spring/Fall 1998): 25-70.
Schaflechner, Jürgen "'The Hindu' in Recent Urdu Horror Stories from Pakistan (2016)." *Academia.edu*. Accessed June 19, 2018. https://www.academia.edu/27523878/_The_Hindu_in_Recent_Urdu_Horror_Stories_from_Pakistan_2016_
Schaflechner, Jürgen. "Why does Pakistan's horror pulp fiction stereotype 'the Hindu'?" *The Conversation*. Last modified March 14, 2017. https://theconversation.com/why-does-pakistans-horror-pulp-fiction-stereotype-the-hindu-73885.
Schuetz, Verna. "The Bizarre Literature of Hanns Heinz Ewers, Alfred Kubin, Gustav Meyrink, and Karl Hans Strobl." PhD diss., University of Wisconsin, 1974.
Seunghee, Sone. "The Mirror Motif in the *Crow's-Eye View (Ogamdo)* Poems*." *Seoul Journal of Korean Studies* 29, no. 1 (June 2016): 193-217.
Shimokusu, Masaya. "A Cultural Dynasty of Beautiful Vampires: Japan's Acceptance, Modifications, and Adaptations of Vampires." In *The Universal Vampire: Origins and Evoltion of a Legend*, edited by Barbara Brodman and James E. Doan, 179-194. Madison, NJ: Fairleigh Dickinson University Press, 2013.
Simsone, Bārbala. "A Cloud of Vapour, the Cool of the Cellar: the Horror Genre in Latvian

Literature." *Interlitteraria* 19, no. 2 (2014): 307-320.
Skvorecký, Josef. "Some Contemporary Czech Prose Writers." *NOVEL: A Forum on Fiction* 4, no. 1 (Autumn, 1970): 5-13.
Smith, Verity, ed. *Encyclopedia of Latin American Literature*. Chicago, IL: Fitzroy Dearborn, 1997.
Stableford, Brian. "The Cosmic Horror." In *Icons of Horror and the Supernatural*, edited by S.T. Joshi, 65-96. Westport, CT: Greenwood Press, 2007.
Stableford, Brian. *Glorious Perversity: The Decline and Fall of Literary Decadence*. Rockville, MD: Wildside Press, 2008.
Straub, Pater. Introduction to *The Wine-Dark Sea*, by Robert Aickman, 7-10. New York: Arbor House, 1988.
Sullivan, Jack, ed. *The Penguin Encyclopedia of Horror and the Supernatural*. New York: Viking, 1986.
Suppia, Alfredo Luiz. "Horror in Literature and Film in Latin America." Oxford Bibliographies. Last modified July 24, 2013, http://www.oxfordbibliographies.com/view/document/obo-9780199766581/obo-9780199766581-0124.xml.
Süssekind, Flora. "Deterritorialization and Literary Form: Brazilian Contemporary Literature and Urban Experience," Working Paper Series, University of Oxford Centre for Brazilian Studies, June, 2002.
Suyofie, Fadia. "Magical Realism in Ghādah al-Sammān's 'The Square Moon.'" *Journal of Arabic Literature* 40, no. 2 (2009): 182-207.
Swart, Sandra. "'Bushveld Magic' and 'Miracle Doctors'–an Exploration of Eugene Marais and C. Louis Leipoldt's Experiences in the Waterberg, South Africa, c. 1906-1917." *Journal of African History* 45 (2004): 237-55.
Taljaard-Gilson, Gerda. "Die inslag van die Gotiese in die Afrikaanse literatuur: 'n ondersoek na 'n eiesoortige Afrikaanse Gotiek aan die hand van die Faust-motief." *LitNet Akademies* 13, no. 1 (May 2016): 185-208.
Taratko, Carolyn. "'Jules Verne Would Roll over in His Grave,' or Döblin on the Future." *JHIBLOG*. Last modified Mar. 11, 2015. https://jhiblog.org/2015/03/11/jules-verne-would-roll-over-in-his-grave-or-doblin-on-the-future/.
Teeuw, A. *Modern Indonesian Literature*. Leiden: Springer-Science+Business Media, R.V., 1967.
Van Graan, Mariëtte. "Die rol van ruimte in Afrikaanse spookstories." PhD diss., Noordweis-Universiteit, 2008.
Vandermeer, Jeff. "The New Weird: 'It's Alive?'" In *The New Weird*, edited by Ann VanderMeer and Jeff VanderMeer, ix-xviii. San Francisco, CA: Tachyon Publications, 2008.
VanderMeer, Jeff and Ann VanderMeer, eds. *The Weird*. New York: Tor Books, 2012.
Vargas Llosa, Mario, and Roger Williams. "A Morbid Prehistory (The Early Stories)." *Books Abroad* 47, no. 3 (Summer, 1973): 451-460.
Vasconcelos, Sandra Guardini T. "Leituras Inglesas no Brasil oitocentista." *Crop* 8 (2002): 223-

247.
Versins, Pierre. "Maurice Renard." In *Encylopédie de l'utopie, des voyages extraordinaires, et de la science fiction*, edited by Pierre Versins, 734-735. Lausanne: L'Age d'Homme, 1984.
Villareal, Isaí Mejía. "El Cuento de Horror Fantastico Visto por Seis Narradores Mexicanos." Thesis, Universidad Autónoma Metropolitana Unidad Azcapotzalco, 2015.
Vines, Lois Davis. *Poe Abroad: Influence, Reputation, Affinities*. Iowa City, IA: University of Iowa Press, 2002.
Wa Kabwe-Segatti, Désiré K. *Écriture de la jeunesse: mutations et syncrétismes (1990-1996)*. Paris: Éditions Publibook, 2011.
Wagner, Tamara S. "Ghosts of a Demolished Cityscape: Gothic Experiments in Singaporean Fiction," In *Asian Gothic: Essays on Literature, Film and Anime*, edited by Andrew Hock-Soon Ng, 46-60. Jefferson, NC: McFarland, 2008.
Walcott, Derek. *Derek Walcott: The Journeyman Years, Volume 1: Culture, Society, Literature, and Art*. New York: Rodopi, 2013.
Wedell-Wedellsborg, Anne. "Haunted Fiction: Modern Chinese Literature and the Supernatural." *The International Fiction Review* 32, no. 1-2 (2005). Accessed May 23, 2017. https://journals.lib.unb.ca/index.php/IFR/article/view/7797/8854.
Wessels, Andries. "Intertekstualiteit en modernistiese kompleksiteit in Henriette Grové se Linda Joubert-romans." *Tydskrif vir letterkunde* 48, no. 2 (2011): 32-49.
Whitehead, Angus. Introduction to *The Wayang at Eight Milestone: Stories & Essays by Gregory Nalpon* by Gregory Nalpon, i-xix. Singapore: Epigram Books, 2013.
Wisker, Gina. *Contemporary Women's Gothic Fiction: Carnival, Hauntings and Vampire Kisses*. London: Palgrave Gothic, 2016.
Wisker, Gina. "Showers of Stars: South East Asian Women's Postcolonial Gothic." *Gothic Studies* 5, no. 2 (Nov. 2003): 64-80.
Xiaohuan Zhao. *Classical Chinese Supernatural Fiction: A Morphological History*. Lewiston, NY: E. Mellen Press, 2005.
"Yasunari Kawabata." In *Contemporary Authors Online*. Detroit: Gale, 2005. Contemporary Authors Online. Accessed June 20, 2018. http://link.galegroup.com.lscsproxy.lonestar.edu/apps/doc/H1000052623/CA?u=nhmccd_main&sid=CA&xid=01b9b01d.
Young, M.J.L. "The Short Stories of George Sālim." *Journal of Arabic Literature* 8 (1977): 123-135.
Yücesoy, V. Özge. "Korku Edebiyati (Gotik Edebiyat) Ve Türk Romanindaki Örnekleri." Thesis, İstanbul Üniversitesi, 2007.
Zarei, Rouhollah. "Axes of Evil Live Evermore: Brother Poe in Iran." *The Edgar Allan Poe Review* 4, no. 2 (Fall 2003): 14-21.
Zell, Hans M., Carol Bundy and Virginia Coulon. *A New Reader's Guide to African Literature*. New York: African Publishing Company, 1983.

Index

Abbadie, Luis G., 148
    El último relato de Ambrose Bierce, 148
Abe Kōbō, 101
Abimael Pinzón, José, 84
    El Vampiro, 84
Achebe, Chinua, 6, 124
    Things Fall Apart, 6, 124
Agapit, Marc, 111
Aguilera-Malta, Demetrio, 86-87, 141-142
    Don Goyo, 86
    El secuestro del general, 142
    Siete lunas y siete serpientes, 86-87, 141-142
Ahmed, Humayun, 152
Aickman, Robert, 92
Ajidarma, Seno Gumira, 160
    "The Mysterious Shooter Trilogy," 160
Akutagawa Ryūnosuke, 29, 30
al-Sammān, Ghāda, 199
    al-Qamar al-Murabba', 199
    Beirut Nightmares, 199
Alekseev, Gleb, 60
    Podzemnaia Moskva, 60
Allende, Isabel, 138
Amadi, Elechi, 127-128
    The Great Ponds, 127-128
Andersen, Hans Christian, 41
Anderson Imbert, Enrique, 75-76
Andrés, Elena, 191
    Trance de la vigilia, 191
Andreyev, Leonid, 56
    Chernye maski, 56
    "Dnevnik Satany," 56
Ángel Herra, Rafael, 139-140
    La guerra prodigiosa, 139-140
Angerhuber, Monika "Eddie," 176, 182
Angola, 5, 65
Ansky, S. 58
    Tsvishn tsvey veltn--der dibek, 58
Anttila, Leo, 42
    "Destiny," 42
Argentina, 10-11, 75-79, 132-134

Argüello Mora, Manuel, 15
Argueta, Manlio, 143
    Un dia en la vida, 143
Aridjis, Homero, 148
    La leyenda de los soles, 148
Armijo, Roberto, 142
    Jugando a la gallina, 142
Arredondo, Inés, 145-145
    Los Espejos, 145
    La señal, 145
    Río subterráneo, 145
Aslan, Levent, 199-200
    Geceyarisi Kabuslari, 199-200
    Karanliğin Gozleri, 199-200
Aurobindo, Sri, 98
Austria, 34-37, 175
Bakhtin, Mikhail, 78
Baliński, Stanisław, 54
    Miasto księżyców, 54
Balzac, Honore, 149
Banaphul, 98
Bandopadhyay, Bibhutibhushan, 25, 97, 152
    Pather Panchali, 97
Bandopadhyay, Tarashankar, 98
    "The Witch," 98
Bandyopadhyay, Sharadindu, 97
Bangladesh, 152
Barbados, 79-80
Barker, Clive, 179, 180
Baroja, Pio, 61
    El hotel del cisne, 61
    Vidas sombrías, 61
Barreto, Lima, 13
    "A nova Califórnia," 13
    "Sua Excelencia," 13
Barreto, Paulo, 12-13
    O bebe de tarlatana rosa, 12-13
Barrios, Eduardo, 14-15
Basu, Manoj, 98
Baudelaire, Charles, 14, 21, 28, 29, 49, 89, 93
    "Les Fleurs du Mal," 21
Beaulieu, Natasha, 150
    L'Ange écarlate, 150

Beckett, Samuel, 146, 147
Bedoya y Lerzundi, Manuel Augusto, 18
    La señorita Carlota, 18
    El tirano Bebevidas. Monstruo de America, 18
Bei Cun, 154-155
    Shixi de he, 154-155
Belgium, 37-39, 107-109, 175-176
Bely, Andrei, 57-58
    Peterburg, 57
    Serebrianiyi golub', 57-58
Bemba, Sylvain, 121
    Tarentelle noir et diable blanc, 121
Bendrupe, Mirdza, 52
    "Helēna," 52
Benet, Juan, 190-191
    Una Tumba, 191
    Volveras a Región, 191
Benitez-Rojo, Antonio, 140
Béraud, Henri, 45, 46
    Lazare, 45
Bernanos, Georges, 113
Bernanos, Michel, 113-114
    La montagne morte de la vie, 113-114
Bertin, Eddy C., 176
Bierce, Ambrose, 29, 45, 148
    "An Encounter at Owl Creek Bridge," 45
bin Ishak, Yusof, 103
Bioy Casares, Adolfo, 77
Blade, 177
Blatty, William Peter, 158
    The Exorcist, 158
Bolduc, Claude, 151
    Les yeux troubles et autres contes de la lune noire, 151
Bolivia, 80-81
Bombal, Maria Luisa, 15
Bond, James, 159
Bond, Ruskin, 159
    A Season of Ghosts, 159
Borges, Jorge Luis, 15, 76, 77, 78, 79, 85, 86, 89, 90, 91, 92, 117, 140, 145, 148, 154, 155, 157, 161, 183
    Historia universal de la infamia, 15
Bosch, Hieronymous, 34, 37
Bouquet, Jean-Louis, 108

Bourne, J.A.V., 87
    Dreams, Devils, Vampires, 87
Boutet, Frédéric, 45
Bradbury, Ray, 85, 108, 163
Brandorff, Walter, 175
Brazil, 11-14, 16, 81-83, 134-138
Breton, André, 95, 112
Breughel, Jan, 37
Breughel the Elder, Pieter, 34, 37
Brontë, Charlotte, 56, 73
    Jane Eyre, 73
Brontë, Emily, 56, 73
    Wuthering Heights, 73
Bruss, B.R. 111
Brussolo, Serge, 180-181
Bryusov, Valeri, 57
    Ognennyi angel, 57
Buffy the Vampire Slayer, 177
Buitrago, Fanny, 139
    La otre gente, 139
Bulgakov, Mikhail, 39, 57, 59
    The Master and Margarita, 57, 59
Bunin, Ivan, 58
    "Sukhodol," 58
Busson, Paul, 36 37
    Die Wiedergeburt des Melchior Dronte, 37
Buzzati, Dino, 108, 114-115, 176, 183
Byron, Lord, 170
Calcaño, Julio, 19
    Cuentos escogidos, 19
Calvino, Italo, 93, 115
Calvo de Aguilar, Isabel, 117
    La danzarina inmóvil, 117
    Doce sarcófagos de oro, 117
Campbell, Ramsay, 182
Camus, Albert, 76, 132
Can Xue, 155
Cannibali, 185
Caravana, Nemesio E., 104, 105
    Ang Puso ni Mathilde, 105
    Exzur, 104, 105
Cardona, Jenaro, 15
    "La caja del doctor," 15

Cardona Peña, Alfredo, 85
Carrington, Leonora, 145
    Le Cornet acoustique, 145
    La Porte de pierre, 145
Carnacki the Ghost-Finder, 45
Carrere, Emilio, 62
Carter, Angela, 192
Catcher in the Rye, 116
Cerruto, Oscar, 80-81
    Cerco de penumbras, 80-81
Chaianov, Aleksandr, 58-59
    "Veneditkov," 59
Champetier, Joel, 151
    L'Aile du Papillon, 151
    La Mémoire du lac, 151
    La Peau Blanche, 151
Champion, Jeanne, 180
    Dans les jardins d'Esther, 180
    Les Gisants, 180
    Vautour-en-Privilège, 180
Chart Korbjitti, 174
    Chon Trok, 174
    Khamphiphaksa, 174
Chaudhuri, Pramatha, 98
    "Sacrifice by Fire," 98
Chaviano, Daina, 140-141
    Casa de Juegos, 141
    La Habana oculta, 141
Chekhov, Anton, 56, 63
Chesterton, G.K. 45
Chettur, Sankara Krishna, 25
    The Cobras of Dharma Sevi and Other Stories, 25
    Muffled Drums and Other Stories, 25
Chile, 14-15, 83-84, 138-139
China, 20-22, 152-157
Christie, Agatha, 117
Clauzel, Robert, 178-180
Cocteau, Jean, 107
Collier, John, 108
Colombia, 84-85, 139
Collymore, Frank, 79-80
Congo, 65-66, 120-123
Conrad, Joseph, 87

Constantini, Humberto, 133-134
    De dioses, hombrecitos y policias, 133
    La larga noche de Francisco Sanctis, 133-134
Cortázar, Julio, 78-79, 93, 117, 140, 145
Costa Rica, 15-16, 85, 139-140
Croatia, 39
Cruz Cornelio, Mateo, 104
    Doktor Satan, 104
Cuba, 16, 85-86, 140-141
Cuevas, Alejandro, 18
Czech Republic, 39-41, 109-110, 176-178
Dadié, Bernard, 67-68, 70
    Le pagne noir, 67-68
Dahl, Roald, 108
Dario, Ruben, 14
Dashkov, Andrey, 194
    Necromancers' Wars, 194
    The Pale Horseman, Black Jack, 194
    The Servant of Werewolves, 194
Dávila, Amparo, 91, 92-93
Dawn of the Dead, 179
de Alencar, José, 11
de Assis Júnior, António, 5, 65
    O Segredo da Morta, 5
de Azevedo, Álvares, 11
de Beauvoir, Simone, 76
de Burgos, Carmen, 62
    "La mujer fría," 62
    "El perseguidor," 62
de Campos, Humberto, 13-14
    Monstro e outro contos, 13-14
de Ghelderode, Michel, 107, 108
    "The Devil in London," 107
    "The Collector of Relics," 107
de Goncourt, Edmond & Jules, 46
de Lautreamont, Comte, 95
de Lisser, Herbert George, 17-18
    The White Witch of Rosehall, 17-18
de Lorde, André, 46
de Loyola Brandão, Ignácio, 136-137
    And Still the Earth, 136-137
    Não Verás País Nenhum, 136
    Zero, 136

De Maria, Giorgio, 183-184
    Le venti giornate di Torino, 183-184
de Maupassant, Guy, 11, 19, 39, 45, 50, 63, 104, 113
de Nerval, Gérard, 49
de Oliveira, Nelson, 137
    Naquela época tínhamos um gato, 137
de Sá-Carneiro, Mário, 55
de Sade, Marquis, 113
de Unamuno, Miguel, 61
de Warren, Raoul, 110
    La Bête de l'Apocalypse, 110
    L'Énigme du Mort Vivant, 110
    Rue du Mort-qui-Trompe, 110
del Mundo, Sr., Clodualdo, 105
    Tuko sa Madre Kakaw, 105
del Paso, Fernando, 86
del Valle-Inclan, Ramón, 61
    Jardín umbrio, 61
    Tirano Banderas, 61
Delgado, Antonio, 147
    La hora de los unicornios, 147
Denmark, 41-42, 178
Dey, Panchkari, 24
    Mayabini, 24
    "The Poet's Lover", 24
Dharap, Narayan, 157-158
Díaz Llanillo, Esther, 85-86, 141
    El Castigo, 85-86
    Cuentos antes y después del sueño, 141
Dinesen, Isak, 41-42
Diop, Birago, 65, 70
Divov, Oleg, 189-190
    The Dog Master, 189-190
Djarens, S., 25
do Rêgo, José Lins, 82
    Água-mae, 82
do Rio, João, 13
    Dentro da noite, 13
Döblin, Alfred, 48-49
    Berge Meere und Giganten, 48-49
    Berlin Alexanderplatz, 48
Donoso, José, 138-139
    El obsceno pájaro de la noche, 138-139

Dostoyevsky, Fyodor, 56, 63, 191
    Crime and Punishment, 56
Doyle, Arthur Conan, 28, 42, 63, 181
    "The Hound of the Baskervilles," 42
Drayton, Geoffrey, 80
    Christopher, 80
    "Mr. Dombey the Zombie," 80
    Zohara, 80
Droguett, Carlos, 83
Du Maurier, Daphne, 46, 56, 73, 183
    Rebecca, 56, 73
Du Plessis, I.D., 9, 71, 74
du Plessis, P.G., 74
    Die nag van Legio, 74
Duan Chengshi, 20-21
    Youyang zazu, 20-21
Dueñas, Guadalupe, 91, 92
Dumas, Alexandre, 18, 46
Dürrenmatt, Friedrich, 194
    Der Auftrag, 194
    Die Panne, 194
    Der Verdacht, 194
Dutt, Toru, 23
    Le Journal de Mademoiselle d'Arvers, 23
Easmon, R. Sarif, 130-131
    The Feud, 130-131
Ebnou, Moussa Ould, 126-127
    Barzakh, 126-127
Eco, Umberto, 184
Ecuador, 86-87, 141-142
Edogawa Rampo, 28, 29
    "The Caterpillar," 28
    "The Human Chair," 28
    "The Hell of Mirrors," 28
    "The Red Chamber," 28
Eekhoud, Georges, 37
Egbuna, Obi, 70
    Daughters of the Sun and Other Stories, 70
Egypt, 63, 197
Eisenstein, Sergei, 93
El Salvador, 142-143
Elizondo, Salvador, 93
    Farabeuf, 93

Emechata, Buchi, 129
    The Rape of Shavi, 129
Erckmann-Chatrian, 44
Eshun, J.O., 123
    Adventures of the Kapapa, 123
Ewers, Hanns Heinz, 34, 37, 47
Ezeriņš, Jānis, 52
Fagunwa, Daniel O., 6-7, 68, 69
    Ogboju Ode ninu Igbo Irunmale, 6-7, 68, 69
Fantouré, Alioum, 123-124
    Le récit du cirque, 123-124
Fatanmi, D.J., 69-70
    K'orimale ninu igbo Adimula, 69-70
Faulkner, William, 84, 87, 95, 190, 191
Fernández Cubas, Cristina, 191-192
Ferré, Rosario, 149
Finland, 42-43, 178-179
France, 43-46, 110-114, 179-181
France, Anatole, 5
Frey, Alexander Moritz, 48
Frondaie, Pierre, 45
    "The Dancing Dead," 45
    "The story of a ghost and the two arms of Venus," 45
Fuentes, Carlos, 91-92
Fuks, Ladislav, 109-110
    Spalovač mrtvol, 109
    Variace pro temnou strunu, 109-110
Fumiko Enchi, 100-101
Gangopadhyay, Sunil, 98
Gao Xingjian, 156
    Lingshan, 156
García Márquez, Gabriel, 84-85, 93, 139, 154
    "Espantos de Agosto," 139
    La Hojarasca, 84-85
    One Hundred Years of Solitude, 84, 139
García Morales, Adelaida, 192
    El sur seguido de Bene, 192
García Sánchez, Javier, 192
    El mecanógrafo, 192
    Los otros, 192
Garmendia, Salvador, 151
Gascar, Pierre, 112-113
Gautier, Theophile, 46, 49, 59, 63

Ge Fei, 156
Germany, 46-49, 114, 181-183
Ghana, 123
Giardinelli, Mempo, 133
    Luna Caliente, 133
Gilman, Charlotte Perkins, 57, 117, 166
    "The Yellow Wallpaper," 57, 117, 166
Gippius, Zinaida, 56-57
    Chertova kukla, 57
    "Ivan Ivanovich I chert," 57
    "Sumasshedsha," 57
Goethe, Johann Wolfgang von, 41, 58
    The Sorrows of Young Werther, 41
Gogol, Nikolai, 29, 56, 59, 115
    "Viy," 56
Goh Poh Seng, 170
    If We Dream Too Long, 170
Gokhale, Namita, 159
    The Book of Shadows, 159
Gómez Windham, Guillermo, 32-33
    "Tía Pasia," 32-33
González León, Adriano, 95
    País Portátil, 95
Gorey, Edward, 164
Goya, Francisco, 164
Gozzano, Guido, 50
Grabinski, Stefan, 53, 54, 115, 176
Gracq, Julien, 111-112
    Un beau ténébreux, 112
    Au château d'Argol, 112
Grīns, Aleksandrs, 52
Grové, Henriette, 73-74
    Meulenhof se Mense, 73-74
Guatemala, 143-144
Guimarães Rosa, João, 82
    Grande Sertão: Veredas, 82
Guinea, 66-67, 123-124
Gürpınar, Hüseyin Rahmi, 64
    Cadı, 64
    Gulyabani, 64
Guyana, 87-89, 144
Guzmán, Humberto, 146
    Manuscrito anónimo llamado consigna idiota, 146

Haasse, Hella S., 99
    Oeroeg, 99
Habib, Muhammad, 25
    The Desecrated Bones and Other Stories, 25
Halim, Tunku, 167-168
    Dark Demon Rising, 167
    The Rape Of Martha Teoh and Other Chilling Tales, 167
    Vermilion Eye, 167
Halloween, 179
Hamidullah, Zaib-un-Nissa, 104
    The Young Wife and Other Stories, 104
Harris, Wilson, 88-89
    The Palace of the Peacock, 88-89
Hawthorne, Nathaniel, 49, 82
    "Rappaccini's Daughter," 49
Hearn, Lafcadio, 28, 140
Hadāyat, Sadeq, 63-64
    Būf-e Kūr, 63-64
Harahap, Abdullah, 159-160
    Demonic Dances, 160
    Hell Calls, 160
    The Mystery of Satan's Children, 160
    Redeeming the Sins of Derivation, 160
    Werewolves, 160
Heath, Roy A.K., 144
    Kwaku, 144
    The Ministry of Hope, 144
    The Shadow Bride, 144
Heike Monogatari, 26
Hellens, Franz, 37-38
Hemingway, Ernest, 50
Henry, O., 85, 112, 169
Hernández, Felisberto, 93-94
Hernández Catá, Alfonso, 16
Heym, Georg, 48-49
    Der dieb, 49
Hideyuki Kikuchi, 164
Hino Hideshi, 163, 164
Hitchcock, Alfred, 105, 153, 184
    The Birds, 153
Hloucha, Joe, 40
    "The Doll Under the Hat," 40
    Pavilón hrůzy, 40

Hoeane, Z.L. 68
    Pale tse hlomolang le tse tshehisang, 68
Hodgson, William Hope, 45, 113
Hoffmann, E.T.A., 34, 36, 37, 43, 44, 46, 47, 49, 54, 55, 59, 63, 183
Holmes, Sherlock, 28
Honduras, 16-17
Houssin, Joe, 180
    Locomotive Rictus, 180
Howard, Robert E., 182
Huerta, Alberto, 147
    Ojalá estuvieras aquí, 147
Hugo, Victor, 5
Huysmans, J.K. 43, 46, 57
    À Rebours, 43
    Là-bas, 57
Hyakken Uchida, 27-28
    Meido, 27-28
India, 23-25, 96-98, 157-159
Indonesia, 25, 98-100, 159-160
Invernizio, Carolina, 49
    La Vergine dei veleni, 49
Iqbal, Muhammed Zafar, 152
    Pishachini, 152
    Pret, 152
Iran, 63-64
Israel, 118, 197-198
Italy, 49-51, 114-115, 183-185
Ito Junji, 164
Ivory Coast, 67-68
Jackson, Shirley, 50, 92
Jamaica, 17-18
James, Henry, 80, 149
James, M.R., 87, 139, 141, 182
Japan, 26-32, 100-103, 160-165
Jean-Charles, Jehanne, 108-109
Jelinek, Elfriede 175
    Der Kinder der Toten, 175
Joaquin, Nick, 169-170
    Tropical Gothic, 170
Jordan, 198
José Arreola, Juan, 89, 91, 145
Joubert, Linda, see Henriette Grové
Joyce, James, 75, 78, 93, 95

Kafka, Franz, 35, 36, 53, 63, 67, 84, 85, 86, 89, 92, 95, 112, 113, 115, 132, 141, 147, 152, 154, 155, 157, 161, 183
"The Metamorphosis," 36
Kaijaks, Vladimirs, 186
Kallas, Aino, 42-43
Sudenmorsian, 42-43
Kanai Mieko, 161
Kasongo, Maurice, 66
Kongono, esclave des nains-démons de la forêt, 66
Kast, Pierre, 180
Les Vampires d'Alfama, 180
Kawabata Yasunari, 101-102
"Kataude," 102
Nemureru Bijo, 102
Kazuo Umezu, 103, 163, 164
Kemp, T.L., 9
Karásek ze Lvovic, Jiri, 39-40
"Romány tří mágů" trilogy, 39-40
Kaschnitz, Marie Luise, 114
"Vogel Rock," 114
Kazuo Umezu, 103
Ken Asamatsu, 164
Kenya, 124-125
Kho Ping Hoo, 100
Kim Tongni, 32
"Munyŏ-do," 32
King, Stephen, 103, 150, 151, 157, 158, 159, 164, 168, 177, 179, 180, 185, 187, 190
Kipling, Rudyard, 19
Kivinen, S. Albert, 178
"Keskiyön Mato Ikaalisissa," 178
Klíma, Ladislav, 40-41
Utrpení knížete Sternenhocha, 41
Koji Suzuki, 164
Ringu, 165
Konjaku Monogatarishū, 26, 29
Koontz, Dean, 179, 187
Korea, 32
Kubin, Alfred, 35
Die Andere Seite, 35
Kulhánek, Jiří, 177
Vládci strachu, 177
Kuni, Ibrahim, 125-126
The Bleeding of the Stone, 125-126

Kurahashi Yumiko, 162
Kuwait, 198-199
Kyōka Izumi, 26-27, 29, 30
Laforet, Carmen, 116-117
    Nada, 116-117
Landolfi, Tommaso, 114, 115, 183
Langenhoven, C.J. 8-9, 71, 74
    Aan Stille Waters, 9
    Geeste op aarde, 9
Langstrup, Steen, 178
Latvia, 51-52, 185-187
Lawrence, D.H., 92
Laye, Camara, 67
    Dramouss, 67
Leandoer, Kristoffer, 193
    "De Svarta Svanarna," 193
Lebakeng, D.P., 68
    Sekoting sa lihele, 68
Lee, Russell, 172
    Almost Complete Collection of True Singapore Ghost Stories, 172
Lee Woo-hyuk, 173
    Toemarok, 173
Lehtimaki, Konrad, 42
    Kuolema, 42
Leipoldt, C. Louis, 8, 71, 74, 131
    Die rooi rotte, en ander kort verhale, 8
    Waar spoke speel, 8
    Wat agter le en ander verhale, 8
    "Die wit hondjie", 8
Leonnier, Camille, 37
Leroux, Gaston, 44
    Le fantôme de l'opéra, 44
Lešehrad, Emanuel, 40
    Démon a jiné povídky, 40
    Záhadné životy, 40
Lesotho, 5-6, 68
Letailleur, Édouard, 45
    La Demeure de Satan, 45
    Perkane, le Démon de la Nuit, 45
    Le Squelette de la rue Scribe, 45
Level, Maurice, 44-45, 46
Levi, Primo, 115
Lewis, M.G., 41, 49

The Monk, 41
Li Jinfa, 21
    Wei yu, 21
Liang Xiaosheng, 153
    Foucheng, 153
    "Zheshi yipian shenqi de tudi," 153
Libya, 125-126
Ligotti, Thomas, 107, 176, 182
Lim, Catherine, 171
    Or Else the Lightning God and Other Stories, 171
Lim, Shirley, 165-166
    "Haunting," 165-166
Linde, Marie, 9
Liu Suola, 155
    "The Quest for the King of Singers," 155
Lobato, Monteiro, 13
    "Negrinha," 13
Lomami-Tshibamba, Paul, 65-66, 120-121
    Ngando le Crocodile, 65-66, 120
    La Récompense de la Cruauté, 120-121
London, Jack, 19
Lopes de Almeida, Júlia, 12
    "A colha," 12
Lorrain, Jean, 43-44
    Monsieur de Phocas, 43-44
Louw, Anna M. 131
    Vos, 131
Lovecraft, H.P., 20-21, 40, 42, 45, 49, 53, 54, 93, 105, 111, 117, 137, 141, 148, 163, 164, 176, 178, 179, 180, 182, 183, 199
    "The Shadow Out of Time," 45
Lu Xun, 21-22
    Ye cao, 21-22
Luft, Lya, 134, 135
    The Red House, 134
Lugones, Leopoldo, 11
    "Cábala práctica," 11
    Las fuerzas extrañas, 11
Machado de Assis, Joaquim Maria, 12
Machiko Hasegawa, 102
    Sazae-san, 102
Maeterlinck, Maurice, 37
Mahadoo, C.S., 127
    Twilight Escapism, 127

Maillu, David G., 124-125
    Kadosa, 124-125
Majumdar, Lila, 98
Majumder, Dakshinaranjan Mitra, 23-24
    Thakurmar Jhuli, 23-24
Malaysia, 103, 165-168
Mallarmé, Stephane, 93
Maluenda Labarca, Rafael, 83-84
    Vampiro de trapo, 83-84
Maniam, K.S., 167
    Haunting the Tiger, 167
Marais, Eugene, 9, 71, 74, 131
    Die boom in die middle van die tuin, 9
    Dwaalstories en ander vertellings, 9
Mariko Koike, 164
Martínez Tolentino, Jaime, 149
Martinho, Carlos Orsi, and Miguel Carqueija, 137-138
    Medo, mistério e morte, 137-138
Matheson, Richard, 108
Matoš, Antun Gustav, 39
    Umorne Priče, 39
Mauliņš, Jānis, 186
    Ragana, 186
Mauritania, 126-127
Mauritius, 127
Maurois, Andre, 45-46
    Le peseur d'âmes, 45-46
Mayoral, Marina, 191
McCullers, Carson, 146
Medek, Vladimir, 177
    Krev na Maltézkém náměstí, 177
Meissner, Janusz, 54
Mercedes Levinson, Luisa, 79
    La casa de los Felipes, 79
Merimée, Prosper, 39
Mexico, 18, 89-93, 145-148
Meyer, Stephanie, 41
    Twilight, 41
Meyrink, Gustav, 34-35, 47
    Der Golem, 35
Mičanová, Daniela, 177-178
    Modrá krev: O upírech a lidech, 177-178
Mirandoli, Franciszka Pika, 53-54

Tropy, 54
Mishima Yukio, 30, 164
Mistral, Gabriela, 14
Mitra, Premendra, 96
Mittelholzer, Edgar Austin, 87-88, 144
    The Adding Machine, 87
    Corentyne Thunder, 87
    Eltonsbrody, 87
    A Morning at the Office, 87
    My Bones and My Flute, 87, 88
Mizuki Shigeru, 102-103
    GeGeGe no Kitaro, 103
Mo Yan, 156
    Jiuguó, 156
Mocoancoeng, J.G., 68
    Meqoqo ea phirimana, 68
Moey, Nicky, 171, 172
Mofokeng, S.M., 73
    Senkatana, 73
Mofolo, Thomas, 6
    L'Ange déchu, 6
    Chaka, 6
Monteiro, Jerônimo, 82-83
    Fuga para parte alguma, 82-83
    Visitantes do espaço, 82
Monteiro, Domingos, 115-116
Montemayor, Carlos, 145
    Las llaves de Urgell, 145
Montero, Mayra, 149-150
Moo, Z.Y., 172
    The Weird Diary of Walter Woo, 172
Moravcová, Jana, 177
    Dračí krev, 177
    Nemrtvý, 177
    Trůn pro mrtvého, 177
Morohoshi Daijiro, 163-164
Motsamai, Edward, 5-6
    Mehla ea malimo, 5-6
Mujica Láinez, Manuel, 75
Mukerji, S., 24
    Indian Ghost Stories, 24
Mukhopadhyay, Troilokyanath, 23
Murakami Ryu, 165

Murasaki Shikibu, 26
    The Tale of Genji, 26
Murena, Hector A., 77
Murnau, F.W., 41
    Nosferatu, 41
Nabokov, Vladimir, 38, 57
Nadir, Kerime, 119
    Dehşet Gecesi, 119
Nakagami Kenji, 161-162
Nalpon, Gregory, 170
Nasrallāh, Ibrāhīm, 198
    Barārī al-hummā, 198
Natsume Sōseki, 27, 101-102
    Yume jūya, 27
N'Diaye, Amadou, 130
    Assoka, ou les derniers jours de Koumbi, 130
Negri, Ada, 51
    Di giorno in giorno, 51
    Le strade, 51
Nenonen, Kari, 178
    Ken kuolleita kutsuu, 178
    Noitarovio, 178
Neto, Coelho, 13
    Esfinge, 13
Neudecker, Christiane, 182-183
Nezval, Vítězslav, 41
    Valérie a týden divů, 41
Ngandu Nkashama, Pius, 123
    Yakouta, 123
Nienaber, P.J., 74
    Geeste en gedaantes, 74
Nietzsche, Friedrich, 18, 40, 58
Nigeria, 6-7, 68-70, 127-129
Nodier, Charles, 90
Ōba Minako, 162
    Urashimaso, 162
    "Yamanba no bisho," 162
Ocampo, Silvina, 77-78
O'Connor, Flannery, 146
O'Donnell, Elliott, 72
Ofoli, Nii Yemoh, 123
    The Messenger of Death, 123
Ogundele, J. Ogunsina, 69

  Ejigbede Lona Isalu Orun, 69
  Ibu Olokun, 69
Oguri Mushitarō, 30
Okri, Ben, 129
  The Famished Road, 129
Oliphant, Margaret, 17
Onyeama, Dillibe, 128
  Godfathers of Voodoo, 128
  Juju, 128
  Nigger at Eton, 128
  Revenge of the Medicine Man, 128
  Secret Society, 128
Orbitowski, Łukasz, 187-188
  Złe Wybrzeża, 188
Ortese, Anna Maria, 184
  L'Iguana, 184
Orwell, George, 67
Osamu Tezuka, 102
  Tetsuwan Atomu, 102
Owen, Thomas, 107-108, 176
Pacheco, José-Emilio, 146-147
  El principio del placer, 146-147
Page, Norvell, 37
Pakistan, 103-104, 168-169
Palma, Clemente, 18
Palma Soriano, Manuel Ricardo, 18
Papini, Giovanni, 89
Parashuram, 97-98
Pardo Bazán, Emilia, 61-62
  "La resucitada," 61-62
  "Vampiro," 61
Pavić, Milorad, 190
Paz, Octavio, 89, 145
Pedraza, Pilar, 192
Pereira, Ana Teresa, 189
Peru, 18
Perutz, Leo, 36
  Der Meister des Jüngsten Tages, 36
Pessoa, Fernando, 55
  Um jantar muito original, 55
Peters, Lenrie, 71
  The Second Round, 71
Petruševskaja, Ljudmila, 189

Songs of the Eastern Slavs, 189
Philippines, 32-33, 104-106, 169-170
Pilniak, Boris, 59-60
    "Mat' syra-zemlia," 59-60
Pink Floyd, 147
Pira Sudham, 174
Pishacho ki Mallika, 159
Poe, Edgar Allan, 8, 10, 12, 14, 18, 19, 28, 29, 34, 36, 38, 39, 40, 42, 44, 45, 46, 49, 50, 52, 53, 54, 55, 58, 59, 63, 78, 80, 82, 86, 87, 89, 90, 91, 92, 93, 99, 104, 108, 113, 115, 117, 140, 141, 149, 157, 159, 169, 182, 183, 190, 191, 199
    The Narrative of Arthur Gordon Pym, 113
Poland, 53-54, 187-188
Polidori, John, 83
    "The Vampyre," 83
Portugal, 54-55, 115-116, 188-189
Pound, Ezra, 93
Pratikto, Rijono, 99-100
    Si Rangka dan Beberapa Tjerita Pendek Lain, 99-100
Prévot, Gérard, 108
Pritchett, V.S., 69
Proust, Marcel, 75
Pu Songling, 21, 22
    Strange Tales from a Chinese Studio, 21, 22
Puerto Rico, 149-150
Puriņš', Andris, 187
    Ar skatienu augšup jeb Vampīru sazvērestība, 187
Pushkin, Alexander, 59
Qasim, Qasim Khadir, 198-199
    Madinatt Al-Reyaah wa Qissas Okh' ra ann Al-Ar'waah wa' Al- Ash'baah, 198-199
Québéc, 93, 150-151
Quiroga, Horacio, 19, 91, 93, 94, 140
Radcliffe, Ann, 49, 50, 64
Raffles, Sir Thomas, 148
Rahat, M.A., 169
    Kalu Jahad, 169
Ramos, Graciliano, 81
    Insônia, 81
Rappoport, Shloyme Zanul, see S. Ansky
Ray, Jean, 37-38, 107, 111
    Malpertuis, 38
Ray, Satyajit, 23, 157, 158
Raychowdhury, Upendrakishore, 23
Reeve, Clara, 49

Régio, José, 116
    "Os Alicerces da Realidade," 116
    Há Mais Mundos, 116
Rellergerd, Helmut, 181
Renard, Maurice, 44
    Le docteur Lerne, sous-dieu, 44
    Les mains d'Orlac, 44
    Le Peril Bleu, 44
Rendell, Ruth, 111
Rey Rosa, Rodrigo, 143-144
    El cuchillo del mendigo, 143-144
Reymont, Władysław Stanisław, 53
    Wampir, 53
Ribas, Oscar, 65, 67, 70
    "O Praga," 65
    Uanga (Feitiço), 65
Rice, Anne, 138, 177, 180
    Interview with the Vampire, 177, 180
Richter, Anne, 108
Rimbaud, Arthur, 95
Robbe-Grillet, Alain, 93
Rodenbach, Georges, 37
Rodoreda, Mercè, 117
    Del que hom no pot fugir, 117
    La mort I la primavera, 117
    La plaça del diamant, 117
Romania, 55-56
Rosenthal, Eric, 72
    They Walk By Night, 72
Rosny, J-H, aîné, 44
Rothmann, Maria Elizabeth, 71-72
    Uit en Tuis, 71-72
Roy, Hemendra Kumar, 25
    Names Feared By All, 25
Rubião, Murilo, 135
Rulfo, Juan, 90, 91
    Pedro Páramo, 90
Russia/Soviet Union, 56-60, 189-190
Ruti, Antoine M., 129-130
    Affamez-les, ils vous adoreront, 129-130
Rwanda, 129-130
Ryō Hanmura, 160-161
    Ishi no ketsumyaku, 160-161

Sábato, Ernesto, 76-77, 132-133
    Abbadón, el exterminador, 132-133
Sadji, Abdoulaye, 70-71
    Tounka, 71
Saki, 108, 179
Salarrué, 142-143
    Catleya luna, 142-143
    Cuentos de Barro, 143
Sālim, George, 118
Samperio, Guillermo, 147-148
    Textos extraños, 147-148
Sanchez Boudy, Jose, 140
    Cuentos a luna llena, 140
Santos, Bienvenido N., 105-106
    Villa Magdalena, 105-106
Saramago, José, 188
    Ensaio sobre a cegueira, 188
Sarduy, Severo, 86
Sartre, Jean-Paul, 76, 111, 132
Saulietis, Augusts, 51-52
Savinio, Alberto, 50-51
    La casa ispirata, 50-51
Scanners, 179
Schulz, Bruno, 53
Schulz-Sembten, Malte, 182
Schwob, Marcel, 89
Sclavi, Tiziano, 184
    Dylan Dog, 184
Seignolle, Claude, 112
Seishi Yokomizo, 32
    Dokuro-Kengyo, 32
Seixas, Heloisa, 138
    A porta, 138
Senécal, Patrick, 150, 151
    Le Passager, 150
    Sur le Seuil, 150
    5150 rues des Ormes, 150
Senegal, 70-71, 130
Senghor, Léopold Séddar, 70
Serao, Matilde, 49-50
    Il delitto di via Chiatamone, 50
    La mano tagliata, 50
Serbia, 190

Shakespeare, Billy, 41, 199
Shelley, Mary, 41, 49, 50, 104, 105
    Frankenstein, 41, 83, 104, 105
Shelley, Percy, 41
Sheridan Le Fanu, J., 17, 22
Shi Nai'an, 22
    Water Margin, 22
Shi Shuqing, 173
Shi Zhecun, 22, 27
Shirato Sampei, 102
Siefener, Michael, 182
Sierra Leone, 71, 130-131
Simões Lopes, João, 12
    "Contrabandista," 12
Sin, Damien, 172
    Classic Singapore Horror Stories, 172
Singapore, 170-172
Siraj, Syed Mustafa, 158
Smith, Clark Ashton, 42
Socé, Ousmane, 70
Sologub, Fyodor, 59
    Melkii bes, 59
Somers, Armonía, 94
Sosnkowski, Jerzy, 54
    Żywe powietrze, 54
South Africa, 7-9, 71-74, 131
South Korea, 172-173
Spain, 60-62, 116-117, 190-192
Steeman, Stanislas-André, 107
Steiner, Kurt, 110, 111
Stevenson, Robert Louis, 17, 104
    Dr. Jekyll and Mr. Hyde, 104
Stoker, Bram, 18, 148, 159
    Dracula, 17, 18, 83, 119, 148, 159
Stradiņš, Jānis Ivars, 187
    Dēmonu villa, 187
Strobl, Karl Hans, 34, 47
Suárez, Alicia, 79
    "Samantha," 79
Süskind, Patrick, 181
    Das Parfum, 181
Švandrlík, Miloslav, 176-177
    Černí Baroni, 177

Sweden, 193
Switzerland, 193-194
Syria, 118, 199
Tabassum, Abdur Rashid, 169
    "The Man With Dusty Shoes," 169
Tagore, Rabindranath, 22, 24-25, 96, 152
    "The Lost Jewels," 24
Taiwan, 173
Takahashi Takako, 163
Tanizaki Junichirō, 28-29
Tansi, Sony Lab'ou, 121-123
    Conscience de tracteur, 121-122
    La vie et demie, 122-123
Tarantino, Quentin, 185
Tario, Francisco, 89-90
    Jardin secreto, 89-90
Tawfik, Ahmed Khaled, 197
    Ma Waraa Al Tabiaa, 197
Telles, Lygia Fagundes, 134-135
Tenniel, John, 164
Teodoreanu, Ionel, 56-57
    Fata din Zlataust, 56
    Golia, 56
    Turnul Milenei, 56
Thailand, 173-174
Thiry, Marcel, 109
    "Un Plan Simple," 109
Thomas, Dylan, 69
Tieck, Ludwig, 37
Topor, Roland, 113
    Joko fête son anniversaire, 113
    Le Locataire chimérique, 113
Tremblay, Michel, 93
Turcios, Froylán, 17
    El vampiro, 17
Turkey, 64, 118-119, 199-200
Tutuola, Amos, 6, 68-69
    Palm Wine Drinkard, 68-69
Ueda Akinari, 26
    Ugetsu Monogatari, 26
Ukraine, 194
Ulasi, Adaora Lily, 128-129
    Who is Jonah?, 128-129

Unno Jūza, 30
Uruguay, 19, 93-94
Váchal, Josef, 40
    Krvavý román, 40
Vainonen, Jyrki 179
    Tutkimusmatkailija ja muita tarinoita, 179
Valenzuela, Luisa, 132
    "Aqui pasan cosas raras," 132
    Cola de lagartija, 132
    El gato eficaz, 132
    Realidad nacional desde la cama, 132
Valéry, Paul, 93
van Reenen, Reenen, 8
Vargas Vila, José Maria, 14
Vaswani, Bulchand Jhamatmal, 96-97
Veerendranath, Yandamuri, 158
    Tulasi Dalam, 158
Velvet Underground, 93
Venezuela, 19, 94-95, 151
Verhaeren, Emile, 37
Verne, Jules, 48
Vicente, Angeles, 61
    Los cuentos de Sombras, 61
Villiers de l'Isle-Adam, 18, 19, 45, 46
Vinci, Simona, 185
    Dei bambini non si sa niente, 185
von Adlersfeld-Ballestrem, Eufemia, 46-47
    Ca'Spada, 47
    Die dame in gelb, 47
von der Gabelentz, Georg, 47
    "Gelber Schädel," 47
    Das Rätsel Choriander, 47
von Frankenstein, Victor, 13, 31
Walcott, Derek, 80
Walpole, Horace, 50, 90
Waltari, Mika, 42, 178
    "Isle of the Setting Sun," 42
    Kuollen silmä, 42
    "Mummy," 42
    "The Red Triangle," 42
    Sinuhe, egyptiläinen, 42
Wang Shuo, 155
    Wanr de jiushi xintiao, 155

we Kang'ethe, Karanja, 125
    Mission to Gehenna, 125
Weird Tales, 42, 54, 127
Wellman, Manly Wade, 112
Wells, H.G., 44, 82, 105
    "The Empire of the Ants," 82
    The Island of Doctor Moreau, 44, 105
Wheatley, Dennis, 128
Wildberg, Bodo, 35-36
Wilde, Oscar, 28, 50
Wok, Othman, 103
Xu Dishan, 22
Yahp, Beth, 166-167
    The Crocodile Fury, 166-167
Yarbro, Chelsea Quinn, 180
Yasutaka Tsutsui, 164
Yi Sang, 32
    Kkamagwiui Siseon, 32
Yu Hua, 156
Yumeno Kyūsako, 29-30
    Dogura Magura, 29-30
Zamacois, Eduardo, 62
    El Otro, 62
Zameenzad, Adam, 169
    The Thirteenth Hour, 169
Zárate, Jose Luis, 148
    La ruta del hielo y la sal, 148
    Xanto: Novelucha libre, 148
Zarchi, Nurit, 198
Zariņš, Kārlis, 52
    "Remember You Will Die, Heidenkranc!", 52
Zhizhmore, Maks, 60
    Posledniaia zhertva, 60
Zhong Ling, 173
Zhu Lin, 154
    Nu Wu, 154
Zigmonte, Dagnija, 186-187
    Gausīgais Nazis, 186-187
Zola, Emile, 18
Zong Pu, 152-153
    "Wo shi shei?", 152
    "Woju", 152-153

Made in the USA
Middletown, DE
29 August 2018